"Damn you, woman, a man has limits," he growled, leaning against her.

"Let go of me. Stop this." Pinned between the cold wall and the hard muscles of his chest, Laurien could scarcely breathe. She turned her head away from his harsh gaze, but he gripped her chin and brought her eyes back to meet his.

"I told you once I wouldna hurt you." His lips were very near hers, his voice barely a murmur.

"Let me alone!" Laurien was trembling now, and knew he could feel it. "I willna give you what you want."

He pulled her away from the wall, crushing her against him, and Laurien gasped. "I hate you . . ."

With a groan, Connor lowered his head to hers. "Hate me, then." His lips captured hers.

FALCON ON THE WIND

SHELLY THACKER

AVON BOOKS ◆ NEW YORK

AVON BOOKS
A division of
The Hearst Corporation
105 Madison Avenue
New York, New York 10016

Copyright © 1991 by Shelly Thacker Meinhardt
Inside cover author photograph by Jim La Moore
Published by arrangement with the author
Library of Congress Catalog Card Number: 90-93195
ISBN: 0-380-76292-7

First Avon Books Printing: January 1991

AVON TRADEMARK REG. U.S. PAT. OFF. AND IN OTHER COUNTRIES, MARCA REGISTRADA, HECHO EN U.S.A.

Printed in the U.S.A.

RA 10 9 8 7 6 5 4 3 2 1

To Mark
*You are the wind
beneath my wings*

ACKNOWLEDGMENTS

Heartfelt thanks to Angie, Carol, and Suzie for support and encouragement above and beyond the call of duty. My dreams couldn't have come true without the three of you. Score one for TLMB.

Thanks also to GDRWA, and to Annabelle and her Thursday night scribes, for their critiques.

Prologue

Strathfillan Abbey, Scotland, 1291

T he rain soaked Sir Connor of Glenshiel's tunic, carrying tiny rivulets of blood down his back and over his horse's flanks. The violent gusts of wind that whipped over the lowland fields nearly tore him from the saddle, as lightning split the night sky. He blinked hard, wiped his blond hair from his eyes, and peered at the murky shadow just beyond the river. Aye, it was the abbey. *Finally.* Grabbing a handful of mane, he urged the destrier into one last, bone-jarring trot. Fresh pain sliced through his body.

He reached the cloister and, using the last of his strength, slid off the horse's back into the mud. He nearly passed out from the effort. Limping to the doorway, he stood there, swaying, a full minute before Malcolm looked up from the maps he was studying.

His friend's grizzled, stocky form straightened in surprise. "Connor!" Malcolm blurted, his voice more a question than a greeting. Connor had been gone but three days.

"Summon Wil . . . William." Connor could barely force the words past his lips. The chamber was filled with the smell of incense and the monotone chants of the monks on their way to evening prayers. "William," he repeated, lurching into the dimly lit cloister.

Malcolm was already at his side, helping him to
seat near the warmth of the fire. "God's teeth, lad! Wha
happened?" Several of the brothers rushed into the ha
at the sound of a disturbance. "Fetch some salve an
bandages," Malcolm called to them. "And rouse Wil
liam." He turned back to Connor. "The others, lad
Galen and the others, where are—"

"Dead." Connor shook his head, trying desperately t
ignore the physical pain and the much deeper, sharper pai
of grief. He had to stay conscious until he could see Wil
liam. "All dead. We were just over the border . . . Am
bush." The scene two days ago came flooding back. Wha
was to have been a friendly meeting had turned into
bloody slaughter. His brother Galen—young, reckles
Galen—had raced into the clearing first.

And had been the first struck down by the Englis
arrows.

"No weapons . . . they said no weapons. Englis
bastards! 'We'll crush the Scots just . . . just like th
Welsh.' Saints' blood, why did I let Galen come? . .
My fault." Connor was almost babbling now, trying t
resist as the pain from deep gashes and cracked ribs an
a broken wrist tried to drag him into soothing black
ness. "English dogs . . . They sent me back so I coul
tell . . ."

Sir William of Lanark entered the hall at a run. A ta
man of more than two score years, he had paused onl
long enough to don his chemise at the news that Con
nor—and only Connor—had returned. "Saints' blood!"
He turned to Malcolm. "What befell—" Conno
grabbed his tunic and pulled him down to where he coul
hear.

"You were right," Connor rasped, sadness and ange
almost choking him. "No peace with the English . .
They mean to put Balliol on the throne . . . Crush u
. . . just like the Welsh." One of the monks steppe

forward, bandages in hand, but Connor shook his head, spitting out words as fast as he used to skip stones over Loch Shiel as a boy. "The French, William—we must go to the French. The Auld Alliance . . . Might still be . . . loyalties. You were right." And with one bloody hand still gripping his friend's shirt, he finally sank into unconsciousness.

Chapter 1

Chartres, France, 1295

Dawn came cool and clear, crushing Lady Laurien d'Amboise's fervent hopes that rain might postpone her wedding. She had cried herself to sleep last night, for the first time since her mother's death. Now she sat watching as the sun crept up behind the delicate spires of the newly rebuilt cathedral where ''the event,'' as she had come to think of it, would take place.

She scanned the late September sky one last time, looking for any hint of clouds. Nay, the sun would be beating its fullest upon her as they stood before the cathedral doors, exchanged rings, and recited their vows before moving inside for the Mass.

Three maids arrived in the guest room as the first rays reached her window. Patiently, silently, she withstood the preparations as they bathed her with the gentlest wood-ash soap, combed out her honey-brown hair, and began plaiting it. The sun was high above the waking town when they finished. Already, freemen and serfs gathered around the castle walls, ordered in from the fields to pay homage to this girl who would be their lord's next wife. Laurien was beginning to feel like the main course at a St. Michaelmas feast.

None of this would be happening, she thought bitterly, had she been able to complete her quest, begun years before, beside her mother's deathbed.

She had been six then, trembling with cold and fear on that night, her little brother Henri beside her. They'd clasped hands with their mother, who whispered her last words to Laurien—secret words that had changed Laurien's life.

"Louis d'Amboise is not your father, Laurien," she had said, speaking quickly as death drew her into its dark grasp. "I am afraid that, once I am gone, Louis might . . . hurt you. Find your real father. He is a kind and loving man. He will welcome you . . ."

She had died before revealing his name.

Laurien stared out the window, squinting in the morning-bright sun. She had been so close to finding her real father, after thirteen years of searching. If only Henri had not betrayed her.

She banished the memory. Thinking of Henri would only bring more tears, and she had no more time to cry. She needed to think. The maids wound the last plait into place at the back of her neck, secured it with netting and a slim gold circlet, then brought out the gown.

That accursed gown, Laurien thought—that gown of azure and topaz-colored silk, the finest Louis d'Amboise could find. He had ordered the best seamstress in Amboise to make it in the latest style, with a tight-fitting bodice, a flared skirt that trailed along the ground in full folds, and long, tight sleeves with jagged edges. He had the seamstress make a mantle of matching silk, with a jeweled clasp and ermine lining. He'd ordered both to be embroidered with the de Villiers coat of arms. *And ordered me to wear them,* she thought bitterly. Well she would not be the main course of Louis's little feast! She threw up her hands just as the maids were about to slip the gown over her head.

They jumped back quickly. "M-milady?" one ven-

tured. The maids and servants had learned to be wary
of this girl since her arrival a sennight before. In those
seven days, they had discovered that her delicate beauty
and bright green eyes hid an angry storm that swirled
just beneath the surface.

Laurien slipped quickly back into her nightdress. "I—
I am ill. Tell milord that the ceremony must be post
poned." The lie had worked before. Comte Jacques de
Villiers had had no opportunities to show off his betrothed this past week, as an unexplained illness had
kept her away from the many celebrations.

She had spent the time trying to think of some way
to get to Tours. Days before leaving Amboise, Laurien
had received a message from her old friend and tutor
Sister Katherine. It contained but two lines: *I have news
of your father, and must see you. Meet me in Tours
immediately.*

Had Sister Katherine found him at last? Her father—
her *real* father—would surely help her break this betrothal. That very day she had tried to slip unnoticed
from her home, but Henri had seen her leaving. *Damn*
him for stopping her. She chewed thoughtfully on her
lower lip.

She must find a way to Tours.

The three servants had made no move to leave. They
looked at one another, then the brave one spoke again,
her voice quivering. "We c-cannot tell the comte you
are ill, milady. H-he will be displeased. It is best if
you—"

Laurien's sharp look cut her off. "Out! All of you!"
They dropped the gown over a chest at the foot of the
bed and scurried out.

Laurien had had but a moment to herself when her
husband-to-be stormed into the room.

She had hated the idea of marrying him before, but her
reluctance was naught compared to the loathing she had

felt upon meeting Jacques de Villiers. His face was like a moon, his body like a great bowl of frumenty pudding, stuffed into his fine blue and gold silk tunic and leggings. Her gaze traveled down his ridiculous outfit and finally rested on his feet. He wore matching silk shoes—one blue, one gold—with long curled toes in the latest fashion. The image of a goblin from a childhood tale struck her, and despite her black mood, she began to laugh. It was the wrong reaction.

De Villiers crossed the floor in two strides. "Enough!" he yelled and slapped her across the face. Laurien fell to the floor, stunned, her hand on her hot cheek. De Villiers came at her again, grabbing her shoulders and wrenching her to her feet.

"You have embarrassed me enough!" He shook her violently. "You refused to appear at the feasts I have held in your honor and now this!"

He was close enough that she could smell him, and Laurien wanted to retch. De Villiers had made his fortune trading silks and spices, but that was not all he sought on his trips to the East. He brought back something else, a flower called an opium poppy that he had ground into a special snuff. It had rotted his teeth—and his mind, she thought.

She broke free and stepped back, thinking quickly. "How dare you intrude in my chamber!" She tried to sound haughty and brave; in truth she felt so frightened her heart was running a frantic race. Her cheek still tingled. "It is most unseemly for us to be alone together—"

"Unseemly!" he snarled. "*You* speak to me of unseemly? You, who have not the slightest idea of how a proper maiden conducts herself. Once we are wed, I shall teach you!"

"I will *not* wed you!"

"Dare you to think you have a choice? Willful, stubborn little fool. I shall brook this temper of yours no longer!'' In the expanse of flesh his gray eyes glowed at a sudden thought, and his voice lowered to a purr. "You shall say your vows willingly, my dear, because I wish it, and because your father wishes it. But most of all"— he brought out something from his belt—"because I can convince you how unwise it is to resist."

Her gaze locked on the object in his hand—a gilt riding whip.

He snaked out his other hand and grabbed Laurien about the waist, clutching her to him. She glared at him and tried in vain to pull away. "You would not dare! My family—"

"Will not help you now." He brought his mouth savagely down on hers to silence her scream as he ripped the nightdress from her body. The sour taste of rotted teeth and wine invaded her mouth, sending fear and disgust twisting through her; fat fingers pawed her naked limbs. Chilled to her very depths, she fought in outrage to break free. De Villiers cruelly tweaked one rose-tipped breast and brought the whip up to her neck.

He released her mouth at last. "Now, Laurien, you will find, as others have found, that it is best to grant me what I ask." She gasped as he wrapped the thin strip of leather about her neck and began squeezing. "Otherwise, I become . . . unpleasant."

The world was beginning to turn silver-gray at the edges when he suddenly unwrapped the whip and trailed it down her back. She choked and gasped and, for the first time in her life, felt what could only be described as terror.

"If I wish," de Villiers continued as he clutched her again and drew his whip across her buttocks, "I can be most gentle. But displease me . . ." The whip struck home with an expert touch. Laurien cried out as the sharp sting brought tears to her eyes. "And you shall find me disagreeable." He ran his soft fat hands over her smooth curves. "Such wonderful skin. It would be a shame to damage it."

Laurien's anger welled up and overcame her fear. "You animal," she rasped. She was trembling now, not from fright, but from the idea of spending the rest of her life controlled by a man who knew how to hurt her so expertly, a man who obviously enjoyed her pain.

The whip shot out again, snaking across her smooth belly, but this time she bit her tongue to stifle her cry. "Laurien," he said in mock surprise, a smile creeping across his face. "What a vile thing to say about your husband-to-be. We are late, my dearest. Now, put on that gown and come downstairs."

He started for the door. With his hand on the latch he stopped and turned to face her, all traces of false mirth gone. "You have a bruise on your cheek, beloved. See that it is covered before you leave this chamber. And do not make me come back here a second time."

Laurien stood in stunned silence for a long moment after he was gone, her mind racing, trying desperately to think of some way, any way, out of this nightmare. Then, slowly, she picked up the silk wedding gown and began to dress.

The throng spilled into the castle courtyard and lined the street leading to the cathedral, grumbling among themselves. Time spent in town today meant time in the furrows on Sunday if they were to get the harvest in before it rotted. But the lord had demanded a crowd for his wedding, and had issued an order that any caught in the fields on this day would spend the rest of the week in his dungeon.

Vendors were taking advantage of the sullen mood, offering roast mutton, sweetmeats, dark bread, and cool cups of ale to cheer the milling townspeople. Jugglers and mimes earned few coins, but cutpurses found the pickings good.

Near the castle wall, two men in particular attracted attention, despite their best efforts to avoid it. Like many in the crowd, both wore the rough brown broadcloth and simple hoods of pilgrims. The stockier of the two sat on a dappled gray horse that would have been called a nag in even the poorest of families. But the other man, the one with the broad chest and a shock of blond hair falling over dark blue eyes, was mounted on a huge black stallion that pranced impatiently.

"I told you to use a less spirited mount." Malcolm nudged his friend in the ribs with a leg of mutton, as yet another child paused to stare up at the tall pilgrim on the great, black horse.

"I shall need his speed, since I have only this." Connor patted his back, where his shortsword was lashed beneath his cloak. He gave the lad a wink and a smile as his mother pulled him away from the odd pair. "Or would you rather that day's end finds me a wedding guest in de Villiers's dungeon?"

"Nay," Malcolm growled through a mouthful of mutton. "I wouldna wish anyone into that knave's hands."

Connor suddenly turned serious. "I am sorry you had to come, Malcolm—"

"I am the only one who knows the area, even though 'twas long ago," Malcolm cut him off. "So leave it be." He finished his repast and tossed the bone in the dirt.

Connor reined in his nervous charger as a dog dashed out of the crowd to snatch up the bone. "Aye," he said, quickly changing the subject. "I wonder what causes the delay."

From their vantage point near the gate's barbican tower, the two had a clear view of the wedding party assembled in the courtyard. De Villiers had appeared and mounted his white horse, when a servant suddenly called him back inside. Moments later the portly man reappeared, and now he stood talking quietly to his guards.

"Mayhap the lady has reconsidered," Malcolm ventured.

"Reconsidered? A position as wife to the king's most favored adviser? Jewels? Wealth? Any female would give her front teeth for— Wait!" Connor stiffened. "There she is." A low whistle of appreciation escaped him as the girl stepped into the courtyard. She seemed a pleasantly manageable package.

The tall, slim figure walked unescorted toward the waiting horses. Nay, she fair glided, a wisp of softness and silk. She stood out among the glittering nobles like a graceful angel among gaudy statues. Connor shook his head, wondering where that poetic thought had come from. Verse was not one of his talents.

He returned his attention to the girl. Her throat and cheeks were hidden beneath a tightly wrapped wimple, her hair draped in a veil, but he caught a glimpse of delicate features, and her clinging gown revealed full curves. She moved slowly toward her small brown mare, stiffly refused the guard's offered hand, and mounted without help.

De Villiers stood staring at her for a long moment, and she returned the look. From where Connor watched, he could not make out her expression. Finally, the comte remounted and motioned to his guards. The party moved toward the street and the impatient throngs.

Connor turned to Malcom. "Away, my friend. And remember, if I dinna arrive within the hour—"

"I am off to Calais, aye." Malcolm nodded, then added under his breath, "For Scotland, lad!" He maneuvered the dappled nag toward a side street.

Connor's expression hardened. "And for Galen," he whispered.

He turned his black stallion and disappeared into the crowd.

A breeze cooled Laurien's face, chilling the sweat that trickled down her back and under her arms as the wedding party rode through the chateau gates. The air was cold, but she felt as though she were suffocating, her silk cloak an unbearable weight on her slim shoulders. Guards positioned along the route urged the crowd to cheer as she passed into the street, but she heard naught except the steady clop, clop, clop of her horse's hooves on the dirt; felt naught but the slow thud of her own heart.

The autumn sun glinted on gold and jewels as the long line of horses moved through the crowd, a stream of silk-clad ladies in purple and green and red, and knights in clinking chain mail. Laurien rode in the middle of the procession, boxed in by guards on either side, one in front, and one behind. Her numbed mind wondered why they rode in this unusual arrangement, rather than two before and two behind. She watched her betrothed's mount at the head of the line.

De Villiers waved to the crowd on both sides of the cramped street, smiling broadly, twisting left and right in the saddle. He looked like some kind of trained bear waiting to be tossed a fish. Laurien stared blankly at the scene about her, feeling as if she had become only a player in someone else's strange dream.

They passed tiny buildings, clustered about the edge of the chateau like grimy children clinging to their mother's skirt. She looked across a sea of haggard faces, open mouths with missing teeth forming a soundless, gaping O as the spectacle moved past. Hundreds of pairs of dull eyes stared, filled with . . . What was that look? Jealousy? Envy?

They would not envy her so, Laurien thought, if ever

they chanced to spend a few minutes alone with the comte and his whip.

The procession passed into the marketplace at the town's center, and the sea of peasants went on, all clothed in gray fustian or sackcloth colored with yellow and green vegetable dyes. Pilgrims dotted the crowd in their hooded brown cloaks. She knew Chartres and its cathedral was a popular destination—many did not want the risk and expense of a trip to the Holy Land. But she had never seen so many pilgrims in one place.

And there were children everywhere. Some stood on upturned carts, others sat on their parents' shoulders for a better view. One urchin, wailing, caught Laurien's attention. The girl evidently had hurt her knee; her father picked her up and cuddled her, kissing away her tears. Then he kissed her knee, as if to take away the pain.

Laurien quickly looked away, her own eyes filling with tears. What was it like, she wondered, to have such a caring father? If she could know that feeling for only a moment, she would gladly trade places with a peasant girl.

Laurien's chest felt heavy. The passage narrowed on the way out of the market and the wedding party squeezed through a street of timber-framed hovels, where more onlookers leaned out of windows. The air seemed to grow thick with the smells of sweaty bodies, roast meat, and spilled ale, and, over all, the refuse that lined the streets. She tugged at the gold chain fastening her mantle, wanting to throw it off, trying to breathe. She heard a liquid splat as someone tossed a bucket of slops out a window on one of the side streets.

The cathedral loomed before her.

She had seen it up close only once, during the betrothal ceremony. Before that, in distant Amboise, she had heard much of what many said was France's most beautiful cathedral. They approached from a hill to the east, and the midday sun shone through the huge windows so that the luminous reds and blues and violets seemed to dance. But the delicate beauty was wasted on her: inside that cathedral her fate would be sealed. They were close enough now that she could see the outlines of the statues above the doors.

A commotion on the right drew Laurien out of her grim musings. A man on horseback, the largest pilgrim she had ever seen, was jostling for position on a side street. He quieted his mount—a fine stallion—and looked up to stare straight at her. His angular face was young and handsome, and a thatch of blond hair fell over his forehead, giving him a boyish charm despite the broad shoulders and muscular frame that nearly filled the space between buildings.

But what struck her were his eyes, the most vibrant blue eyes she had ever seen, blue like the sheer glass of the cathedral windows. Those eyes held a look unlike any of the other villagers', a look of absolute *determination*. She could not tear her gaze from his. An unfamiliar and unsettling sensation rippled through Laurien's body, searing her like a flash of lightning. The most outlandish idea struck her that, somehow, all his fierce determination was directed completely at her.

One of the guards noticed her stare and broke out of line to question the man. But when Laurien craned her neck to watch what happened, she saw that the strange rider had melted away into the crowd.

The sight of the odd pilgrim scrambled her thoughts. Could it be that de Villiers did not dominate everyone in the city? The thought made her sit taller in the saddle, the anger and fear she had felt that morning flooding back. She would not give him the opportunity to control her! As long as she had a horse under her and her wits about her, she had a chance.

Already her detested betrothed was greeting the priest.

She would have to be quick. If she could break out of the procession and push her way through the crowd, she could be away before any would have a chance to react. She would ride to Tours, to Sister Katherine. She would find her real father. Mother had said he would welcome her; he would save her from this marriage. She had to get away from here, from that animal.

She looked again at the four guards surrounding her. She realized now why they were there—not to protect her, but to keep her in. She could kick one, grab his reins. No, she thought, these bulky men-at-arms would be more than able to fend off her attack. She would need to think of something . . .

Her *aumoniere!*

Like all noble ladies, Laurien wore a large embroidered bag to carry alms for the poor. But hers held more than coins. Laurien had but one possession in the world that mattered to her, and she carried it always: her knife, a slim silver blade with a glimmering emerald in the hilt and a strange runic inscription. Her mother had pressed it into her hand before she died, along with a matching ring, whispering, "He would want you to have these."

Laurien had given the ring to Henri as a token of her love and loyalty. The knife she had kept for herself, a precious reminder of her real father. Last night she had slipped the delicate weapon into her *aumoniere*. Her hand moved slowly to the bag hanging from the silken rope that girdled her waist. She felt the outline of sharp metal.

Stabbing the guard would not work, but she could nick his horse. She didn't want to hurt the animal, but if she could just make it rear, mayhap toss its rider, she would have an open path to freedom. It was her only chance.

She started to open the bag and slip her hand inside when she heard a surprised cry on her right that rippled through the crowd. She turned, and what she saw made her breath catch in her throat. She froze as the blond pilgrim on the huge black stallion came charging straight toward her.

The guards at her side spun their mounts to face the onslaught a moment too late. The rider plunged out of the crowd and plucked her from the saddle.

Laurien screamed as she felt herself ripped from her horse, her waist held in a grip so strong she could not take another breath. The crowd scattered with cries of terror, and from the direction of the cathedral she heard a roar like that of an animal pierced by a huntsman's arrow.

The blond madman shifted her to an awkward position over his lap, and she could see stunned faces watching as the stallion bolted toward a side street. One of the guards managed to wheel his mount and block their path, his weapon ready. She heard the metallic ring of a sword being pulled free of its scabbard.

The horse reared, and she screamed again as she heard the clash of steel on steel just above her head. After only four thrusts, the guard was gripping a bloody wound on his shoulder and they were racing down the street. Behind them she heard another bellow that could only be de Villiers, then the sound of many hooves pounding after them. Terrified peasants flattened themselves against buildings as the horse thundered past.

They rounded a corner, the stallion's muscles bunching and straining, and she could see two guards pushing a haycart into their path. She screamed again as the lunatic spurred his neighing mount onward. She felt the horse's hooves leave the ground—and was suddenly looking down into the guards' startled faces, then at the street rushing up to meet her.

She squeezed her eyes shut, bracing for the inevitable impact, but instead she had the wind knocked out of her by the pilgrim's knees as they landed. He urged the horse on, and they raced through the streets, scattering chickens and pigs from their path. They quickly reached the edge of town and sped across the open fields, a half dozen guards only an arrow's flight behind.

She heard the airy whoosh of a crossbow bolt, then another. The rider hunched down over the horse's neck, squeezing her between his chest and his knees. Despite the protection of her thick mantle, she felt as though he would crush the life from her. She gasped short, terrified breaths, watching flying hooves and meadow grass rush by several feet below. Lather from the horse's shoulder flecked her gown.

Soon the arrows stopped, and Laurien knew the guards were falling behind as the rider headed into the forest. He straightened as they left the path and charged through the trees. She could hear the guards crashing into the underbrush far away. She struggled to sit up.

He stopped just long enough to right her so that she was sitting astride in front of him. She had opened her mouth to beseech him to release her when he brought out a piece of cloth from his tunic and whipped it around her mouth as a gag. Helpless and mute, she could only hold on for sweet life as he spurred the stallion onward.

They plunged faster through the woods. Branches whipped past, tearing at her veil and dress. The pilgrim wrapped his arms around her waist, shielding her with his large frame. Pressed against the hard muscles of his chest, she grew more frightened as they rode deeper into the wood. The gloom thickened around them, the sun only occasionally breaking through the branches overhead. What plans did this wild rider have for her?

It flashed through her head that, for the first time in a sennight, she was free of de Villiers. But the idea only struck new fear into her heart as she pictured what he would find after several days searching the forest: her body, raped and bloodied, hidden beneath a tangle of underbrush.

The trees became a blur, and her eyes focused on the sword still in the pilgrim's hand, the reddened blade resting across her knees. Though her mouth was bound, her mind screamed in a single, endless shriek as a cold wave of fear drenched her. She thought she would faint.

But even in shock, her mind refused to sink into darkness. The rider kept changing directions, turning left, left again, right, then back along their own trail until she no longer heard the sounds of other horses. She longed to close her eyes and waken alone in her room at Amboise, to find that this was only a nightmare. Instead, she was intensely aware of her captor's every move as they galloped onward. She felt his powerful thighs easily guiding the charger, felt the pounding of his heart against her back—or was that her own heart?

They raced through the forest, his body surrounding her with the scent of sweat and leather and horses. Would there be much pain when he took her? Or would she finally black out? Her mind had only begun to imagine what torment possibly lay ahead, when the ride came to an end as suddenly as it had begun.

The pilgrim slowed to a trot and gave an unusual whistle. A moment passed, then she heard an answering whistle rise eerily from the trees to their left. The stallion turned toward the sound. A few paces further on, the rider stopped, eased her to the ground, and moved off.

She felt disoriented, breathless. She put out a hand to steady herself against a tree, but a rough hand took her own and a masculine voice rumbled from the shadows. "So this is our prize." She hadn't heard that language in years, but recognized it as Gaelic. The speaker stepped forward, and she found herself looking not at the rider but at a second pilgrim, an older, stocky man with sandy-brown hair. "Did they follow, lad?"

She spun to her left and saw the fair-haired rider saddling a fresh mount. "Lost them in the trees. We had best not linger."

The shorter man reached toward her with a knife in his hand. Her eyes widened, but he merely cut the cloth that gagged her. She spat out a mouthful of damp fuzz and turned on the blond madman.

"Who—What—Who are you?" she finally sputtered. Her captors looked surprised that she spoke in their tongue. "Whatever you want, my—my family will pay a large ransom for my safe return." She wondered briefly whether that was true.

Both men burst into laughter. " 'Tis not your family's or your betrothed's money we want." The blond man smiled, easily swinging up on his new horse. His companion also mounted a second stallion while the blond man rode over to Laurien.

"Forgive me, but there wasna time for introductions." He gave her a mocking half bow. "I am Sir Connor of Glenshiel. And this"—he indicated his friend with a nod—"is Sir Malcolm MacLennan. And you, Lady Laurien d'Amboise"—he reached down with one arm, lifting her easily onto his saddle—"you are now mine."

Chapter 2

A full moon cast eerie shadows through the branches as they finally left the twisting forest pathways and ventured onto a side road. Laurien still had no explanation of why they had abducted her. What did they want if not rape or ransom? She had asked such a flurry of questions that the Scotsman had gagged her again soon after they left the clearing.

He hadn't bothered to blindfold her, not that it made any difference. The sun had set on her left an hour or so ago, so she knew they were heading north. But they had made so many turns and backtracks in the forest that, even if she had been in her native region of Touraine, she would have been thoroughly lost. The two men slowed their mounts to a trot as they left the forest.

They edged along the side of a rut-carved road, the blond man riding slightly behind and to the right of his companion, holding Laurien firmly in front of him. His right hand moved from her waist to the sword on his back at the slightest sound, but when Laurien made any attempt to slip from the horse, she found her captor's unyielding arm locked about her instantly.

Several times he stopped to peer into the darkness behind them. Laurien peered as well, certain at one point that she saw the shape of a rider melting into the trees. Her heart leaped with hope. Mayhap it was Henri. But she wondered if her brother would even try to rescue her. And what if it were de Villiers's men? Which was better—to go back to that animal or to take her chances with the fair-haired giant who held her captive?

She had no time to think on it further. The stocky man reined in and gestured to a broken-down building that loomed out of the darkness at a fork in the road ahead.

Connor stopped beside him. "The Front de Boeuf."

"Aye. No lord or lady would set a slipper through her door. There's none but knaves and cutpurses inside that dark belly."

Laurien felt her captor's tense muscles relax. "Good. Just our kind." He gave his friend a crooked smile and his teeth shone in the moonlight. Laurien shivered.

They rode around to the back of the inn, where a ramshackle lean-to served as a stable. Connor leaped to the ground and reached up for Laurien. She was uncomfortably aware of the strength and warmth of his hands as he lifted her easily from the saddle. His hands lingered at her waist until she got her balance. She tried to break free, but he grabbed her wrist and pulled her back against him.

"Dinna try anything, I warn you. 'Tis far to the nearest town and you will find no help inside these doors." His voice was low and his piercing blue eyes reinforced the threat. His fingers circled her wrist like talons, as though her arm were no more than a twig that he could snap at the slightest whim.

She would much prefer a night alone in the forest to a night in this place with him. She would tell him as much, she assured herself with a bravery even she did not believe, were her mouth not gagged.

As if reading her thoughts, he grinned and relaxed his grip ever so slightly. "For your own safety, 'twould be wise to stay near me." Leaving Malcolm to see to the horses, he headed for the inn's rear door, tugging her along behind.

The door opened onto a tiny cooking area filled with smoke from an open firepit and the smell of hot broth. Strips of dried cod and venison hanging from the rafters hit Connor in the head as he strode through the entrance. A plump serving girl looked up, startled, nearly dropping the emaciated chicken she had been plucking.

"Good eventide." Connor smiled, pulling Laurien close as she tried again to wrest her arm free. He did speak French, she realized. Could this hulking pilgrim truly be a knight? A noble? "Have you a chamber for milady?"

The wench could not tear her eyes from Laurien's gown and fur-lined mantle. Laurien tried to catch her gaze, her eyes pleading for aid, but the girl pointed to a door at the far end of the room. Looking at the gag in Laurien's mouth, she held out her hand. *"Un argent."*

Frowning, Connor reached into his tunic and tossed her a coin. "Indeed there are thieves here," he muttered in Gaelic. *"Merci."* He bowed and pulled out another silver coin. The girl grabbed for it, but he snatched it back. "On a cold night such as this, there would be travelers warming themselves within?"

The girl nodded, her eyes on the gleaming circle of metal.

"If you were to entertain them, mayhap dance for them, I would be most grateful." He slipped the silver onto the feather-covered table where the girl sat. "And this will be here when you are finished."

Smiling, the wench stood and smoothed her ragged skirts, pulled at her bodice to reveal more of her considerable bosom, and ambled out. Connor waited until the sound of a stringed instrument reached them, then flipped his hood up, did the same for Laurien, and hurried toward the door.

The inn's main room hosted only a handful of travelers, and by this late hour, all were well into their cups. Some sat with their heads on the tables, jaws slack, hands still gripping their tankards. The rest were engaged in grabbing at the serving wench as she spun to a drunken tune played on a lute that was obviously missing several strings. None of the bleary eyes took particular notice of the unusual pair making their way up the stairs.

Connor picked a room at the end of the hall, looked around as he opened the door, and stepped inside. Relying on light from the hall, he opened the shutters of the room's only window. Moonlight spilled across the floor, illuminating their surroundings.

The chamber was strewn with filthy rushes that looked as though they hadn't been changed since the inn had been built. A hand-hewn pallet bed filled one corner, and a tiny fireplace took up the adjacent wall. The only other furniture was a three-legged stool. Connor closed and bolted the door behind them and knelt by the fireplace. At least the innkeeper had supplied a small amount of firewood, along with flint and iron.

Laurien looked out at the moon and shivered despite her mantle. Now that her captor finally had his back to her, she began to fumble with the gag knotted at the back of her head. Where were they? She had been searching her memory for the name Front de Boeuf since Connor said the words, but she had never heard of this place.

She considered the distance to the open window, wondering how far it was to the ground below. It could not be that high, she decided; from outside, the inn appeared a squat little building. And mayhap the Scotsman had lied. There might be a town nearby where she could find aid and obtain directions to Tours. If she could get to the stables . . .

Connor started a fire and turned toward Laurien, pulling a knife from his boot. She backed against the far wall, fear making her stumble. So he did intend to rape her at knifepoint! For an instant she thought of her own little knife, then just as quickly discarded the idea as she marked the size of his blade.

Well, she was not going to stay around to give him the chance to use it on her! He reached for her, but she slipped to one side. Darting under his arm, she scrambled out the window before he could catch her.

She heard an angry oath behind her as she hit the thatched roof of the first level and slid off, clutching two handfuls of straw. She slammed into the ground on her side and sucked in her breath at the pain.

For a squat little building, the inn was awfully tall.

Staggering up and lifting her heavy skirts, she ran for the stables. She heard Connor hit the ground behind her.

She had barely cleared the corner when she ran straight into Malcolm, tumbling them both to the ground. His green eyes widened. "Saints' breath—"

Laurien didn't even have time to untangle herself. A now-familiar arm looped around her waist, and she felt herself lifted into the air.

"How did she get out?"

Laurien caught only a glimpse of angry eyes as Connor threw her over his shoulder and headed for the stables. "She leaped out the window." She kicked her legs wildly and pounded on his back to no avail. She remembered the sting of de Villiers's whip that morning and could only imagine what kind of punishment the Scotsman would mete out for her attempted escape.

Still sitting in the dirt, Malcolm laughed. "The lass leaped out a window? God's teeth, what a handful!"

Connor grabbed a length of rope from the lean-to, turned on his heel, and carried Laurien back past his laughing companion. "Get us some ale. I need it after this day.'' She was still pounding on his back as they reentered the inn.

He shrugged to the two or three revelers who looked their way this time. ''Unhappy bride.'' The comment sent a wave of laughter through the room. One man gave him a drunken salute with a broadsword.

Connor took the stairs in three strides, opened the door with his shoulder, and lowered Laurien onto the pallet bed, pinning her with his weight as he pulled out his knife again. ''You have naught to fear from me. And if you call out you will get no help from those below.'' She felt the cold metal against her cheek as he cut away her gag.

Laurien moved her jaw, the muscles sore and strained. Her breath was ragged, her heart pounding, but she glared into the indigo eyes just inches from her own. ''I-I do not fear you. I despise you, you knave!'' She struggled to throw him off. She did not like the way he held her helpless, the way his sinewy arms pinned her so easily.

He ignored her angry words. ''Anything broken?'' He pulled aside her mantle and boldly probed her left side. Even through the thick silk of her gown, she felt a warmth tingling down her body as his fingers moved along her ribs. She inhaled sharply, not from pain, but from surprise at the unfamiliar sensation, and fear at what might happen next.

''I cannot breathe,'' she lied. He sat up, and with a single desperate motion, she pushed off the bed and snatched the little blade from her *aumoniere*. The green jewel glimmered in the firelight. ''If it is rape you intend, you will find me more than able to defend myself.''

The crooked grin curved across his features as he slid from the bed and moved toward her. ''I dinna make a habit of forcing myself on spoiled, pampered, unwilling damsels.''

"Aye, *pilgrim*,'' she sneered, ignoring his jibe, her knife and the distance between them loosening her tongue. "And next you will tell me you are as chaste as a monk.'' She backed slowly toward the door.

"Nay.'' His smile widened. He edged around to the right, his gaze traveling over her body and finally resting on her face. She felt warmth rising in her cheeks at the unspeakably blatant appraisal. His expression sent the clear message that he wouldn't care if a damsel were spoiled and pampered, as long as she was willing. When those luminous blue eyes rose to her face, she unwittingly stopped moving away.

Taking the advantage, he grabbed her hand and twisted the knife from her grip. The blade clattered to the floor, and he kicked it away into the rushes. "Never draw a weapon unless you intend to kill. And if you intend to kill me, I suggest you find a weapon larger than that sliver.''

He still held her hand, looking down at her with eyes that conveyed not anger or thoughts of punishment, but mirth. The tingling warmth again spread from his fingers into her own and up her arm, making her tremble. Had he told her true? Did he mean her no harm? She tried to pull away but he held her tight, and for a moment she had the strangest feeling that he was going to kiss her. Instead, he finally stepped away and picked up the rope where he had dropped it by the door. After tying her hands in front of her, he led her back to the bed.

"Sit.'' He pulled up the three-legged stool and sat nearby.

He spoke as one used to having his orders obeyed— just like her stepfather, Louis. The thought sparked her anger, drowning the tingling sensations that still tickled her skin. "I am not some trained bear who will jump at your every command." She remained standing.

He glowered at her. "I would explain—"

"Why have I been taken against my will, manhandled, dragged on a mad ride through the forest in the dead of night—"

"If I must gag you again to get you to listen, woman, I shall."

She rubbed her jaw, the muscles still sore from having been gagged the better part of the day. She sat. Leaning back against the wall, she decided she had best keep her temper in check. Hard experience with Louis—and, lately, de Villiers—had taught her that to show defiance only earned her a beating. But she felt a tiny grain of trust that this Scotsman would not hit her. He had certainly had ample opportunity to harm her, if that was his intention. But thus far his touch had been quite . . . She could not think of a word to describe it or how it made her feel.

Except, mayhap, *uneasy*.

She gazed at her hands in her lap. "I am ready to hear your explanation, milord."

Connor grinned again. Her voice still held a measure of fire despite her suddenly meek expression. It was unusual for a woman to show him defiance. Most tried to get what they wanted from him either by whining pleas or coy lies. And none had dared pull a knife on him before. "Malcolm was right. You are a handful."

She shrugged.

He leaned back against the edge of the fireplace, studying her features, deciding how much he could afford to tell her. Framed by the silken veil and wimple, her face was a pale oval, graced by large eyes, a long, straight nose, and delicately sculpted lips. When he did not speak, she looked up at him and arched one brow.

Haughty wench. This was a girl used to days spent

trying new plaits for her hair, a pampered pet whose biggest concern before now was choosing what color floss to use in her needlecraft. She was obviously impatient to return to her wealthy betrothed: she had done naught but try to escape since her feet touched the ground.

"My task is to get us to . . ." He paused, looking at her through narrowed eyes. "To where it is we are going with our skins intact. 'Twill be much easier if I dinna have to worry about you leaping out of windows at every opportunity."

"Aye. So?"

"So I will tell you why we are doing what we are doing. And you will agree to cooperate—"

"I shall not agree to anything," Laurien said.

Connor sighed. There was much to be said in favor of docile, quiet women. "Stop interrupting. Scotland is trying to secure her freedom from the English. Five years ago, the last heir to the Scottish throne died, and Edward I of England insisted he had a feudal right to choose our next king—"

"And he chose John Balliol." She shook her head, obviously irritated that this was turning into a history lesson. "What has it to do with me?"

Connor gritted his teeth. Her knowledge surprised him, but he was beginning to regret having unleashed the bold tongue behind those exquisite lips. "Saints' blood, woman, let me finish. Edward thought Balliol would be naught but a puppet, and we feared the same— but Balliol surprised us all. Edward wanted to garrison English troops in our border castles. He demanded that Balliol come to London, help pay for the English army. But our king refused."

Connor stared into the flames. Laurien noticed the way the light accented the strong, straight line of his jaw, the rough-hewn angles of his cheekbones. She low-

ered her eyes again, perplexed. Why could she not seem
to stop looking at him? She cleared her throat to urge
him to finish his explanation.

He frowned at her impertinence and continued. ''Balliol repudiated the homage he had sworn to Edward. He
called together a small group of trusted knights, including myself and Malcolm.''

Connor remembered that day vividly, how he had surprised his friends by arguing for peace. But even at the
age of one-and-twenty, he had already seen more than
his share of bloodshed, in the battles he had fought as a
mercenary on the continent. And Scotland had settled
with the Norse but thirty years before. He was loath to
see that kind of bloodshed return to his homeland.

He looked again into Laurien's puzzled eyes, thinking
ruefully how their entire plan hinged on this one recal-
citrant female. ''The meeting went on for hours. We
were evenly split—some argued for war, some thought
we should form an alliance with France.''

Laurien nodded. ''Our two countries formed an alliance over a hundred years ago—''

''The Auld Alliance. Aye. But some of us thought to
sue for peace. So a small group was sent to meet with
the English.'' He moved his stool closer to the fire, remembering another cold autumn night, a desperate ride
over rain-soaked roads, his brother Galen's blood soaking the English soil.

''I was the only one who returned.'' He paused, ran
his fingers through his hair, rubbed his tired eyes, and
finally continued. ''After that, a handful of us traveled
to France to meet with the king and his advisers. To
negotiate an alliance. Well, that dragged on and on, until last year we thought we had finally closed the agreement. We returned to Scotland. Then we received a
missive from Comte Jacques de Villiers.''

Laurien shivered, her nails digging into her palms at

the mention of the name. She was completely lost again, unable to see any connection between herself and this alliance.

Connor watched her odd reaction and went on. "The note was a demand for a bribe. Five thousand silver marks, or de Villiers would oppose the treaty. As I am sure you know, your betrothed has the king's ear. We had no doubt he would make good his threat, and our chances would be ended. We paid."

Laurien thought of her own strange dowry, how de Villiers had offered to accept coin in place of land. "But why would de Villiers want such a huge sum—"

" 'Twas not the end. After we paid what he asked, he demanded more. Another ten thousand marks. Well, Scotland hasna the wealth to fill his coffers, and we dinna have the time to waste. In the past few months, English troops have been seen along our border. There is fear that they will soon attack our lowland castles unless we have French support."

He turned to face her again, and Laurien thought he seemed oddly divided—moonlight playing over the left side of his face, firelight illuminating the right. His teeth gleamed in a sly smile. "Then, a few weeks ago, we heard through our friends here that de Villiers was to marry again. A girl from the provinces, a girl he went to great trouble and expense to woo and win."

Laurien stared at him, openmouthed, as realization struck her in a sudden bolt. "So you thought—"

"So Malcolm and I were sent back to France, but this time on a different mission. By holding you hostage, we mean to assure de Villiers's quick cooperation. You shall come to no harm, and you will be returned anon to your beloved's arms."

Laurien leaned forward on the bed, shaking her head in disbelief. Any thought of holding her temper in check had just been reduced to cinders. "You mean to win an alliance by force? How like a man!"

"I dinna ask for your opinion of our plan. I require only an answer to my question: will you cooperate, or would you prefer to spend the next several weeks bound and gagged?"

He stood, towering over her, his eyes suddenly fierce, the shadows from the fire making him seem like some Viking warrior risen from ancient flames.

She raised her chin and returned his gaze squarely. "I will give you an answer, Scotsman. I am not going back to de Villiers. Ever."

Now it was Connor who blinked in confusion. "Not go back—"

"Just being in the same room with him makes me want to retch. He is cruel and brutal. The first time I saw him he was nearly choking a servant to death for daring to spill broth on a new tablecloth."

Connor stared at her. She must be lying, but he could not discern what she hoped to gain by it. He believed that de Villiers was capable of such violence, but what would that matter to a woman offered position and wealth as his wife? "Many lords punish their servants with blows. 'Tis his right."

"His right? To gain obedience by the pain of his fist and his whip? To win loyalty by force?" Her anger made her forget her bound hands, and she leaped to her feet. "Aye, I suppose you admire that. You two are much alike."

He grabbed her shoulders and stared into her furious eyes. "Nay. You know naught of me." She was not lying. The hatred that burned in those green depths could only be real.

"But I know much of him. And I will not go back!"

"That wasna one of your choices. You will be returned to de Villiers. Our alliance depends on it."

"I wish you could have your alliance. Believe that. But I will not be your pawn."

"Very well, then. You have made your choice." He released her and stepped back. "I shall simply keep you bound."

"Then watch your back, Scotsman." Her lips curled into a mocking imitation of his lopsided grin. "For I shall run when I can. I shall watch for every tiny opportunity to escape."

He nodded, his lips a grim line. "Thinking only of yourself. How like a woman." He pronounced the last four words distinctly, then turned on his heel and departed.

Surprised at his sudden exit, left with no target for her anger, Laurien stood, looking at the door, at the window, and back again. He hadn't even bothered to close the shutters. Was he mocking her threat to escape? But then, she thought, she would have a hard time making an exit with him in the hall below. And with her hands tied, she did not want to risk a second attempt through the window. Her ribs still ached from her first jump.

The ache brought back memories of his soothing touch, the tingling path of his probing fingers. Never had a man touched her in that way. It was not the clammy pawing of de Villiers, or the greedy fumbling of the younger knights and swaggering squires she had met. His touch had been a soft caress. Her thoughts drifted on, and she wondered how his fingers might have felt on her bare skin . . .

She shook her head, amazed at her own musings. What was she thinking of? Of course he had been concerned about her. He would not want his prize damaged. She would have to be in perfect condition when returned to de Villiers. Aye, despite his handsome face and charming smiles, this Scotsman was just like every other man she had ever known. He was using her to his own ends, demanding that she bend to his will. When the door opened and Connor strode in, carrying an armful of clothing, she had worked herself back into a fury.

"For me? How kind." Her words dripped with false sweetness.

"I know these are not what you are used to, milady." He returned her sarcasm. "But they are necessary for our disguise."

"Disguise?" She watched as he set each piece in a neat pile on the bed. All matched the brown homespun that her captor and his friend wore. There were a pair of leggings, a long tunic, a belt, gloves, and dark leather boots.

"Aye. Those searching for us will be looking for a pilgrim traveling with a finely dressed lady, not pilgrim men returning from their journey to Chartres."

"Clever," she said tartly, though she really did think it was a workable plan. "But I have already said I will not help you."

He sighed, sat on the bed next to the garments, and rubbed his eyes. "Milady, I willna argue any more this night. 'Twould be so much easier if you would cooperate—"

"Easier for you."

"Think on it," he snapped. " 'Tis foolish to resist. You dinna know where you are, and if you did, where have you to go? De Villiers has every one of his guards out searching for you by now. You would stand no chance on your own."

She stiffened. "You do not know where I might run. And I am certainly not going to tell you."

He shook his head in exasperation. "Very well then, do what you will. But be warned, you willna get far." He rose from the bed and again drew his knife. This time Laurien did not back away.

"So you trust me that much." He reached for her hands. "Shall I trust you as well? Shall I leave you unbound tonight? You would be better able to sleep."

She looked up. Was he holding the promise of comfort before her like a carrot before a hare, only to jerk it away at the last moment? She echoed his words. "Do what you will."

He looked down at her through half-closed lids. Her eyes were as dark and cool as the night sky. His lips parted in a whisper. "Is that an invitation?" From the moment he had first held her in his arms, he had been aching to steal a kiss. The girl was too lovely for her own good. She obviously had parents who had humored her every whim and given her free rein much too often. Her spirit had never known a master. Her pride cried out to be humbled.

"Nay, churl." Laurien tried to push him away, but her bound hands were little help. He pulled her to his chest and raised a hand to her cheek. When she winced as if in pain, he withdrew it.

"Something wrong, milady?" He smiled at her reaction. Did she think that acting coy would make him stop? She tried harder to push him away, but he held her tight and pulled back the silk wimple that covered her cheek. His eyes narrowed at the sight of a large dark bruise.

"What is this?" She turned her face away. Holding her chin with his free hand, he brought her eyes back to meet his. "Is it from the rough journey today? Truly, Lady Laurien, I didna intend to hurt you."

She jerked her chin free, ignoring the tickling warmth that was beginning to melt through her. His concern was false. What matter to him that she had tasted of a man's brutality? It had not been the first time, and she doubted it would be the last. "Nay. It was another man who caused that little pain."

"De Villiers?" Connor's voice lowered to a growl. Only the weakest of knaves would attack a defenseless person. A picture flashed into his mind of himself, lying at the feet of the English on that cold autumn night, beaten bloody while bound hand and foot, helpless while his brother lay dying, only inches away.

"Aye. De Villiers." She raised her brows and blinked innocently. "You are surprised? After all, as you said, it is his *right*." She stopped struggling to get away. "Now release me."

But Connor seemed not to hear the last words. The women of his acquaintance were mostly shallow, self-interested creatures; the stubborn dignity in this girl struck a chord deep within him that had not been played in a long time. He found himself responding to the pain and anger in her eyes before he even had time to consider what he was doing. Instead of releasing her, he wrapped one arm around her and gently stroked her unbruised cheek.

The tension in Laurien's stomach spread upward as he traced strong fingers along her jawline. His eyes flickered over her face, the firelight reflecting an almost sad tenderness that made Laurien feel weak. Their fight, her anger, everything was lost in that bright indigo gaze. Strangely enough, the tension began to leave her body. Her silk-clad form seemed to mold naturally to his hard, lean lines. The rough cloth of his sleeve tickled her bare neck where her wimple had fallen away. She shivered and tried to clear her thoughts. "You . . . you had noth—"

His kiss silenced her whispered words. He lowered his head to hers and covered her mouth with a gentle sweetness, bending her slightly backward so that her body arched into his. The tingling warmth of his fingers was naught compared to the sensations that swirled through her as his lips moved over her own. She felt as though she had been enveloped in a cascade of sparks, as if every part of her body had at once become brilliantly alive. Then as suddenly as it began, the kiss ended, leaving her dizzy, as if she had drunk a tankard of honeyed wine all in one gulp.

He stood her upright and sliced through the ropes that bound her wrists. "Now, milady"—his voice was a husky whisper—"I will spend the night below your window, and Malcolm will be outside the door. And when I return on the morrow, I suggest you be dressed in your new garments." Still holding her arms, he pressed his cheek against hers, and she could feel his rough beard against her skin, his warm breath tickling her ear. "And if you dinna wish to change, I shall be more than willing to help."

Releasing her at last, he left Laurien alone with her jumbled thoughts and only the cold moon for a companion. What an infuriating man! How could he demand her obedience one moment, then turn gentle and teasing the next? His moods were as hard to follow as the twisting forest pathways they had ridden earlier, making her feel equally lost.

She bent over and fished through the dirty rushes. He hadn't even bothered to take her knife. She found it near the fireplace and slipped it back into her *aumoniere*. Did he think her so weak and defenseless? Frowning, she sat on the bed and rubbed her wrists. Was leaving her free for the night truly for her comfort, or to show his disdain? The thought of being subject to this man's will made her angry all over again.

She thought once more of the question she had asked herself earlier that night. Was it better to go back to de Villiers or to take her chances with her captor? Well, that choice—like all the other choices in her life—had been made for her. She could only choose to cooperate, or fight him every step of the way.

She flung herself across the bed and pounded clenched fists into the straw sack that served as a mattress. She heard a small tearing sound as she did so and rolled back to a sitting position, looking at her gown. That accursed gown! Only this morning one man had been trying to force her into it, and now another was trying to force her out of it!

As she examined her raiment by the firelight, her anger almost turned to laughter. The fine silk gown that her stepfather had given so much concern was utterly ruined. The de Villiers gold and blue was stained by the sweat of Connor's horse and dirt from the roads, torn in a hundred places from the branches along the forest paths. It gave her an odd sense of satisfaction to have ruined the one thing about her that her stepfather had cared for.

Cared? Nay, that was the wrong word. She wasn't certain Louis truly cared for anything. Certainly not for her.

Until this summer, he had never even broached the subject of choosing a husband for her. It was not out of respect for her restless nature, Laurien knew, but from a desire to hold on to her wealth. For when Mother died, they discovered that she had willed to Laurien her own dower lands, rich tracts along the Loire.

As long as Laurien remained unmarried, her stepfather managed the manors and pocketed the profits. But when she wed, the lands would pass into the hands of her husband. Though Louis seemed to despise his stepdaughter, rather than cast her out and lose his income, he simply tolerated her presence.

He had always driven suitors away . . . except Comte Jacques de Villiers. The memory brought a lump to her throat, and she walked to the window, letting the cold night breezes chill the pain. She had waited for Louis to send the prancing fool on his way, but de Villiers had made a most unusual proposition.

He had proclaimed he was so taken with her that he would accept coin, rather than the usual pledge of land, for her dowry. He had also promised to make his new bride sign her lands over to Louis. She would never forget her stepfather's delighted face when he informed her that a betrothal had been arranged.

Clenching her hands into fists, Laurien returned to the bed. The fire was low, and she stared into the dying flames.

Where have you to go? Connor's words burned into her.

Tours, she wanted to cry out. Mayhap her real father awaited her there even now. Laurien had been educated at the convent at Tours, and become friends with her favorite tutor, Sister Katherine. It was Katherine who had discovered that the strange runes on Laurien's knife were Danish. They had been searching for Laurien's father in Denmark, through messengers and friends, ever since.

Mayhap Sister Katherine had located him at last. Mayhap that was why she had insisted, *Meet me in Tours immediately.* It would be just like Katherine to plan such a surprise.

Laurien fingered the brown cloth of the garments piled on the bed. The beginnings of a smile tugged at her lips. Very well, she would play the Scotsman's game for now. She would not try to hinder their journey. But she would not return to de Villiers, she promised herself. As soon as she figured out where they were, she would escape and make her way to Tours. Betrothals could be broken. Her real father would help her. Mother had said he was kind.

Without another thought, Laurien unfastened her ermine mantle, pulled the ruined silk gown over her head.

and dropped both to the floor. Sitting on the bed, she slipped off the circlet, wimple, and netting. The night wind caressed her bare skin as she begun unplaiting her hair. Beyond her window she saw that silvered clouds had at last drifted into the sky, making it seem as though the blue stars winked at her. Her somber mood melted in a laugh.

"You may find, Sir Connor of Glenshiel"—she smiled, shaking free her hair—"that you have gotten more than you wagered on."

"The miller went where?" Connor turned to Malcolm, blinking, realizing his friend had been speaking.

"Nay. I said the miller's two daughters take the traveler by the hand and lead him . . ." Malcolm sighed, wrapping his cloak tighter against the night wind. "Oh, leave it be. 'Tis a jest, and you are obviously in no mood."

Malcolm finished his bowl of greasy broth with a loud slurp and followed it with a swig of ale. "Cold broth and warm ale. I shall have the stomach ills tonight, I tell you. Wouldna feed this to a cat. I knew I should have bought some extra mutton from that vendor in Chartres when I had the chance . . . Connor? You havena heard a word I've said, have you? Twenty English riders are coming over the hill, Connor."

"What about the mill?" Connor turned to him again with the same vacant stare. "Sorry, Malcolm. I am tired. Or mayhap 'tis the food and ale they serve in this place. You should have bought some extra mutton from that vendor in Chartres." He emptied his cup onto the grass with a frown. A bowl of broth sat untouched by his side.

Malcolm laughed, keeping his voice low so as not to waken the lady above. Since he hadn't heard a loud crash, he assumed her to be abed. He had balanced a large serving platter borrowed from the kitchen against her door and joined Connor for a quick meal below Laurien's window before resuming his guard. "My friend, I have seen you tired, and I have seen you drunk, and I have seen you addled over many a pretty face—and I can tell you this is definitely the last. Why, I remember the first time you bedded Ceanna, you were like this for a sennight—" He suddenly thumped down his tankard and looked at his friend, alarmed. "Connor, tell me you didna—"

"Nay, Malcolm." Connor smiled at the older man's inference.

"Good." Malcolm sat back, still regarding Connor with a suspicious frown. "De Villiers will expect the lass back in the same condition in which she left, or the whole thing will be off."

"Fear not. She is untouched." Connor's smile faded, remembering the sight of Laurien standing defiant in her torn gown, her green eyes bright with hate. "Except by de Villiers's hands."

"You think he took her after the betrothal? She told you that?"

"Nay, but she has the bruises to prove it."

"That son of a whore. Trust a serpent like him to beat a woman. Why—" Malcolm paused with his cup halfway to his lips. "Wait a moment. How do you know she has bruises when she is swaddled in silk from head to toe?"

"I saw but one, on her cheek, and I can guess the rest. Oh, leave off, Malcolm." He shook his head and looked away from his friend's still-suspicious gaze. "She is no different than the pampered little lackwits at home. I have no feelings for her." But even as his mouth formed the words, he was thinking of the determined set to her chin as she defied his demands, then the sweetness of her lips against his own, the way her curves molded to his body. Why had he kissed her?

"Well, see that you dinna. After all we have been through to get this far, you can ill afford to become attached to the lass."

"You know me better. She is the shortest path to our alliance, no more." He never should have kissed her. The thought had plagued him since he left her chamber. Why had he given in so easily to his desire? Was it because he saw mirrored in her eyes his own pain? Or did he simply want to bend her body to his will as he could not bend her spirit? The worst part was that he had been fighting a mental battle all night, fighting the urge to return to her room and take her in his arms . . .

Either way, Malcolm was right. Concern or attraction, he could ill afford to have feelings for the girl.

Especially since he would be alone with her all day on the morrow.

". . . and the sooner we have done and make for home, the better I shall feel," Malcolm said.

Connor tried again to bring his thoughts back to the problem at hand. " 'Twill not be as easy as we thought, my friend. She doesna want to go back."

"Why ever not?"

"She dislikes him." Connor shrugged. "He offers her wealth and position and one of the finest castles in all France, and she doesna want a bit of it."

"Does she think she will find better?"

"I dinna pretend to know what any woman thinks." Connor stretched out his legs, folded his arms across his chest, and settled back against the cold inn wall as Malcolm rose to leave. "But she has to go back. That is simply that."

Malcolm laughed, slapping his knees.

"And what is there to laugh about?" Connor gave his jovial friend a dour look. "We have enough to worry about with a long journey ahead of us, and she plans to fight us at every turn."

Malcolm stopped chuckling long enough to do his best imitation of Connor. " 'Simple.' " He spoke in a growl through a lopsided smile. " 'Kidnap one provincial lady, bring her to Scotland, and return her to the love-hungry de Villiers after he delivers the goods. Wonderfully simple.' Didna you say that less than a fortnight ago?"

"Aye. Well, 'twould seem I have gotten more than I wagered on."

"Duty before beauty, lad."

"Thank you." Connor tossed the empty wooden tankard at him. "I shall have that added to the family coat-of-arms. Wherever would I be without you to remind me?"

Malcolm chuckled again and turned to leave, pointing emphatically to the room above.

Chapter 3

⟡

$\mathbf{T}$he bright light of early morning filled the chamber, and Connor blinked at the vision before him. He had expected to find milady still lazing abed, or at best wearing her gown and spitting defiance. For a moment he thought he had stepped into the wrong room.

Laurien stood beside the window, the first rays of dawn warming her face. Her unbound hair tumbled to her waist in a riot of spice-colored curls. The simple brown garments did much more for her figure than had the silk gown that lay in a heap at the end of the bed. He'd had them made in a small size, not expecting to find de Villiers's bride to be a tall girl with womanly curves. And what curves! The rough cloth clung to her full breasts, the loosely cinched belt revealing a tiny waist with a swell of hips below. His eyes traced every line of her long legs and finally returned to her face.

Laurien smiled and gave him a jaunty salute with one gloved hand. "Well?" She squared her shoulders. "Do I pass? Do I make a convincing man?"

She tilted her head as she spoke, and a stray curl fell over one eye, adding a taunting charm to her grin. It was as if some woodland revelers had come in the night and replaced the young woman with one of their own. His gaze roamed over her body once more.

"Only from a distance . . ." Aye, and he'd best remember to keep *his* distance. God's teeth, this was go-

43

ing to be a long day. "But that will have to do. Malcolm is waiting below with fresh mounts." He handed her the brown cloak he had brought. "This will help."

He watched as she quickly fastened the cloak about her neck. Her eagerness was an act, he knew, a game meant to lull him into unwatchfulness so she could escape. He usually enjoyed such diversions, but women made poor opponents, for they were unable to parry more than a few well-aimed thrusts. He bent to pick up her discarded dress and mantle.

"Nay, they are ruined. Leave them." Laurien stopped him, her tone flat. She pointed to the *aumoniere* hanging from her belt. "I will take only my coins. They might be useful."

He straightened and looked at her with mock surprise. "My, but you *are* helpful this morn."

She shrugged. "As you said yourself, I have no chance to escape."

"I see." Connor nodded. Did she think he would be so easily fooled? He had no intention of relaxing his guard—or leaving behind a trail of clues. He would send Malcolm back for the garments. "We will leave them, then."

She smiled in satisfaction.

He decided to see how much rope was needed to trip her up.

"I am pleased you have decided after all to cooperate. Will you swear you shallna attempt escape?" Say it, he urged in his mind. Make a vow you have no intention of keeping. Just like— He broke off his own thought. *Sibylla.* How many times in the last nine years had he used that name as a curse? He looked at the girl standing before him, the dawn light making stray tendrils of her hair glow in a halo about her face, innocent features masking her easy untruths. That was who she reminded him of, he thought with a suddenness that was like someone throwing open a door. *Sibylla*.

"I swear." Laurien sighed, as if annoyed that he would even ask. "You were right. It is foolish to resist. I am better off going with you to— Where is it you said we are going?"

He shook his head. She was like a troubador, thinking to play him as if he were a pipe, but she would find his notes sour when blown with the breath of falsehoods. "I did not."

Her hair was darker than Sibylla's, her skin paler, but she had that same haughty pride, that way of eagerly twisting her lips around a lie. It brought to mind an image of his once-beloved Sibylla, her belly fat with another man's babe.

Was that the chord this girl had struck in him last night, a memory that both filled him with tender longing and gave him an almost violent urge to break her spirit?

Laurien shifted uncomfortably under his hard stare. "Why will you not tell me? I have promised I shall not hinder you—"

He held up a finger to cut her off. "And that leads us to a second oath. You will, of course, follow my orders. You will"—he leaned closer, putting the full force of his deep voice into the last words—"obey me."

He caught the faintest twitch of a taut muscle in one smooth cheek, and instead of a quick flurry of words, this time she answered slowly. "Aye," she breathed, her voice soft, her manner meek.

He looked down at her in silence, and a slow grin spread across his features. "Then, milady, let us begin our journey."

Sir Malcolm was waiting for them below. Laurien saw only two horses and stifled a groan. After Connor's kiss last night, spending another day in his lap would be more than she could bear. And it would afford her no opportunity to escape.

She waited silently, doing her best to appear the humble and obedient female, while Sir Malcolm regaled them with the story of how he acquired the horses. It seemed he had to explain to the stableboy three times, that, aye, he wanted to trade the two fine stallions for nags.

As he finished the tale he handed Connor a bundle of food. "Safe journey, my friend. Keep an eye for de Villiers's guards. The roads are likely full of them by now."

"Aye, and see that you heed your own advice."

"When would you say 'twould be best for me to head back?"

Laurien had impatiently walked over to the horses, but she spun about at Malcolm's question. "Back? Back to Chartres?"

Connor ignored her. "I think we can let de Villiers sweat another day, mayhap two. But do not tarry here overlong, lest he lop off your head when you bring him the demands."

Malcolm nodded. "I will leave tomorrow afternoon, and meet you at Gaston's by the end of the week."

Laurien's heart started an odd fluttering beat as she absorbed this news. She would have her own mount after all.

But she would be traveling alone with the Scotsman.

She mounted one of the horses, resolutely telling herself this was not a cause for concern. She might have believed it, were it not for the prickly warm sensation that started at her toes and ran all the way up to bring a blush to her cheeks. What was it that caused these strange feelings in her body whenever she looked at the Scotsman, or thought of him, or—Sweet Mary forbid—touched him?

It was not fear, or anger, for she had felt those before,

and never had they affected her thus. Trying to puzzle it out, she watched him approach.

Connor tied the bundle of food to his saddle, not even sparing her a glance, then turned to wish his friend farewell. They spoke in hushed tones this time, and she could not make out what they were saying.

Connor quickly explained to Malcolm about the gown, then grasped the older knight's forearm, emotions roiling through him. Someone had to deliver their demands to de Villiers, and Malcolm had insisted, pointing out that he knew the roads best, for he had spent time here during the Crusades. But since the age of two-and-ten, when Connor had been made Malcolm's squire, this man had been more father than friend. Malcolm had taught him the principles of honor and chivalry, and as a naive, idealistic boy he had embraced them fervently.

If only to spare Malcolm the disappointment, he wished he could still believe in them.

"Speed be with you, my friend." Connor's eyes said what he could not. "And, by nails and blood, you had better arrive at Gaston's in one piece."

"Aye?" Malcolm grinned. "And you had better have a full cask of ale waiting for me." He looked at Laurien. "And see that the lady doesna come to *any kind* of harm, you rogue."

"She will be completely safe," Connor insisted before starting toward the horses. He scowled upon hearing Malcolm's response, a soft but decidedly less than confident grunt, behind him.

"He is not accompanying us?" Laurien asked when Connor reached her side.

"Does that make you nervous?" Connor asked without looking at her.

"Nay," she said quickly. Even as she said it, she knew that she lied. Truly, she *should* be relieved, for it would be easier to escape from one captor than from two.

But her mind was being as uncooperative as her body this morn. All she could think about was the feel of Connor's arms about her the night before, the warm touch of his lips, the intriguing spark of mischief in his eyes when he kissed her.

She forced herself to set such distracting thoughts aside and put her mind to planning her flight, as Connor called a final farewell to Malcolm and led her into the forest.

Laurien inhaled the fresh autumn air, already feeling fatigued. She had gotten no sleep the night before the wedding, and little last night, but a cold wind and the effort to keep her ill-trained mount at a trot kept her awake.

The midmorning breeze carried the smell of leaves and grass, crushed beneath the horses' hooves on the damp ground. The scent and her man's garb made her smile, thinking of her younger days with her brother Henri.

With Louis often away managing her lands, she had picked up her brother's love of hunting and hawking, and had become skilled in handling a sword. Henri had shared with her all he learned from his expensive tutors. And whenever her stepfather struck her in anger, it was Henri who soothed her pain. He would find her curled up in one of her secret hiding places—for he knew each one—bringing a cool cloth for her bruises, saying just the right words to wring a smile from her lips. But in the end, he too had betrayed her. Laurien's smile faded as she remembered that.

Banishing the memory, she glanced over at Connor. Thus far he was sticking to her like a wet cloak. He rode close, his leg occasionally brushing against her own.

She stared at him accusingly after the third time, but he only looked away, ignoring her unspoken reprimand. She reminded herself for what seemed the fiftieth time that morning that she must hold her rebellious impulses in check. He must not suspect she was planning her escape.

Morning turned into afternoon, and they ate dried fish and beef from the inn, rather than stopping for a meal. Connor offered his flask, and Laurien accepted it gratefully, letting the cool water soothe the salty taste from her tongue. A few drops trickled over her chin, and she wiped them away with a gloved hand.

When she handed the flask back, she saw Connor gazing at her with *that* look, the same he had had last night before he kissed her.

"You need not watch me every moment." She turned away, willing herself not to blush, pretending interest in the thatch of branches that formed an arch over their heads. "I shan't disappear into the air."

"Until I return you to de Villiers, you are mine to do with what I will. Watch you, or . . ."

Connor smiled as the unfinished comment brought a flush of color to Laurien's pale cheeks, and she clenched her teeth to stop a retort. 'Twas a seductive temptation, watching her. Indeed, he had been trying to avoid it all day. But he could not resist noticing the shape of her lips when she spoke. And his whole body tensed when he watched the droplets of water slip from his flask and glide over her chin, making her shiver as they headed for the warm hollow of her throat.

The more she acted the humble maiden, the more he was driven to goad her into showing her temper. 'Twas a perverse notion, for docile females were usually the best females, but it seemed unnatural on her. He tore his gaze from her blushing profile. This was torture, pure and simple, and getting worse by the minute.

"Our destination is Calais, is it not?" She tossed off the question like a volley from a catapult.

"Now what makes you think that?" Connor managed a laugh. By nails and blood, the girl was clever! That had been too easy.

"It is the closest port to Scotland. You want to hasten me out of France, rather than tarry and risk that de Villiers's men will pick up our trail."

He only laughed again, shaking his head. "Nay, milady, you have it all wrong. Keep trying, though. Your version is most amusing." Saints' blood, she had followed the path of his reasoning flawlessly!

Laurien smiled at his hasty denial. He only confirmed her belief when he urged the horses to a faster pace. Now that she had a better idea of their whereabouts, she knew it was time for her escape. For more than an hour she had noticed the sound of a stream off to her left. The gurgling water gave her the idea she had been looking for. She asked the Scotsman to stop a moment.

He gazed at her quizzically. "What do you require?" At her silence he became impatient. " 'Tis near dark, and we have a long way to go. Find your tongue."

"I have to . . ." She lowered her eyes, as she imagined a shy maiden would. "It has been a long time . . ." She stumbled over the words as if she could not say them.

"If you need to relieve yourself, there are a number of trees to choose from right there." He pointed to the oaks lining the path. He was in no mood for games. Now that she knew where they were going, she obviously had thought of somewhere to run.

Laurien looked at him with wide eyes, embarrassed by his blunt reply. The color that suffused her cheeks was no act. "At least allow me to go down by the stream, milord."

"Very well." He dismounted. "But I shall accompany you."

"Thank you, *milord,*" she ground out, "but I need no assistance." The churl was not going to allow her a moment to herself. She wondered if she could outrun him. The muscular feel of his legs pressed against hers was uncomfortably fresh in her memory. But this might be her best chance to flee, and every mile they traveled was taking her farther from Tours.

"You have two choices." Connor crossed his arms over his chest. "Sit your horse 'til we arrive at our destination, or accept my escort."

She sighed and dropped her reins. Now that she had started this, she would see it through. He reached up to help her dismount, but she set her teeth, ignoring the proffered hand, and swung easily to the ground and strode into the woods.

She found a small stand of bushes next to the stream and had worked her way into the center by the time Connor caught up with her.

"If you would like a bath as well, I would be willing to hold your clothes," he quipped. Before she could launch a retort, he flashed a smug grin and moved past her to the stream.

Connor shook his head. Women were so easily foiled. After taking off his gloves, he bent and refilled his flask. He still hadn't heard her move out of the bushes.

He turned to toss off another barb and saw her hurrying into the trees.

Swearing, he leaped after her. She moved as swiftly and silently as a deer, breaking into a run at the sound of pursuit. She almost made it to the horses, but it took only a few long strides for him to catch up. He dove for her legs, toppling her roughly to the ground.

"Damn you!" she cried, twisting around to scratch him.

He dodged clear and grabbed her arm, pulling her to her feet. "Have you forgotten your promise so soon? You swore you wouldna escape."

"Burn you!"

"What language." He plucked a leaf from her hair, unable to choke back a laugh. The lass was full of surprises, and far too deceitful to be trusted. He would not make the mistake of turning his back on her again—no matter what her state of undress. "Where is my obedient lady of this morn?"

For once Laurien was at a loss for words as the full weight of her failure hit. He had been expecting her to try something all along! She hadn't fooled him for an instant, indeed had provided him with one long jest. His laughter burned her like a brand.

Connor spun her around and pushed her ahead of him toward the horses. "I shall let this pass, but I warn you, I willna be so forgiving the next time."

Laurien refused his help in mounting, and glowered at him silently when he took her horse's reins from her. He mounted his own nag and tugged hers forward so she rode directly beside him.

"A lady cannot be expected to keep an oath to a knave," she snapped in her best haughty voice, staring straight ahead. Her intended insult only earned her another infuriating chuckle.

As they traveled on, they encountered no one wearing the de Villiers blue and gold, though they passed the occasional serf heading for his lord's manor, leading a team of oxen or carrying huge, curved scythes for the autumn harvest. At dusk, they skirted the walls of a large town—mayhap Crécy, Laurien thought, or Agincourt—and picked their way through the fields beyond, where long rows of barley, rye, and maslin were falling under the serfs' tools.

Nightfall found them deep in the forest once again.

Connor slowed the horses to a walk and they rode silently, the only sounds the snapping of frosted branches beneath the horses' hooves and the squeak of saddle leather.

Several times they saw distant lights flickering in the gloom around them. Cookfires, Laurien reasoned, probably warming travelers like themselves. But the hair on the back of her neck stood up, and she had a distinct feeling they were being watched.

By the light of the full moon, she could make out the shape of a large keep perched on a hill just ahead. Laurien thought they would ride around it as they had the town, and was surprised when Connor turned onto an almost hidden track that branched off the main path. He was heading directly for the castle. She started to question him, but decided to save her breath. She was quickly learning that Connor was not a man to explain himself, certainly not to a *mere* woman.

Riding single file, they were halfway to the castle when three horsemen charged out of the trees to block their way.

"Hold!" the leader challenged. "Your name and your destination!"

Laurien's heart beat so hard it hurt—they were closed in on three sides, the path too narrow for them to wheel and run.

"LaRoche. A torch!" The voice bellowed. They heard the click of flint and steel and a brand flamed to life in the gloom.

By the light, the riders quickly assessed one another. Laurien saw that their tunics were not blue and gold, but yellow marked with a red shield and a white dragon. Dressed in chain mail, all three had longswords lashed to their saddles and bows across their backs. The leader brandished a steel-tipped pike. The two men behind him rested battle-axes across their knees. These were not men on a search, but warriors equipped for battle.

Connor drew the same conclusion in an instant. "We are but humble pilgrims, Sir Knight," he said placatingly. "We seek only shelter from the cold."

"Liar!" The leader leaned over his saddle with a smirk. "I have seen this trick before. I say you are a mercenary, thinking to sneak through in disguise and help Varennes. The lad hidden beneath the cloak there is doubtless your squire."

"Nay, sir," Connor insisted. Now he knew where he had seen the sign of the dragon before. So, his old friend Gaston de Varennes still had not settled the feud. "We know not who is lord of yon castle. We were caught in a storm to the south and thought to make it to Boulogne by nightfall—"

"Two men traveling this deep in the forest, at night, heading for this particular castle? Do not mistake me for a fool." The man drew his sword.

" 'Tis knavish, Sir Knight, to so accost travelers on holy pilgrimage." Connor felt the too-familiar sensation of blood rushing through his limbs, his muscles tensing for a fight. There was no room to turn around, and they certainly could not get away by backing up. If these men insisted on a battle, he would have no choice but to comply. He slowly moved one hand to the shortsword hidden on the back of his saddle.

Laurien saw the movement. He would get them both killed! She spurred her mount forward suddenly, forcing Connor's horse behind hers. "Please, sir," she appealed to the leader. "He tells you true." She threw back her hood, releasing a cascade of honey-hued tresses. "I assure you, I am no squire."

The man gaped and appeared to forget all about the sword he had drawn. When he finally spoke, his voice had lost much of its belligerence. "I would know your name, milady."

Connor didn't know whether to strangle the girl for taking such a risk or to thank her. The revelation seemed to be having quite an effect on their would-be attackers. He held his tongue but rested his hand inches from his sword.

"I am Katherine de Poitiers." Laurien took the name of her friend and tutor, struggling to keep her breathing even as her heart pounded. Thinking quickly, she nodded to Connor. "This is my husband."

The leader snatched the torch from his man-at-arms and peered at them more closely. Laurien knew that any knight was honor-bound not to interrupt pilgrims on their travels. Unfortunately, this one seemed to want more proof before releasing them.

"Why do you travel in men's garments, Lady Katherine?"

"The fault of a thief, sir. We chanced upon a river one evening and I stopped to wash myself, and a peasant woman stole my gown." The tale had worked on her stepfather, the first time he caught her coming back from a ride wearing clothes borrowed from her brother.

"And you traveled with only one gown?"

"Nay, two, sir. But I had brought the spare to wash it as well. She made away with both, and I have worn my husband's extra garments ever since." She held the man's gaze for a long moment, then lowered her lashes shyly for effect. She hoped he was a more trusting soul than the Scotsman. Her mouth had gone dry, adding an appealing note of frailty to her voice. "Please, kind sir. We are nearly home and need only shelter for the night."

The leader scrutinized them, stone-faced.

"I pray you, sir, I am most fatigued." Laurien interrupted before he could pose another question. She tried unsuccessfully to force a tear. "If you refuse to let us pass, I shall simply collapse here on this path."

Measuring them one last time, the leader at last moved his horse out of the way. "Pass," he said finally. At a flick of his hand, his men melted back into the trees.

Laurien immediately spurred her horse forward, not wanting to give him time to reconsider. Connor galloped after her.

Antoine de Mayenne watched the pilgrims moving down the path. When they had disappeared, he turned his horse and followed his men, wondering if he had made the right decision.

But surely, if the blond giant *was* a warrior hired by Varennes, he would know better than to bring such a lady into a castle that was to be attacked on the morrow.

Chapter 4

Laurien released a long-held breath. She could almost feel Connor's eyes glaring at her as they rode on through the darkness. She smiled. She did not care if he was angry. Men always became angry when a woman dared to take control, regardless of the end result.

If she had turned in her saddle, she would have seen that Connor was not glaring, but smiling. He almost laughed aloud. How ironic that, for once, a woman's lies had worked to his advantage.

The path widened, then emptied into a clearing as they approached the wide moat surrounding the castle's massive curtain wall. Laurien started to raise her hood when Connor's voice halted her.

"Leave it," he rumbled.

She shrugged. If giving orders assuaged his male pride, so be it. It wasn't worth fighting over.

A helmeted head appeared at one of the gatehouse towers near the edge of the water. "Your name and your task?" the guard bellowed.

He reinforced his challenge with a crossbow aimed at Connor. Laurien also noticed steel arrowheads glittering in the moonlight, as guards hidden on the parapet drew their bowstrings. Her breath caught in her throat, and she began to tremble, the strength ebbing from her limbs, and the last of her courage along with it. She turned to Connor with questioning eyes. He had come here apurpose. Did he not have a plan for gaining entry?

As if in answer, Connor put two fingers of one hand into his mouth and whistled, the same odd sound he had made yesterday in Chartres. The guard instantly disappeared, and a moment later the drawbridge clanked down, landing with a thud at their feet. Connor motioned for Laurien to ride across. Puzzled, she complied, wondering what she would find inside.

They passed under the gatehouse and into the outer bailey, where the same man who had challenged them from the parapet waited to greet them.

"Good eventide, milord." As soon as they dismounted, he handed their reins to a servant who led the horses away. "My apologies for the trouble. We were not told you were coming."

Laurien pulled her cloak tighter with one hand, feeling awkward. The guard could not seem to keep from staring at her. She guessed it was her unusual garb.

Connor also noticed the man's gaze. A sudden, possessive impulse seized him, and he took Laurien's arm and pulled her close to his side. "The trouble is quickly forgotten. Especially if you ease my humor with some fresh venison and hot bread. And mayhap a flask or two of wine?"

"Aye, come, you must be tired. And I am sure milord will be eager to see you."

Despite Laurien's best efforts to twist away, the Scotsman kept her pressed to his side. The guard led them across the open practice ground, past the stables and granary and over the drawbridge of the second gatehouse. After entering the keep and climbing what seemed to Laurien's aching legs an impossibly long spiral stair, they came at last to the great hall.

It was like opening the door into a battle scene, she thought, as an incredible din burst upon her senses.

Burly warriors ate at haphazard trestle tables, pounding their sword butts on the tabletops to emphasize their shouted demands. Servants scurried to bring more food, more wine.

In one corner, a cheering crowd swept cups and trenchers to the floor and assembled around a pair of arm wrestlers. In another, a pair of huge, shaggy dogs snarled over remnants of venison. Feminine squeals punctuated the masculine roar as serving girls were pinched or tumbled into laps for slobbery kisses.

As they entered, a tall man at the table before the fireplace rose and, arms wide, crossed the room in a few strides. He drew near, and Laurien saw that his fine linen tunic and silk surcoat strained over his broad chest and thickly muscled arms. Dark brown hair curled below his ears, and a stubble of beard accented his angular jaw. Brown eyes crinkled at the corners as a smile lit his deeply tanned features. When Connor released her to grab the man by the forearm, Laurien stepped back involuntarily.

"Welcome back, my friend. How go the negotiations?" The man turned toward Laurien as if noticing her for the first time, though his eyes had not left her since she stepped into the chamber. "I see you have brought me a gift! Most generous, Connor."

The noise in the hall lowered to curious murmurs, as more and more heads turned to see what was happening at the entrance. "Nay, my friend." Connor quickly slipped an arm around Laurien's waist. " 'Tis the girl we spoke of before. The one from the provinces? My new wife."

This last he said loud enough for his voice to carry to the ends of the hall. Shocked at such bold teasing, Laurien tried to push him away, but Connor held her locked to his side.

Apparently disappointed that the girl would not be

offered for their pleasure, the warriors turned back to their pursuits, and the hall was soon drowned in a fresh din.

The dark-haired man looked at Laurien, a confused frown furrowing his brow, then his features brightened with apparent understanding. He laughed so loudly that the sound echoed to the chamber's ceiling. "Aye, of course." He clapped Connor soundly on the back. "I must hear the whole tale. Come, we will eat in the solar."

The three of them walked to the rear of the hall and the passage leading to the solar, a spacious meeting chamber just off the great hall. As in her own home, the solar boasted a large window with clear glass, which made it the warmest room in the castle by day, while its nearness to the main hearth held the heat at night.

As soon as Connor released her, Laurien moved to the chamber's hooded fireplace, glad for a chance to thaw herself and gladder still for an excuse to break away from the Scotsman's grasp. What did he mean by claiming her as wife in front of the entire room? He was only mocking her for the story she told in the forest. And after she had saved their skins! She shot him an angry glance and found him looking at her with that crooked grin.

Ignoring him, she turned back to the hearth and removed her cloak and gloves. The warmth of the room seemed almost steamy after she had spent an entire day in the autumn chill. Connor's friend summoned a servant to bring food and a trestle table, then turned his attention to his guests.

"Sir Gaston de Varennes." Connor pulled Laurien back to the door. "I present to you the Lady Laurien d'Amboise."

Gaston swept to one knee, taking Laurien's hand in his. *"Ma demoiselle,* I pledge myself to your service. If there is aught you have need of, simply ask and it shall be yours.''

Laurien looked down into his dark eyes and smiled hopefully as he kissed her hand. ''I do not imagine you would include my freedom in that offer?''

''Nay, I am afraid yon blond villain would strike me down if I dared.'' He sighed. ''But if you ever tire of this husband, you now know where to find better.''

He gave her a wink and turned to where Connor stood with crossed arms, frowning at Gaston's performance.

''Now, my friend,'' Gaston continued. ''Why did you send no message that you were coming? From your last note I gathered you were returning to France to deal with de Villiers, but I cannot believe that even you would attempt this.'' He glanced again at Laurien, his eyes devouring her in the full light.

''None but Malcolm know that we are here. I didna want to trust a messenger with the information.''

''Aye,'' Gaston agreed, turning serious. ''But I could have warned you. This is not the best time for you to have come.''

''You are still having trouble with Beauvais.''

''His men stopped you, did they?'' Gaston shook his head. ''Aye, he still refuses to acknowledge me as lord of this castle. I have had to hire those you saw in the great hall to defend it.''

Servants arrived with benches, a trestle table, and what seemed to Laurien enough food to feed every reveler in the keep. There were platters of hot venison and rabbit, bowls of thick soup with bacon, a wheel of cheese, trenchers of hard bread, and three tankards of warm spiced wine. The mingled aromas made her stomach growl, reminding her she had not had a hot meal in two days.

Gaston politely motioned her to take a seat. Laurien smiled at him and complied, unable to remember the last time she had been treated with such consideration. She briefly thought of suggesting that the Scotsman take lessons from his friend. The idea made her smile widen.

Gaston returned her smile and started to sit beside her, only to be nudged out of the way by Connor.

Frowning, Laurien sat as far to the left as possible, but when Connor sat, his bulky frame filled the rest of the bench and she found herself pressed against him. She refused to voice the biting remark that sprang to mind, determined not to be baited into any further arguments. She had provided more than a fair share of his entertainment for one day. God's truth, the man could exasperate a saint!

"Those men are a ragged lot, Gaston." Connor moved his leg to rest against Laurien's, smiling when his action made her drop the piece of cheese she had just picked up.

"Well, since you and I retired, my friend, there are no decent fighters available." Gaston smiled wistfully.

" 'Twas your idea to retire." Connor jerked his leg away as Laurien trod on his foot, then leaned toward her so his shoulder rested against hers.

"I could not bear to pass up this castle," Gaston continued, frowning at his friend's teasing of the lovely girl. Why did he always delight in making women uncomfortable? They were much more amenable when treated chivalrously. Glenshiel was only succeeding in making her angry. He watched as a stray lock of Laurien's hair trailed onto the table and Connor covered it with his fingers before she could jerk it away.

"Aye, but you have done naught but fight for it ever since you got it."

Gaston sighed. "And this time I have had to settle for what fighters I could get. Most of my liegemen have been called into service, and it seems our friend de Villiers has been gathering up every warrior for hire on the continent."

"He is gathering men as well as coin?" Connor forgot Laurien for a moment, just long enough for her to extricate herself from his touch. "That bodes ill. He sounds like a man preparing for war. But against whom? I care not for the sound of it."

"Nor do I. With most of my regular men away, Beauvais thought it an ideal time to start up his old feud. It seems he is still upset with the way I acquired my keep."

"Acquired it? You stole it from him." Connor laughed, helping himself to a slab of venison.

"Most untrue." Gaston leaned over to Laurien, who was doing her best to finish a bowl of soup while ignoring Connor. "Believe not what this knave tells you, milady. I won this castle in a tournament."

"You cheated," Connor reminded him.

"Not true," Gaston defended himself, still gazing into Laurien's extraordinary eyes—green with flecks of gold around the dark center. What a shame to waste such beauty on de Villiers. "I unhorsed Beauvais in fair combat. A hundred saw it."

"And I suppose that potion you dropped into his drinking water just beforehand had naught to do with it?" Connor grinned. "He was so drunk, had you not unhorsed him quickly, he would have fallen out of the saddle on his own."

"Any man foolish enough to wager a castle in a tourney deserves to lose it."

"You have never been an honorable man, my friend." Connor laughed.

"But unlike you, I never wanted to be," Gaston shot back. He was sorry as soon as he said it. Connor's smile faded, and an uncomfortable silence feel over the table.

Connor broke it at last, changing the subject. "You expect Beauvais to attack soon?"

Gaston nodded. "Aye. On the morrow. He sent another ultimatum two days past which I, of course, ignored. My sentries have been reporting troops moving into the woods all day now. They will come at dawn."

Connor glanced at Laurien. He hated to have her—*any* woman, he quickly corrected himself—in the midst of such danger. But there was no help for it now. He turned back to Gaston. "Malcolm will arrive in a few days. Is there any way you can bring him in through their lines?"

"You mean *if* I have not finished Beauvais by that time." Gaston gave him a wounded look. "Aye. When I acquired this keep five years past, the first task I undertook was to start digging a tunnel. We have a secret sally port to the north."

Laurien had finished her meal and sat with her head resting on one hand, feeling all the fatigue of two sleepless nights combined with a day in the saddle and the warm meal in her stomach. Her eyelids had started to droop, but she was not so sleepy that she missed Gaston's answer. She tucked the bit of information away in her mind, then gave in to the urge for a most impolite yawn.

Gaston clucked his tongue. "Connor you have run this poor *demoiselle* ragged. When will you realize that women are delicate creatures who need to be pampered and handled with care?" He ignored Connor's muttered expletive and nodded to the door at the far end of the chamber. "The lady obviously needs her sleep. She can stay in my chamber. It is the best protected. I will sleep on the floor, of course—"

Laurien opened her mouth to protest, but Connor leaped in first. "Nay, Gaston. I know you too well. You sleep in the solar. I will stay with her."

Laurien had no chance to object to that either, as Gaston spoke quickly. "But you are an unchivalrous knave when it comes to women, Connor. She will be better off with me.''

"Aye, if you consider bedded better off."

"What say we let the lady decide?"

Both turned to look at Laurien, who had given up trying to get a word in and was thrumming her fingers on the table. With her dust-smudged face and her hair in wild disarray, Connor thought she looked like an errant child who had come home late after a day playing in the woods.

"I say you both can stay here and argue all night while I go and sleep." She yawned again.

Not giving Gaston a chance for further argument, Connor stood up and scooped Laurien into his arms in mid-yawn. "She is, after all, supposed to be *my* wife." He shrugged to Gaston, ignoring Laurien as she pushed at his chest and demanded to be released. He called over his shoulder as he headed for the door. "Good night, Gaston."

The sleeping chamber was almost as large as the solar, except that its window had shutters rather than glass. Laurien finally gave up protesting and allowed herself to be carried in. She surveyed the chamber from where Connor held her on the threshold. A fireplace and fur throws on the floor added warmth, while candle sconces on either side of the bed offered a little extra light. Hung with silk that had been elaborately embroidered with Gaston's crest, the large bed beckoned with a thick mattress, pillows, and several blankets.

Laurien objected again when Connor kicked the door shut but gave no sign of releasing her. "You can put me down. I do not need to be tucked in like a child."

Smiling, Connor started to drop her, and she threw her arms about his neck with a yelp of surprise.

"I like a willing wench." He chuckled, starting for the bed.

Laurien snatched her arms back. "Release me," she pleaded, too weary to come up with a clever counter-stroke. "Please."

"As you wish, wife." He complied with a grin, laying her gently on the bed. Taking a pillow, he went to sit on the furs before the fire.

"And you can stop mocking me, too," Laurien grumbled.

"Mocking you?" Connor slipped his tunic over his head, and Laurien lost her line of thought as the fire reflected along his skin, making the rippling muscles of his chest look like a river of hot gold.

"Aye," she continued at last. Rolling on her back, she concentrated on the canopy of silk overhead. "For what I said to the men in the woods. About you being my husband."

"You think that is why I said it? Nay, 'twas for your protection from the men in the hall. You must understand how they think. A woman alone is fair game."

"I know quite *well* how men think," Laurien hissed, remembering the warriors' hungry gazes raking her body. She did not exactly relish the idea of sharing a sleeping chamber with Connor, but at least he offered her protection from those in the hall. She curled up on her side, unable to suppress a shiver. "I know more than I ever care to know about men."

Connor's eyes narrowed and he stared at her a moment. When he spoke again, his voice had softened slightly. "You are safe here. Most of them know me, either by acquaintance or reputation. They willna come near you if they think you are mine."

"Good." Laurien responded, her limbs feeling like unbearable weights. She was too tired to argue that *most* men thought of any woman as fair game. The warriors below were just like the knights and squires who had come to Amboise, seeking the hand of an heiress. They had praised her virtues with honeyed verses, all the while trying to pull her into a dark corner. She had always been able to fend them off with a slap or—at worst—a nip from her ever-present knife.

But while she had found their false words and coarse tricks annoying, she'd hated their hungry gazes most of all. For when they looked at her, they saw not a woman with thoughts and hopes and feelings, but her hair and her skin and, most of all, sacks and coffers filled with silver and gold from her lands.

Of all the men she had known, only Henri had ever treated her as if she had a mind in her head . . . Why must she constantly remind herself of Henri? She rubbed her temple absently, as if soothing away the memory. With a sigh, she turned her attention back to the Scotsman.

He had removed his boots but left his leggings on. The tight material clung to his lean muscles, leaving little to the imagination. Did this Glenshiel have such a reputation that men who had never met him would fear him? He leaned back against the fireplace, looking as if he had been sculpted from the same rugged stone. Nay, he was not boasting. At rest, he looked more like a country swain than a threatening warrior. But what was his fury like unchecked? She could only imagine. And to think that she had believed him a pilgrim. A giggle nearly bubbled to her lips.

Despite the weariness that pressed upon her, Laurien found herself unwilling to look away, feeling a tingle, deep inside, of something she could not name. She caught his gaze, and the tingling became a languor that stole over her, softer and warmer than the thickest furs. Finally, fatigue won against her curiosity at watching the play of muscle on muscle as he stretched by the fire, and she closed her eyes—just for a moment, she promised herself. She dare not fall asleep until *he* had gone to sleep. She could not trust him.

Connor mused over her slim form. From where he sat, he had a delightful view of her long, tapered legs and the fawn-brown tresses that spilled over the edge of the bed. Her hair glistened like copper in the firelight. He had the strongest urge to sneak over and take a handful, to feel it against his cheek, to surround himself in her scent.

"Do you always sleep fully clothed?" he asked softly.

Laurien didn't even bother opening her eyes. "Do you always ask rude questions of those you barely know?"

"I only meant," he replied, the glimmer of an idea coming to him, "that if you dinna intend to use the blankets you might be willing to spare one."

"Will it quiet you?" She raised herself on one elbow and eyed him with annoyance.

"Aye." He nodded earnestly.

"Will you then go to sleep?"

"Aye."

She swung her legs over the edge of the bed and gathered up one of the blankets. "Toward that end, I will do anything." She walked over to where he lay stretched before the fireplace like a great cat surveying its territory. Stiffly, she offered him the blanket.

Reaching up, he grabbed not the blanket, but her hand. He pulled her down to him, holding her arms behind her back with one hand while pulling the blanket over them. "Now that is much warmer." He grinned.

Anger twisted Laurien's features. "Release me!" Would the churl never cease?

"You said you would do anything," he protested, eyes wide with innocence.

"That did not include warming your bed!" She managed to free one arm and drew it back to slap the grin from his face, as she had been longing to all day. He caught her hand as it came at him, rolling over so that she was trapped beneath him.

He held her motionless despite her struggles. "Then you should learn not to say what you dinna mean." She was breathing heavily from her anger and the effort to throw him off, and he could feel her breasts heaving against his chest, feel the softness of her full curves, of the furs beneath them, of her hair splayed over his arm like a silken storm.

"Men should learn that women do not enjoy being tricked!" His full weight pressed her back into the plush skins, and she was acutely aware of the strength in every line of his body. She hated his strength for reducing her to helplessness, hated the idea that she could never be a man's equal because of that simple fact of bulk and sinew that held her wishes captive to his whim.

"I didna mean to trick you. But you are right. I know naught of you. So, tell me something." He *had* meant to trick her, and he knew it. It was just that he could not stand to sleep alone. When he was six-and-ten, there had been Sibylla. Later, as he warred across the continent with Gaston, he had spent the nights in his cups with his fellows, or in some camp follower's bed. After he returned home, he'd had a long string of short entanglements, never lacking a bed partner but never keeping any one for more than a few months. He always kept moving, kept his energies focused on whatever battle needed to be fought at the moment. Still, there was something about the night. While he could wear his invisible armor by day, the night brought out in his soul a longing for human contact that even he could not overcome.

"I have no desire to tell you aught of myself," Laurien spat. Her struggles were only succeeding in entwining her further as he covered every wiggling limb.

"Must you ever be averse to my simplest request?"

He tickled the pale underside of one wrist, thinking of planting a kiss where his fingers traced. He quickly discarded the idea, not wanting his eyes any closer to those quick nails. He would seek a safer spot. "Give away but a humble trait. Where did you learn Gaelic?"

Laurien rested her aching muscles, and he relaxed his grip ever so slightly. Mayhap an answer or two would make him release her. "At Tours, at the Sisters of St. Benedict. One of my tutors was Welsh."

"You were educated in a convent?" The image of a mischievous little girl surrounded by silent, stiff-faced nuns made him laugh. "And what else did they teach you?"

"Other languages." She sighed. "History. Healing and a bit of herb lore. They kept a lodging for the poor and infirm. Will you release me now?"

He ignored her plea and traced his finger up her arm and along her shoulder to her neck. "And that was where you were when de Villiers offered for your hand?"

The mention of that name turned her stomach. "Nay I . . . I left."

"You were dismissed?" He grinned. "Allow me a guess . . . You had trouble with the rule of silence?"

It irked Laurien that he guessed the truth so easily. He ended his slow exploration with his finger beneath her chin, and tiny beads of perspiration broke out on her upper lip, whether from her masculine blanket or something else, she knew not.

She summoned a final reserve of strength for a last effort to break free, but he held her as though she were a moth fluttering beneath his finger. She wanted to scream or cry, but her pride would not let her resort to the traditional feminine weapons. "I am too tired to play any more games, and I am too tired to fight you. So if you mean to rob me of my maidenhood, do it and get it over with!"

He chuckled at her ire. "You are, without question, the most adept liar I have encountered. You needna play the blushing virgin to save yourself. 'Tis not rape I intend."

This was too much. "I am a maiden still. What makes you think I am not?"

"You said you knew the ways of men."

"That was *not* what I meant—"

"And did not de Villiers take you after the betrothal?"

"Nay. I was . . . I told him I was ill."

Her hesitant answer only confirmed to him that she was lying again, thinking to save herself from his lovemaking. "You needna lie. If I wanted you, we would already be making love."

A burst of strange heat spread through Laurien at his bold words. "You said you never took a woman by force."

"In my experience, that has never been necessary." His crooked grin disarmed her, as he twirled a lock of her hair around one finger. "You see, 'tis all a matter of striking the right bargain. Women alternately offer or withhold their bodies to get what they want. If I offered you your freedom, say, would you give in then?"

"Such arrogance!" Her eyes widened in disbelief. "There are some things that have no price."

"So you willna give in, and we have no bargain . . . and there is also the matter of your betrothal. Though you belong to me for a time, in truth you belong to de Villiers."

Anger clouded her features. "You are wrong, Scotsman. I belong to no man. I never shall."

He raised his eyebrows and chuckled. "I see. And what will you do out in the world without a husband?" He tickled her chin with the end of the lock of hair.

She twisted her face away, exhaustion doubling her annoyance at his teasing. "I have my mother's lands along the Loire. They are mine by inheritance. There is a small keep, and I shall live there."

"You would live there alone?" His smile faded.

"There will be serfs, and perhaps a small retainer—"

" 'Twas not what I meant."

"Better to live alone than with some fat merchant who cares for naught but his accounts. Or a knight who is always away seeking his fortune in some foreign land—"

"You have never wished for a man . . . to love you?" He shook his head in wonderment.

"Men do not love." She looked away, staring into the flames, thinking of the father who had never come to find her, and of the stepfather who had unwrapped a grieving six-year-old girl's arms from around his neck, leaving her alone outside her mother's chamber, her cries echoing louder than his footsteps.

Connor gently brought her eyes back to meet his, caressing her cheek. "Nay, Laurien. 'Tis you who are wrong. Dinna want to be alone. 'Tis not a thing to be wished for."

His lips stole her reply as they lowered to her mouth in a gentle kiss. She fought to throw him off, fought the delicious sensation that coursed through her, but he held her still and kissed her deeply. His tongue parted her lips and explored her mouth, his tender possession weakening her defenses until at last she ceased her struggles. The tingling she had felt before bloomed into a flame that spread to every hidden region of her body. His lips finally left hers and traveled along her jawline to her ear, his delicate nuzzling sending a shiver to clash with the fever that continued to rise within.

"That is what you were meant for." His voice was a

bare, husky whisper. "Not to live alone in some musty keep, but to be held, to be caressed . . . to be loved."

He continued his searing path along her neck, tickling her skin with the stubble of his beard, soothing with lips and tongue. At last he came to the hollow of her throat, and he lingered on that spot where her life's blood pulsed so close to the surface.

Deep in her mind, Laurien cried in outrage at being so completely at his command, but she closed her eyes and relinquished her resistance, a more intimate part of her awakening joyfully to his call. She felt as though she were floating on a river made hot by the sun, knowing she was heading for the ocean, but too utterly at home in the water to care. And then the sensations stopped. She waited a moment, shivering at what might come next, but naught happened.

She opened one eye, then the other. He was propped on one elbow, gazing down on her with his disarming grin back in place. She blinked curiously. "W-why do you stop?"

"I have had many reactions to my lovemaking, Laurien, but never has a lady gone to sleep." In truth, 'twas not her fatigue but his own will that had stopped him. He had done it again, given in to a desire that quickened his very blood and made him throw nine years of hard-won control to the wind! And what spell did she use to wrest soft words from his lips? They seemed to leap, unbidden, from his mind to his tongue.

He struggled to right his thoughts. Malcolm had spoken truly. He would have to guard against these foreign feelings, lest he throw their entire plan awry. She had to be returned to de Villiers. Everything—their alliance, his country's freedom, his revenge for Galen's death—depended on it.

Laurien felt a more familiar warmth rising in her cheeks. And now that the pleasant sensations had stopped, she felt the full force of her sleepiness. "I—it is . . ."

"Nay, charm me no more." He stroked one blushing cheek as her eyelids drooped seductively. "For you are tired and the hour is late." He settled beside her, drawing the blanket around them once again. "Sleep, milady. Tomorrow there will be—"

A gentle snore interrupted him, and again he smiled. He wrapped one bulky arm about her slim waist. For tonight, at least, he would not be alone. But he must keep his mind on what lay ahead, he admonished himself.

For though they were safe at the moment, their journey had only begun.

Chapter 5

*A*s always, Connor was up before dawn. Dusky hues of blue and red and yellow had just begun lapping at the black edges of the night sky as he leaned against the sill, looking out through the open shutters. He watched the furtive movements of those below. Shadowy clumps moved about in the inner bailey, breaking up to reveal themselves as men taking their positions along the wall. Rising out of the forest beyond, tall dark shapes lumbered toward the castle, like great dragons waiting to unfurl their wings and spit fire on any in their path. Siege towers, he knew. How many times had his day begun thus? He pulled on his tunic and glanced again at the woman curled before the fire.

He had been up for some time, but she still slept soundly, her head nestled where his shoulder had been. He should have left already, he admonished himself. There was much to be done and little time. He would need to borrow chain mail and a helm from Gaston. He should be below by now, helping direct the placement of men and weapons, choosing the best positions for the pots of boiling pitch and animal fat, discussing with Gaston whether it was best to concentrate their defense on the gatehouse or curtain wall . . .

Without thinking, he crossed to the hearth and crouched beside Laurien. Even in sleep, she held her hands balled into tiny fists. What ill humors must invade her dreams to vex her so? He reached out and gently uncurled each slender finger. She moved not a whit, but a small sound escaped her, whether from a dream or his touch, he knew not. He smiled, remembering the night before, the warmth of her lips, the way she had trembled in response to his kiss. By day, she held herself haughty and distant. But last night he had felt something else, something that called to him . . .

Her hair lay in tangles across the fur throws, irresistibly beckoning his touch, and he ran his hand over it, enjoying the softness. He really should be off. The lass would be safe enough here.

"Connor?" A rap at the door interrupted his thoughts.

"A moment," he called softly, recognizing Gaston's voice. Moving back to the window, he closed the shutters and lowered the bar. He picked up his boots from before the hearth and stoked the fire until it flamed anew. Then, as if it were the most natural thing in the world, he tucked the woolen blanket closer about Laurien's slim shoulders, admonishing himself even as he did so. Her comfort should not be uppermost in his thoughts.

Standing, he lingered still, looking down at the girl. 'Twas not for him, such softness, never for more than a brief time, he reminded himself harshly. Not any woman, and especially not this one. His was a world of sharp edges and steel blades, of battles to be won and an empty castle to return to. Thus it would be, forever. Sibylla had seen to that. Ever since that night ten years ago—

"Connor." Gaston's voice was insistent this time.

"Aye," Connor hissed, with more than a hint of irritation. "To the battlements. *As ever,*" he added under his breath.

She was warm. That was all that mattered. Her bed felt warm and delightful, and she knew Henri would be coming soon to waken her, but she would not go. "Not today, Henri," she murmured. She had no desire to take her usual ride this morn. Why should she leave her bed when she had this wonderful warm wall to lie against? "Nay, I said." Why was Henri still calling for her? And why had her sheets taken on a sudden chill? Someone had stolen her warmth away and she was . . .

. . . Alone.

Laurien sat up with a start, blinking in the shadowy room. Of course she was alone. She had awakened every day of her life alone. Why should it bother her today? She shook her head, suddenly aware that she lay not in her bed of linens and silks, but on the Scotsman's pallet of furs. Everything came back in a rush. How long had she slept?

The flames in the fireplace had burned low, and the place beside her felt cool to the touch. Through cracks in the barred shutters, the full light of morning seeped into the chamber. How long had he been gone?

Fully awake now, she threw back the blanket and stood, listening to the rising echoes of the battle outside with a mixture of horror and fascination. She heard the clamor of shrill war cries pierced by the screams of the wounded, the clash of weapons and the steady *whump* of catapult stones finding their targets. Never had she been so close to a real battle. Every story she had ever heard crowded into her mind, tales of men burned by boiling pitch, of bristling weapons at every turn, of unlucky warriors who chanced to fall into a moat, only to be dragged to the bottom by their own armor. She shivered. Glenshiel would be in the thick of it.

She shook her head suddenly. "Do not be a fool," she said aloud. He was more than able to take care of himself. Why was she wasting valuable time worrying about him? She should be thinking of this as an ideal opportunity to escape.

Most of the castle's occupants would be busy—she hoped. Now was her best chance.

She thought of Gaston's words from the night before. *We have a secret sally port to the north.* Her host did not guard his words as carefully as the Scotsman. Obviously he was a more trusting soul. She went to the door, and was surprised to find a parchment note tacked to it. On it were only two words, both underlined:

Restez ici. Stay here.

With a frown of disdain she snatched the note down, crumpled it into a ball, and sent it sailing into the fireplace. Surely the Scotsman realized by now that she was not to follow his orders. She reached for the latch, then paused.

Aye, the man was no fool. He almost certainly would have posted a guard. But would they spare a man from the battle solely to watch her?

She cautiously lifted the latch and opened the door a crack.

Hearing no cry of alarm, she stepped into the solar.

She squinted as her eyes adjusted to the bright light, then realized with relief that she was alone. Her cloak and gloves lay where she had left them last night, and she quickly put them on, pulling the hood well forward to conceal her face. Finding naught else of use to take along, she moved to the door and tried the latch.

Locked. She grimaced.

And likely watched by someone in the chamber beyond. She gritted her teeth. She would have to talk her way past him. But first, she must get past the lock.

Reaching for her *aumoniere,* she felt the familiar outline of her knife. Glenshiel had made a mistake in underestimating her. She smiled. Too late, he would realize he had erred by allowing her to keep the little weapon.

She knelt before the door and began working at the wood surrounding the metal bolt. Easing the blade into the fastenings, she wiggled it back and forth until the wood began to splinter. She repeated this process all the way around the square of iron until, at last, she had it loose. It took only a little extra effort to use the blade as a lever and gently, gently slip the bolt free.

She placed her knife back in her bag. Then, taking a deep breath for courage, she opened the door.

She paused, still as a statue, fully expecting to be subjected to a rain of masculine outrage; but, glancing around, she exhaled in relief. It seemed they could spare no one from the battle, for no guard had been posted.

Obviously the Scotsman considered one lock sufficient to hold a mere female. She smirked. The man's contempt for women would be his undoing some day. A pity she would not be around to see that.

Her eyes took a moment to adjust again as she walked into the shadowed great hall. How eerie it seemed, empty and silent after the revels of the night before. The refuse had been swept away, the trestle tables neatly placed along the walls. A small fire crackled on the hearth, untended. The servants must all be occupied in the kitchens beyond, she realized, preparing food and drink for the tired, and poultices for the wounded. She would need to move quickly and cautiously; she did not want to have to stop and explain herself to a servant or—worse—one of the warriors who might happen to enter.

There was no way to reach the main door except by crossing the open hall. She picked her way toward the door, the yellowed rushes crunching beneath her feet. She barely breathed, alert for the slightest sound.

A few more steps . . . The door was almost in reach. A crack sounded behind her and she froze, her heart pounding. She slowly swung her head around to see the fire flaring and sparks drifting up the chimney. A log had shifted. She smiled at her own foolishness and continued on her way. Finally, she reached the door. Casting one last look behind to see that no one had noticed, she slipped out into the stairwell tower.

As in most French chateaux, this tower was one of four that offered access to the various floors. A spiral stair led above and below, a single door on each level the only entry to the rooms beyond. A torch sputtered in a sconce next to Laurien's head. She pulled it from the wall and started downward, quickly, softly, the occasional click of her heels on the hollowed-out stone steps echoing like the crack of a whip.

Her heart was beating madly with excitement and anticipation by the time she reached the ground floor, where another torch flickered in the gloom. On her right she saw that the portcullis had been lowered, the thick, iron-wrapped wooden grating blocking the portal that led outdoors. The door on her left, she guessed, led to the now-empty garrison quarters. She hurried past, heading for the huge underground storage chamber, the most likely place to find Gaston's tunnel.

The staircase spun onward, coming to an abrupt end at a large door flanked by two more torches. She reached for the iron ring, her hand shaking, then stopped and took a deep breath to calm herself. If she let her eagerness overtake her, she would rush and make a mistake and be discovered. She could not bear that, not now. She was too close to freedom—from Glenshiel and the plans he had for her, from de Villiers, from her stepfather.

All she need do was locate the tunnel and flee to the forest beyond. In just days, she could be safe in the welcoming arms of her real father.

That exquisitely sweet thought brought a smile to her lips, but she willed herself to concentrate. Intellect failed her when she let emotion get too tight a hold—and that had happened too often these past days. Levelheaded once more, she gripped the torch tightly and opened the door.

The flame in her hand illuminated only the smallest circle of light compared to the size of the chamber. Two pairs of blood-red eyes flashed in the brightness, then disappeared into the shadows. Laurien shivered at the skittering of countless tiny paws and retreated a step. Choking back her fear, she forced herself to move forward.

Where to begin? The chamber was much larger than she had expected, wider across than even the great hall. Every corner overflowed with the bounty of Gaston's larder—barrels of wine and ale, casks of dried fish and beef, sacks of flour and cakes of salt. The scents of pepper, ginger, and cloves spiced the clammy air.

As she looked about, the enormity of her task nearly overwhelmed her. But what had she expected, she reasoned, a bright red arrow pointing to the entrance? Setting her teeth in determination, she decided to start with the wall to her left.

She held the torch at eye level, peering at the stones and moving slowly, looking for some crack or line that would reveal itself to be a door. Intent on her search, she did not notice the flame suddenly dance wildly.

But she did hear the footstep behind her.

She spun about and ducked as a silver-clad form charged her. A sword bit into the wall where her head had been. She dashed to one side, taking in all at once the figure's size, chain mail, and yellow and red tunic—one of Beauvais's knights!

"Defend yourself, lad," he boomed as Laurien scrambled backward. "You shall not live to tell your lord I have discovered his tunnel."

He attacked instantly, wielding his sword with the deadly skill of a practiced warrior. A cry ripped from her throat, and she swung the torch in desperation only

to have him knock it from her hand. It sputtered out i
the dirt, and she dashed for the entrance, enveloped i
darkness. She fumbled for the door, tore it open, an
leaped up the stairs with the man on her heels. H
tripped her and she fell, the edges of the steps knockin
the breath from her.

She rolled to the wall as the sword came down again
sounding like a smithy's hammer on an anvil as i
glanced off the stone. Still at the foot of the stairs, h
jerked it back to deliver the killing stroke and stopped
the weapon suspended above his head like some unbal
anced unicorn's horn.

At the amazement on his face, Laurien suddenly real
ized her hood had fallen away as she rolled, revealin
both her features and her hair. She took advantage o
the opening and launched a kick with both feet into hi
midsection. He fell backward with a grunt of surpris
and lost his grip on his sword. Laurien turned and scur
ried up the stairs, fumbling with her *aumoniere* to fre
her knife. She heard a snarl just behind her.

She threw herself into the door to the first level an
slammed it behind her, only to have it smash open be
fore she could secure it. Her knife flew from her hand
and she tumbled headlong across the room, her hea
smacking the rush-strewn floor. She staggered to he
feet and looked madly about for a weapon, a ringin
sound filling her ears. The garrison quarters were empty
the racks picked clean, the only weapons left behind
pair of pages' training swords on the far wall.

Still leaning against the door, the man sheathed hi
blade and slid the bar into place, blocking any servant
who might have heard her cries. An ugly grin wrinkle
his mouth. Laurien backed away, her head spinning from
her fall.

"Varennes has scraped the barrel indeed if he ha
taken to hiring women to fight his battle," he snarle

as his dark eyes raked her body. "For once, I count myself fortunate to have been chosen scout. Never did I expect to chance upon such a choice morsel in his larder." He pulled off his mail gloves and moved toward her.

The ringing in Laurien's head swelled to a horrible buzzing, as though a swarm of bees droned around her. Her tongue refused to utter any of the words her mind was screaming.

"Come, wench." He kept advancing. She edged toward the far wall. "I shall know the pleasures of your body before I give you the kiss of my sword."

Laurien's back came up against the cold stone. She blinked, trying to clear her mind, and seized her one chance. She snatched one of the short page's swords from the wall and held it out, breathing hard, putting all the menace she could into her stance. The room tilted crazily before her eyes, a silvery fog threatening to close off her vision completely.

The man laughed and moved closer, batting at the sliver of metal like a cat playing with a mouse's whiskers. But with a movement born of years of practice, her arm whipped the sword up as he reached out. He snatched his hand back, roaring in surprise and pain, blood dripping through his fingers.

She ran for the window, threw back the bar, and tore open the shutters. She was not fast enough. His fingers closed on her shoulder and he spun her around, rage twisting his features. On instinct alone, she slashed upward again as she came about, opening a fresh line of red along his cheek. He screamed this time, his blood-ied hand moving to his eye. She launched herself toward the window and leaped out, the page's weapon still clutched in her hand. The shock of the cold air made the pain in her head unbearable and she knew only that she was falling . . .

* * *

Connor slumped down behind the wall, exhausted After several hours of fighting, neither side was making any progress. The leather jerkin beneath his borrowed chain mail was sodden with sweat. He pushed back the metallic coif that protected his head, along with the padded leather cap underneath, savoring the cool touch of the wind in his damp hair. He was concentrating on holding the moat and battlements, while Gaston saw to the defense of the main gate.

He licked his cracked lips, as a familiar voice repeated the litany of battle in a singsong voice through his thoughts . . . Keep them from gaining the outer bailey. If that fails, keep them from the inner bailey. If they take that as well, defend the castle to the last man . . . 'Twas an ancient game, a living, breathing, bloodied chessboard. The winners took the prize, and the losers picked up the pieces and went home. He had played this out too frequently, both from the attacking side and the defending side. Another blow from a catapult shook the wall-walk he was sitting on, and he put out a hand to steady the man beside him, who had just taken aim and now teetered precariously at the edge.

Connor stood and peered over the top of the wall wiping the edge of his silk surcoat over his face to clear the soot that stung his eyes, coughing on the fetid steam from the caldrons of boiling pork fat to his left and right At the edge of the water below, relays of red and yellow clad warriors struggled to fill the moat with soil and stones and branches. One of Beauvais's siege tower stood just beyond the reach of the defenders' arrows waiting for the makeshift bridge to be completed. It could take all day, Connor knew, for the moat was well within his men's range, and they kept the fillers pinned down with a rain of arrows and scalding liquid. He was more concerned about the scaling ladders.

A sudden high-pitched sound broke into his concentration and he spun about. It was the falconer's whistle, ringing high and clear above the din, the secret warning that he and Gaston had devised during their mercenary days. His friend was in trouble. Half crouching, he sped back along the wall, scanning the area near the gate as he went. At last he saw Gaston, standing in the middle of the practice field, apparently fit and healthy, pointing at—

"God's teeth!" A string of profanities tumbled from Connor's lips as he beheld an unbelievable image: Laurien, sword in hand and hair flying, leaping along the wall of the inner bailey, with one of Beauvais's men on her heels! "How the—What in God's name is she *doing out here!*" The man behind her reached forward and caught her hair, savagely jerking her backward. Connor was already running toward them as fast as his chain mail would allow.

Antoine de Mayenne paced up and down along the moat, his mood growing more sour with each step. He had expected this to be a quick assault, over in a day, mayhap two. But Varennes had many more warriors than he had counted on. His men were outnumbered at every turn. They were dying like dogs merely to satisfy Beauvais's vain, idiotic need to settle the score with young Varennes. He had been watching his best men fall all day, men he had honed like fine weapons from the time they were lads. It left a bitter taste, like a metal coin on his tongue. If only he had been able to keep more of Varennes's mercenaries from getting through.

The scaling ladders seemed to be succeeding, at least. A score of his men had finally scrambled up onto the wall-walk. They fought valiantly despite the odds, battling with swords, now, instead of arrows. De Mayenne crossed the moat, striding over the boards they had hastily thrown down as a bridge, and grasped the lowest rung on one of the ladders. Only blood could quench his bitterness.

He gained the wall and quickly dispatched the man who came at him. He turned to take on another when a movement in the inner bailey caught his eye. A *woman.* Struggling with one of his men. And one of Varennes's hirelings was running toward them. The fool had thrown off his coif, exposing his head . . .

It took but an instant for the image to form in his mind. Last night. A woman dressed as a lad and the hulking blond man who claimed to be a—

"Pilgrim!" he bellowed, cursing himself. He had let one of Varennes's warriors trot in right under his nose! De Mayenne whipped his crossbow from his back, loaded it, and pushed his way through the battling men along the curtain wall. He would correct this error personally.

Laurien screamed in terror as the knight caught her hair and jerked her down. She had twisted her ankle when she landed on the wall-walk, and fresh pain shot through her leg. The man grabbed her by the collar, shaking her in his fury, blood from his wounded hand soaking her tunic. He threw her down, and she tried to scramble away, crablike, but he unsheathed his sword and raised it, smiling through the blood that dripped down his cheek.

"To hell you go, wench."

She squeezed her eyes shut and bit her lip. But to her amazement, the pain did not come. She heard the sound of metal scraping metal and looked up to see the Scotsman standing over her, his sword interrupting the stroke that would have sliced her through. With terrifying strength, he forced the man's weapon up and away from her. Pushing the other backward, Glenshiel stepped neatly around her, silent, deadly. Undaunted, her attacker feinted, and then the two were locked in battle.

She lay frozen, the pain in her head and leg forgotten, watching in horror as the men struggled. This was nothing like the showy fighting she had seen at tournaments; this was a death match. Each stood his ground, hacking and slashing, intent on killing the other. They balanced precariously on the scant yard of space that was the wallwalk, Beauvais's man at a disadvantage because of his wounded eye. He snaked out a leg to trip Glenshiel but the Scotsman danced back, amazingly light despite his heavy armaments.

Beauvais's man jabbed his weapon forward, trying to catch his opponent unaware, but Glenshiel parried and they came together, sword hilt braced against sword hilt, sinew against sinew. They stood still, like figures in a painting, until finally Beauvais's man gave out. His foot slipped ever so slightly and, with a final shove, the Scotsman sent him over the wall. A scream rose, shrill over the droning sound in Laurien's head, only to be cut short suddenly.

She lay where she had fallen, unable to move, barely able to breathe, watching the black lion on the back of Glenshiel's tunic rise and fall as he gasped for air. He turned toward her, and his expression choked the breath in her throat. His eyes glowed bright with a killing fire. Blood gleamed on his sword, his tunic, his cheeks. The angles of his face sharp with anger, he strode over to her and extended a hand to jerk her to her feet.

Suddenly Laurien heard a hiss of something flying over her head, and Connor stumbled backward, as if a giant, invisible hand had slapped him. He staggered and sank to his knees, putting a hand to his chest. His jaw went slack with pain, and the hard lines of his face dissolved into complete amazement.

The end of a crossbow bolt stuck out from the front of his tunic, a bright crimson stain spreading around the wound.

Chapter 6

"**B**urn you, man, take it out!" Connor rasped the words, then clenched his teeth as another wave of pain coursed through him. Images floated before his eyes, of Gaston and the girl hovering near, and a balding man he did not recognize. He did not remember being carried inside to Gaston's chamber, could make no sense of the melee of voices around him. It was all he could do to keep from crying out, as hot needles of agony radiated from the crossbow bolt in his chest. But, he comforted himself, at least he could feel, at least he was still awake. Because, with a terror that stripped all reason, he felt that if he closed his eyes, he would not waken again.

"He is right," Laurien appealed to Gaston. "We must get it out." She gingerly examined the wound, feeling sick that she had been the cause. Had she not been trying to escape, had he not been fighting to save her . . . Sweet Mary, it was *her* fault that he had been wounded.

Gaston had seen Connor's attacker a moment too late, and killed him just after the man fired. With Laurien's help, he had carried the wounded Scotsman inside, quickly tearing away the silk surcoat and taking off his boots and chausses. But they could not remove the mail shirt or leather tunic beneath, for fear of hurting him even more.

The balding man frowned at Laurien and shook his

head. "The bolt has a barbed end made of steel. If we take it out, it may injure him further."

Laurien spun, making no effort to hide her disgust for the mercenaries' barber. The skinny man reeked of ale, and the only contribution he had offered thus far was to ask what star Connor had been born under. "We must close the wound," she hissed. "If we do not he may bleed to death."

"You summoned me for my opinion, milord." The barber shrugged and turned to Gaston, making no effort to lower his voice. He folded his arms over his blood-stained brown tunic. "I say the best we can hope for is to make him comfortable."

Gaston looked from the girl to the man, utterly at a loss as to what order to give, what decision would save his closest friend. The girl claimed to have some healing skill, learned in a convent. Yet he had never before doubted the word of a barber, for they were well versed in battlefield surgery.

But this man believed that all they could do was watch Connor's life slowly seep away. It seemed like a macabre jest, that after all the battles Connor had been through he should die in a dispute over a castle won in a tourney—

"Gaston," Connor's voice was barely more than a whisper now, and his body was drenched in sweat. "If you dinna take this accursed bolt out now I shall do it myse—" The rest was lost in a gasp that dissolved into a groan. Connor turned his head to try and hide the pain that etched his features.

"Guard!" Gaston was at the door in a moment, spurred to action at last. "We shall need your assistance. And you." Laurien jumped at the ferocity of his voice. "Bring the ewer and bandages over. And one of those." He pointed to a pair of wooden candlesticks displayed above the hearth.

Gaston quickly arranged the group about the bed, the guard holding Connor's legs, the barber holding his left arm, Laurien holding the right.

Glenshiel's eyes sought Laurien's and locked there as Gaston wrapped both hands about the short wooden shaft. She tried a tremulous smile of reassurance, but could not quite manage it. Instead she slipped her hand into his and returned his unblinking gaze, thinking again how his eyes seemed like the sheer glass of a cathedral window, sturdy yet breakable. Someone slipped the candlestick between his teeth, and for a moment she saw a flicker of something most disconcerting in his gaze. He knew what was coming, she realized with sudden clarity, and it frightened him.

"Strength, my friend," Gaston whispered.

Laurien bit her lip to stifle her cry as Gaston pulled at the bolt. Connor's eyes clamped shut, and he bit down on the piece of wood in his mouth as if he would snap it in two. A roar sounded from deep in his throat. His fingers interlaced with hers with bruising force, and his every muscle tensed in a convulsion of agony. The sudden burst of strength nearly pitched the burly guard across the room.

At last the bolt came free. Connor slumped back into the pillows, the tension in his body replaced by the weakness of a newborn. The lines eased from his face. His eyes opened, sought Laurien's, and lingered there for a moment, then slid closed as he slipped into unconsciousness.

Laurien exhaled, realizing that she had been holding her breath right along with him. She slowly unlaced her fingers from his, trembling. Gaston tossed the bolt and candlestick aside and hurried to remove the chains and jerkin and cover Connor with blankets. Laurien felt another wave of guilt at the sight of all the blood. The strangely metallic smell filled the air.

To think she had once feared the Scotsman would hurt her; instead *she* had caused him harm! With a fresh linen towel and water from the ewer, she quickly began to bathe him, cleaning away the blood. Truly, she reflected, he had not mistreated her. She tried to remember that he was her captor, and an infuriating, arrogant man, but all she could think of was how he had protected her from the warriors in the hall last night, and from her attacker this morn . . .

And the gentleness in his voice when he whispered sweet words to her after kissing her . . .

And the fact that it would be her fault if he died.

Nay, she would not let herself think on that. She forced her guilt to the back of her mind and set about using the skills she had learned at the abbey infirmary. She examined the wound closely. The bolt had plunged through both layers of protective garments to make a jagged hole, no bigger around than her thumb, but deep.

Three inches to the right, and the crossbow would have done its job perfectly. "W-we have no time for a needle and thread." She looked at Gaston. "You shall have to use your sword."

Nodding in understanding, Gaston crossed to the hearth. He heated his blade in the flames.

"Before you attempt that," the barber intoned with a critical air, "it is best to apply powdered stag's horn, or ground pearls."

Laurien noticed with irritation that the man still leaned against the bedpost, hands clasped behind his back. She glanced at the guard. "Remove him."

The guard looked at Gaston for direction, but Varennes was already moving back toward the bed. Laurien turned away as he lowered the flat of his sword over the wound. She placed a hand over her mouth and nose as a soft hiss filled her ears and a sickening steam rose. Thank God, she thought, that Glenshiel was not awake.

"The bleeding has stopped," Gaston said quietly.

Nudging him out of the way, Laurien deftly bandaged the wound with soft linen and bound it tightly as the three men watched.

"He still may develop infection," the barber offered as she finished this task. "Or fever."

"Why is this oaf still here?" she demanded in frustration.

"You will want to bleed him later," the man continued, ignoring her and addressing Gaston. "I shall gather my instruments."

"Nay," Laurien cried in disbelief, spinning to stare wide-eyed at him. "It will kill him!"

"You must purge the poisons." The bare-pated man faced her at last, color creeping into his cheeks at her affront. "In order to balance his humours."

"Why do you listen to this?" Laurien appealed to Gaston. "Mercenaries' surgeons are not well known for taking particular care of their wounded. I need not tell you—"

"I will not be insulted by a woman!"

"I have seen the results of his kind of treatment before. Sir Gaston, please. I can help Sir Connor. I need only some yarrow, elder flower, and nettle leaves."

The barber's face turned an angrier shade of red. "Are you going to trust this female and her potions over myself?"

"Cease this, both of you!" Gaston shouted at last, pressing his hands over his ears. He felt as if the walls were slowly closing in around him. The battle still raged outside, and he did not have time to weigh the advantages of one type of ministration against another. He did not like this self-important barber, and astrology and bleeding had always seemed to him an asinine way to help a wounded man.

But could he trust the girl?

He looked at her, standing there in her man's garments that were now stained with Connor's blood. Her face was pale from this day's ordeals, framed by matted hair. But her eyes met his harsh gaze without wavering. She was tough, this one, and strong. A lesser woman would have crumpled into useless tears, but she had steeled herself and helped without question. Helped a man who held her captive. And she *had* shown some knowledge of healing. As if reading his doubts, she repeated softly, "I can help him."

"Very well, I shall have the herbs brought to you."

She gave him the slightest hint of a smile, feeling immense pride in his trust.

"You"—Gaston pointed a finger at the barber, who stood with his mouth pursed tightly, as if he had just swallowed a lemon—"will withdraw to tend your other patients below. Return here at nightfall to see how Sir Connor fares. If aught is amiss, summon me."

With a tight nod and a withering glance at Laurien, the little man stalked from the room.

"Return to the solar," Gaston instructed the guard. "Stand watch and mind that she does not leave this chamber."

As the guard hastened out, Gaston pinioned Laurien with another fierce gaze. "As you managed to make such quick work of my best lock, I shall not leave you unattended," he explained. "I must see to the fighting outside, but I will return before dawn."

He reached out suddenly and grasped her chin, his voice low and tense. "Woman, I have never known a friend more noble or more true than that man." He gestured toward the bed. "If he dies at your hands . . ." His words trailed off but his fingers tightened to underscore his meaning.

Without another word, he released her and left, closing the door firmly behind him. She rubbed her chin, feeling dizzy and hot. Sweet Mary, he had plunked complete responsibility squarely on her shoulders. But had she not asked for it? Sitting on the edge of the bed, she pulled another blanket over her patient. She placed a hand on his forehead, feeling the cool, almost clammy skin.

It sent a chill through her. God's teeth, who did she think she was, to argue with a surgeon, to take this man's life into her hands? He lay so quietly, the only sign of life the slight rise and fall of his chest. His deeply tanned skin, which she had admired only last night, now looked deathly pale. The thick-hewn arms that had held her tightly lay powerless on the blanket. The full mouth that curved so easily into a smile or uttered teasing words was still.

All because of her. She felt another stab of guilt, followed quickly by fear that she might not possess skill enough to save him.

She dipped a fresh cloth in the ewer and smoothed back his damp hair. Her throat felt tight. Coughing, she looked at the window and saw that tendrils of smoke were drifting in the open shutters.

She went over to push them shut, then stopped in mid-motion, her hand raised.

Through the swirling gray smoke, she could see that the walls and bailey were deserted. Gaston's men had burned Beauvais's siege towers to cinders earlier. Two still stood, their blackened skeletons smoldering. She knew enough about warfare to know where the men had disappeared to. The attackers had given up on attaining the wall and moved around to the back of the castle, attempting to tunnel into the bailey.

The late afternoon sun glanced along the wall, sparkling on the bright chain mail of the fallen. But what caught her eye was the scaling ladder, just one, that someone had pulled up onto the walkway. Perhaps a contingent of Beauvais's men had wanted to ensure a way back down in case the battle did not go their way. She knew not . . .

But her mind began to race.

She could lower herself out the window, clamber over the wall, and be well into the forest long before the physician returned at nightfall. The guard outside had not been instructed to check on her, only to keep her from exiting the chamber. Even the smoke would work to her advantage. She felt elation rise within her. At last, a clear chance to escape!

With one hand on the window ledge, she looked back at Glenshiel, and her excitement melted away. He looked so helpless, so completely vulnerable.

She swore under her breath. The wound was deep, and he had lost much blood. He might develop an infection, a fever. The next few hours would be crucial. She was not even certain she could help him—and she did not want to imagine what Gaston would do to her if she failed.

Her fingers tightened on the shutter. Why shouldn't she go?

Because he saved you, a small voice whispered at the back of her mind. *Because you came as close to death today as you ever have in your life. You saw that blade slicing down to cut you in two and* he *interrupted the blow.*

He had his own reasons, she answered her conscience. He had to save his prize. He thinks of me as naught more than booty to be bartered. I owe him nothing.

And if you had stayed in your chamber as he instructed, the voice reprimanded, *you would not have been in danger. And he would not now be lying—mayhap dying—in that bed.*

She looked away, concentrating on the scaling ladder

instead of the silent form wrapped in blankets and bandages. She swallowed hard.

I will never get another chance like this, she pleaded, knowing somehow she had already lost the battle.

If you leave him to that butcher of a surgeon, the man will surely bleed him to death, the voice finished.

"Saints' breath," she said aloud. "I cannot go."

Quickly, before she had time to change her mind, she pushed the shutters closed. She lowered the bar to shut out the smoke—and any chance of escape with it.

"I shall live to regret this." She sighed in the general direction of the fair-haired knight. "Of that, I am certain."

Chapter 7

"Why should I not have you killed this instant?"

Sir Malcolm did not turn around as de Villiers, bellowing, banged open the door and strode into the great hall at the Chateau de Chartres.

Instead, Malcolm lounged in the high-backed chair at the head table, stretching his legs toward the warmth of the fire that crackled on the hearth. When he'd told the castle steward what he had come to discuss, he had been quickly ushered inside.

"Greetings, milord," he replied coolly as the footsteps of several men drew near.

"You whoreson!" De Villiers slammed a fist on the table. "You are five kinds of a fool, coming here without escort. You will not leave alive—"

"As you wish, milord." Malcolm turned toward him at last, a slight smile playing around his lips. "But if I fail to meet my companions within two days, you willna see the girl again."

De Villiers stood puffing, nostrils flaring, his beady eyes boring into Malcolm. He looked like a mad bull on a rampage, his pale face appearing twice its normal size as his red cheeks pulsed in and out. It was two days since Laurien's abduction, but he still wore the blue and gold silk wedding garments, now stained with sweat about the collar and under the arms. He appeared every inch the distraught bridegroom. Good, Malcolm thought.

Any idea that de Villiers might not care to bargain for the girl disappeared.

He quickly measured the two men who stood at de Villiers's side. One Malcolm took to be an adviser of some sort; he was tall and thin, with gray-tinged brown hair, and an elegant tunic of cream-colored linen.

The other looked to be a mercenary—hired directly from hell. He wore a tunic and leggings of fur, and a cloak cut from the same grizzled hide. His neatly clipped beard offered an odd contrast to the black-brown hair that hung in a shaggy mass to his shoulders.

De Villiers, sneering, motioned the two men forward. "I do not know who in the devil's name you are, but you will find I deal harshly with those who steal from me."

Before Malcolm could reply, the shaggy-haired man jerked him from the chair and threw him up against the stone wall of the hearth.

"Call your mongrel to heel," Malcolm ground out, once he caught his breath, "if you value the Lady Laurien's safety."

"Fear not, I will send you back to your friends," de Villiers snarled. "But I will send you in several pieces!"

"Send me back unharmed or find yourself a new betrothed!"

"You will tell me where she is. A bit of torture will loosen your tongue—"

"*If* you could get the information from me, 'twould be too late. She will be killed in two days—unless I return safely."

De Villiers paused. "If your friends kill her, they would have naught to bargain with."

"Meet our demands quickly, else we may simply kill her out of spite." Malcolm matched de Villiers's sneer and hoped he sounded suitably ruthless. "Believe me when I tell you we are determined men."

At that, de Villiers fell quiet, his fists clenching and unclenching.

"You canna marry a corpse, milord," Malcolm said tightly.

A tense silence gripped the chamber. No one moved.

Malcolm glared at the shaggy warrior who held him pinned. He noticed with revulsion that the end of the man's nose was missing; a scar snaked up the remainder to end on his forehead.

Far more disturbing, though, were his eyes—clear and gray, like dirtied snow that would not melt. They stared with a stark, almost palpable intensity that Malcolm could only describe as . . . evil. He felt a sudden chill wash over him, as if Death himself had swept into the chamber on a January wind.

Finally, the comte settled his bulk into a chair on the far side of the table. "Release him, Balafre."

The grizzled giant complied and went to stand behind de Villiers's chair. Malcolm smoothed his brown tunic, feeling a great deal of relief, not a speck of which he allowed to show. The elegantly clad adviser, who had watched the scene with a look of silent amusement, glided into a seat at the comte's right.

"Let us begin with your name," de Villiers growled.

Malcolm reclaimed his seat in the high-backed chair. "Sir Malcolm MacLennan." He leaned back and put his feet up on the table. "From Scotland. I am here to inform you that you willna be receiving the ten thousand in silver you demanded of us."

De Villiers's face, which had been flushed with anger, now drained completely of color. "Good Christ—"

"Allow me to put it plainly. We want the alliance between Scotland and France signed, and quickly. If you choose not to help us, the Lady Laurien d'Amboise will meet an untimely end. If you wish to have her returned, you will sway your King Philippe—"

"I will not be ordered about." De Villiers surged to his feet.

"Aye, you *will*. Sway your king quickly to favor our request. You have already impressed upon us the influence you hold. Now use it. When the alliance has been signed, send word to Strathfillan Abbey in Scotland." Malcolm swung his feet to the floor and stood. "You have a fortnight. No more. The brothers will know where to locate us."

"What assurance have I that you will hold to your end of the bargain? How do I know whether you have her at all?"

"When we are certain the alliance is signed, she will be returned to you immediately." Malcolm picked up the bundle beside his chair and pushed it across the table. This last bit of dramatics had been Connor's idea. "Consider this a token of our intentions. Do as we say or the girl will suffer the consequences."

De Villiers tore open the fastenings and stared silently at the tattered remains of Laurien's wedding gown. His jaw worked, making the swollen flesh below his chin quiver like a coxcomb. "I will have her back in a fortnight?"

"Aye." Malcolm picked up his cloak and gloves, signaling that the matter was not open to further discussion.

"She *will* be returned to me untouched," de Villiers snapped. "Do not dare to soil what belongs to me!"

Malcolm thought of the girl's bruised face and tried to keep a note of sarcasm from his voice. "She will be as perfect as the day she left."

"She had better be." De Villiers shoved the package away from him. "It is agreed, then."

Malcolm nodded his farewell and headed for the door, satisfied. "Dinna try to have me followed, milord."

"Wait," de Villiers called. He was still hunched over

the table. "Know this before you depart, MacLennan:
my enemies live very short lives." He looked over his
shoulder then, his eyes burning with frustrated rage.
"And you have made an enemy this day."

Malcolm returned his glare with a contemptuous look,
which he cast upon the adviser and the hulking mercenary in turn. In truth, he felt the comte's threat to his
very bones and could not think of a single clever reply.
There were entirely too many things that could go wrong
with this mad plan.

"A fortnight, milord," he said as he strode from the
hall, his voice booming with a cheerful confidence he
did not feel. "Mark it well."

No sooner had the Scotsman departed than another
angry voice sounded at the door. "I demand to know
what you are doing to find my sister!"

De Villiers glared over his shoulder as Henri d'Amboise stalked across the chamber. With his black hair
and blue eyes, few would believe him to be Laurien's
brother. The man gave new meaning to the word "pest."
"As I have told you the past two days, my best men are
searching for her."

"Your *best men,*" Henri said with a look of disgust,
"could not even protect her in the first place."

"Then ask your father to send out his own guards. I
grow weary of your harping!"

"My father has been in hiding the last two days, for
fear that you would seek him out to break the betrothal.
At the moment he is dead drunk." Henri was nearly
shouting by this point. He gestured to the two men at
de Villiers's side. "As no one else here seems capable
of rescuing my sister from God knows what sort of hell-
ish captors, I shall search for her myself. I have come
to tell you I am leaving."

"Go then," de Villiers snapped at him.

Henri turned on his heel and stalked toward the door,

muttering half to himself as he left, "Saints' blood, what a mistake I made!"

De Villiers could not discern what he meant by that, and did not particularly care. The hotheaded young idiot would probably be lost in the woods by morn, and good riddance.

Turning back to the table, the comte stared at Laurien's torn wedding gown for a long moment.

Then a rumble began in his stomach, gurgled upward, and came out as a laugh.

"The Scots! And to think I worried it was some madman carrying her off." His laughter came harder and faster until he could barely breathe. He wheezed, coughing, and wiped his face. "And they wish to force my hand on the alliance! If only they kn-knew," he sputtered, tears trickling down his plump cheeks, "that I want the alliance as much as they!"

He threw back his head and laughed until his stomach hurt. Indeed, their alliance fit neatly into his plans. He had been persistently urging Philippe to sign, almost to the point of irritating the monarch, a thing he never risked.

"I doubt your mercenaries will find it so humorous, milord," Paxton muttered in his clipped English accent, flicking at a piece of lint on his cream-colored sleeve. "They are waiting for the ten thousand in silver you promised them."

De Villiers sat up straight, half choking. The echo of his own laughter seemed to mock him.

Paxton looked at him in complete calm. The Englishman was one of de Villiers's two best assassins. As always, he cut straight to the heart of the matter. "Since you will not be receiving the money from the Scots, where do you plan to obtain it?"

De Villiers uttered a vicious oath. He had several thousand warriors for hire waiting in the south, and they were a notoriously impatient lot. They demanded payment in coin. "Damn them!" he shouted. "Damn the accursed Scots for interfering!"

Balafre, the other of de Villiers's best assassins, offered a rare opinion, his voice rumbling like a winter storm. "You have brought us here to deal with these thieves. Leave them to us. In time—"

"Time? I have no more time!" De Villiers pushed his chair away from the table with a savage motion when he rose, sending it tumbling. He began to pace. "I will not be denied any longer! I have already waited too long to have what I want—what is *owed* to me!"

Far too long! Growing up as Philippe's illegitimate cousin, de Villiers had existed on the fringes of the court, close enough to see the grandeur, but never allowed to touch it. He had always been stout, with no skill at weapons or fighting; his youth had been spent suffering endless jests, derision . . . and, worse, laughter.

Now he was inches away from silencing that laughter forever.

He crossed to a side trestle and poured himself a cup of wine from a waiting pitcher. When dear, gullible cousin Philippe had appointed him an adviser, he'd begun at last to gain acceptance among those who had disdained him for so long. He had indulged his every desire—wealth, women, power. But they only sated his appetite for a brief time. He'd satisfied his every lust, but could not wipe that echo of laughter from his memory.

He secretly longed to rule them all, to beat them down as he had been beaten. To crush them. Brutally.

Philippe had made his fatal error last year, entrusting de Villiers with a very useful post: head of the army. Then the most golden of opportunities presented itself when the Scots began to pester Philippe about an alliance.

De Villiers tossed off the rest of the wine in one gulp. He had already called all of his liegemen into service. He would send the army to Scotland, on pretense of defending France's new allies from the English. Philippe would then be an easy target for de Villiers's hand-picked mercenaries. He, Jacques de Villiers, once the object of scorn and laughter, would install himself as king. His first order would be to tell his army to seize the Scottish throne.

But the mercenaries were still in the south, waiting for ten thousand silver marks he did not have . . .

De Villiers threw the goblet to the floor and stalked back to the table, snatching up the wedding gown in one shaking fist. "No one bests Jacques de Villiers!" He grasped both sides and ripped the silk in two, casting both pieces away with a vicious snap. "No one!"

"The girl is the key," Paxton said calmly. "Once you have her wealth, the plan will work. Money is the only obstacle."

"The only obstacle?" de Villiers snarled. "I was depending upon the profits from her autumn harvest *and* the ten thousand to cover my debts!"

He threw himself into a chair and stared up at the faded tapestry on the wall above the hearth. Money had been a problem from the start. When he began to assemble the mercenaries, he had found his coffers almost empty. Bribes and favors and discreet assassinations were expensive, and he had sorely neglected his trade in the east while looking after his interests at court. That was when he had decided he must marry again. Not any girl, but an heiress.

The fact that he had a wife at the time presented no difficulty. An arranged accident had taken care of her. And then he had set out after the wealthiest available girl, the beautiful maid of Amboise.

He had even tricked her father into giving him several

hundred marks in dowry. He had, of course, no intention of handing over her lands after the wedding.

"I must get her back quickly," he growled. "I must marry her and get the funds from the harvest into my pocket. Then I shall send the army to Scotland and take every last piece of silver the accursed Scots have. I will force them to pay ten times ten thousand!"

De Villiers smiled at that thought and looked at his two assassins. In all the uncountable tasks Balafre and Paxton had undertaken for him, they had never failed. Paxton had the mind of a master chess player, Balafre the heart of a hunter. In the end, they always ran their quarry to ground and dispatched it with ruthless efficiency. "I want the girl back within a sennight."

"Seven days?" Paxton raised an eyebrow. "To find her so quickly will be difficult. And costly—"

"I will give you whatever you want—jewels, opium, women."

A jackal's grin curved the Englishman's lips as de Villiers said this last word. "I am told this Lady Laurien is a great beauty—"

"You shall not lay a hand upon her, do you understand me?" de Villiers snarled. "No one takes what belongs to me! You may have as many others as you wish, Englishman—pale little virgins, none older than three-and-ten. Are they not your favorite? I can obtain boys as well, if you prefer."

Paxton shrugged, the intended insult not affecting him in the least. He still smiled in the slightly insolent way that never failed to ignite de Villiers's temper.

"Jewels," Balafre interrupted before de Villiers and Paxton could start arguing. "We will accept payment in jewels."

De Villiers glanced at Balafre's ring, a ruby large enough to make the heart of a queen beat faster. He remembered the months of time and trouble he had gone through to obtain it. But the payment had been well earned.

"Done," de Villiers said. He leaned over and picked up the scraps that had been Laurien's wedding gown. He held them in his fists, then began twisting them one around the other, tighter and tighter. "Bring me my heiress."

Paxton, still smiling, rose and bowed deeply in a manner that seemed somehow mocking, then walked toward the door. Balafre paused before following his partner.

"And her abductors?"

Still holding the twisted fabric, de Villiers rose and crossed to the fireplace. He dropped the pieces of ruined silk into the flames, one by one, watching them curl, then blacken.

"Kill them."

Chapter 8

❧⟩⟨❧

"S ibylla?"

Laurien awoke with a start, surprised that she had fallen asleep so quickly. She had just closed her eyes, intending to rest but a moment. A fire blazed on the hearth beside her; a caldron of bubbling water suspended over the flames emitted warm steam that swirled about the chamber. By the light of the sconces on either side of the bed, she could see that Connor had managed to throw off his blankets again.

"Sibylla?" He repeated the odd word he had whispered, then groaned, a low sound of torment.

Laurien leaped to her feet, quickly regretting her haste as pain stabbed up her left leg. She had not thought she'd seriously injured her ankle yesterday morning, but it had become swollen and tender, making each step a sharp reminder of her attempted escape.

After limping over to the bed, she pulled the blankets up to Connor's chin. A full day had passed since he had been entrusted to her care, but his condition had not improved. In fact, she thought uneasily, he seemed to be getting worse.

Last night he had been quietly asleep when the barber returned to check on him, still intent on bleeding him. Laurien had placed herself at Connor's side and refused to move, calling the barber a half-witted butcher and saying he would have to bleed her first. Enraged, the

108

man had given up and stormed out, yelling that she would pay the price for her insolence—when Connor died.

"Nay, you will not die," Laurien whispered fiercely, focusing on her patient as if her will alone could make him well. Connor's tangled hair stood out in pale contrast to the dark slashes of his eyebrows and the light brown of his beard, which had grown thick with the passing days. A sheen of sweat glistened on his flushed skin.

She felt Connor's forehead. Concern furrowed her brow when she found his skin hot beneath her fingers. Throughout the day, he had been half delirious, mumbling and tossing on the bed; now, as night fell once again, it seemed her worst fear was coming true.

Fever.

She poured fresh water from the ewer and dipped a clean cloth, bathing his face, neck and shoulders. Her worry deepened when she saw that his skin was flushed all the way down his chest. She checked the poultice she had placed over his wound. The bleeding had stopped— that was a good sign—and the fragrant balm of yarrow and elder flower should prevent infection.

Why, then, was he fevered?

Frustrated, Laurien tossed the cloth into the pile of damp and bloodstained rags by the hearth, and sat on the edge of the bed. She had no more answers. For a day and a half now she had concentrated her best efforts on the Scotsman. She was exhausted, her ankle throbbed, and though she wracked her brain, she could not think of what else to do for him. Mayhap he was meant to die.

She put her hands over her eyes, unable to explain why that thought brought sudden tears. She blamed it on fatigue. She was upset because this was so unfair, she reasoned. She had given up a perfect chance to escape.

And he was going to die anyway.

She balled her hands into fists and glared at him, wanting to strike him or shake him—to somehow force him to respond to her ministrations. "Die, then!" she railed. "Die if you insist, you accursed Scotsman. I do not care. It does not matter to me!"

She flung herself from the bed, turning her back on him, and gave in to her tears. Even as she stood there, crying and angry at herself for crying, she knew she had not spoken the truth.

It did matter. God help her, she *did* care. She realized with no small surprise that she was not sobbing out of fear for herself, at what Sir Gaston might do to her, but out of fear for Glenshiel. By all rights she should hate him, but she found that particular emotion did not number among the confusion of feelings she had for him.

She could not deny, at least to herself, that he had become . . . important to her, somehow.

Wiping away her tears, Laurien turned back toward the bed. She did not have time to think about herself. She must think of some way to save him. She must—

Connor shivered suddenly, a violent frisson that made her heart sink.

"C-cold," he murmured, his voice a dry whisper. A second shiver coursed through him.

Laurien felt the first pang of true despair. Cold? The chamber was almost stifling, and she had covered him with two woolen blankets and a fur wrap. Yet he complained of cold.

She limped to his side and lightly brushed his hair from his forehead. What should she do? She had been so sure of herself, puffed up with her own skill, certain that she could save him. Now she felt helpless, her confidence completely shattered.

She could think of only one other way to warm him, and the idea brought a flush of color to her own cheeks.

He shivered again, and she hesitated only a moment more. With fever clouding his mind, she thought hopefully, he would likely remember none of this.

She moved to the far side of the bed. The sound of her heartbeat, thrumming in her ears, drowned out the crackle of flames on the hearth. The firelight and the candle sconces on the wall cast dancing shadows across Connor's still form.

Before she had a chance to change her mind, she slipped under the blankets and eased herself down beside him.

She edged closer, slowly, admonishing herself all the while that there was no reason to be nervous. The man was unconscious.

But her heart thumped wildly in her chest when her breasts came in contact with the too-hot skin along his ribs. He groaned again, and she felt the deep, pain-filled sound reverberate through her. Willing herself to relax, she pressed herself against the full length of his body and pulled the blankets closer about them.

Gingerly, she lay one arm across his midsection. Even through the cloth of her sleeve, she could feel the warmth of his skin, and beneath her bare fingers she felt a raging fever. The heat from his body, combined with the warmth of the blankets, her snug tunic and leggings, and the steam swirling about the chamber soon had Laurien perspiring.

She thought of removing her garments, but just as quickly discarded the idea. The rough material was all that now separated her from Glenshiel's naked form, his smoothly muscled maleness.

Instead, she held him tighter, watching the steady rise and fall of his broad chest.

"Do not dare to die on me, Scotsman," she whispered urgently.

She pushed the disturbing thought from her mind. Unable to think of aught else to do, she decided to pray, but she could not find any words to express what she felt. Nor could she remember any of the litanies that Sister Katherine had tried to make her memorize years ago. She silently offered up a few lines of one that came to mind.

Then she gave up, closed her eyes, and whispered a single word aloud, putting her heart and soul into it.

"Please."

Laurien awakened in the darkness, guessing the hour to be long past midnight. Connor had been tossing fitfully and kept trying to throw off the covers; it took constant effort to keep him still, lest he reopen his wound. To her dismay, she could feel that his body was still ablaze with fever.

She slid out from under the blankets and limped to his side of the bed. Twice now she had risen to prepare a valerian root tea to deepen his slumber, but had only managed to get a few drops into him. He seemed to be sweating more heavily, at least. Laurien took that as a good sign, and hoped it meant his fever was nearing a breaking point. She dipped a cloth in the water basin beside the bed, and began to bathe his face and chest again.

She was near a breaking point herself. She had caught only brief snatches of sleep, coming fully awake at the Scotsman's every move or sound, fearful she would find him suffering some awful, final crisis. Her nerves were close to snapping; she would soon be no good to him at all.

"Fight, damn you," she admonished him as she moved the cloth over his neck and shoulders.

He made a small sound, deep in his throat.

But this was not a groan of pain, more a sound of pleasure. "Feels . . . good."

Laurien stopped in mid-motion, her hand upon his chest. Had he actually spoken, or was she losing her mind?

He opened his eyes. "S-smell . . . What is that?" He wrinkled his nose and gave a perturbed look at the poultice on his wound.

Laurien almost laughed with relief and joy. His speech was slurred and his eyes were glassy and staring, but he was conscious. And he had uttered a complete sentence! It was enough to make her giddy. "A poultice," she answered his question at last. "It will help your wound heal more quickly."

He blinked up at her as if trying to see through a fog. "You look terrible."

"*Merci.*" She smiled at what was likely a very accurate appraisal. "You are a most charming patient." She put down the cloth and picked up the half-full cup of dark tea from beside the bed, holding it to his lips. "Finish this and I shall think about forgiving you."

With Laurien supporting his head, he drained the cup of its sharp-smelling brew, but not without a few sputtering protests, which Laurien found encouraging. Mayhap, she thought with a silent word of gratitude, she might have skill enough to save him after all. He lay back and closed his eyes, and was silent a long moment. Laurien thought he might have fallen asleep.

Suddenly he shivered. "Head . . . feels . . . strange." He opened his eyes again and frowned, trembling now. " 'Tis . . . so cold."

Laurien's rush of cheerful confidence abruptly stilled. "Your head feels strange because the drink is supposed to make you sleep more deeply," she said softly. "So be an obedient patient and cease your struggles against it."

His lashes drifted downward again and Laurien moved back to the far side of the bed. She waited until his chest was rising and falling evenly; then she gently lifted the covers and eased herself down upon the mattress.

The slight movement, however, was enough to waken him. He blinked at her in disbelief and mumbled at her, his speech growing more slurred as the sleeping potion began to affect him. "She means to . . . tor-torture me.'

"I mean only to warm you until your fever breaks,' she admonished as she inched closer. "So put any other thoughts from your mind." Slowly, she moved against him, her eyes never leaving his.

He made a low, masculine sound of appreciation as her body fitted neatly to his.

She stared at him accusingly. "This is for your benefit. And by that I mean your health. And since, as you so ably pointed out"—she placed one arm about his midsection again—"I look less than appealing at the moment, I am certain you will not find cause to attempt aught untoward."

"But 'twould be . . . m-much more e-effective," he said, grinning weakly, "if you . . . remove your garments."

"Never mind that." She ducked her head so he could not see her smile. For once, to her wonderment, she found humor in his teasing. "Go to sleep."

When she reached up to tuck the blankets back into place about him, she saw that, for once, he had followed her orders.

Chapter 9

It was late morning by the time Laurien awakened again. She lay with one hand on Connor's uninjured shoulder, and she slid her fingers along his chest, smiling upon finding that his skin had regained its normal warmth.

"I do believe you will recover, Scotsman," she murmured, giving in to the urge to remain where she was just a moment longer.

He chuckled softly, his eyes still closed. "I shall do my best. But that homespun tickles. I think you should take it off."

"I thought you were asleep!" She snatched her hand away.

He opened one eye. " 'Tis near impossible to sleep with you scratching away at my side."

Laurien noticed that his words were quite distinct. She suddenly felt a surge of uneasiness at lying this close to him, and an intense awareness of the fact that he was not wearing a stitch of clothing.

She started to rise. "Since your fever has cooled, you are welcome to have the bed to yourself."

But before she could move away, he reached beneath her shoulders with his good arm and pulled her back, uttering a sound that was half growl, half sigh. Laurien's heart began to beat a wild rhythm. Mayhap her minis-

trations had worked too well. He seemed to be regaining
his strength with alarming speed.

"Let me up."

Her words went unheeded; it appeared he had lost the
all-too-brief tendency to follow her orders. Their roles
had suddenly reversed, and she was now the one at his
command.

He gazed down at her, his sleepy eyes still bright with
the last of his fever and the lingering effects of the potent
drink she had given him. He was unpredictable under
the best of circumstances; there was no telling what he
might do with the potion clouding his reason. He was
probably not even aware of who she was or what he was
doing.

His hand moved from her shoulders to her back. She
tried to pull away, keenly aware of where Glenshiel's
actions were leading. He held her fast. Laurien stiffened.
She knew a single quick jab to his ribs would gain her
freedom, but she could not bring herself to hurt him.

"With my valerian root tea in your blood, you haven't
the wits of a turnip just now," she told him firmly, determined to regain control of the situation. "Nor do you
have the strength to do what you are thinking of doing,
so let me g—"

She gasped as he tugged at the back of her tunic and
his hand touched her bare skin. His fingers caressed the
curve of her spine and ignited her body, sending a flame
to awaken every hidden region, bringing a flush to her
face. He pressed her hips against him, and all of her
intentions to remain controlled and distant went up in
flames.

"You are so soft," Connor whispered, his voice husky
and urgent, filled with tenderness and an almost painful
longing. "So soft and so beautiful."

"Now I *know* you are not in your right mind," Laurien insisted, even as she felt her heart quickening. "Release me."

"Nay," he replied, his fingers moving higher beneath her tunic to boldly stroke the underside of one breast. "I think I shall keep you."

Laurien barely breathed as his hand rested possessively where it had ceased its wandering. She seemed to have lost the capacity for reason. Connor's gentle explorations were filling her not with outrage, but with longing, an ache that was at once delightful and frightening. His tone and actions were almost certainly the result of the medicine she had given him, but his words made her feel strange inside nonetheless. "Y-you will remember none of this on the morrow—"

"Then I should not miss an opportunity," he said, lowering his head to hers, "to take advantage of the situation."

And before Laurien knew what was happening, he was kissing her, his mouth hot upon hers, his tongue darting out to part her lips. She lost the last shred of her own control, and responded with equal fervor. It was as if she had become a stranger, an entirely different Laurien, not a defiant girl but a woman, willing—nay, eager—to revel in the feel of this man's claiming her. He filled her with an unfamiliar hunger, a *wanting*—

Suddenly he lay back upon the pillows, gasping for breath.

Laurien quickly wriggled out of his grasp and placed some much-needed distance between them. She turned away, shaken, and took a deep breath to cool the feelings that had risen so quickly within her. "There," she gasped. "W-was it worth nearly passing out?"

"Aye," he breathed, turning his head toward her. "If I were to know no sustenance but the sweetness of those lips and the soft gaze of those eyes, I would live long and happily."

He reached out for her, but she pulled away from his eager fingers. She scrambled out of the bed before he could make any further effort to catch her. "Verse? You make a most unusual poet, Scotsman." Her own voice sounded strangely husky to her ears. Her tongue darted out to soothe her slightly swollen lower lip.

Connor groaned. "Do you know what you do to me, woman? To have you a hair's breadth away, and be unable to do aught about it?"

"Think you I would have come so willingly to your bed if you *were* able to do aught about it?"

"Oh, lass." He smiled wickedly. "We shall see, anon. By God we will." He closed his eyes. The brief expenditure of energy had obviously cost him dearly.

He murmured on sleepily. "And if I die before I have the chance to do aught about it . . . Saints' blood, I shall kill myself."

"Shhh," Laurien whispered, her insides still churning from his bold words and soft entreaties. "Go to sleep, turnip-wit."

"You will but torture me endlessly. In my dreams, my defiant *demoiselle*. In my dreams . . ."

Sleep claimed him again, leaving Laurien to wonder if he had even realized it had been she in the bed beside him—

My defiant demoiselle, he had called her.

"You *did* know it was me," she accused the slumbering form. She noticed he wore the slightest trace of his familiar grin.

But for some reason, his boldness left her feeling more pleased than angry.

For lack of aught better to do, and to distract herself from the disturbing path her thoughts were taking, Laurien set about tidying up the chamber.

That occupied the rest of the morning, but by midnoon she was still feeling restless. She drifted to the window and opened the shutters. Leaning out, she inhaled deeply of the cool, foggy air, tasting the autumn scent of damp leaves mixed with the clinging, burnt odor from the destroyed siege towers. Below, a mason and his apprentices were working to repair the damaged curtain wall. As the men patched the jagged gaps left by catapult stones, she noted, with a pang of regret, that the scaling ladder had been cleared away.

She chewed her lower lip thoughtfully. It was time to turn her thoughts back to planning an escape. She had certainly paid her debt to the Scotsman.

She glanced at the bed, where the object of her thoughts was sleeping peacefully. She had relented in her struggle to keep him covered, and he lay with the blankets pushed down to his waist.

What had God been thinking, Laurien wondered, when He created so handsome a face and form, and gave both to one man? She supposed the Scotsman could not help but be arrogant with such looks and such strength. His well-muscled arms attested to long days handling a sword, just as several scars, large and small, marked many a battle long past. A mat of golden hair peeked out at the lower edge of the bandage, narrowing to a trickle of curls over his rib cage, down his lean stomach, and—

Laurien glanced away, feeling a sudden tightening in her own stomach, amazed that Connor could elicit a response from her without even a word or movement. How was it that this man should affect her so, when others had not? She had known many young men in her life, some equally handsome, and they had left her with a firm sense of their lot as selfish, brutal, greedy. Yet the more time she spent with Glenshiel, the more she came to see that he shared none of those qualities. She knew so little of him, but each new trait she discovered only increased her appetite to know more.

How was it that he had become important to her, in so short a span of time?

Laurien jumped at the sound of the door swinging open. Sir Gaston, his helm and gloves still tucked under one arm, strode in. His eyes swept over her charge with a somber glance. He placed a hand to Connor's forehead, then nodded. "You have done well."

After Varennes's earlier threats, Laurien felt more than a little relief at his words. She kept it hidden. "You did not expect such skill from a mere female?" she asked tartly. "I told you I could help him."

"That you did." Gaston gave her a wry smile and slipped the coif from his head, running a hand through his matted black hair. "Glenshiel has cheated death more than his share of times, and someday, I am afraid, it will catch up to him. But not this day, thanks to you."

Laurien gave him an indifferent shrug and turned back to the window. "He should be well enough to move about in a few days."

"Good. But knowing him, he will not wait that long." His mood obviously lightened, Gaston moved to the chest against one wall. He began rummaging through it after tossing in the helm and gloves. "I bear other good tidings, milady. Beauvais has given in. The battle is ended."

"So soon?" Laurien tried to keep her voice steady, but her heart thumped strangely at the news. Warfare was normally a slow business. Even small battles usually lasted a fortnight or more. With the siege over and Connor on the mend, they would be leaving soon.

The Scotsman would have her on a ship and whisked away in a trice. She had no idea what manner of dangers awaited in traveling across the sea, what Scotland was like, or how the Scots rebels might treat her—and she had no desire to find out.

She must find a way to escape before they reached the coast.

"Beauvais has lost too many men," Gaston explained as he took a number of garments from the chest and closed the lid. "He sent word that he is prepared to discuss a peaceful end to our troubles. We are to meet at his castle."

"It sounds like a trap." Laurien crossed the room and leaned against one of the bedposts.

"It may be." Gaston sat on the stool beside the door to pull off his boots. "But I would rather meet the old wolf in his castle than invite him and his pack inside here. And I am taking the mercenaries along in case things turn sour." He leaned forward, elbows on his knees. "I will, of course, leave your guard here." He indicated the door.

"How could I possibly escape?" Laurien crossed her arms and looked down at her patient. "He thwarts me at every turn."

Despite the bitterness in her voice, her eyes held an unmistakable softness as she gazed at Connor, a fact which did not escape Gaston's notice. It surprised him only for a moment. She would not be the first unsuspecting maid to fall victim to his friend's rough-hewn charm. Yet this particular lady, Gaston felt, deserved at least some warning of what lay ahead in such a course.

"Lady Laurien." His voice was low, barely above a whisper. "Your eyes reveal to all the world the contents of your heart. Be careful of that."

"I do not know what you mean." Laurien turned to him with an honestly amazed stare.

He grinned and looked down at his steepled fingers. "Heed me, milady. Connor and I met when we were fighting for a lord of Aragon. We had a disagreement over the division of booty in a captured castle. You see, a serving girl was discovered hiding in the loft above the kitchens—

"I do not wish to hear tales of your . . . your *exploits*." Laurien frowned.

"Nay, milady, listen on. You will see my point. The Aragon lord declared that, to avoid a fight, she be given to the man who had made the most kills that day." He raised his eyebrows. "Me, of course. Connor did not agree."

Her irritation warring with curiosity, Laurien sat on the edge of the bed. "So you challenged him to fight."

"Fight we did." Gaston nodded. "The better part of the afternoon. But I simply could not best the man. Our swords were evenly matched. Finally, I declared that no woman was worth such effort, and that the Scotsman had made the most kills. We spent the rest of the night drinking, and the rest of four years fighting on the same side."

He looked over at his sleeping friend. "I wanted to make sure I would never find myself on the sharp end of his sword again. And he felt the same."

Laurien blinked in confusion as Gaston stopped, seemingly finished with his tale. "But what happened to the girl?"

"Aye, the girl. Therein lies the lesson, milady. Connor slipped away at dawn and spent the better part of the next day and night with her. But I still believe, to this day, that I *did* make the most kills that day. And he knew it . . . He just wanted the girl."

Laurien furrowed her brow as Gaston rose to leave, unable to see what lesson she was supposed to discern from that. Gaston walked over and placed a finger gently beneath her chin, tipping her gaze up to meet his.

"And he left the next day and never saw her again." His eyes became dark and serious. "You see, he was willing to fight for her, *but not to keep her*. Remember milady, remember to tread most carefully. I have seen too many maids cry too many tears, and feel I cannot leave you unarmed, so I give you at least a warning. Do not give this one your heart, for he cannot accept it."

She jerked her chin away. "You may keep your ridiculous warnings! The only feelings I have for the Scotsman are loathing and contempt."

Gaston's reply to that was a soft chuckle. Before she could rant at him further, he bent down and kissed her, the briefest touching of lips, a chaste whisper compared to the demanding kisses of the Scotsman.

Laurien tried to slap him, incensed that he had no more qualms about taking liberties than his infuriating friend. Her hand met only air. Gaston was already at the door.

"Yon blond villain would have knocked me flat had I attempted that while he was awake." He smiled at her and sighed wistfully. "But it would have been worth it. Fare thee well, *ma demoiselle.*"

Laurien sat fuming as the portal closed behind him. *Do not give this one your heart!* What gave him the absurd idea that she had any intention of doing so? She might feel a certain—and quite understandable, she assured herself—*gratitude* that Glenshiel had saved her life. But she certainly was not . . . She certainly would not . . . Nay! She would never give her heart to any man, especially not one who had so ruthlessly taken her captive, who saw her as naught but booty to be traded off like a sack of grain.

She frowned down at Connor with an accusing glare. Remembering the soft emotions she had felt for him only moments before, she sprang up from the bed, suddenly wanting to be as far from him as possible.

Aye, it was much too dangerous to linger overlong near this Scotsman. He aroused too many unfamiliar, confusing thoughts. Better to keep a goodly space away from him. Especially if, as Sir Gaston seemed to be trying to tell her, the knave could indeed be heartless when it came to women.

She was still pondering Gaston's warning when a soft knock sounded at the door. At her acknowledgment, a tiny woman clothed in gray homespun bustled in, a trencher of food in her hands. Two young girls followed her, one carrying a length of fabric, the other a large bowl and a steaming ewer.

"Good 'noon to you, *ma dame,*" the woman said, her elfin figure dipping into as much of a curtsy as she could manage. "Milord said you were tired and hungry, and asked me to bring you some fare from the kitchens."

The serving woman motioned for the girls to deposit their burdens on the trunk against the wall. They did so and curtsied before leaving. Laurien accepted the trencher of food with a grateful smile. "Thank you," she said, sitting on the stool by the door. She nibbled at a warm beef pastry.

While Laurien ate, the woman unfurled the length of cloth, revealing it to be a gown of amber-colored velvet, trimmed with brown marten fur at the neck and cuffs. "This will be much more fitting for Sir Connor's lady."

Laurien almost choked on a mouthful of grain pudding. It was exasperating, the way everyone seemed intent upon linking her to the Scotsman! "I am *not* S—"

She stopped herself, remembering that Glenshiel *had* called her his bride, for her protection. With Sir Gaston gone and Connor incapacitated, Laurien decided she'd best let the story stand.

The serving woman stood looking puzzled, waiting for Laurien to finish her sentence.

Laurien smiled at her. "I am not so hungry anymore," she said lamely. "This is very good." She finished the rich almond-flavored pudding.

The woman looked pleased. "Thank you, milady. When you are finished with your meal, I shall leave you to your bath."

"Bath?" Laurien coughed on the last of the meat pastry and looked uneasily at Connor. "Here?"

"Milord instructed us that you are not to leave the chamber. He does not wish to tempt trouble, no doubt, with some of the men still about and Sir Connor unable to protect you." She hefted the metal ewer the girl had carried in, poured steaming water into the shallow bowl, then handed Laurien a small cake of soap. "I am afraid this will have to do. But you will be much more comfortable." She cast a critical gaze at Laurien's stained tunic and leggings.

"But . . ." Laurien still looked at Connor, the soap held awkwardly in her upturned palm.

"A new bride, are you not?" The woman smiled knowingly. "Ah, how well I remember. But the shyness will pass anon, *ma belle.*" She held out her hands expectantly. "I will have your garments washed for you."

Her meal finished, Laurien hesitated. The hot water looked appealing indeed, and she could smell the light, spicy scent of sandalwood oil rising on the tendrils of steam. She sniffed the soap and found it, too, smelled of *bois de santal*. The thought of indulging herself in such a luxury brought a guilty smile to her lips. While she disdained most feminine fripperies, she had always harbored a secret weakness for fragrant oils and soaps. And it would feel *so* good to wash away the grime of the last two days.

"All right," she said at last.

Moments later the serving woman was carrying out the trencher and Laurien's tunic and leggings, leaving Laurien standing in the middle of the chamber with only a crisp linen towel for covering.

With one last glance to ensure Connor still slept

soundly, Laurien moved to the farthest possible corner of the room. She rubbed the soap until the basin frothed with bubbles, then closed her eyes and splashed her face. The hot, heady lather felt unbelievably rich as she ran her hands over her cheeks and throat. Leaning over, she removed the towel and washed her hair leisurely. Then she dipped a corner of the cloth and scrubbed herself from head to toe until her skin was pink.

With a sigh, she at last toweled herself dry, and slipped the velvet gown over her head. The soft material clung to her body, making her delightfully warm, and fell to the floor in a short train edged with gold embroidery. The neckline dipped scandalously low between her breasts; the fur trim tickled her skin. Had she a mirror, she knew she would present a most wanton image. She wondered, with a wry twist to her lips, what kind of women had enjoyed Sir Gaston's hospitality in the past.

Picking up a bone comb that the serving woman had left for her, Laurien settled cross-legged on the furs before the hearth and set about removing the tangles from her long tresses. After she worked the last knot free, she tossed her head back and closed her eyes, running her fingers through her hair with a sigh. It felt so good to be clean and warm and dry; she could almost imagine she was safe at home in her own chamber. Reluctantly, she opened her eyes, and was startled to find herself looking into Connor's intense blue gaze.

The knave was watching her every move from where he lay on the bed!

She started to speak but could not find her voice. His eyes were fierce, dark with an emotion she had seen before in the gaze of men. She sat pinioned, her breath escaping between parted lips, her heartbeat unnaturally quickened. She felt an embarrassed warmth creeping into her cheeks, and she silently cursed both herself for giving in to the pleasures of a bath, and Sir Gaston for providing her with such a revealing gown. She might be clean and warm and dry, but Connor's eyes told her she was not safe, not safe at all.

His sultry regard finally left her face, but she only felt more uncomfortable still as his eyes traveled to the depth of the wide bodice. Though he lay several feet away, wounded and powerless, Laurien had the most unsettling sensation that he was next to her, running his strong hands over her body, tracing the furred edge of her bodice with his fingers instead of his eyes. Her mind refused to work, but her senses seemed to have sharpened. She was aware of the sound of her blood rushing in her ears, the scent of *bois de santal* filling the room, the feeling of his gaze lingering over every inch of her body.

"H-how long have you been awake?" she managed at last.

His lips curved in a familiar grin. "Long enough."

She turned away from him, the spell broken by their voices. "You might have told me." Standing, she tossed her hair in a show of haughty anger, trying to hide her frustration. Even when she kept her distance from him, it seemed impossible to gain an equal emotional distance. She turned her back to him and retreated to the corner, pretending to busy herself with tidying the room.

"Aye," Connor said belatedly. He closed his eyes, feeling weak, not sure how long he had lain asleep. More than that, he was still shaken by the sight he had awakened to.

It had taken him a good minute to realize he was experiencing reality and not another half-dazed dream as he had watched Laurien at her bath. God's teeth, what a vision . . . Laurien, bathed in light from the fire, her naked limbs moist, glistening, her head thrown back as she wrung the cloth over her face. He had watched every drop of water trickle down her neck and over her body, as her breasts peeked impudently between wet strands of her long hair.

Even as he remembered, desire shot through him, swift and urgent. The dull throb of his wounded shoulder was nothing compared to the ache she caused in his loins. Whether it was simple joy at finding himself still alive, or Laurien's earthy beauty, or something else about her, he wanted her. Now. Every sinew in his body cried out to have her in his bed, warm and yielding, to feel her body beneath his, to lose himself in her softness. A low moan of frustration escaped him.

Laurien turned instantly. "Are you in pain?"

He opened his eyes and almost laughed at her concerned face. "Nay," he assured her. He watched the soft sway of her hips as she moved toward the bed. It was not an affected, practiced motion, as with some women, but simply the way she walked. He frowned, noticing that she was favoring her left foot. "You are hurt."

"It is naught." She reached for the ewer of water beside the bed.

"Dinna tell me 'tis naught," he insisted. "Sit down."

When she made no move to obey, he reached up, caught her skirt, and pulled her down beside him.

He regretted it almost instantly, not just because the movement sent pain flashing through his shoulder, but because his entire body sprang to awareness with Laurien so close. He found himself entranced by the scent of sandalwood clinging to her, and by the way her damp, dark hair made her skin seem as pale as fresh cream.

He struggled to bring his wandering thoughts back to more pressing matters. "How long have I been asleep?"

"A long time," Laurien said slowly. "What do you remember?"

Connor searched his mind, sorting through the dreams, shadows, and half-formed visions that floated before him, then vanished like smoke in a strong wind. It was like being lost in a cave, listening to echoes but unable to tell who was speaking, or from which direction.

Suddenly an image materialized: of Laurien, running along the curtain wall, sword in hand, hair flying. "You were out in the bailey. You were trying to escape." Anger flooded through him as his rapidly awakening memory put the chain of events together—the girl, the battle, the crossbow bolt that came from nowhere as he bent to pull her to her feet. "God, woman, how much of a fool are you? Were you that desperate to escape that you would plunge into a battle?"

Laurien's own temper flared at his accusation. "Nay, I was running from Beauvais's man. He found me in the tunnel when I—Very well, I *was* trying to escape. But when you were hurt I helped you. I could have escaped then, but I stayed." At the look of disbelief on his face, she clenched her fists. "Fie! You must remember. I have been here every moment these past days. You were talking to me. You were . . ." She blushed suddenly and stood, turning her back on him. "You do not remember?"

Connor was wondering what could possibly make Laurien blush so profusely, when another memory came to him.

He recalled a warm, soft shape beside him, holding him, soothing him when he thought himself lost in a timeless blur of agony and heat and terrifying darkness.

He remembered a voice, whispering, forbidding him to die.

Laurien's softness, Laurien's voice.

She spoke the truth. She *had* helped him. He did not believe that she had given up an opportunity to escape, but he could not dispute that she had saved his life. He reached out toward her, started to thank her, the sudden

mix of gratitude and pleasure and desire he felt almost
unnerving. Then he stopped himself.

His reason promptly launched into the fray. He must
not allow himself to have feelings for this woman. For
years he had avoided any such entanglements, concentrating on the Scottish cause until it blocked out all other
thoughts and emotions. He could not change now, could
not let a woman distract him from his goal. Too many
lives were depending on him, men and women and children who would be slaughtered by the English—cut down
as his brother Galen had been cut down.

Connor shook his head, the image of Laurien at her
bath, soft and glistening and tempting, warring with the
image of Laurien leaping along the curtain wall, racing
headlong into a pitched battle. She confused him. Con-
founded him. But if his plans for the alliance were to
succeed, he must gain control over himself. He must
not soften toward her in any way.

Laurien turned toward him with questioning eyes.
Connor knew she would be angry at the lie he was about
to tell. He tried to convince himself that was for the
best, but it did not keep him from feeling like the lowest
kind of knave.

"I cannot remember any of it," he said abruptly.

"You must!" Laurien insisted.

"Nay, I dinna remember what happened. If you are
the one who saved my life, then you have my gratitude—"

"*Merci,* oh great and noble sir," she hissed at the
cool indifference in his voice. "You knew who I was
when you awakened this morn! You . . . you said . . ."

"Well? What did I say?" Connor snapped, wishing
she would let the subject drop. The throb in his shoulder
had been joined by an equal throbbing in his head.

Laurien suddenly lowered her eyes, and Connor could
not help but notice that her lashes looked like dark shad-

ows on a field of fresh snow. He silently railed at himself for his weakness. Why could he not steel himself against these maddening feelings?

"You said I was beautiful," Laurien said sullenly. "You called me your defiant *demoiselle.*"

Silence reigned for a long moment.

Connor managed a sarcastic chuckle. "Did I? I must have been delirious."

Laurien's head came up, and Connor saw a quick, sharp glimmer of pain at his cruel remark. Then her hurt melted in an emerald-green glare of pure loathing.

"I had a perfect opportunity to escape, you ungrateful cur. I stayed to save your worthless life!"

"Really?" Connor said sarcastically. "You wish me to believe you would do that, give up what you want above all else, to help me?

"Believe what you will." She turned her back on him again and went to the window, opening one of the shutters. "I wish to God I had left you to die!"

Connor found her actions more disturbing than her words.

Had she not leaped out a window—twice now—in her efforts to escape?

Indeed, had she not shown time and again that she was determined to have her freedom? She had pulled a knife on him, lied to him repeatedly. And she had a most disturbing tendency to slip through locked doors . . . and out windows. Saints' breath, with her ability to concoct a believable tale, she could likely even talk her way past the guard.

Connor gritted his teeth. He could not allow her to escape. And she would try, of that he was certain. Just as he was certain he would not be able to stop her, weakened as he was.

He dare not trust her.

Worse, he dare not trust himself. If she stayed in this

chamber, her beauty and her scent and her fiery glances driving him mad, her every movement so innocently enticing, he was not going to heed his reason much longer.

He would end up finding some way to get her into his bed.

"Summon Gaston," he growled.

Laurien dismissed his order with a wave of her hand. "Sir Gaston is gone. When the fighting ended, he went to negotiate the peace with Beauvais."

"Then call for the guard."

"Why—"

"Call him."

Laurien knew Connor well enough by now to recognize that tone. He was turning more surly by the minute, and would brook no more argument from her. Annoyed at being so sternly silenced, she turned on her heel, and stalked to the door in a swirl of amber velvet, muttering a few less-than-feminine words about the Scotsman.

When she came back with the guard, Connor refused to even look at her.

"Are any of the upper chambers without windows?"

"Nay, sir," the guard replied with a puzzled look.

Connor cursed softly under his breath, hating what he was about to do. "Then take her to one of the upper chambers and tie her—"

"Nay!" Laurien spat as the guard took her arm. "You cannot mean to do this!"

"Whether you helped me or not, it changes naught," Connor shot back. "I willna give you another chance to escape. What did you expect? Did you think that I would open the door, give you my thanks, and set you free?"

Laurien could find no words to reply. What had she expected? For him to treat her gently now, with some consideration for her feelings? Some small part of her had expected things to be better between them. It was obvious she still meant nothing to him, that she would never be more than a pawn in his plan.

He was ruthless, single-minded: all in all, very much a man.

"I thought you were different," she said with bitter ire. "I see now that I was wrong."

While Connor did not clearly understand what she meant, her words struck him. Part of him still ached to keep her here with him and damn the consequences. He wanted to tumble her into his bed, to ease that soft gown from her shoulders and kiss the pale skin scented with sandalwood . . .

He savagely motioned for the guard to take her away.

"Burn you, then!" Laurien yelled as she was taken from the chamber. "I will not forgive you for this!"

Chapter 10

The fire burned low in the little chamber, and Laurien curled herself into a tighter ball to ward off the chill, cursing Glenshiel's name with every oath she knew. She had already rubbed her wrists raw trying to loosen the tight ropes the guard had tied her with that afternoon. At last she had given up and thrown herself down on the stiff pallet in frustration.

She knew not how long she had lain thus, her mind devising various plans of delicious revenge to exact upon the Scotsman. She thought it heartless of him to order her tied up; the chamber was so high above the ground she would have to be ten kinds of a fool to even think of trying to escape by the window.

But then, a fool seemed to be precisely what he thought her to be. An untrustworthy, foolish female. Well, if he meant for this imprisonment to make her docile and repentant, he would find himself sorely mistaken. Her stomach growled again. She guessed the hour to be long past dinner.

The sound of voices outside the door brought her to her feet. She was more than a little surprised when Glenshiel's friend, Sir Malcolm, stepped inside.

"Your guard was most unwilling to open the door." He slipped the torch he carried into a sconce beside the portal. "He seems to think you might slip away if he but cracked it an inch."

"Have you not heard? I am a fearsome threat. I make full-grown knights and well-armed guards quake in alarm."

He laughed at her sarcasm. "We have more to fear from milady's sharp tongue and quick wit than aught else, I am certain."

"Tell me, what is the word from the comte?" she asked bitterly. "Did he agree to your demands, or has he already found himself another wealthy heiress to take to wife?"

"He agreed," Malcolm said flatly.

Laurien felt a cold, unpleasant wave of anger and vexation roll through her. She had dared to hope de Villiers would simply replace her and tell the Scots to go hang. Unfortunately, it seemed she was still useful to her captors.

Malcolm moved to the hearth to stoke the fire. "I no sooner arrived here than Connor sent me to see how you fare."

"Truly?" She raised her chin. "You can tell *milord* that I am well, no thanks to him, and that he had best not let me out, for I have thought of all manner of ills which I would like to see befall him."

"I see." Malcolm grinned. "And would you like to tell me your version of the tale?"

"To what end? Naught will change." She chafed at his mild attitude, at the knowing smile that seemed to say he understood. Understood what? She stepped into the light and nodded toward the door. "You need not waste your concern on me."

Malcolm ignored her dismissal and added another log to the fire. "Saints' blood, but you're a stubborn one—" Looking down at her, he noticed the bindings and the traces of blood about her wrists for the first time. "What is this?" He reached down and took her hands.

"It was by *milord's* command." Laurien scowled.

Malcolm quickly drew his knife and sliced through the ropes. "More likely the guard was overzealous in fulfilling Connor's orders." He gently examined her raw skin. "I will bring some salve."

"You need not worry about me."

Malcolm ignored her again and left. Laurien plunked herself back down on the pallet. She heard him address heated words to the guard beyond the door, and her benefactor returned anon, carrying not only salve and bandages, but an extra blanket and some food.

"Here." He sat beside her and placed an apple in her hand. "Eat." Not waiting for a reply, he took her free hand and applied the salve with gentle strokes.

Laurien thought of refusing the food, but her growling stomach warned her not to be disagreeable on that particular point. She bit into the apple while Malcolm wrapped her wrist in a length of linen.

"You could order a servant to do this," Laurien said tartly. "I should think it beneath a knight's honor to render aid to a mere woman."

" 'Tis my experience that a knight must choose for himself what is honorable and what is not."

She shifted the fruit to her bandaged hand as he took the other. "But are you not afraid of raising Glenshiel's ire?"

Malcolm made a sound that was half chuckle, half disapproving grunt. "He didna mean for you to be treated thus. And if he did, I shall box his ears. 'Twas the quickest way to straighten him up when he was a lad."

Laurien almost smiled at the image of the tall blond knight having his ears boxed. It might do him a world of good. The mention of Connor's childhood reminded her of the word that had piqued her curiosity. As she watched Malcolm deftly fastening the second bandage, she blurted out the question before she had even completed the thought.

"Sir Malcolm, what does 'sibylla' mean?"

Finished with his task, Malcolm sat back and eyed her with a suddenly serious gaze. "Where did you hear that?"

Regretting her quick tongue, Laurien shrugged. "He called it out in his fever. It matters not. I only wondered—"

" 'Tis not for me to tell." Malcolm's voice seemed oddly harsh. "And I wouldna suggest you bring that name up with Connor."

Discovering that the word was a *name* only made Laurien's curiosity burn brighter, but Malcolm's tone told her he considered the matter closed. She shrugged again and finished her apple as Malcolm rose to leave.

"I shall have your other garments brought to you in the morn." His voice had easily shifted back to its gentler level. "We must leave on the morrow."

"But he should not be riding so soon—" Laurien stopped, realizing her tongue had again outpaced her.

Malcolm smiled and eyed her with a probing gaze. "So you are concerned for him."

"Nay," Laurien snapped, tossing her head. "I merely do not wish to see all of my hard work go for naught."

"I see," he said again with that irritating note of understanding. "Dinna worry over that. We must leave at first light. We have a ship to catch, and we may already be late."

Laurien nodded. When he did not leave, she raised her eyebrows and gave him a questioning look.

Malcolm hesitated, then smiled. "Mayhap you would allow me to show you something. Place your fingers, so." He put two fingers of his left hand in his mouth.

Laurien frowned. "Why should I want to do that? I—"

"Be agreeable for once, milady." He demonstrated again. With an indulgent sigh she imitated him. "Now purse your lips. Aye. Now blow—softly."

She did as he said and was amazed at the high-pitched whistle that filled the chamber. "That sound!" She was suddenly interested. "That odd sound that you and Glenshiel made in the forest. What is it?"

"A falconer's whistle," he explained. "If you blew any harder you would hear it through the castle."

She looked at her fingers. "But what has whistling to do with falcons?"

"You have gone hawking, have you not? How do you induce the bird to return with its kill?"

"With a lure, of course."

"Aye, but if he flies too high or too far in search of the prey? He loses sight of his home. He canna see the lure, and becomes lost."

"But the whistle carries on the wind." Laurien nodded, impressed.

"Aye. So, milady, if you have need of aught else, and your guard proves irksome, call for me." He started for the door.

"But . . ." Laurien looked after him in surprise. "But why would you do this for me?" She looked down at the bandages on her wrists. "Any of this."

Malcolm turned in the doorway, and Laurien thought his gaze seemed sad. "Have you been so ill used all your life, milady, that you wonder at a simple kindness?" Then he smiled at her, a smile that reflected no hint of teasing or sarcasm, but an honest warmth. "You deserve better."

Alone after he left, Laurien pulled the blankets about her. It indeed caused her no small amount of wonderment that a man could be gentle and kind when he had no need to be. She set about finishing the food he had

brought for her, thinking that she must remember to
thank him on the morrow.

The next morning Laurien dressed in her man's disguise, eager to be free of her cell, her mind working on
escape plans even as she donned her cloak and gloves.
Mayhap, she thought, if she had a decent mount she
could break away and lose her pursuers in the forest.

She was still considering the idea as the guard es-
corted her to the great hall. The hour was early, and the
hall empty but for a few servants and Connor, who
waited at the door.

He seemed pale, she noticed, and he moved slowly
as he walked toward them, but otherwise he looked
healthy enough. She raised her chin and bestowed an
insolent smile upon him, determined to show that her
brief imprisonment had achieved nothing. But when he
took her elbow and those indigo eyes looked down at
her, Laurien felt a flutter in her stomach. She quickly
subdued it and tried, unsuccessfully, to jerk her elbow
away.

"You rested well, I trust?" Connor led her out the
door. Malcolm had railed at him for mistreating the girl,
but she looked no worse for the experience. In fact, she
looked as defiant—and as tempting—as ever. He did not
care for the determined set to her chin. And he liked the
mischievous gleam in her eyes even less.

"Listen to me, Scotsman." Laurien finally managed
to wrest her elbow from his grip and turned to face him
at the top of the spiral stair. "You are mistaken if you
think locking me away for a night will frighten me into
obedience."

Connor shook his head and looked toward the heavens. "Too much to hope for? I thought as much." His
fingers closed about her arm again. "You have my per-
mission to *feel* disobedient all you like. But you will do

as I say. I willna have any more trouble from you." He pulled her along behind him down the stair, doing his best to ignore the burning ache in his injured shoulder.

"Stop wrenching me about." Laurien tried to break his grip on her arm but was forced instead to concentrate on keeping up with him as he hurried down the steps. "I will not be handled thus by the likes of you!"

"I am afraid I shall be 'handling' you all day." He smirked, ignoring her struggles. "You willna have your own horse this ride."

"Why not?"

"Because I said you willna."

"I shall ride with Sir Malcolm, then."

"Nay." Connor felt a little stab of annoyance that she would choose to ride with Malcolm over himself. They had reached the ground floor, and he tugged Laurien toward the open portal that led outside.

Having endured all she could of masculine tyranny, Laurien dug in her heels. "Why not?"

Jerked to a stop, Connor winced and spun about, his humor fading quickly. "Because I said you mayna! Some of the best men on two continents have followed my orders without question, and now I must explain my every command to a woman?" He took her by the shoulders, barely restraining himself from trying to shake some obedience into her. "I'll not have it."

In truth, Connor could not explain his vehemence even to himself. He did not feel half so strong as he was trying to appear. If Laurien had her own mount and tried to escape, he wasn't at all sure he would be able to stop her. And for reasons he did not want to examine too closely, reasons that had naught to do with the alliance, this mission, or his duty, he could not stand the thought of letting Lady Laurien d'Amboise go free.

Laurien glared at him a long moment, not liking the warmth that shimmered through her body as his strong fingers curved about her shoulders. The flutter, doubled in strength, had returned to her stomach. "Why not just tie me again?"

"Do not tempt me, woman," he growled.

She wanted to kick his shin but settled for stamping her foot. It was a hopelessly feminine gesture and only made her feel silly. "You have no reason to treat me like this, you dull-witted, ungrateful, muddleheaded turnip! I saved your life."

Connor laughed. "Oh, aye, you would have me believe that you gave up a chance to escape in order to save me. Then I would shower you with gratitude, and have pity on you and let you go free. Is that what you hoped for?" He pulled her against him, his hands slipping beneath her cloak. "Woman, there are other ways to work your wiles on me, and I assure you they would be much more effective. Why not tempt me with a sample?"

"Burn you!" She twisted in his arms, and this time when she stamped her foot, her heel landed squarely on his boot top. With a cry of surprise, he released her.

Laurien sprang back, and before she knew it, the name that had been tickling her curiosity leaped to her lips. "If that is what you want, you will have to get it from your Sibylla—"

Connor stiffened instantly, his face transforming into a mask of fury. His eyes became cold, unseeing. Laurien froze, surprised and frightened at the sudden change, at the ready violence that was suddenly unleashed and aimed at her. He closed the distance between them, one hand coming up as he moved.

Her every muscle twitched to turn and run, but she stood still. "Go ahead," she whispered. "You would not be the first. Smite me. Prove yourself a man."

Connor stopped immediately. "Damn you." Anger and guilt warring within him, he lowered his arm and pushed her back against the wall, his weight trapping her against the stone.

He flinched as he did so, and Laurien realized his injured shoulder must pain him terribly despite his outward show of strength.

"Damn you, woman, a man has limits," he growled, leaning against her. "You *know* that, yet you strike out again and again. 'Tis as if you wish to force me to strike back."

"Let go of me. Stop this." Pinned between the cold wall and the hard muscles of his chest, Laurien could scarcely breathe. Her heart thrummed like that of a captured bird. She turned her head away from his harsh gaze, but he gripped her chin and brought her eyes back to meet this.

"I told you once I wouldna hurt you." His lips were very near hers, his voice a bare murmur, his eyes darkening. "But that isna what you want, is it? You would like for me to hurt you just as other men have hurt you. Then 'twould be easy to believe us all worthless, cruel, hateful bastards—"

"Let me alone!" Laurien was trembling now, and knew he could feel it.

"That is exactly what you *think* you want, is it not? To be alone. You have believed it so long you can no longer see aught else. Nay, I willna give you what you want; I willna be what you think me to be."

He pulled her away from the wall, crushing her against him, and Laurien gasped, "I hate you—"

With a groan, Connor lowered his head to hers. "Hate me, then."

His lips captured hers, seeking, demanding, and Laurien's knees gave way; clasped firmly in his embrace, she did not fall. Heat flamed through her and a myriad of emotions weltered in her mind—anger, resentment, pride, fear that he spoke the truth, and fear that her truth could be a terrible weapon in his hands. Just as swiftly, a much stronger feeling overpowered the rest. She felt an irresistible longing, a secret joy at the way he hungered for her. Casting aside the warnings that sounded in her mind, she closed her eyes and surrendered to Connor's kiss.

Her lips opened beneath his. With a moan, he trailed one hand down her back, pressing her hips to his as his tongue darted out to explore her mouth. Laurien trembled as she felt his body go taut, straining against her. Fire bolted through her at his ungentle possession, and her arms raised to circle his neck, pulling him closer. His lips never leaving hers, Connor lowered her gently to her feet. His fingers pushed back her hood and tangled in her hair. Laurien arched into him, consumed by the fire that raced through her.

A call from the courtyard shattered the spell woven between them like a stone smashing a window. Connor's head snapped up, his passion-dazed mind clearing quickly as Malcolm's voice floated in from a discreet distance beyond the open portal.

"If we tarry here all day, we shall have to swim the Channel, and I, for one, am not a good swimmer."

"I . . . had some trouble managing the stairs." Connor coughed. He added a wheeze. "But the lass was most generous with her assistance. We will be along in a moment."

Darting beneath his arm, Laurien stumbled away from him, trying to steady her breath.

" 'Twould seem, milady''—Connor turned toward her, his eyes full of regret and his voice full of promise—"that we must finish this another time."

Laurien hoped he could not see that her knees were still shaking. Free of his touch, she felt pride and anger replacing the less familiar emotions she had briefly surrendered to.

But she also felt fear. For each time he kissed her, each time she let her defenses weaken, it was becoming a little bit harder to hate him.

She wiped her mouth with the back of one hand. "Do not ever," she hissed, "*ever* try that again."

Connor's only response was a soft, mocking chuckle as he followed her out.

The man stalking the streets of Calais caught the notice of many. He looked neither left nor right, but strode straight ahead, parting the crowd like a spear cast into the sea. At first glance, he seemed a mercenary, or a sailor just arrived from some distant land. But he wore garments of fur, chains of silver and gold wrapped about his black boots, and a ruby ring upon his right hand. His nose was horribly disfigured, but most disturbing of all were his eyes; the few that felt the touch of his gray gaze quickly looked away and hurried about their business. More than a few crossed themselves as he passed.

Balafre at last turned down a side street and left the pier, satisfied that his quarry had not yet arrived. He and Paxton were taking a chance in concentrating all their efforts in Calais, but the puzzle pieces supplied by de Villiers had brought them straight to the little northern port. Relying on Balafre's instincts and Paxton's logic, they decided to gamble that their quarry would flee, running headlong for home. They were looking for one man and the girl, possibly two men and the girl. All probably disguised, the men more than likely Scottish.

Aye, focusing on Calais was a risk, but if this ambush failed, they would try something else. Balafre was a patient man. In the end, he would have them.

He ducked into the little hovel that had served as his quarters for the past two days. "Paxton."

At his summons, the Englishman strolled in from an antechamber, frowning, bare to the waist. "Am I to have no rest? All is in readiness. What more is there to be done?"

"Have we a man on every gate?"

"Aye, and the pier. And all roads leading to the city."

Paxton glanced back into the chamber he had just left. "Stay where you are," he said sharply over his shoulder. Then he turned back to his partner. "The four who guarded the wench during the wedding procession have been placed at the south gate. Those who chased the blond rider into the forest are at the main gate and along the pier—"

"Why have you not changed?"

"It was my task to *think* of a plan," Paxton replied with a slight sneer, "not to don the garments of a beggar and *participate*. We have more than enough men. I thought I would remain here—"

"You know better than to anger me, Paxton." Balafre pinned him with an unyielding gaze. "Change. I want every man ready."

Paxton was about to object when a movement behind him caught his eye. Uttering at oath, he darted back into the antechamber. A moment later he reappeared, holding a young girl by her hair.

She was naked and so wide-eyed with terror that she did not even struggle in Paxton's grasp. Balafre guessed her to be not a day older than ten.

"Sneaky little wench was reaching for my knife." The Englishman shook her and looked up at Balafre with a smile. "I found her in the market square this morn. She asked me for assistance, said she could not find her *maman.*" He jerked the girl's head back to give Balafre a better view. "Not a bad-looking little piece, once I washed off the dirt."

"You will find another one later. Garb yourself, and join the men at the pier."

With a sigh of disdain, Paxton nodded, shoving the

girl back into the other chamber. "I will need a moment to finish her, lest she wander back to *maman* and begin telling tales."

Balafre's only reply was a grunt. In an absentminded gesture, he began fingering the necklace he always wore about his throat. Paxton felt a surge of disgust. He had heard many strange stories whispered about Balafre over the years, including one to explain that necklace. But he had always thought the dozens of white nuggets must be the teeth of squirrels, or some other small animals. He could not believe each was a trophy—

Without another word, or any sign of farewell, Balafre turned and left just as quietly as he had entered.

Shaking his head at the man's lack of manners, Paxton returned to the antechamber and his interrupted entertainment.

Balafre strode back along the pier to take up his position near the town's main gate. As the crowd soundlessly parted before him, he turned the ruby ring upon his finger. If this task went well, by the morrow the girl would be on her way to de Villiers and her abductors would be dead.

As always, he meant to ensure that all went well. That efficiency was what accounted for his popularity, he mused as he walked. The nobles always came to him when their problems got out of hand—an enemy to be silenced, an errant wife to be disposed of, an agreement to be secured with the assistance of a little discreet torture. They came to him, he knew, for one simple reason.

He did not fail.

Reaching the main gate, he nodded to the two guards positioned there, one disguised as a beggar, the other as a merchant selling religious relics. Balafre sat under a shade tree. Patience. That was the key, he thought with a smile. He watched the steady stream of people entering the city. As he liked to do in his free moments, he took out his knife and the small whetstone he carried. His eyes never leaving the gate, he began to sharpen the blade with fast, even strokes.

The hunt had begun.

Chapter 11

Laurien paced the small clearing where she and Sir
Malcolm waited. As soon as they had ridden within
sight of Calais, Connor had insisted on going in alone
to check on the ship that would take them to Scotland.
Leaving his horse behind, he'd carried only the sword
hidden beneath his cloak.

He hadn't given her a single chance to escape all day,
holding her snugly in his lap during their ride. He'd
teased her about the way she held her back so straight
and stiff. In truth, she had not done it from anger, but
from a desire to avoid hurting his injured shoulder.

Sir Malcolm sat beside his horse, half asleep, just
alert enough to stop her should she try to slip away. She
knew because she had already tried.

Laurien plopped down beside an oak at the edge of
the glade. Her hand went to the *aumoniere* at her waist,
and she felt her eyes well anew with tears. She had
briefly toyed with the idea of somehow threatening Sir
Malcolm with her knife, only to realize that the little
blade was missing. In her fight with Beauvais's man, she
remembered, it had flown from her hand and into the
rushes in the guardroom. By now, one of Varennes's
mercenaries had claimed it for his own.

She fought the bitterness that washed over her. After
all she had suffered in the past days, it was silly to cry
over something so small as losing her knife. But it had

been a final gift from her mother, and a link with her real father. She had carried it with her from childhood. Must she leave everything behind? Every step they took was carrying her farther away from Tours, from finding her father at last.

Angrily, she wiped her eyes and cast a look of longing at the horses. Her chances for escape were dwindling rapidly. Once on the ship, once in Scotland, how would she ever make her way back to France? She could almost feel her fate closing in around her, like a noose tightening about her neck. Great white birds with gray-and-black tipped wings wheeled overhead, screeching down at her as if mocking her thoughts. She scowled up at them, then turned her angry gaze down the path the Scotsman had taken.

He'd left at midday. Now the sun glanced low through the trees, spreading shadows in long, dark fingers across the grass. She felt stirrings of concern at his long absence, and tried to shake them off. What matter to her if something befell her captor? What matter if he never returned? It would be so much the better for her, would it not?

But despite all her efforts, she could not stop worrying about the Scotsman. She resumed her pacing.

She was about to ask Sir Malcolm if they shouldn't search for Glenshiel when a movement at the edge of the trees caught her eye. Malcolm was on his feet in an instant, sword drawn.

He smiled and sheathed the blade as Connor strode into the clearing. "I was beginning to think you had tired of us and sailed alone for home."

Connor's features were grim and he ignored his friend's jest. "Our ship has gone. It sailed yesterday."

Malcolm frowned. "I feared so. We wait for another, then."

"Nay, we had best not linger." Moving to his horse,

Connor started untying the pack behind his saddle. "De Villiers's men are about. They are watching the city."

"Fie! how many?"

"I couldna tell. I was about to enter the main gate when I saw one of the guards who chased me out of Chartres. The man was dressed as a beggar. That clever bastard has them disguised." He slipped his remaining weapons into his belt. "I went in through the north gate instead. I didna recognize anyone, but he would be a fool not to have men at every entrance."

"Which, unfortunately, he isna." Malcolm quickly gathered a small bundle of food. "Have you a plan?"

Looking at Laurien, Connor nodded to the discarded pack on his horse. "Take whatever you need and let us be on our way," he said brusquely.

"There is naught that *you* have that I need," Laurien answered in an equally surly tone.

Connor eyed her suspiciously, then motioned for her to walk ahead of him down the winding dirt path. He turned his attention back to Malcolm as the three of them set off toward the city. "We shall enter through the south gate. It seemed the least crowded."

"You have found us another ship, then?"

"Aye, a merchant cog. A bit ragged, but seaworthy enough. None were aboard but the mate, and he was agreeable to taking passengers once I gave him a handful of our silver."

"Fortunate to find another ship headed for Scotland."

"Nay, she is bound for Hull."

"Hull?" Malcolm stopped in his tracks, staring at Connor as if the younger man had lost his senses. "Hull is in *England*. If you will recall, we are not on the best terms with our neighbors at the moment."

" 'Twas the only vessel sailing near Scotland for a sennight at least. All others are bound for London or Southampton."

"And 'tis sure the authorities in Hull will give us a warm welcome—before they toss us in the darkest dungeon they can find."

"Nay, 'twould seem the captain shares our distaste for the English. The mate said they have had trouble bringing their goods through the southern ports, so they are most careful." He started down the path again. "We shall land in Hull and ride up the coast for home. None will know we were ever in England."

"What kind of trouble?" Malcolm persisted. "What might these goods be?"

"I didna ask. But of the casks and crates I saw, the markings had been rubbed off. I'd say they are carrying choice trinkets lifted from traders all over France."

"A ship of thieves, then, sneaking their booty out of the country?"

Laurien's imagination was already picturing all manner of dangers. "Sir Malcolm is right. I have no desire to get killed in this venture—"

Connor rounded on the pair of them. "If the two of you prefer, we can stay here a sennight—or more—and hope to find a ship bound for Scotland. And then we can hope them agreeable to taking passengers. 'Tis certain de Villiers's men would be most happy to provide us accommodations while we make our inquiries."

Not waiting for further comment, he walked onward, leaving the chastened Malcolm and Laurien to follow. The three of them reached the edge of the forest a few minutes later. From the hill where they stood, they could see the city's southern gate below. As an important port, Calais had elaborate defenses. The curtain wall was several feet thick, the gate actually a tunnel, with an iron portcullis at either end. A steady stream of travelers pushed through, dispersing on the far side into the markets and streets. Many headed for the far edge of the city, where a line of masts marked the wharf.

A handful of men lingered about the curtain wall—sailors looking for crew, tradesmen selling food and trinkets, beggars, and merchants. It would be impossible to tell which were de Villiers's guards.

"Well, then." Malcolm sighed. "How do we get through?"

Connor gave him a satisfied smile. "They seem most interested in those traveling in pairs or threes. We shall go through one by one—"

"A ruse would make more sense," Laurien interrupted. "We might start a fire, or some form of trouble, and while they attend to that, we could sneak through."

"Or we might stand on the wall and wave a flag to tell them we have arrived." Connor retorted. "They would be after us like a pack of wolves. Nay, we shall make a quiet entrance, then be gone before they ever know we were here."

He turned back to Malcolm and nodded toward the road. "Take care, my friend. I shall follow with the girl. Once you are inside, dinna tarry. We sail at high tide, so make straight for the wharf and find the ship. 'Tis a Venetian. You will know it by the triangular sails."

Malcolm shrugged and flashed a teasing grin. "Simple." Giving Connor a hearty slap on the back, he slipped down the hill. They lost sight of him as he moved into the throng.

Silent, Connor and Laurien waited several anxious moments until he reappeared. Finally they spotted him, emerging safely on the far side of the tunnel. Nudging Laurien ahead of him, Connor started down the hill.

As they neared the road, he stopped short and turned Laurien around to face him. "Give me any trouble, woman, and I will see that you regret it."

"Save your threats, Scotsman," Laurien hissed. "Much as I dislike my present company, I have no desire to find myself in the hands of de Villiers's mongrels.''

"Then for once, do as I bid you. Keep your head down. And for Sweet Mary's sake, be silent." He pulled her hood farther forward and bent her head. "Remember, I shall be right behind you. Dinna even think of running once you are through those gates."

With that last warning, he pushed her ahead of him into the crowd of peasants, nobles, traders, and sailors jostling into Calais.

Laurien shuffled toward the gate, carefully keeping her eyes on the road at her feet. Billowing clouds of dust made her cough and stung her eyes. The squeaking of cartwheels competed with the screeching of those awful birds overhead, and the patter of many foreign tongues. From all sides, she could hear the cries of vendors calling attention to their wares and swearing at the little thieves that swooped from the sky. The smells of salt and fish hung heavy in the air.

The people pushed closer and closer together as they neared the entrance, prodding and bumping one another in their impatience at the slow pace. Every little nudge made Laurien flinch in fear that one of de Villiers's guards was grabbing at her. She steadfastly kept her head bowed.

It seemed to take a lifetime to reach the entrance, but at last daylight turned to shadow and the throng pushed its way into the tunnel. A steady roar echoed strangely in the crowded passage. It sounded much like a waterfall, except that it ebbed and swelled. Laurien realized with a twinge of foreboding that it must be the sound of the sea. She was listening intently to the odd sound when she bumped into the woman ahead of her.

The line had come to a stop.

Within moments, those around her began grumbling at the delay and cursing in several languages, shouting

at those in the front to move forward. Laurien's throat
went dry. What was happening? She longed to look up,
but did not dare. She was only partway through the tunnel, closed in on all sides. If the guards recognized her
now, she would be utterly trapped.

Those behind kept trying to shove forward and Laurien found herself squeezed up against the fat peasant
woman in front of her. She chanced a look over the
woman's shoulder.

That single quick glance made her heart begin to hammer. Three men were questioning someone at the front
of the line.

And one of those men had been her escort in the
wedding procession in Chartres.

Frozen for an instant by a cold rush of fear, Laurien
hunched over and pulled her hood closer about her face.
She tried to push backward into the crowd, but could
not move against the crush of people. She started to
elbow her way through when the line began to move
forward again.

Helpless, she was swept along—directly toward de
Villiers's guards.

She huddled deeper into her cloak, trying to appear
as small and unworthy of notice as possible. She stared
wide-eyed at the ground, too frightened to even breathe.
Please, please, please, she prayed, *look at someone else.
Do not look at me. Not me.*

It almost worked.

"Arretez!"

The barked command was accompanied by a pair of
dusty black boots that stepped into view, neatly blocking
her path. The river of people parted around them and
continued forward. Her mind riffled through a string of
commands. Cry for help. Run. Fight.

But she had no weapon.

"Regardez-moi."

Laurien shook her head as if unable to comprehend the man's order. If she looked up, she was lost. Where was Connor? Her blood rushed in her ears. If she tried to flee, the guard would be on her in an instant. And in another moment he would lose patience and seize her anyway. He would cry out to his fellows that Lady Laurien d'Amboise had been found. The guards would descend on her. They would carry her back to the comte.

It was over. She was trapped. Unable to stop herself, she slowly began to raise her head.

What happened next occurred in the span of a heartbeat, but to Laurien it felt like an hour. She looked up in dismay at the guard from the wedding procession. Eyes widening in recognition, he reached for her and opened his mouth to call out to his companions. She recoiled in fear, only to see his expression of triumph turn to one of horror. Connor's sword flashed into view and felled the man with a single stroke.

Laurien heard a scream and realized the voice was her own. The cry woke her from her stupor as chaos broke out around them. The other two guards spun toward them, and another pair appeared from out of the crowd, drawing swords from beneath the shabby garments of their disguises. The throng of people dissolved into panic, tripping over one another in their efforts to squeeze through the narrow passage, and flee the violence that had erupted in their midst. Buffeted one way and another by the frenzied surge, Laurien was carried almost out of the tunnel. She fell and would have been trampled, but suddenly Connor was there once more, pulling her into the light inside the city walls. The guardsmen were almost upon them.

"Run!" Connor pressed a knife into her hand and pushed her in the direction of the wharf. "Defend yourself. Run for the ship!"

Laurien stumbled away as he turned to face de Vil-

liers's guards. The four swordsmen split up to come at
him from two sides. With neither shield nor armor, she
knew he could not hope to defend himself from all of
them at once. Without even thinking, she started back
toward the men. Their full attention directed at Connor,
they did not heed when she raised her hand and sent the
blade flying. Her target staggered and toppled like a tree,
the knife buried in his gullet.

In the moment of confusion, Connor lunged toward
one of the others. The man recovered his senses an instant too late and met his end on the second thrust from
Connor's sword. Connor instantly threw himself at the
other two, slashing out and badly wounding one, then
turning upon the other like a madman. Laurien was
stunned at the speed and ferocity of his attack. The battle had barely begun when it was over; the guard fell,
and she and Connor were standing in the middle of the
gateway, panic all around them, staring at one another
in mutual surprise.

They stood there only an instant, both breathing hard,
and Laurien saw a feeling far more intense, far more
intriguing than surprise, come into Connor's gaze. He
started to speak when a cry from further along the wall
interrupted. A group of surly-looking men were hurrying toward them, all brandishing arms.

"Farewell to our quiet entrance." Connor grabbed
her hand and ran for the tangle of hovels that made up
the city of Calais.

Dodging in and out of the crowd, they ran until Laurien felt certain her lungs would burst. They passed lines
of mud-and-wattle buildings, skirted the market square,
and finally approached the wharf. They hurried toward
the pier, slowing to a fast walk as they tried to blend
into the varied mixture of travelers and sailors.

At last, ducking into a small passageway, they

stopped. "Have we lost them?" Laurien's breath rasped in her throat. She bent over, trying to stop puffing.

"For the moment." Connor sheathed his sword, rubbing his left shoulder. "We must get to that ship, lest we find ourselves permanent guests here."

"H-how much farther?"

"There."

She looked up and saw that they had come all the way to the water's edge. The sea stretched away before her eyes, a mass of dark blue with no end, only a darker line where the water met the sky. The sight made her dizzy. Sweet Mary, but it was enormous! She could see no land at all, no other side. Scanning the dozens of ships that crowded the piers, she spotted the one with triangular sails.

"That one?" she puffed. "We are going to sea in *that?*" Smaller than the others, the boat Connor had pointed to seemed more like a pinecone bobbing in a pond than a vessel fit for traveling upon that great expanse of water.

He took her hand again, tugging her toward the street. "Aye, and we had best be about it, else 'twill sail without us—"

Suddenly he stopped and stepped in front of her, nudging her back into the shadows. Following his grim gaze, Laurien saw that an odd-looking group of men were running along the pier. The weapons in their hands and the determined looks upon their faces marked them as more of de Villiers's guards, despite their disguises. Moving to the first ship at the end of the wharf, they forced their way aboard and began to search it, ignoring the outraged complaints of the crew.

Connor swore softly. There were about ten ships between that one and theirs, but they could not get to the Venetian without being noticed.

He could think of only one plan. He would have Laurien sneak toward their ship while he distracted their pursuers. He was about to tell her to go when another man appeared on the wharf and began yelling at the guards. Though weaponless, he was apparently their leader, for the guards stopped ransacking the ship long enough to heed him. He was dressed as a beggar, but he was tall and thin, almost elegant-looking, with gray-brown hair and an imperious attitude. Grumbling, the motley-looking group of de Villiers's men left the ship, gathered on the dock, and were soon engaged in a loud disagreement with him.

Connor grabbed Laurien's hand. "We willna have a better chance." Before Laurien could reply, he walked into the large clear area that separated them from the ships.

Moving quickly, they threaded their way through the sailors working in and around the time-worn vessels. Laurien thought her heart must surely give out, it was pounding so hard. De Villiers's men were only yards away. She could no longer feel anything except the cold knot of fear in her belly, and the strong warmth of Connor's large hand clasped about hers, tugging her onward.

Then they were on the pier, and she saw Sir Malcolm waiting before the Venetian, his way blocked by a burly man garbed in faded green homespun. As they approached, the man turned his attention to Connor. He gestured toward the ship, his pointed cap bobbing over his forehead as he spoke.

"Cannot take three. Ze cabin ees not big enough."

"I *told* you there were three," Connor said tightly. He glanced over at the guards on the wharf. For some reason, the leader had split the group up, sending most back into town. But the remaining four had resumed searching, ship by ship.

They had no time to barter. "We have paid more than enough," Connor snapped.

"M'hap your *français* ees not so good. I thought you said two." The man shrugged and turned to board the ship. "No room for three."

Connor felt his ire rise as a sense of helplessness hit him. This sea whelp would happily keep their silver and leave them stranded on the wharf. He had not come this far only to see their plans end on a pier in Calais. Reaching into his tunic, he withdrew the small pouch that held the funds he had brought from Scotland. Tearing open the strings, he withdrew the rest of the coins and caught the man's arm. "Will this clear any more space?"

The mate smiled at the flash of silver in the late afternoon sun. His grizzled jaw worked back and forth.

" 'Tis all we have." Connor added urgently. "You shall have more *when* you deliver us safely to our destination. We have friends awaiting us."

The sailor quickly pocketed the circles of metal. "For ze passengers, I have room only for two." The man eyed Malcolm with a critical air. "But m'hap I 'splain you as a new crew member, *mon ami*. You look enough like an old salt of ze sea." Apparently pleased with his plan, he urged them toward the thin wooden plank that served as a bridge between ship and dock. *"Vite, vite,* eh? Hurry. Ze rest of ze crew coming along soon."

Malcolm walked across, and the mate pushed Laurien forward. Halfway across the moving plank, she made the mistake of glancing down. She stopped short, transfixed by the waves that lapped about the wooden hull a goodly drop below. Her next step wobbled.

The mate placed a hand at her back. "Move along, *garçon*. Zere ees no time."

His shove sent Laurien tumbling headlong onto the deck. Her knee smacked into a crate, drawing a most unboylike yelp of pain from her lips. Their host stepped nimbly aboard and pulled her to her feet.

"Alors, what ees thees?"

Connor was too late to stay the man's hand. The sailor grasped her hood and pulled it back, releasing a cascade of hair. "A woman!" He turned toward Connor. "You said not'ing of a woman. Zey are bad luck on a ship. *Mon capitaine*, he will skin me if he finds her. Bad luck. You and ze other can go, but not thees one."

Laurien protested as he poked at her, hurrying her back toward the plank. "*Allez*. Off. Off."

Connor could see—and hear—that de Villiers's men were engaged in a heated discussion with the crew of a cog six berths over. He pushed Laurien behind him and grabbed for the *aumoniere* hidden beneath her cloak.

"Mayhap," he said, pouring her coins into the thief's quickly extended palm, "this might balance your bad luck. And do not forget, you will receive a great deal more when we arrive safely."

The mate examined the pile of coins with a cocked eyebrow and a twist to his lips. He looked from his hand to the empty *aumoniere*. "A'right, zen. You and ze wench come with me."

Connor gave Malcolm a quick, keen look, silently asking him to keep an eye on their decidedly untrustworthy host. Malcolm responded with an almost imperceptible nod. Indicating that Malcolm was to remain on deck, the mate led Connor and Laurien to the mast, bending over to pull aside a small hatch.

The opening revealed a ladder that led into the hold. Connor quickly followed him down, hunching over as they moved toward the bow. He turned in exasperation when he noticed Laurien had lingered behind.

She stood at the bottom of the ladder, looking forlornly upward at the small square of daylight. Bathed in the golden hues of the setting sun, she stole his breath, and he forgot for a moment the dangers that lay behind them and those that surely lay ahead. In that instant, she looked as she had that first morning at the Front de

Boeuf, soft yet strong, like a wild thing plucked untamed from the woods. The look of sadness and longing on her face melted his anger and filled him with regret. He knew too well what it felt like to leave one's homeland behind. Suddenly, he wanted to enfold her in his arms, to soothe her hurt, to protect her . . .

Instead he moved back to the ladder, caught her arm, and called her name gruffly. "Laurien, we must hurry."

She turned to look at him, the sadness in her eyes instantly replaced by a glare that chilled him. She withdrew her arm from his touch as if she thought him diseased. "Then move along, Scotsman."

Laurien followed him forward into the darkness, struggling against her fear. The mate had lit a small flame in a bowl filled with the sticky, oily substance called pitch. She felt her way forward, the tiny flicker of light not enough to help her identify the dark shapes that filled the hold. From the smells, Laurien guessed the cargo included fruits and spices, and a goodly amount of costly woods from Navarre and Aragon.

The mate led them toward the pointed front end of the ship. A few steps brought them to the far wall. Handing the little torch to Connor, he grinned at them like a small child about to reveal a prized secret. He felt along the wall, then pulled at the bottom of one of the boards. It loosened, and he yanked it free to reveal his secret. The solid wood of the bow had been hollowed out to create a tiny chamber.

"What *mon capitaine* cannot see, he cannot take a portion of," the mate explained in low tones. He hunched over and moved inside. "You stay here, and no one will know you are on board. After we get to ze port and unload ze other cargo, I come get you out, eh?"

Laurien peered inside. The "cabin" was triangular in shape, no larger than a stall in a stable, filled with thick furs of every description and diaphanous silks shot with metallic thread. The mate shoved his private cargo into the corners to clear a place for them.

She eyed the chamber with dismay. "But how are we to breathe?"

The mate grunted, pointing to the wall he had just passed through. On closer examination, Laurien could see what appeared to be decorative carving, cut deeply into the wood, jagged like the crenellated top of a castle wall. From the inside, one could tell that the design had been cut right through. Obviously, it was not the first time the man had smuggled human cargo under his captain's nose.

"Ze air, she come in through zere," the mate added as explanation. He took the fire bowl from Connor and fitted it into a small sconce attached to the point of the bow.

Laurien had no time for further questions. At the sound of many footsteps above, the man backed out and urged them inside. "Ze crew ees coming." He picked up the board, and his face appeared at the opening one last time. "Until I come back, you keep *silence*, eh? *Mon capitaine* find out about zis, he throw us all three over ze side."

With that cheerful thought, he slipped the secret panel into place and shut them into their makeshift cabin. They could hear him rearranging the cargo in front of the door.

The space was so cramped that Laurien had to hunch over, and Connor was bent almost double beside her. She prayed that the footsteps were indeed the crew coming aboard, and not de Villiers's men. Her heart thrumming, she slipped off her cloak and sat, hugging her knees, her back to one of the plush piles of furs. She pressed herself as far away from Connor as she could manage, but only gained a scant foot of space between them. She tugged at the neck of her tunic. Already, the air seemed too close, heady with the scent of wood and spices and the sea.

She watched Connor as he set his sword aside, slipped off his cloak, and slouched down across from her, stretching his legs as much as was possible.

"I am so pleased you are able to relax," Laurien hissed, trying her best to keep her voice low. "If those guards find us now, we are trapped!"

"Nay, since their leader divided the group, 'twill take them longer to search. And I dinna believe our host or his *capitaine* are going to allow anyone to force their way on board and search *this* ship." He cast a wry glance at the rich booty surrounding them, then nudged off his boots, closing his eyes on a sigh. He wriggled his toes in the furs. "We are safe enough . . . for now."

"For now?" Laurien squeaked.

"We should be sailing momentarily, and I dinna see how they could find us after that. By the time de Villiers's men figure out what has happened, we shall be riding up the coast to Scotland."

Laurien flinched as his leg brushed hers. Connor's eyes opened, glittering unnaturally blue in the firelight. "I give you my word I willna bite you."

Laurien looked away, his soft teasing making her more uncomfortable than his anger ever did. "And how do we know our *host* will not simply slit our throats and throw us into the sea?"

Connor shook his head. "His kind is more interested in coin than killing. I have promised him more when we arrive. That should be enough to secure our passage. For now he has all my silver."

"Not to mention *mine*," Laurien added tartly.

"A small price to leave this place and de Villiers and his mongrels, as you put it, behind. Does your knee hurt?"

Laurien slapped his hand away as he reached out to touch her. "Your prize is undamaged."

He examined his tingling fingers with a frown. "Listen to me, milady. We are likely to be here well into morn, so what say we call a peace, if just for now. I am willing to forgive you—"

"I have done naught to be forgiven for."

"And what of your attempt to escape at Gaston's?"

"I have already made up for that. The fault is not mine if you cannot remember that I saved your life."

Feeling a little stab of guilt, Connor slid closer. "Can you not bring yourself to be good-tempered, if only for a short while? You might even become used to it."

Laurien only felt more incensed. Finding herself boxed in by piles of furs on two sides, the bow on the third, and Connor's large frame on the other further fueled her ire. "And who are you to talk to me of temper? I have been abducted, dragged across the countryside, tied up, locked up, pushed about, and now I find myself in the hold of a ship that will more than likely sink long before we reach land. Is all of this supposed to put me in a good humor?"

He regarded her with his infuriating crooked grin. "I saved you from your impending marriage. Is that not worth something?"

"I was not in need of saving at the time, you muddleheaded turnip. I was about to make good my own escape. But for your interference, I would be free now, not cramped into some thieves' ship, being taken to a land and people I know naught of."

"You would never have made it out of Chartres on your own. You would be Lady de Villiers now were it not for my interference."

"As if my fate matters to you. You have never given a single thought to what will happen to me when I am returned to him. Do not pretend that you have. Nay, so long as Sir Connor of Glenshiel wins the day, woe be to any who block his path.''

"What I have *done,*" Connor defended himself, stung by her words, "I have done for my country. For my people. Can you not understand that?''

Before Laurien had a chance to reply, the boards above their heads reverberated with the stomping of a booted foot.

Connor turned so he was sitting next to her, their shoulders touching. He whispered in her ear. " 'Twould seem our host wishes to remind us of the need for quiet.''

Laurien held her tongue. The two sat in stubborn silence.

She listened to the increasingly louder sounds above, and again hoped it was the crew moving about—not de Villiers's men forcing their way aboard. She relaxed only slightly when she heard someone start whistling a jaunty sailor's tune to accompany the thump of ropes being moved about the deck.

She tried to ignore the warmth of Connor's body so close to hers. The little cabin was beginning to feel terribly warm, and she knew she was breathing too fast. The Scotsman, however, seemed quite comfortable. Though she refused to look at him, she could hear his breathing, steady and deep, could feel his shoulder rise and fall against her own. She wished fervently that he would move away, but he showed no inclination to do so. She would not ask him. She would not let him know that his closeness affected her. She would not—

"I suppose I should thank you for helping me at the gate today,'' Connor whispered in her ear.

Laurien flinched but forced herself to turn her face toward him. They were nearly nose to nose. His eyes had lost their teasing glint, and his lips were no longer twisted in a mocking grin. His expression as he looked at her was almost . . . tender. "I would not ask it of you." She filled her voice with a harshness she did not feel. "I know it would be a terrible strain."

Connor ignored her sarcasm. "Why did you do it? You could have run."

"I . . ." Laurien shook her head, unable to tear her gaze from his. Why had she not taken the opportunity to escape? At the time, the thought hadn't even entered her head. She had seen Connor in danger and reacted without pausing. Even now, she didn't want to consider her reasoning. It brought an odd little flutter of fear to her stomach to think of what might have happened to him. "I do not know—"

The sudden movement of the ship interrupted her reply, throwing her against him. Startled, she tried to brace herself as she felt the bow lurch forward and down. But there was no part of the tiny chamber that wasn't moving.

Connor wrapped an arm around her and held her to his chest. " 'Tis all right. We have moved away from the pier. Dinna be afraid."

"I am *not* afraid." Laurien lied, remembering how small the ship had looked in comparison to the size of the sea.

Connor smiled down at her. She was so busy trying to brace herself against the movement of the ship, she hadn't even pulled away from him. Despite her brave words, she was breathing hard, like a captured rabbit. "Have you never been to sea before?"

Laurien shook her head. She could hear the waves lapping hungrily along the sides. How deep was the sea? Likely more than deep enough to swallow this entire ship and all aboard in one gulp. The bow began to pitch up and down with disturbing regularity, making her stomach feel quite queasy.

Even in the dim light, Connor could see Laurien turn pale. "You are not going to have seasickness, are you?"

Laurien looked up at him, suddenly aware that he held her and just as suddenly not minding. "What is seasickness?"

Looking at her wide eyes, Connor again felt stirrings of protectiveness. He had been quite ill his first time at sea, with no one to help him through it. "Mayhap 'tis best if you dinna know."

Releasing her, he reached up and lifted two of the pelts from the pile at their back. He nudged her out of the way and unrolled them in the small space. "Lie down with your head toward the bow. You willna feel the movement so much."

Not of a mind to argue at the moment, Laurien did as he bade. She found to her surprise that she had more than enough space to stretch out full-length in this direction, and the furs felt soft and welcoming. The top pelt was wolf, the black-tipped silver fur silky in her fingers. She lay on her side, closed her eyes, and tried to ignore the motion of the ship.

She heard, more than felt, when Connor lay down beside her.

"Do you feel at all better?"

His voice was less than a whisper, but it sounded oddly tense, striking a spark of similar tension in her. Her heart began to beat faster.

"A little." She kept her eyes closed, remembering what Sir Gaston had told her about her eyes revealing her emotions. As she had so many times before, she sensed a softening of her feelings toward Glenshiel. Yet she could not put a single name to the tangle of emotions he evoked in her.

"Roll on your back," he whispered.

At this, Laurien opened her eyes, but he motioned for her to close them again. Fighting a wave of nausea, she complied with his soft command and rolled over. The scant inches of distance between them disappeared, and she could feel the full length of him pressed against her side. A shiver coursed through her. She wondered if it was from this thing he called seasickness.

Connor touched her stomach.

"Nay," she cried, jerking upright, her eyes flying open.

He pulled his hand away. "Do you wish to feel ill the entire journey?"

Laurien shook her head. She was already feeling more than miserable.

"Then lie down and close your eyes, and allow me to help you."

Laurien chewed at her lower lip. Her stomach was now pitching with every roll of the ship. She weighed the merits of spending hours in such suffering against the thought of allowing Connor to touch her. She felt uneasy about it, but if he did indeed intend only to help her . . .

She lay down again, her eyes squeezed shut, her body stiff as a lance.

She flinched when he touched her, but did not pull away this time.

" 'Twill be all right," he soothed.

His hand began to move in a slow circle, up toward her ribs, then down over her stomach. She barely breathed, taking in only short, nervous little gasps of the sea-scented air. Even through the rough cloth of her tunic, she could feel his warmth. She trembled, remembering the strength she had seen him use on more than one occasion, aware that he was holding that strength in check.

Then, to her surprise, the queasy feeling gradually began to leave her. The gentle pressure of Connor's touch actually began to feel . . . good. Very, very slowly, almost against her will, and certainly against her reason, she found herself relaxing.

The ship seemed not to lurch so much, or mayhap she was growing used to it. The rolling motion began to seem peaceful, almost as pleasant as the feeling of Connor's strong fingers moving over her belly. Memories of the anger she had felt toward him only moments before flickered through her mind, but she could not find cause to renew their sparring. She had to admit, just to herself, that he had been right this time.

She much preferred this to arguing.

Connor felt inordinately pleased with himself when he saw a smile touch Laurien's lips. She felt so small and soft beside him, her wildness and temper soothed away. He could feel her muscles gradually relax beneath his hand. He watched, fascinated, as her breasts rose and fell softly. Her breathing slowed and deepened, and her lips parted. Lying in the flickering, golden glow of the single flame that lit their cabin, she looked like the princess of some troubador's tale, awaiting a kiss to awaken her.

Dare he? For so long he had secretly ached to see her respond to him like this. Her defiance had bewitched him from the moment they met, and this sweetness tempted him almost beyond his endurance. Dare he disturb this gentled creature? Barely completing the thought, he bent his head to hers.

Her body now languorous from his ministrations, Laurien lay still as his kiss caught her unawares. His hand had stopped moving, and his tongue teased at her lips, seeking entry. She uttered the barest little squeak of protest. Then, as had happened time and again at his touch, her body responded before she had time to think.

She allowed his kiss, then returned it, and his ardor deepened. Their tongues met, teased, explored. The prickly silk of his beard felt rough against her chin, tickling, then scratching as he grew more aggressive. Laurien felt a flame of desire deep within her. His mouth moved lower, and her tongue darted out to soothe her swollen, bruised lower lip, tasting the salty tang of him that lingered there. He nipped at her tongue, then covered her jaw with wet, openmouthed kisses, laving her tingling skin. The contrast between his demanding kiss and the teasing, cool moistness of this new onslaught made her shiver.

His hand began to move higher, and fire blazed through her limbs. A very small, very distant voice cried out that she was being brazen, wanton, that she should resist as she had resisted the advances of other men. She should not be enjoying the caresses his hands and lips and tongue lavished on her body.

Her heart silenced the voices with a single thought. This man *was* different, this one who made her feel as no other had. She had desperately tried to deny the power he wielded over her, a sweet power that brought her every emotion into play and every passion to the surface. Like the sudden fury of a summer storm, her heart overwhelmed her reason, demanding that she deny herself no longer. Uttering a soft cry of surrender, she wrapped an arm about his neck, her fingers tickling the curls at his nape.

Growling in pleasure, Connor slipped one arm beneath her, crushing her closer. The briefest flicker of hesitation tugged at his conscience, then disappeared. His need for Laurien burned so brightly, so clearly, that it made duty and promises fade into half-formed shadows. *She* was all that mattered now. Her arms circled his neck, pulling him closer, drawing him toward the softness and solace that he had longed for, it seemed, all his life. Hungrily, he accepted all that she offered and demanded more.

His free hand resumed its wandering path across her

belly, gradually tugging her tunic upward until his fingers met bare skin. She made the smallest whimper of objection; he continued his circling, soothing pattern higher, over her ribs, until his hand met the softness of one breast. Full and taut, it filled his hand, and his fingers caressed its tender curves. She trembled in response. He flicked at the peak with his thumb, then his tongue, and her whimper deepened into a moan. Raw need seared through his veins, so intense he thought his body would splinter into shards.

His senses were flooded with the scent of her hair, the silken glory of her skin, the dark, sultry pleading in her eyes. His pulse raced, but he desperately sought to hold himself in check. He must not hurt her as de Villiers had. He must go slowly, drawing her ever upward in a spiral of unspoken pleasure. He rained a trail of tiny kisses down her neck. His free hand found its way beneath her tunic, and he slipped the garment over her head.

Laurien lay half naked beneath him, but found that she felt no shame, only a tingling heat that suffused her skin. He placed a lingering kiss at the hollow of her throat, then traced lower. Never had she known so many sensations at once—the warmth of the furs beneath her back, the roughness of Connor's tunic against the delicate skin of her breasts, his spicy masculine scent, the sound of his breathing, now ragged with desire. A tempest of feelings coursed through her, like hunger and thirst and longing all at once, all centered on this man.

He impatiently tossed his own tunic aside. His eager fingers quickly loosened the rest of their garments and they lay naked, dark limbs mingling with pale. She ran her hands over his ribs, through the mat of hair on his chest, marveling at his hard-muscled strength. His body was so different from hers, so angular and solid, so unfamiliar and intriguing. Her fingers encountered the healing wound on his shoulder and she pulled away, pained by the memory that she had caused him to be hurt.

Connor caught her wrist, touched by the sadness in her eyes. He turned her palm upward, kissed it slowly, and placed it over his heart, covering her hand with his own. His heart seemed to turn over as he looked down at her, and he longed to tell her . . . What? What would he say if he could find the words? The soft speech of lovers had never come easily to him. With a grin, he settled for what came more naturally.

His hand skimmed over the curve of her hip, then lower. His mouth returned to hers, devouring, plundering. He thrust his tongue against hers and she hesitantly, innocently suckled it. He thought he would burst.

Laurien gasped as Connor's fingers trailed down her bare leg to her knee, then slowly, tantalizingly, back up toward the thatch of hair between her thighs. He lingered there for an instant, just long enough to moisten his fingers on her dampness, then stroked down her other leg, more slowly this time. By the time his fingers moved upward again, she was squirming beneath him, the tension that curled inside her belly almost beyond bearing.

She felt a desperate, feminine yearning she could not put into words. Connor again touched the soft triangle of curls and she squeezed her eyes shut, biting her lower lip to hold back the pleading, wanton words that leaped to her tongue. His fingers massaged her intimately this time, finding a sensitive spot that sent an explosion of delicious sensations rippling through her limbs. A cry of longing tore from Laurien's throat, and she raised her hips, arching against his hand.

Sweet Mary, how she wanted this man, needed him . . . *loved him*.

The thought flitted into her mind like a bright-winged butterfly, making her open her eyes in amazement. She gazed up at Connor, his tousled blond hair, the startling blue of his eyes. Could that be the name for the tangle of feelings she had for him? She barely had time to consider the question when a trembling began deep inside her. Connor's fingers moved lower, stroking the wet cleft between her legs, then slipping inside her.

In the span of a heartbeat, all reason fled as a spasm shook her body. A sudden wave made of both ice and flame swept from her toes to her fingertips. Her every muscle tensed, tighter, tighter, until she thought she would faint with the sheer rapture of it. Then just as suddenly the most delicious sensation of release washed over her, stealing her breath away. No sooner had the first wave receded than a second followed, more intense, leaving her gasping with pleasure.

She arched against Connor, and he gently pressed her back into the furs, lowering his hips against her. He lay suspended above her for a moment, holding her absolutely still, kissing her temple, her cheeks, her chin. Laurien could feel his manhood teasing between her thighs, and she moved against him, longing for him to end this sweet torment. She knew now what she wanted: to feel him inside her, not his fingers but this blunt, velvety steel that was the pure masculine essence of him.

Her wriggling at last broke Connor's endurance. Covering her mouth with his, he plunged home with a single thrust. He stilled instantly as Laurien stiffened beneath him with a sharp cry of pain. A numbing flash of reason struck him. There was no mistaking what he had just felt. She was a *virgin*.

That brief rational thought had no chance to take hold, but burned to a cinder in a blaze of sensual excitement as Laurien instinctively relaxed, her body adjusting to his invasion. He struggled for control, the muscles of his arms and back straining, slick with sweat, but there was no holding himself back. She felt so tight, so wet, so absolutely perfect. She made a small sound deep in her throat and began moving her hips in an ancient lovers' dance. He groaned at the exquisite torture of her movements, trembling, and matched her strokes, withdrawing almost completely, then gently sheathing himself.

He pushed into her, moving his hips in a slow circle, and kissed her again, drinking in the petal softness of her lips and the music of her small moans of ecstasy. Her body opened to draw him deeper with each thrust. He moved faster, harder, and she responded with equal passion, her legs curving around his. The rolling motion of the ship mirrored their movement, the crash of the waves covering the gasps of surprise and pleasure that came from both of them. She wrapped her arms about his neck, nibbling and biting his shoulder, now so wild with desire he knew she must be leaving marks.

She drove him mad with her teeth and tongue. With a growl, he lowered his mouth to her breast, and his lips found one pebble-hard nipple. He grazed it with his teeth then sucked at it, punctuating each ungentle kiss with a deep thrust that left her moaning his name, her voice husky and sweet to his ears.

Far more quickly than he would have liked, the pressure in his body built to breaking. His very blood seemed to be afire. He gathered her to him and plunged deep within her, shuddering. The tension that tortured him shattered at last, and he moaned her name, over and over, as he found release. He knew the pleasure of taking Laurien with him, for she cried out softly, nipping his neck as a third spasm wracked her body.

Breathing hard, he rolled on his side and pulled Laurien close, brushing a kiss in her hair. He stroked her back and she closed her eyes, murmuring an exquisitely feminine sigh of satisfaction.

Laurien snuggled against Connor's chest and gave in

to the delightful drowsiness that overtook her. Lying in the hold on a ship of thieves, on a stolen wolf pelt, naked and defenseless, she felt safe in his arms.

Long after she had fallen asleep, her breath a warm whisper against his chest, Connor lay awake, disturbing thoughts robbing him of slumber.

Chapter 12

⟨∽◡◠◡∽⟩

C onnor was still awake half an hour later. Laurien had lied to him before, but on one particular point she had told him true. She was indeed a maiden. Or had been, he corrected himself. God's teeth, what had he done?

She lay in his arms, soft and trusting. Her cheeks were flushed, her lips still slightly swollen from the shared passion of their kisses. A light sheen of perspiration glistened on her skin. As he watched her sleep, Connor was caught between two emotions—tenderness and regret. Malcolm's words of a few days past rang in his mind.

De Villiers will expect the lass back in the same condition in which she left . . .

Connor knew with terrible certainty that he had betrayed her. When de Villiers discovered his betrothed was no longer a maiden, he would make her life miserable, punish her cruelly for having lain with another.

Connor felt ill. Laurien had been right. He hadn't given a thought to her possible fate upon returning to de Villiers. And now he had made that fate worse. He hadn't considered the possibility that she had been telling him the truth about her virginity. What a selfish, thickheaded fool he was.

He slipped away from her side, pulled on his leggings, and shrugged back into the rest of his clothing.

176

Laurien rolled onto her stomach and sighed, a whispered accompaniment to a sweet dream. The sound tugged at his heart.

He ran his fingers through his hair, feeling an intense desire to flee. That was his usual habit; simply give the lady a cool farewell and slip away at morning's first light without so much as a kiss. But there was no way out this time, no escape from the shambles he had made.

He mused over a sudden notion—what if they did not return the girl?

He could almost hear what Malcolm's response to that would be. They had no choice. Without the alliance, Scotland would be in flames before year's end. Connor knew too well what had happened when the English had descended upon Wales. Castles cut off from food and supplies until the occupants starved to death. Crofts scorched and families burned to death as they struggled to save their villages. Women and girls raped when King Edward loosed his soldiers on the survivors. When surrender finally came, the Welsh had little left to surrender.

Was it not better that one girl suffer than thousands? Connor felt his chest tighten as his guilt deepened.

Watching Laurien sleep, he devised and discarded one plan after another. At last he gave up in frustration, unable to see any way he could save the girl without losing the alliance. He lay beside her again, wanting to sleep, to forget. But instead of lulling him, the motion of the ship and the sound of the waves taunted him, tormented him with memories of his first ocean crossing, the first time he had fled from a woman . . .

He was seven-and-ten, a lanky whelp of a boy, still living at Malcolm's keep. Half drunk and completely exhausted, he stumbled down the tower steps to his wife's chamber, his way lit only by the occasional flash of lightning. He flung open the door and sent her maids scurrying out.

"Whose is it?" he spluttered, a flask still clutched in one fist. He kept his eyes on a point above Sibylla's head, trying to ignore the newborn cradled in her arms. The window shutters rattled with the violence of the November storm. "Tell me his name, damn you. I will cut the bastard's heart out!"

He had expected fear, resistance, at least some battle to protect her lover's name. Sibylla smiled at him. "The babe is Duncan's."

The sound of his brother's name sliced through Connor's heart like a steel blade. "Sibylla, nay," he whispered lamely, unable to find words dark enough to hold his pain.

"I love him. I have always loved him."

Connor stood speechless, the breath knocked out of him as if a battering ram had hit him squarely in the midsection. She hummed a lullaby and pulled back the swaddling to reveal the babe's tiny head, a dusting of blond hair, sleepy blue eyes. None would doubt that the boy was Connor's own. Only the two of them knew that Sibylla had not lain with him since their wedding night almost a year ago.

"Sibylla, why . . . What have I done that you could do this to me?" Tears burned his eyes, threatening to spill over. He blinked hard to hold them back. "My God, how could you do this to Eda, to your own sister?"

She shrugged. "You have been gone so often. Eda insisted I accept her hospitality. I was lonely here."

"So lonely that you would lie with Duncan?" He shook his head in denial. "I asked you to come with me to Edinburgh. I should have insisted."

"I care not for the annual tourneys." She yawned. "The city is too hot and crowded to spend the summer there.'' The baby began to fuss, and she set him beside her on the bed.

"And when I was nearly killed by Sir Fergus's lance, fighting for my life," Connor whispered accusingly, "all along you were growing fat with my brother's babe—" His voice broke, and he could not continue.

"You had the king's physician himself to see to your comfort. And Malcolm. You did not need me by your side for all those months."

"What a fool I was." When Connor could find his voice again, his words sounded small and weak, easily swallowed by the noise of the wind raging outside the keep. "I didna understand why you wouldna come to me. I hastened home because I feared you were ill."

She gazed at him unblinking, her blue eyes cool. Even the strain of childbirth had not lessened her beauty. Only one who knew her well would note the lines of fatigue marring her skin, the tendrils of blond hair in disarray, clinging to the perspiration about her neck and shoulders.

How easy it had been to fall in love with Sibylla, how quickly she had become everything to him.

Since the night he met Sibylla at Duncan and Eda's wedding, he had been like an overeager puppy trotting at her heels. Her name was his last thought as he fell asleep each night, the first in his mind each morn. When she consented to wed him, he envisioned a life filled with joy. He was still squire to Malcolm, but he made plans to win his knighthood and build a grand keep that he and his new bride would fill with laughter, with children.

"Sibylla, you told me that lovemaking was too painful for you. You said that you loved me, that you only needed time . . ." Connor hung his head, suddenly more weary than he could ever remember being. As young and inexperienced as he was, he could understand that, somehow, she had planned to hurt him this way. She had wanted him to *know* the babe was not his.

As he stared at the floor, his vision blurred with tears. His spurs, silver-bright in their newness, shone against the dark brown of his boots. He hadn't taken the bits of metal off since he arrived home three days ago. He hadn't done much but drink to numb his shock at seeing his wife.

He hated the spurs suddenly. He had nearly gotten himself killed in his eagerness to win them. Now he wanted to rip them off and throw them against the wall. "How could you lie to me?" he choked out. "Why?

"I have told you what you wanted to know. If you wish to learn more, I suggest you speak to Duncan. Will you not leave me to rest now?"

Connor raised his head and looked at her in stunned silence a long moment, a tear trickling down his cheek. Not taking his eyes from hers, he reached up and untied the long piece of fabric knotted about his left arm. He held it out to her. When she made no move to retrieve her favor, he let it slip from his fingers, and it fell to the floor in a tiny pool of green silk.

He strode from the chamber to seek his brother.

Outside the keep, the storm threw him back against the wall. The wind nearly tore his cloak away. Rain and ice pricked his skin like needles as he fought his way toward the stables in the darkness. Volleys of lightning stabbed out of the sky, making the onslaught of sleet glow with a silvery light.

His destrier followed the familiar path from Malcolm's keep to Castle Glenshiel. Nearly numb by the time he arrived, Connor ignored the guards' greeting. Later he would not remember dismounting or entering the keep or taking down the twin Norse blades from the hearth in the great hall. He found himself standing in his brother's chamber. Duncan slept soundly, curled beside his wife, Eda.

The ancient steel felt cold and heavy in Connor's hand. He dropped the second blade on the floor. The clatter startled his brother and sister-in-law awake.

Duncan quickly soothed his wife. "Go back to sleep, my love. My brother has chosen an odd hour for one of his pranks."

Eda smiled sleepily and snuggled back into the covers. Connor stared into his brother's knowing eyes. "Outside," he said, and turned on his heel without awaiting a reply.

Lightning danced along the ground, illuminating the practice ground where Connor waited. He felt terribly calm as Duncan walked toward him. His brother was three years older, at least two inches taller, and had the advantage in weight and experience. And he hadn't spent the last three days emptying wine flasks.

But Connor could feel rage bubbling beneath his thin layer of calm, mingling with a hurt sharper than any pain he had known, until his blood fair burned.

Duncan had sheathed the sword. The chemise and leggings he had donned were already soaked. He approached with open arms. "Connor, please," he shouted above the storm, "allow me to explain."

Connor brandished the blade to warn him away. "Tell me but one thing, damn you," he cried. "Is it yours?"

Duncan circled, his palms up in a pleading gesture. "I never thought this would happen. She isna what you think—"

Connor slashed the air and stepped closer. "Burn you, you bastard, is it yours?"

Duncan stopped moving away. His hands still outstretched, he looked the image of a saint from a church tableau. An eruption of thunder drowned the roar of rain spattering across the cobblestones. As the sound retreated, Duncan nodded. "Aye."

With a cry that was half growl, half scream, Connor launched himself at his brother. The rain and sleet blinded him and he slashed out madly. Duncan leaped clear and slipped on the slick cobbles. Connor was on him in an instant. Duncan drew his sword to fend off the blow. Their blades met, scraping together with a metallic screech. Duncan pushed upward, his greater strength sending Connor tumbling.

Connor leaped to his feet and charged again. His last thread of control had snapped, and he was driven by a rage as pure and cold as the sleet. His opponent parried. Connor sliced his blade up, down, right, seeking an opening and finding none. He drove forward with a flurry of blows, the sword seeming almost to move with a life of its own, thirsting for blood. His woolen garments were sodden, but he moved swiftly, like a warrior born, every muscle in his body tensed for the battle at hand.

He kept his eyes focused always on the sword in the other's hand. He felt a prickle of pain on his skin, then another. He ignored them, not caring what wounds he received this night, not caring if he died here. The fire in his blood could only be quenched by the death of his opponent.

Time spun onward and he fought with animal fury, but he could not score a hit, could not break through the other's defenses to draw blood. Finally, fatigue and too much wine began to take their toll. He was slowing down, leaving himself open, once, twice, a third time. But never did his opponent use the advantage to deliver a blow. Connor stumbled and fell to his knees. He struggled to rise and slipped again.

He looked up, expecting to feel a blade instantly biting into his skin. Instead he saw his brother standing scant inches away, gazing down, shoulders slumped. Though he was uninjured and showed little sign of tiring, Duncan threw down his sword.

Connor sat gasping for breath, drinking in as much rain as air. At last, he heaved himself to his feet, sword still in hand. A flash of lightning lit the sky, and Connor saw the look of utter sadness in his brother's eyes, the haggard cast to the features so like his own. He saw the image of a man lost in regret.

Connor struggled to piece together the scattered ruin that was his heart. At last, he blurted the question that had driven him like a madman into the night. "Do you love her?"

Duncan shook his head, and a sad smile twisted his lips. "Nay. I love Eda."

Even before he heard the answer, Connor knew the blood lust had cooled. The fever that had driven him lifted, and he shivered. He dropped his sword. "Go to Eda, then."

The need to hunt had been replaced by a much stronger desire to flee. Connor backed away from his brother, then turned and ran, throwing himself against the wind with the last scrap of strength left in his body. He found his horse and flung himself into the saddle, urging the stallion into a gallop.

Connor let the animal have its head, not caring what direction he took. He rode blindly through the glens and hills. The horse slipped in the darkness, pitching him from the saddle, into the mud. He lay still for a long time, and wept, until he felt completely wrung out, as if he were a bucket that someone had kicked over and all his life were draining away. His tears mixed with the rain in a cold, salty wetness that did naught to numb the ache within him.

Dawn was a blue line along the horizon before he managed to pull himself up. As he did so he felt a jab

of pain on his ankle. Looking down he saw that his left
spur had bent into a misshapen triangle. He slipped it
off, then the right one, and clutched them in his fist until
the steel edges dug into his flesh. The bits of metal had
represented the ultimate prize to him, a badge of chivalry and honor that would win the heart of his lady fair.
Now they meant only pain. He unclenched his fist and
looked at the left spur. His beloved Sibylla had twisted
and ruined what was noble and good.

The right spur, though, was still whole. He stared at
it, thinking of the years of work and sweat and blood
that had gone into earning it. Those hard-won skills of
knighthood were still his.

He closed his fist over the cold pieces of metal and
felt an equally cold resolve grip him. To hell with the
hearts of faithless females. There were battles to be
fought, causes far more worthy than women. Love did
not last, but muscle and steel would never desert him.
Still holding his spurs, he found his horse and threw
himself into the saddle with all the strength he could
muster.

As morning broke, he found himself at Malcolm's
keep once again. He strode to his wife's chamber, trailing mud up the stair. He did not know what he would
say, but he knew what he would do. From now on he
would keep to himself, fight for his own reasons, and
stay as far distant from love as he possibly could. He
swung open the door.

The chamber was empty.

Her belongings were gone, her chests of garments,
the fine gold plates she liked to display above the hearth.
Only a worn pair of shoes remained, apparently discarded in her haste. Those, and the trinket box he had
given her as a wedding gift . . . and the babe. The boy
lay sleeping in a tangle of blankets on the bed.

One of Malcolm's retainers rushed in behind him.

"She has left, Sir Connor. She gathered the lady's maids and fled. Naught that we said could stop her. And she wouldna say where she went, or for how long." He looked lamely at the babe. "We didna know what to do with the child."

Connor observed the tiny figure on the bed. The lad had wakened at the commotion and was crying lustily, struggling to kick free of the swaddling.

Sibylla had left. It only made things simpler. He cared not where she had gone, cared even less what became of her. He certainly was not going to batter what was left of his pride by chasing after her.

Why had she abandoned the boy? He could only wonder. Connor looked about the ravaged chamber and found that he felt . . . nothing.

"Find a wet nurse for the child. Ask in the village." He turned and started for the stairs.

The guardsman followed him. "But, Sir Connor, what of Lady Sibylla? And what am I to tell Sir Malcolm when he returns from Edinburgh?"

Connor stopped when he reached the great hall. This has been a place of joy for him. Now he only wanted to escape it. Sibylla's lies had twisted his memories into a mockery of happiness. "Tell Malcolm I have gone to the continent. And as for the Lady Sibylla, I dinna think you shall see her again soon."

The man stopped him again as he headed for the door.

"But, sir, your son . . . By what name are we to call your son?"

Connor turned in the door, a sarcastic retort on his tongue, but he stopped himself. Why should the boy be made to suffer for his mother's sins? Sibylla obviously did not want her child. And Connor doubted that Duncan would step forward to claim the babe and thus trumpet his adultery to all. The boy would have no one. But if Connor were to claim him, no one would ever question that the boy was his own. Nor would any question his leaving. Many younger sons went to seek their fortunes as mercenaries.

"Sir Malcolm will see that my son is well cared for," Connor said at last. "You are to call him . . . " He paused, then decided upon his grandfather's name. "My son is to be called Aidan. Mayhap *he* will grow to be a man of honor one day." With that, he left . . .

And he had not seen Sibylla since. Connor gazed into the single, tiny flame that illuminated the cabin, morosely watching the shadows flicker over Laurien's slim curves. What would it be like, he wondered, to keep her for himself, to take her to Castle Glenshiel and make her his own. To make love to her every night and wake to her every morn, to raise fine, strong sons and beautiful daughters with spice-colored curls—

He quelled the futile longing, the desire that warmed him, and the softer feelings that overlook him so easily when he thought of this lovely, bold, exasperating girl. Such softness could never be his, never for any more than a moment's brief pleasure.

In the nine years since that storm-wracked night, Sibylla had never come back. He hadn't heard from her; hadn't been able to locate her or a single member of her retinue. Nor had he received any word of her death.

Sibylla's silence was her final cruelty, for that silence condemned him to a life alone, for unless he could prove that Sibylla no longer lived, the Church still considered him married. He could not take another wife. Duncan's death in a hunting accident had made Connor lord of Castle Glenshiel, but he would never have a Lady Glenshiel by his side, nor a family of his own. From afar, he had watched Aidan grow to a fine lad any man would be proud to call his son. Yet he couldn't bring himself to be close to the boy, couldn't even bear to think of

him; the memories of Aidan's birth and his mother were
just too painful.

He felt Laurien shiver as she reached out to the now-
cool space where Connor had lain beside her. He shifted
away from her hand, and gently covered her with another of the wolf pelts. He knew what he must do. It
was unfair to Laurien to pretend there could be aught
between them. And after the way she had saved his life,
and fought beside him in Calais, she deserved more than
to be just another of his brief dalliances. She would be
hurt, but he could not undo what had already happened.
He could only ensure that it would not happen again.

Since that night nine years ago, he had learned to
keep his emotions on a short rein, to think only of the
task at hand—his people, his duty. He would need to
exercise all that control now, for he would not allow
himself any further affection for the girl. She was going
back to de Villiers, and he was powerless to change that.

He had to distance himself from her, stop up his feelings with a determination stronger than a cork in a bot-
tle. She would hate him for his coldness, but better she
should hate him; if she were to fall in love with him she
would only be hurt further, and she had already been
hurt too much.

The sounds of a commotion on deck startled Connor
out of his contemplations. He heard the sounds of running feet, then shouted commands. He could not make
out the words. His first thought was that somehow de
Villiers's men had followed them. But mayhap the English had been searching for smugglers and waylaid the
ship. Either way, he did not wish to find himself cor-
nered in the tiny cabin. There was no room to fight if
the need arose.

The ship heeled suddenly to one side, and a resounding scrape of wood against wood reverberated through

the hold. Laurien was tossed against the pile of furs at her back and jarred awake.

"What happened?" She looked at him in sleepy confusion.

Connor had already picked up his shortsword and loosened the hidden door. Laurien looked rumpled and sweet, unmindful of her nakedness as she rubbed at her eyes. Before Connor knew what he was about, he slipped an arm about her waist and crushed her to his chest. His lips caught hers in rough, demanding possession. One last kiss, he decided. Who knew what fate awaited him above? He wanted one last kiss.

He released her at last and moved the portal aside. "Something is amiss on deck. Stay here." He moved into the hold, pushing aside the stack of crates their host had piled in front of the entrance.

"But what has happened?" Laurien wrapped a fur about her shoulders and stuck her head out before he could replace the plank. "What was that sound?"

"I think we have been boarded. Get back inside," he hissed.

Fully awake now, Laurien could recognize the sharp edge of displeasure in Connor's tone. But she was not going to let him charge off by himself. She reached out to stop him. "You have no idea of how many there are. Wait a moment and I will accompany you."

"I have no need of assistance." Connor prodded her none too gently back into their hiding place. "For once, do as I say. Stay in there, no matter what happens. And keep silent."

Before she could object, Connor slid the door into place. She could hear him pushing the crates back in front of it to block her exit. Though she knew he thought to protect her, she fumed at his surly command.

She strained to hear anything more from the hold, or from above, but the ship had taken on an eerie silence.

After several tense moments holding her breath, she gave up trying to discern what was happening. She decided a peek into the hold would do no harm.

Laurien dressed quickly, warmth suffusing her cheeks as she donned her tunic and noticed that the cloth felt rough against the too-sensitive skin of her breasts. It irked her that Connor seemed able to change his emotions as easily as the wind changed directions. Hours before he had been gentle with her, almost loving, filling her with the most wondrous joy she had ever known. Yet upon awakening, he greeted her with a bruising kiss and a brusque dismissal. She stepped back into her leggings, blushing again when she felt the tenderness between her legs.

She ignored the soreness and wrapped her cloak about her shoulders, feeling terribly unhappy all of a sudden. Connor was not so inexperienced as she. She had given herself freely, surrendered completely, certain he cared for her. Now she was unsure of his feelings. She kicked at the furs they had lain upon, her temper rising. Had he been this way with other women, melting them in a heat of passion only to leave with a farewell kiss and cool words? Did she mean naught more to him than the diversion of a quick tumble? It was suddenly important to her to know the answer, and equally important that the answer be no.

The sounds of a struggle broke out above. She heard voices raised in anger, quickly followed by the now familiar clanging of swordplay. She jumped when something heavy hit the planks just above her head. The sound was followed by a second *whump*, placing a most disturbing image in Laurien's mind of a body landing full force on the deck.

She reached instantly for the portal to the hidden cabin, only to have it ripped open from outside. She fell back in terror when a fearful-looking giant of a man thrust his head through the opening. Nay, he looked more beast than man, with a great mass of grizzled hair hanging to his shoulders, and a necklace of *teeth* about his leathern garments. A slow grin spread his lips in a gruesome leer, curving upward until his scarred nose wrinkled.

"At last." He reached in and grasped her arm, jerking her forward. She screamed, striking him about the head and shoulders with her free hand. He grabbed it easily and twisted it back with cruel force, then pulled her against him to study her face. "At last I have the honor of meeting the Lady Laurien d'Amboise."

Laurien cried out again as he lifted her and dragged her out, into the hold. Unable to free her arms, she kicked wildly at him. One toe struck solid muscle but barely elicited a grunt.

"Do not struggle so," he rumbled. "I am to return you to your betrothed, milady. The comte would be most displeased if I were forced to harm you."

He thrust her up the ladder and out the hatch, where other hands caught at her limbs. She blinked in the bright light of torches that illuminated the night.

A second ship had been tied alongside their craft, but Laurien paid no attention to it or to the blue and gold garbed men who pressed forward to look at her. She stared in horror at the bodies sprawled across the deck—Connor and Malcolm and the ship's mate, and others she guessed were the rest of the crew. Her eyes quickly grew used to the light, and her heart beat painfully in her chest when she saw the dark splotches that stained the planks. Splotches of blood.

"Nay! What have you done? Bastards!" She struggled against the man who now held her, desperate to run to where Connor lay unmoving. The man spun her around and struck her with such force that she half fell to the deck.

He jerked her upright and snarled at her in French that was heavily accented with English. "Hold your tongue, wench, lest I be forced to silence you." He brushed her hair from her face and murmured an appreciative comment she could not make out over the ringing in her ears.

"She is indeed a prize, Balafre," he said as the grizzled giant stepped free of the hatch. "It is a pity the comte is unwilling to share."

The one called Balafre moved forward to take her from her present captor. "Aye, a pity. But the sooner we take her back to Calais, the sooner we shall have our reward."

Laurien recoiled in fear, but the Englishman held fast to her arm. "Nay, Balafre, it makes little sense to turn about tonight. We are less than an hour from England, and I find myself suddenly longing to see my homeland."

Balafre gave him a savage look and moved forward until his face was only inches away. "Some other time, mayhap."

Laurien bit her lower lip as the Englishman tightened his grip and wrapped his other fist in her hair, jerking her head back. "But look at her, Balafre. Be reasonable. It will be days before de Villiers receives the message you sent. We have more than enough time to enjoy her and return to Calais before he arrives."

Balafre did not move, did not blink. "De Villiers wants her back untouched, and I will not disappoint him. We are turning about, Paxton. Now."

"Think, for once in your life," the Englishman retorted. He nodded to the still forms of Connor and Malcolm. "Have you any idea how much the English king would pay for a pair of Scots rebels? There is much more profit to be made here than a handful of gems. Open your eyes, you fool!"

Laurien was terrified at the two possible fates that lay before her, but she whispered a silent prayer of thanks, realizing from Paxton's words that Connor and Sir Malcolm must still be alive. De Villiers's guards—she counted six of them—stood looking anxiously from Balafre to Paxton, as if unsure who was in command.

Balafre glared at Paxton and shook his head in annoyance. He turned to the guards. "You, and you! Get back to our ship and make ready to sail." The two men hastened to obey. Scrambling over the railing to the other ship, they began to cast off the ropes that bound the two vessels together.

Then Balafre bent beside Connor's still form, drawing his knife.

"Nay!" Laurien screamed, amazed when she heard the Englishman's voice echoing the word.

Balafre stopped, his knife at Connor's throat, and glared at Paxton.

The Englishman shouted at the remaining four guards. "What can he offer you? The promise of a few paltry gems, at some time in the future? Why should we settle for such a pittance? De Villiers is desperate. He would pay thousands for the return of such a one. Come with me and I will share the ransom! You will be wealthy beyond your imagination."

Balafre rose, his hand moving to his sword hilt.

The guards already had their own weapons drawn, and Paxton glared at Balafre in menacing silence. Laurien felt her heart hammer as the air grew thick with ready violence.

"Do you know what the comte will do to you for this?" Balafre said softly.

"He will make us rich, if he wants the girl returned." Paxton pulled Laurien in front of him as a shield. "You have misjudged these men, Balafre. They are much wiser than you." He nodded to the guards. "Take him!"

They suddenly closed in on Balafre. Laurien turned her face away from the quick, bloody scuffle. When it was over, one of the guards lay dying on the deck and Balafre, disarmed, was held by the remaining three men.

"I think, my friend, it is past time that we part ways." Paxton chuckled. Still holding Laurien, he walked over to stand in front of Balafre. "But I suppose it would be terribly bad manners for me to kill you outright, after all we have been through together. England is but a few hours' swim to the west—if the cold and the sharks do not get you first."

At a flick of his hand, the guards lifted Balafre and heaved him over the side. Laurien gasped in horror, stunned that murder could come so easily to anyone. She choked back a cry when Paxton ordered his men to carry Connor and Malcolm to the other ship. Sweet Mary, what fate awaited them at this man's hands?

When he turned his attention back to Laurien, she knew with a rush of despair that *her* fate would be most unpleasant. She raised her chin and forced herself to meet his gaze squarely, determined not to show a whit of the fear she felt trembling through her body. He took a handful of her hair and pressed it to his lips. She felt bile rise in her throat.

"Now, then, milady." He ran his hands over her breasts, and Laurien couldn't suppress a shudder. "You intrigue me. I see no hurry in returning you to de Villiers. Nor do I feel any need, as our friend in the water did, to return you in spotless condition."

His hands traveled up her body to her shoulders. He unfastened her cloak and let his fingers rest lightly at her neck. "I simply cannot delay in sampling your charms."

Chapter 13

B y the next afternoon, Laurien had gone nearly numb with raw fear. Clinging to her horse with one hand, she gingerly felt her stinging cheek and nose, her fingers trembling. Paxton seemed to delight in slapping her, and did so if she so much as opened her mouth to speak. Blinking in the steady rain, she noticed, with an odd sense of detachment, splashes of red on her gloved hand. The Englishman's last blow must have left her with a bloodied nose. She let her hand drop into her lap and fell into a dazed silence as they rode northward from the English port of Hull.

Paxton rode ahead of her, holding her horse's reins. She stared at his back through the downpour and desperately tried to keep her mind on Connor and Sir Malcolm. If she let herself think of how this Englishman planned to use her thoroughly and turn her over to de Villiers, she would give in to the sense of helplessness and utter terror that threatened to overwhelm her.

Only a quick lie had saved her thus far. She had managed to convince Paxton that she would please him more if not taken against her will on his ship, and if she had time to recover from her ordeal at the hands of the Scots. Giving her a wolfish smile, he had relented, saying with chilling confidence that he would have many weeks to enjoy her. They had arrived at Hull near dawn, and Paxton eagerly hurried her along the docks, leaving his men to follow later with the Scots.

Laurien shivered, soaked through by the downpour and filled with anxiety. At least Paxton did not strike her again; he seemed satisfied that he had beaten her into obedience. When he stopped to water the horses, he even unwittingly left open an opportunity for her to escape. Her every instinct urged her to flee, but she did not. She did not know where Connor and Sir Malcolm were being taken, and she could not leave them behind, knowing that this barbarian meant to turn them over to the English king. She could not bear the thought of them being tortured and killed; despite Connor's coldness toward her, she cared for him still.

She clung to that feeling as if it were armor against Paxton, against the attack she would face all too soon . . . alone.

By the time they approached the Englishman's fief at dusk, she was frantically trying to devise a plan.

His home was no more than a stone donjon surrounded by scattered outbuildings and a wooden palisade. No guards or servants greeted them, and Laurien guessed from the condition of the place that Paxton had not been home in some time. It was only when he dragged her into the musty great hall that they encountered anyone: a pair of men, sprawled in chairs before the hearth. Their snores echoed loudly, and from the mugs and flasks scattered about the floor, it appeared they were sleeping off a drunk.

Paxton cuffed and cursed them back to awareness, shouting at them for allowing his home to fall into such a state. He then shut Laurien in his chamber on the second floor, allowing her time to wash and garb herself in a worn gown he provided, while he went to talk to the two men.

The moment she had dreaded now upon her, Laurien

resorted to a reckless idea. She managed to beg a flask of wine and two cups from Paxton, along with a few common herbs from the kitchens, explaining they would help her relax after her ordeal.

An hour later, she paced about the chamber, rubbing her temples, trying to soothe the headache that thrummed in her ears. Tension made her every movement awkward, and she stubbed her toe on the broken remnants of a chair that littered the half-rotted rushes. She coughed on the stench of sweat and ale that clung to every corner of the room, then took a deep breath to quiet her pounding heart. *Calm yourself,* she thought. If she could not relax, she would never carry off a pretense of ardor for Paxton.

And she would already need more than a miracle to succeed.

She eyed the cups sitting innocently on a storage chest beside the bed. If the Englishman discovered her ruse, she had no doubt he would beat her senseless. A single candle, flickering next to the goblets, lit the chamber; the tallow had burned almost to its base. She shivered, wondering how soon Paxton would return.

As if in answer, she heard footfalls in the hall beyond the door.

She took a shaky gulp of the stale air and arranged herself on the pallet in what she hoped was a seductive pose, smoothing her gown. The red velvet garment was the most shocking attire she had ever seen, tight enough to reveal every curve, the front cut low between her breasts. She had noted with a shiver that the bodice had been ripped and resewn. She forced a smile to her lips as the portal opened.

Paxton cast an impatient look her way and closed the door. "You look comfortable now, damosel." He peeled off his rain-soaked tunic, prowling over to the bed. "I expect you to prove the delay worthwhile."

Laurien sat up and reached for one of the goblets. Lowering her lashes demurely, she extended it to the Englishman. Despite his slim build, his arms and chest were well muscled. She would be helpless if he decided to use force. "A drink first, milord?" She managed to keep her hand steady.

"This had best not be a trick, wench." He took the cup from her but clenched his other hand into a fist. "I take not kindly to such nonsense. You claimed the herbs were to relax you."

"And so they are." She met his gaze without flinching, but the raw lust she saw there made her look away. She pretended interest in the tattered mattress covering. "For a woman, the drink is soothing. For a man . . ." She paused and lowered her voice to a whisper, as if revealing a secret. "It helps prolong pleasure."

He considered the goblet suspiciously. "And what assurance have I that you are not trying to poison me and help your friends?"

She made a face, but her heart beat faster as the conversation turned to the Scots. "The knaves who abducted me treated me most ill, sir. They mean naught to me."

"You seemed rather concerned for them when you saw them lying on the deck of the ship."

"I was but shocked, sir, at seeing so much blood." She filled her voice with venom. "Naught would please me more than to learn that you have done away with them."

He took her chin and forced her to look at him. "When the English finish with them, they shall wish I had." His eyes lit with anticipation. "If you would you like to take part, I could arrange it."

The cruelty in his gaze made Laurien's stomach lurch. Paxton's fingers sank into her flesh until she felt sure her bones would snap. The ready brutality in this man re-

minded her of de Villiers, but not even in de Villiers'
hands had she felt so defenseless, so very much alone
"I seek only to please you," she whispered.

"Then I will take you along when I deliver them to
King Edward." He released her chin and offered her his
cup. "But now you will drink. Show me that you mean
me no harm."

Laurien felt a tiny measure of relief, hoping from his
words that Connor and Malcolm were somewhere
nearby. She flashed him a smile. She had expected the
request that she drink from his goblet. She took a quick
gulp, tasting naught but the dry snap of alcohol; none
but a healer would know that the wine had been tam-
pered with. And a sip should do her no harm. It took a
larger draught to induce deep sleep. She passed the goblet back.

He sat on the bed next to her, put down his drink
and picked up the other. "Now, from your own."

Laurien could not quell a look of surprise at that. She
dare not drink too much. He leaned over her, and she
leaned away, awkwardly balancing on one elbow. But
he pressed the cup against her lips and forced her to take
a long swallow.

Laurien looked at him over the edge of the goblet as
he withdrew it, managing a tremulous smile. She must
keep him talking, for the liquid would take some time
to render him unconscious, and she herself was now in
danger of suffering the drink's effects.

"You see it is harmless, milord," she whispered in
what she hoped was an alluring tone. "You will enjoy
it most if you savor it slowly."

But before she could stop him, he drank down the
entire contents in one long swallow.

"Enough of the refreshments." He tossed the goblet
to the floor and wiped the back of his hand across his
mouth. "Let us begin the entertainment."

The next instant, Paxton shoved her down onto the bed. Laurien felt a wave of panic as his mouth came down on hers. His fingers cruelly pinched her breasts as he sought to free them from the gown. He bit her bottom lip, and she cried out in revulsion and pain, tasting her own blood. She stiffened with fright, cursing her own stupidity at thinking she could trick him so easily. Then she felt only terror as he pushed the hem of her gown above her thighs.

She must survive this, she swore to herself as fear and humiliation clutched at her. She had succeeded in getting an entire goblet of the potent drink into him. It would take effect eventually. Mayhap too late to save her, but she could still carry out the rest of her plan. Laurien held fast to that thought as a sea of horror pulled her downward. Paxton reached for his belt.

A knock at the door stopped him. He snarled something unintelligible, but the intruder ignored the warning and stormed in. Paxton rolled off her, and Laurien struggled to rearrange her skirts, shame and embarrassment bringing a surge of color to her cheeks.

It was one of Paxton's retainers. "That big Scot broke loose an' 'e's tearin' the yard apart," he declared.

"Get the others and tie him up again." Paxton spat. He made no move to get off the bed but Laurien felt a glimmer of hope as she realized whom they were discussing.

"I did." The man protested. "We can't get near 'im. 'E already knocked down Speares with a kick in the jaw. Keeps yellin' about the girl. 'E thinks we've killed 'er."

"Let him think what he wants." Paxton dismissed the man with a savage gesture.

"But, sir, it'll take all of us to guard 'im with the trouble 'e's puttin up. An' we don't want to sit in the rain all night. I thought if we just show 'im the wench is alive, 'e'll settle down enough so we can grab 'im.''

Cursing, Paxton took Laurien by the arm and dragged her to her feet. "It seems, my sweet, that your distaste for the Scots is not mutual.'' He hauled her roughly out the door and down the stairs, through the hall, and into the cold rain outside.

Icy, almost burning pain assaulted Laurien's exposed skin and bare feet as Paxton dragged her across the muddy yard. Before they had taken a dozen steps, her feet began to go numb. She wished desperately that the potion would take effect and she would pass out. Instead, the scene before her became painfully clear as they splashed toward the small shed that served as a stable.

The guards, still dressed in the blue and gold silks they had worn in de Villiers's service, were arranged in a rough circle around the structure. One of them held a torch. As she drew near, Laurien bit back a cry of concern upon seeing Connor's state. He had been bound and beaten; his face was bruised, and a cut on his forehead was bleeding profusely. Remnants of rope dangled from his wrists. He apparently had broken free, and the five men had not been able to subdue him. A sixth man lay sprawled in the mud on one side of the shelter. Malcolm was nowhere to be seen.

As soon as she and Paxton stepped inside, Connor's eyes locked with hers. His expression of relief quickly changed.

At first, Connor felt only shock at seeing Paxton's state of undress and Laurien's appearance. He had wakened hours before in this stable with a savage headache, and Laurien nowhere to be seen. He'd felt only fear, raw, cold fear that the English bastard had raped and killed her. Concern for his mission or Malcolm or his own possible fate had been overwhelmed by an obsessive need to find out what had befallen Laurien.

And here she was, clinging to the Englishman. The sight tore open old scars and flooded him with feelings of pain and betrayal as hot as his fear had been cold.

"Here is your pretty prize, damn you." Paxton shoved Laurien into the circle of light, then stepped forward and draped an arm over her shoulder, his fingers slipping inside her bodice. "She is quite happy to be with me. So make any more trouble and I shall kill you now and damn the profit to be made!"

Laurien forced herself to keep her eyes on the ground and her features carefully neutral. She could guess Connor's thoughts from his expression of utter rage. Saints' breath, but she longed to throw herself into his arms, to explain everything, to have him protect her from the ugliness around them. But she dared not show a hint of those feelings. If she could not persuade Paxton to return to his chamber quickly, the Englishman would collapse right in front of his men when her potion did its work. Her ruse would be for naught.

Laurien forced herself to smile up at Paxton, and tried not to wince as his arm tightened around her. "Please, milord." She placed a hand intimately on his chest. "Could we not go back inside now?"

"Eager to return to bed, are we?" He pinched her buttocks. "What a wanton you are. If you please me well, mayhap I will not return you to de Villiers for a long, long time."

To Laurien's disgust, he kissed her again. She almost recoiled, her fingers beginning to curl into a fist. But she forced herself to relax and not pull away.

Connor uttered a strangled shout. Blinded by fury, he threw himself forward, not at the guards, but at the Englishman and Laurien. He did not care what they did to him, as long as he could first get his hands around her throat. The guards swarmed over him, dragging him down. His last sight before they pummeled him to the ground was of the Englishman kissing Laurien deeply, and Laurien appearing quite content in the bastard's arms.

The image burned into him, filling him with pain, stealing away his will to fight. The guards he had held off before now wrestled him down easily. He withstood their kicks and blows and curses, unable to think or speak past the white-hot haze of anger and hurt that engulfed him.

When Paxton finally released Laurien, she spun about, terrified by the sounds of the struggle she had heard. She felt like crying upon seeing how the guards had beaten Connor, binding him hand and foot and tying him to a post in the corner of the shed. Despite herself, she started to move toward him—when he stopped her with a glare so filled with hate, it frightened her.

It was a look she had never thought to see in his eyes, for it held no spark of caring, only rage and disgust . . . and the promise of punishment.

Paxton jerked her backward and lifted her in his arms. "I want one of you guarding him at all times," he instructed. "And do not disturb us again!"

With that, he started toward the keep. Laurien's sight and hearing seemed to dim, and with a rush of despair she realized that her own potion had started to work against her. As yet it seemed harmless against Paxton; he might very well be able to finish the rape he had begun. She looked over his shoulder, squinting through the rain, her eyes never leaving the stable as the Englishman carried her farther and farther from Connor.

Her every sinew urged her to fight, but she kept still. She knew exactly where Connor was now. She need only remain calm and pray that the Englishman passed out before she did.

Hurrying up the stairs, Paxton slammed the door to his chamber and dumped her on the bed. She lay frozen in fear as he kicked off his boots and reached for one of the wine goblets. Wrapping one hand about her neck, he wrenched her to a sitting position. Laurien cried out in pain as he crushed her to his chest and pressed the cup against her lips.

"Drink heartily, milady, for I mean to take you again and again this night. You will need a great deal of wine to last under my attentions."

Laurien coughed and choked as he forced her to empty the goblet. He let go of her, and she fell back on the bed, covering her face with her hands, trying not to give in to horrified tears. Already, she felt weak from the drug's effects.

He was upon her the next instant, forcing her down into the mattress with his weight, fumbling with her skirt.

He shook his head as if to clear it. "Saints' blood," he snarled. "I have waited long enough."

He tore the velvet as if it were parchment, ripping the gown from hem to thigh. Laurien squeezed her eyes shut, unable to choke back a sob.

Paxton went completely still.

Laurien opened her eyes to find him glaring at her, his brow furrowed. He shook his head again, then realization dawned on his outraged features.

"What have you done to me, wench?" he bellowed.

His hands fastened around her throat. Laurien never even had the chance to draw a breath to scream. He shook her, wrenching her entire upper body from side to side across the mattress.

"What . . . have . . . you . . . done?"

Laurien gasped for air and found none. She pushed at his chest, frenzied, her mouth opening and closing silently, helplessly. His fingers squeezed tighter and tighter, and her hands grew more and more feeble. The pain in her throat and starved lungs became intense . . . and then it began to fade, and she could feel herself slipping into unconsciousness.

The next instant, the little air in her lungs was knocked from her when Paxton collapsed on top of her in a dead faint.

For a moment, Laurien was too stunned and frightened and relieved to think. She could only lie there and breathe, choking on the fetid air and thinking it the sweetest taste she had ever known. Then, with an effort that took all her strength, she heaved him off and scrambled from the bed.

She backed away across the chamber, her heart thumping against her ribs and her head spinning dizzily. She felt her stomach lurch with nausea. Shaking, she fell to her knees and threw up. She sat hunched over for a long time, her arms wrapped about her stomach, nearly succumbing to the tears that threatened. Wiping her mouth with one shaking hand, she swayed to her feet and looked toward Paxton. He lay unmoving.

She pushed away the thought of what he had almost done to her. There was no time to collapse in a mindless heap. She tore the tattered bedcovering into strips and tied the Englishman up as best she could. Stumbling to the corner, she picked up her brown homespun cloak and fastened it about her neck, her fingers trembling. She clutched the torn edges of her skirt together with one hand and picked up her boots.

She gave Paxton a quick, last look to see that he had not stirred, then hurried to the door and opened it a crack.

Below, the hall was silent. She counted six men, which meant only one was on guard outside. Three of them had already bedded down on pallets that lined the wall. Two were engaged in a game of dice at a trestle table before the fire, while another man watched.

Laurien groaned in frustration and sat down to wait. She could ill afford to waste time. She hoped, with her stomach emptied, that the large quantity of the potion she had swallowed would not affect her, but she could not be sure.

She rose and tiptoed back into the chamber, toward the ewer of water in the corner, darting glances at Paxton, half afraid he would waken and attack her again. She had used most of the water for bathing, but there was a little left. She took several mouthfuls, spitting them out to rinse the sour taste from her mouth, then took a long drink and returned to her position by the door.

It seemed like an hour before the dice players finally finished their game and staggered to their beds. Relieved and nervous at the same time, Laurien slipped out, holding her breath and clinging to the wall in the darkness. Barefoot, she picked her way down the stair.

One of the men muttered something and she froze, her throat going dry. He then snored loudly and rolled over. Swallowing hard, Laurien hurried down the rest of the stairs. She crept to the door, throwing one last look over her shoulder to assure herself that no one had awakened. She hastily put on her boots and went outside.

Inhaling sweet mouthfuls of the chilled, fresh air, she turned her face upward. The rain washed over her, helping to waken her from the drunken feeling that threatened to make her swoon. She longed for a thorough scrubbing to cleanse her from Paxton's touch, but that would have to wait.

The moonless night was impossibly dark. She might as well be blindfolded, Laurien thought in vexation as she squinted at the dark shape that should be the stable. Moving as quietly as possible, she started in that direction, the deep mud nearly pulling off her boots as she inched forward. Her own breathing sounded like a windstorm to her ears, louder even than the splatter of rain on the mud.

She stopped a few yards from the shelter. The man on guard held a small torch at his side, lending just enough light for him to keep his eye on Connor, who lay slumped in his corner, apparently asleep. Laurien felt a tug at her heart, angered at the thought of how the guards had treated him. At the same time, she feared what he might do to her once she untied him. She shook off her uneasiness and tried to think of some way to eliminate the guard.

The man had his back to her. Thinking quickly, Laurien crouched down and removed her cloak, ignoring the bite of the rain on her skin. She gathered up the cloth to fashion a makeshift sack, and placed as many rocks in it as she could find. She crept closer to the guard, approaching from behind him, taking one small, silent step, then another. Her eyes locked on his hunched form, she prayed he would not hear her over the sound of the rain.

When she was as close as she dared, she held her breath, squeezed her eyes shut, and hefted the sack. She brought it down hard on the man's head, and he toppled, groaning. Connor looked up with a start. Before Laurien could grab the guard's torch, it fell and sputtered out in the mud, leaving them in total darkness.

Swearing softly, she felt her way toward the corner.

"I am right here," Connor ground out just as her fingers brushed his shoulder.

Snatching her hand back, she knelt in the mud and tore at the ropes that bound him. She did not like the edge to his voice. "Where is Sir Malcolm?" she whispered.

"The granary." Connor did not utter another word to

her as she fumbled with the ropes. She kept silent as well, knowing she did not have time to explain everything now, and not wanting to unleash the anger she sensed had built to a dangerous level within him.

"You will never untie these by hand," Connor said impatiently. "Look along the wall. There is a shelf of tools."

Laurien felt her way to the shed wall, her hands moving upward until she touched a shelf. It held a jumble of metal that she guessed to be farrier's instruments. She gingerly picked up one with a sharp edge, and soon freed Connor.

As he rose, Laurien backed away a step, half afraid of him in his current humor. She could not see his expression. Silent, he grabbed her arm and pulled her out of the stable toward the wooden palisade.

"Did your Englishman tire of you so quickly that he set you free?" he snarled under his breath.

"I drugged him," Laurien replied indignantly. The churl had condemned her without waiting for an explanation! She tried unsuccessfully to jerk her arm from his grasp.

He gave her a low, sarcastic bark of a laugh. "And where are the guards?" he demanded.

"Asleep in the hall."

When they reached the gate in the palisade, he released her. "Wait here," he commanded. Without another word, without even inquiring as to whether the Englishman had harmed her, he strode back toward the outbuildings.

Laurien struggled to control the anger and hurt that coursed through her. Damn him, then, if he cared so little for her! Let him believe what he wanted to believe. Why should it matter to her? When he returned a few minutes later with Sir Malcolm and three horses in tow,

Laurien was trembling. She blamed it on the cold and the effects of the potion she had drunk.

Sir Malcolm wrapped her in a hug. "I feared for you, lass."

It was the first bit of comfort Laurien had known all day, and her initial surprise was replaced by a sudden rush of affection for the older man. "And I am glad to find you well, Sir Malcolm."

"You will have time for a reunion later," Connor snapped. "We had best leave before the guards awaken."

Laurien stubbornly avoided looking at Connor as he scooped her up and lifted her onto the bare back of the smallest horse. He and Malcolm mounted, and the three of them rode through the gate and down to the road as quietly as possible. Then they turned their mounts toward the north and set off at a gallop.

Clinging to her horse's rain-slick back, Laurien felt wave after wave of dizziness as they thundered along the muddy road. She cursed the wine again, and prayed she would not pass out and fall from her horse. Without her cloak, she was soon half frozen, the rain like icy needles on her neck and chest and hands.

They had ridden only a short while when they reached a fork in the road. Connor and Malcolm pulled up and began to debate what direction to take next. Laurien stopped her horse beside them, less concerned about their plans than about the way the night-cloaked landscape had not stopped moving when her horse stopped. Indeed, she noted with a wave of nausea, it had taken on a most disturbing spinning motion . . .

"Why not follow our original strategy and part company?" Connor was saying.

"Aye, 'twould be best not to bring the lass into Kincardine until we know 'tis safe," Malcolm said. "Make

your way to the hiding place, then, and stay there until
I return with word from William."

With a nod to Laurien, Malcolm turned his horse toward the left fork and set off at a gallop.

Laurien did not watch him go, for she was leaning
over her horse's neck, feeling faint.

"What is it now?" Connor rode over and reached out
for her, his voice harsh.

"Let me alone," Laurien snapped, jerking her head
up to glare at him. Unfortunately, the sudden movement
increased her dizziness tenfold, and she proceeded to
slide off her horse and into the mud.

Before she could rise, Connor was off his mount and
jerking her to her feet.

Laurien started to pull away, incensed that he could
think so ill of her and treat her so roughly when she had
just saved his life again. But when she felt his touch, his
hands warm upon her rain-chilled skin, she did not want
to fight with him any longer. She was frightened and
cold and wet and miserable, and the need to be comforted overwhelmed all her other emotions. She held on
to Connor's arms and leaned against him. "I was so
afraid—"

"Dinna claim you were afraid for me," he snarled,
pushing her away. "Your lies willna work any longer.
You proved exactly what you are when you threw yourself into the Englishman's bed."

Laurien's cheeks burned at the insult, and her temper
quickly dispatched her need for comfort. Shaking, she
glared at him through the rain. "You coldhearted, thickheaded fool! I should have left you to rot. How dare you
condemn me without giving me a chance to explain—"

"Explain what?" His voice was laced with sarcasm.
"That he raped you? I heard no screams of protest. I
saw no struggle to escape him."

He grabbed her shoulders. Before she could object,

he pulled her into his arms. There was no gentleness in this embrace, no sweetness. " 'Please, milord,' " he mimicked, " 'could we not go back inside now?' "

Then his voice changed, shaking with the force of his anger. " 'Please me well and I will not return you to de Villiers.' That is what you hoped for, is it not? It didna work on me, so you thought to try it with him. You cunning wench."

"Stop it!" She pushed at his chest. His words hurt her more deeply than the blows she had received at Paxton's hands. "You do not understand—"

"Oh, I understand you *very* well." He ran his hand up the slit in her skirt, his fingers roaming over her bare thigh. "This gown suits you. 'Tis perfect for a woman who could tumble so easily from my bed to another's. I hate to take an Englishman's leavings, but I can make an exception."

Before she could say a word in her defense, he wound his fingers in her wet hair, forcing her head back. His lips came down on hers in a bruising kiss, utterly devoid of warmth. Gone was the care, the tenderness he had shown her before. She whimpered under the brutal power of his touch, and he only crushed her harder against him. He seemed determined to consume her, to meld her body with his in an unbreakable joining. He forced her lips apart, his tongue plundering her mouth. At last he groaned deep in his throat, broke the kiss, and shoved Laurien away.

She stumbled backward, trembling uncontrollably, shocked by a cruelty she hadn't believed him capable of. Then the tears came, choking, hot tears that left her shuddering. She covered her face with her hands, breathing in great sobs. The tension of her near-rape and her fear for Connor had taken their toll, but this unexpected brutality finally broke her courage.

She jerked away when Connor reached out to touch

her. "Damn you." She sobbed, unable to look at him. "Do not touch me! You would not believe the truth if I told you."

"The truth?" he sneered. "That you drugged him—"

"Aye!" she yelled at him, her voice going hoarse. "I pretended interest in him so I could get him alone, and find out where you were, and then I drugged him. He almost strangled me, not that that matters to you. I could have taken a horse and left you behind, but I did not. Burn you, that is the truth, and I do not care a . . . a pig's back end if you believe me or not!"

Connor did not respond. Laurien stood shaking, struggling with a tumult of emotions that included anger and hurt—and more than a little hope that he would believe her and sweep her into his arms, and soothe her.

But he remained silent, and she could not read his expression in the darkness. Her heart pounded, and she could feel the numbing wine still coursing through her veins. She must steel herself against the drink's power. She was not going to allow Sir Connor of Glenshiel the satisfaction of having her faint neatly into his arms like the fickle wench he believed her to be.

When he spoke at last, his voice was soft and sharp beneath the rhythm of the rain. "That is mayhap the most inventive tale I have yet heard from you."

Furious, Laurien threw herself at him, her hand raised to slap him. Suddenly the ground and sky traded places, tilting crazily before her eyes, and she fell forward.

The last thing she felt before darkness closed about her was the steely strength of Connor's arms catching her.

Chapter 14

The hiding place lay a few hours' ride north of the border. It was little more than a tiny chamber, hidden behind the ruin of a church, carved out of the rocky side of a large hill. After sheltering the horses in a corner of the ruin, Connor carried Laurien inside.

Before leaving for France, he and Malcolm had stocked the hidden chamber with food and blankets. They knew that one of them would have to ride on to the village of Kincardine, the rebels' secret headquarters, to ensure that all was well before bringing the girl in.

He laid her before the hearth, gently removed her ragged gown, and covered her in warm furs. He peeled off his own sodden garments and started a fire, then toweled himself dry with a woolen blanket.

Rain kept up a steady patter, accompanied by the occasional sound of thunder advancing like a charging army and retreating before the wind. With a blanket wrapped about his waist, he stoked the flames and settled back against the hearth. He pillowed Laurien's head in his lap. In truth, he was glad he had a chance to think before facing Laurien's ire. For he knew that he deserved that ire for his treatment of her.

He had felt naught but rage from the moment he saw her clinging to the Englishman, returning his passionate kiss. The sight of his woman in the arms of another . . .

His? Aye, he admitted to himself. He had started to think of her as his. And 'twas not just possessiveness; he had felt that before. This feeling was something new.

Only when she had broken down in tears had a bit of sense squeezed through his anger: Laurien would no sooner give herself to one such as Paxton than she would to de Villiers. Seeing her now in the light, seeing the bruises on her cheek and neck, further convinced him that she must have been telling the truth—and made him feel like the veriest knave. God's teeth, she could have been killed.

Connor looked down at her with concern, then smiled, a grin that was half admiration of her courage, half dismay that she would take such a risk. The ruse with the drugged wine had all Laurien's marks—it was both clever and reckless.

And 'twas not the first time she had risked herself to save him. She had tended him at Gaston's, and stood by him in the melee in Calais. Each time, she might have gained her freedom, the one thing she wanted most in the world. But she had sacrificed that to help another.

To help him.

He brushed her damp hair from her forehead, aware of a new feeling for her, an almost childlike wonder. Sacrifice was not something he had thought a woman capable of.

And instead of showing appreciation, he had only mistreated her. He had stubbornly refused to see the strength and character that lay beneath her beauty and her fire. Believing her as shallow and haughty as other women made his mission less complicated, made it easier for him to think of her as naught more than a playing piece in their game.

But Connor realized now that his determination to feel nothing for Laurien was useless. She buffeted him like a storm, bringing out emotions he had believed—

hoped—long since hidden. The more he resisted his attraction for her, the more easily she seemed to wield her mysterious power over him: the more he struggled to gain control, the more control she seemed to win. Even when she was far from him, she was never far from his thoughts.

And when she was beside him, as she was now, his every sense came alive. He felt not just a physical awareness, but a feeling of completion, of rightness that she be with him. It made him feel vulnerable, and that was not a feeling he liked.

Even worse, he was beginning to hate the idea of returning her to de Villiers.

Connor sighed in frustration. In the years he had lived alone, he had met many women who could elicit a physical response from him, but none able to wring emotions from him like this. Whether he liked it or not, he was caught in an impossible predicament, trapped between duty and desire—with a beautiful, determined woman who had no intention of making things any easier for him.

Trying to sort out what he was going to do about it, he gradually drifted to sleep.

The first thing Laurien became aware of as she floated upward out of slumber was that she felt warm and dry. The second was that she was completely naked.

She opened her eyes to find herself wrapped in furs, her head in Connor's lap. She jerked upright, clutching the fur covering to her chin.

Connor awakened instantly, and she pulled away from him, noticing with an uncomfortable skip of her heart that he wore naught but a blanket draped about his waist.

"Where are we?" Laurien scooted around so as not to provide him with an excellent view of her bare back. She looked about her in confusion.

They were in a small chamber, nay, more like a cave, with rough stone walls, a dirt floor, and not a stick of furnishings. She could hear rain falling, the crack of lightning and thunder competing with the crackle of flames in the fireplace. She remembered arguing with him in the rain, then feeling dizzy . . . She looked at Connor, who gazed at her with an unreadable expression. "What is this place?" she asked. "What happened?"

"You fainted." The confusion and fear in her eyes reminded Connor of the night they had spent on the ship, and he felt anew the urge to touch her, to comfort her. He fought it, determined not to give in to the emotions that threatened his mission. "How do you feel?"

Laurien realized that the room was not spinning and her head felt quite clear. She also felt uneasy with Connor so close, the muscles of his arms and the flat planes of his chest etched into sharp angles by the firelight. The flames' glow burnished his skin to the color of amber.

"Well enough," she said finally. Except, she added to herself, for the too-familiar tickling feeling that began in her stomach. She glanced about her again, looking at the chamber's only door and gauging the distance.

She remembered feeling furious with Connor, but it took a moment to remember the reasons. She forced her gaze back to his face. He did not appear cold, demanding, or intoxicated with rage any longer. But neither did he seem teasing or particularly friendly.

Having exhausted the list of masculine moods she was familiar with, Laurien grew more nervous. She could not measure his current humor, but he had a very odd look in his eyes. "Are you not going to tell me where we are?" she tried again.

"A safe place, in Scotland," he replied with a dismissing gesture. "Laurien, I have had time to think. I have decided you were telling the truth."

Laurien scowled at his lofty tone. "How very nice for you." She tried to wriggle away from him, but found it impossible to move and hold the unwieldy fur about her at the same time.

Connor moved closer as she edged back. He wanted to heal the pain he had caused her, not make her more angry. He wished, and not for the first time of late, that he had more skill with words. "I should have known you would not give yourself to such a man," he persisted. "But when I saw you with him—"

"You showed me quite clearly how you felt." Laurien raised her chin. "There is no need to explain." That must be the look in his eyes, she decided; he could not trust her and he hated her for it. It was quite simple. Yet she was not at all relieved to have made the discovery.

"I regret what happened between us. What I said to you," Connor said in a rush, aware that his voice was too loud, the words sounding more like a reprimand than an apology. But he was unaccustomed to regret, and even less used to voicing his feelings to a woman. He hesitated, then continued in a softer tone. "Did the Englishman . . . Did he hurt you?"

"He did not rape me, if that is what you mean," Laurien spat. She heard what might be taken for concern in Connor's voice, and determined not to let it play upon her feelings. "I suffered no more at his hands than I have at the hands of *other* men."

Yet even as Laurien rebuked him, her gaze was drawn to the bruises on Connor's cheek, the cut beneath the tangle of blond hair on his forehead. She felt an odd little tug at her heart, felt a need to soothe his hurt. But at the same time, the marks reminded her that this was a man used to violence. He was a warrior, swift to anger, slow to forgive, comfortable with the hard edges of life. A man who sought relentlessly to control her. A man she dare not trust.

"I wish I could take back what I did, the way I have . . . treated you," Connor said after a long pause, "but I canna."

He wanted to say more, to reassure her that she was safe with him, to tell her that he was drawn to her like a falcon riding a warm wind toward the sun. But he held back, more willing to face, unarmed, a hundred enemies than risk saying such words.

After nine years of exerting iron control over his emotions, he was not able to speak openly; he wasn't sure he ever would be. But even as he struggled to keep himself silent, he felt an overpowering desire to touch her. She was so unlike any woman he had ever known, selfless and strong and honorable. He wanted to hold her, to treasure her, to show her what he could never tell her. That need he could quell no longer.

Laurien flinched as he raised his hand to her cheek, her every muscle tensing. She remembered too well the brutality that had flared in him the last time he took her in his arms.

Connor swore softly but did not drop his hand. His fingers traced lightly along her jaw, down her neck, coming to rest with the lightest feather touch at the base of her throat. Laurien held her breath, trying to ignore her heart's wild beating.

Connor could feel the reckless pace of her pulse beneath his fingers. "I have made you afraid of me," he said with remorse.

Laurien swallowed hard and clutched the fur to her as if it were a shield—against him, against the hurt men had always portioned out of her.

"Nay." She laughed, but it sounded forced and nervous even to her ears. "I have met with more than enough male tyranny in my life. The past sennight has been no different."

"And I?" He raised his hands to her cheeks, holding

her still so she could not avert her eyes. "Can you tell me in truth I have been no different?"

Laurien closed her eyes to shut out his piercing gaze, concentrating very hard on simply drawing a breath. She was desperately aware of the strength in Connor's hands . . . and the gentleness. He cupped her face with exquisite care, as if afraid she might break. His tender touch filled her with a sweet ache, a longing to let go of the defenses that kept her safe.

Aye, aye, you are different. You can be harsh beyond bearing, yet at times you are gentle beyond measure, and you make me burn with a fire I cannot begin to understand . . . And if ever I allowed myself to dream of tomorrows as other maidens are wont to dream, I might well wish for one such as you.

But when Laurien opened her eyes, she glared at him, angry at herself for foolishly wanting what was beyond wanting. She was not a woman given to girlish dreams. She had learned long ago that such dreams were futile, because men were not capable of love. Even more she was angry at Connor for bringing her so close to admitting all to him. How dare he demand to know her feelings when he kept his own so carefully concealed.

She took a deep breath and told him only half the truth.

"I find you harsh beyond bearing, Scotsman. You order me about. You care naught for my wishes, and when I displease you, you abuse me at your will." Still, it took a lifetime's practice at lying to grate out the next words. "Nay, you are no different than other men."

Connor wrapped his fingers in her tangled hair, pulling her closer. He felt foolish for thinking she could have aught but hatred for him in her heart. Yet he was hurt by her words, and angry at himself for being hurt. "You grant no forgiveness?"

"What would you expect?" she said. "Would you have me forget all in a trice?"

He released her as if she burned his hands. "Nay, forget nothing. Forgive nothing. Hate me, if hating me will please you," he said harshly. "God's teeth, I wish I had never laid eyes upon you, woman."

Laurien laughed derisively. "I did not ask to be abducted, Scotsman."

"And I didna wish to make you part of this!" He stood and stalked away from her.

Surprised at that, Laurien could find no reply. She watched in silence as he leaned against the hearth, hanging his head. Despite herself, she stared, bewitched, at the muscles rippling across his back and shoulders. The blanket that covered him had loosened when he stood, and slipped low about his hips.

When he continued, she had to strain to hear him above the hiss of the fire. "Can you not understand? We tried every possible means to gain our alliance. Mayhap this isna the best way, but 'tis the only—"

"Are you trying to apologize for involving me in this plan of yours, Scotsman?" Laurien mocked him softly. "Lying ill becomes you. In your eyes I have never been more than booty to be bartered."

He did not reply.

The silence stretched out, taut with unspoken words.

At last Connor started to speak, but Laurien leaped in first, part of her not wanting to hear what he might say. "And you dare to call women deceitful. You taunt me with some scrap of kindness now, but you will turn on me the next instant. You care naught for any but yourself. Your only interest is your own skin—"

"God's teeth, this isna about my skin." He kept his back to her. " 'Tis not about coin. 'Tis not about land. Nor is it about you, or de Villiers, or Scotland or England. It is about freedom. For my people. Can you not understand that?''

''Nay,'' she shot back. ''Freedom and I are ill acquainted—''

''And this quest is the one honorable thing I have found to believe in—''

''Honor, then. Your sense of male pride. Women mean less than naught to you. And I do not matter to you at all—''

''Aye.'' He turned to her at last, his hands clenched into fists. ''Saints' blood, you do matter to me.''

A score of sarcastic retorts came to Laurien's mind, but she couldn't squeeze out a one. She could only sit, staring up at him in wide-eyed silence, the fur blanket still clutched against her naked form. In her heart, she knew just how much it had cost him to say that to her. Had she not longed to hear him admit some feeling for her?

His words hung in the air, beckoning, unanswered. Dare she believe them real? Had he not told her before that he knew how to get what he wanted of a woman?

''You are well skilled in telling a woman what you believe she wants to hear, so she will cooperate. What bargain is it you wish to strike, Scotsman? What is it you want of me?''

Connor crossed the chamber in two strides and grabbed her by the shoulders. ''Damn you, woman, I have been trying to apologize. What is it you want of *me?*''

His fingers bit into her arms as he pulled her to her feet. The fur slid down her body until it fell to a pool on the floor.

Laurien was vibrantly aware of the heat of his body. His skin, warmed by the fire, near scalded her everywhere he touched. She looked into his eyes, trying to feel hatred for him, trying to be as defiant as she had been that day in Chartres when a blond pilgrim swept her from her horse. She failed miserably. Somewhere between the forests of Chartres and a tiny Scottish cave, she had come to care for him.

When she finally managed a reply, it sounded less like a cry of defiance than a plea of surrender.

"My freedom."

Connor crushed her to his chest, a small sound escaping him that was half pain, half frustration. He had revealed more to this woman than to any other in years. And she, who was so adept with words, refused him any sweetness in return. He had bared a piece of his heart, however small, and now it lay unrequited and vulnerable. He felt ill at ease, angry with her and afraid of his anger, tortured by the alluring softness of her naked skin against his. He forced himself to release her.

"You ask the one thing I canna grant you," he growled.

The image of Connor wavered, and Laurien realized her eyes were brimming with tears she could not explain. "And y-you have only devised more honeyed words meant to bend my will to your plan."

He reached out for her again, but before he could catch her arm, Laurien jerked away. Her every instinct urged her to run from him, from the emotions that threatened to strip her of all reason. She sprinted for the door.

She barely touched the latch before he was there, behind her, one arm on either side of her so that she was surrounded by him. He leaned his full weight against the portal, then lifted one hand and placed it lightly on the nape of her neck.

"Nay, Laurien, dinna run from me." His voice was hoarse. "Stay . . . please."

Laurien felt a warmth melt through her. She knew that "please" was not a word that often found its way to Connor's lips. He bent to rest his cheek against hers, but made no other move. His every muscle was rigid, nearly trembling with the force of some inner battle. Laurien felt trapped, not by his strength, but by the sensations that spiraled through her body.

The scratchiness of his beard sent pleasant little chills down her spine. The soft mat of hair on his chest tickled the bare skin of her shoulders. She stared at the door, trying very hard to concentrate on the solid wood before her rather than the solid muscle at her back. Without looking, she knew that Connor's blanket had fallen away when he gave chase, and he was now as naked as she.

Laurien shivered, fighting a powerful urge to simply lean back and let Connor's arms close about her. The clean scent of rain clung to his skin, and when he spoke, his voice was a trembling whisper, warm and moist against her neck. "You have every right to hate me for what I have done—"

"Nay," she said softly, failing utterly to cling to her anger and bitterness. "You set out upon this plan to win your freedom, the right to make your own choices, to decide your own destiny." She closed her eyes, feeling the last of her defenses tumbling one by one. "You want the same things as I. How can I hate you for that? But in order for your people to have their freedom I must lose mine."

At the defeat in her voice, Connor felt as if a knife's blade had found his heart. He slid his hand over her shoulder and down her arm, intertwining his fingers with hers. "Laurien, if there were any way to grant you what you wish—"

"Nay, do not speak of what we both know is impossible." She gave in to herself at last and leaned back against him. "I will not think of it, not this night."

His free arm slipped about her waist, and he held her tightly, breathing in the fresh night scents that clung to her hair and skin. He started to speak again, but Laurien turned in his arms and placed a finger on his lips. "Nay, say no more to me, Scotsman," she pleaded softly. "If only for this short time, let us pretend that destiny is ours to decide."

Her eyes slipped closed and he kissed her, melding her body with his in an embrace that bespoke all the restlessness and wanting and desire that burned in him. He deepened the kiss, finding a passion in Laurien that echoed his own. Her tongue darted between her lips to meet his.

When Connor broke the kiss at last, Laurien opened her eyes, sensing his uncertainty. She teased him, running her fingers over his back, arousing him with brief, wet kisses along his chin, his neck, down his shoulder, and into the broad expanse of his chest. He groaned when she gave him a playful nip, and she suddenly found herself lifted in his arms and carried back to the fire.

Connor eased her down to the furs. He felt light-headed, enchanted by the spell of the beauty in his arms, overpowered by his need for her. The storm roaring in the darkness beyond their sanctuary could not match the storm of emotions set free in the tiny chamber. Laurien looked up at him and pulled him closer, her gaze full of sultry challenge.

He began a hungry exploration of her body, first tasting the light sheen of perspiration along her throat, finer than the choicest wine. His mouth, seeking, eager, moved to her breasts, arousing each in turn until they were swollen and tight beneath his lips. Then his tongue swept along the pale, sensitive line of her jaw and settled at her earlobe, where he nuzzled and licked. He whispered, "I want to be inside you."

He took her hand, pressing it against his chest, sliding it over his ribs, then lower, urging her to touch the part of him that was now pulsing with need. "Feel how much I want to be inside you."

Laurien gasped and quivered beneath him, but did not try to pull away. When he released her hand, she began to explore him intimately. He kept his cheek pressed against hers, savoring the silk of her hair, the feminine scent that was uniquely Laurien, the unspeakably sensual feeling of her fingers hesitantly caressing his shaft. She grasped him more tightly and he sucked in a ragged breath, his whole body suddenly taut as a bowstring.

"Yes," he growled. "Hold me." He shifted his weight, thrusting against her hand, the swollen tip of his manhood brushing her thigh. Her free hand moved in tantalizing patterns across his back, her nails tracing his muscles until he thought he would lose his mind. He kissed her again, a rough, urgent coupling this time.

Her fingers brushed along the length of his hardness, bolder now. He caught her hand, knowing he could not last much longer, urging her to release him. She objected at first, and mercilessly lingered to play a moment longer, then finally let go. He touched the soft cleft between her legs. She moaned against his mouth, a deeply feminine sound of longing.

Her breathing came fast and harsh and he tore his lips from hers, wanting to drink in her expression as he stroked her. His thumb flicked against her swollen nubbin of desire, slowly and deliberately, then faster. Her eyes locked with his, the green depths sparkling with passion. She arched her hips, pressing against his hand, biting her bruised lower lip. Her velvety, sensual moans and sharp gasps filled the chamber as his fingers swirled and teased.

Laurien could feel Connor's muscles growing rigid with desire as her own body softened in welcome. The tender, intent expression on his face as he looked down at her touched her more deeply than any words he could speak. At last she could see beyond his mask of determined self-control, catch the barest glimpse of all the love locked away deep within him. She reveled in the branding fire of his kisses, the way passion darkened his eyes to a shade deeper than indigo. She moved her hands along his back, and he wrapped his arms around her, pulling her closer until her breasts were crushed against the bristly hair of his chest. Holding her tight, he thrust deeply inside her.

He threw his head back, squeezing his eyes shut, his mouth opening on a wordless sound of pleasure. The strong column of his neck arched away from her, and she reached up to touch his throat. She could feel his pulse hot and pounding beneath her fingertips, his damp, smooth skin an alluring contrast to the curving muscles beneath. She tangled her fingers in his hair and pulled him down to her. Her mouth opened to accept his tongue even before their lips met. They moved together, rising and falling, sharing one breath, one body.

She felt light, tingling, as if she were soaring with him, two birds on a single wind. He took her higher and higher, the sensations building within her body until she was breathless, wild with excitement, giddy with pure joy. Then he swept her higher still, gliding and diving with her as they strained to break free of the earth and fly beyond the storm toward the heat of the sun. Her hips rose to meet his, and he thrust faster, plunging into her. She cried out at the wondrous feeling of his body, so strong, so powerful, embedded deep within hers.

Tension cascaded from her passion-bruised lips to the sensitive skin of her breasts to the pulsating point where her body and Connor's joined as one. Each exquisite tremor deep inside was stronger than the last. Pure, shimmering sensation swept them upward until they could go no higher. She felt dazed, lightheaded, as if she were looking down on the world from a dizzying height, far above the clouds. Laurien could feel her muscles tightening, tensing, and she held on to Connor, feathering little kisses over his shoulder.

They reached the peak together, hovered there for an exquisite instant, then plunged toward the earth on wings of pure ecstasy. Connor shouted her name, pressing his head against her neck and shoulder. His entire body shook with the force of his release. Laurien threaded her fingers through his hair as his explosion kindled hers. Her head tipped back, and she gave herself over to the torrent of sensation that rushed through her body, his name a soft exclamation on her lips.

In that moment, Laurien found herself able to name the feeling that overwhelmed her, that tied her to Connor even when she could run away, the maddening combination of longing and hunger and tenderness. She loved Connor. Finally admitting it to herself was like opening a door deep within, setting free a host of new emotions to do battle with the mistrust she had felt toward men for so much of her life.

Her body and spirit had been at odds too long; at last they became one, and her heart surrendered up both gladly.

Chapter 15

Balafre's humor had worsened steadily since spending a day half-drowned at sea. The storm clouds drenched him with an unceasing downpour from the moment he stepped off the small fishing boat that had picked him up near the English coast. As he sloshed along the muddy northern roads on a stolen horse, his vengeful thoughts grew blacker. He planned in exquisite detail the retribution Paxton would suffer. The only question left was whether to kill his former partner quickly or slowly. Balafre had begun to favor the latter idea by the time he approached the tiny keep in Morpeth.

A scene of frantic activity greeted him. Paxton was shouting a stream of orders, his voice little more than a hoarse rasp. He had obviously spent the morning yelling. The guards stumbled and slid through the mire, carrying an array of weapons and supplies to their horses. They all came to a halt as Balafre rode through the gate.

All but Paxton. Occupied with saddling his horse, he was oblivious to the murmurs of surprise and fear, and continued snarling abuse at his men. "Be quick there, you lackwits! They have not had time to get far. We will . . ."

He glanced up and froze, the sentence trailing off as Balafre stopped his horse in the middle of the bailey.

"You will what?" the Frenchman queried softly. "How long ago did our captives escape, old friend?"

Paxton stood unmoving a long moment, then returned to his task, answering the question coolly. "I am pleased to find you are still alive, Balafre. We could make use of your assistance." He glanced at his men, his eyes sternly urging them to take some action, any action. They remained where they were, their gazes locked on Balafre.

"Where are our captives?"

"I am afraid you have just missed them." Paxton gave in to the nervous laugh that gurgled up inside him, and instantly regretted it. "But I will have them back anon. I am certain they are bound for the border. If you come inside, we shall eat before we leave—"

"And how did they manage to escape?" Balafre's voice had become as cold and sharp as a shard of ice. He still did not dismount.

Paxton shrugged, trying to think of a story that would not make him look a fool. "These lackwits who call themselves guards did not tie the Scots tightly enough. It is naught but a delay in our plans, be assured."

He had finished saddling his horse but did not move, keeping the animal between himself and Balafre. He gave his partner an impatient glare, trying to look as if he knew what he was about and wanted no argument. Balafre dismounted at last. Paxton breathed deeply in relief and turned to walk back to the keep.

He had not moved ten paces before he heard a click and spun around. Balafre was loading his crossbow.

"It will be a long ride," Paxton said in his silkiest voice. "There is no need to load your weapon just now." He looked again at the guards, only to see them edging toward their horses, ready to flee at any moment. He would find no assistance from that quarter; they looked like frightened pups come face to face with a wolf.

Balafre fitted a bolt to the stock.

Paxton crossed his arms over his chest and slipped his knife from its sleeve sheath to his palm. "Very well." He chuckled, trying to gain time as he edged into a position that would give him a clearer shot. "If it is an apology you want, I apologize."

Balafre raised the crossbow, and Paxton lost all trace of false humor. "Do not try to frighten me, *friend*. You dare not kill me. You need me. You would not begin to know how to conduct this search."

Balafre walked forward, still silent, the weapon balanced on his shoulder.

A little thrill of fear ran through the Englishman. "By Christ," he spat. "You surely do not mean to let my one impulsive act interfere with the task before us. After all the years we have spent so profitably together? Admit it, Balafre, when I found you in Languedoc you could not tell one end of a sword from the other without my assistance."

"I warned you once never to anger me," Balafre said simply. He took aim. "I do not like to repeat myself."

Paxton sent his knife flying at the instant Balafre fired.

The bolt hit Paxton in the shoulder, knocking him to the ground. He felt a blinding wave of pain, quickly followed by rage and an overwhelming relief that he found himself still breathing. Balafre would not miss at such short range; he had not aimed to kill.

"Blind you, you whoreson," Paxton yelled, heaving himself to his knees. Balafre still stood, apparently unharmed.

Paxton gazed up in surprise and alarm—for he *had* aimed to kill.

Balafre plucked the knife from his chest and pulled aside his fur cloak and tunic to reveal a leather hauberk beneath. The blade had made but a small wound that hardly bled.

"The sleeve sheath was one of your more clever ideas." Balafre twirled the small weapon between his fingers, smiling. "But you forget, old friend, that you have taught me all you know."

It was the first time Paxton had ever seen him smile.

"All right," Paxton ground out. "You have taken your revenge. Now help me get this blasted thing out of my shoulder, and we can get on with our search."

Balafre walked toward him, the crossbow slung over one shoulder. Paxton extended a hand in truce.

Instead of reaching down, Balafre loaded a second bolt.

"Sweet Christ!" Paxton struggled to get to his feet, but Balafre kicked him, sending him sprawling. The Englishman scrambled backward, but could find no purchase in the mire. The pain in his shoulder was forgotten in a cold rush of terror. Balafre kept walking toward him.

"I need you no longer, Englishman," Balafre said in the same casual tone he always used. He planted one booted foot on Paxton's chest to hold him still. "Your weakness for women has caused us trouble for the last time. You have become more bother than you are worth." He finished loading the bolt and aimed the weapon at Paxton's chest.

Paxton held up a hand, knowing and not caring that his voice revealed his fear and desperation. "Balafre, half my share—"

"The delay you have caused will make the comte furious," Balafre continued. "But I will clean up the mess you have made, as I always have. De Villiers will give me *all* of your share, old friend." He balanced the crossbow just over Paxton's heart. "You have never understood, have you? Once you accept a task, you must see it finished.'' He released the bolt.

It was only afterward that Balafre remembered he had planned to let Paxton die slowly. Frowning, he pulled both bolts free, cleaned them on the dead man's elegant tunic, and replaced them in his quiver.

He looked at the guards, who were still gathered by the horses. He itched to wreak his revenge upon them as well, but it would have to wait; for now, they were useful to him. ''Are there any here who would care to make another attempt on my life? Or question my orders . . . ever again?''

There was a hasty shaking of heads.

''Then stable my horse and find me some food. Be grateful you have nearly a full day to devise an explanation for your treachery. I sent a message to the comte, and when he arrives here on the morrow, I assure you that he will not be in a forgiving humor.''

Laurien awoke upon finding it difficult to draw a breath, so tight was Connor's arm about her. She opened her eyes and smiled. ''Hold me any more tightly and you will break me in two,'' she objected sleepily.

They lay curled side by side on their bed of furs, sharing one another's warmth against the chill of early morning. Connor relaxed his grip, brushing his lips against her hair in apology. He had been dreaming, an anguished vision of de Villiers carrying Laurien away, while he was powerless, unable to move, unable to stop de Villiers, unable to bring her back.

He opened one eye, just enough to banish the dream and reassure himself that she was indeed here beside him. Then he kissed her bare shoulder and began to drift off into a pleasant doze. He would have been content to hold her thus all day.

Laurien, however, had other ideas. "I am hungry." She yawned and stretched, rolling on her back.

Fully awake now, Connor gave her a mischievous grin. "I, too." He ducked underneath the blankets and began nibbling at her fingertips, making appreciative growling noises.

"I was thinking of food." Laurien giggled, enjoying his show of playfulness, as he nipped his way up her arm.

"Food?" he muttered, his voice muffled by the blankets. "Aye, we have food as well."

He reappeared, his hair tousled from his foray, and pinned her beneath him. Laurien giggled again as he looked down at her with a mock scowl.

"But 'twould require that we leave the bed," he explained earnestly.

Laurien reached up to trace the line of his jaw and ease the frown from his lips. He had made love to her last night until she was too exhausted to move, to speak, to think of aught but her love for him. Morning had chased away the darkness all too soon. She was as reluctant as he to break the spell he had woven around them.

" 'Twould also mean . . ." Connor paused to tease her finger, taking it into his mouth and sucking it gently before he continued. "That we must don our garments, lest we freeze."

Laurien was about to give in to the demand in his darkening eyes when her stomach rumbled most inconveniently.

"However," Connor sighed, "I suppose we must have sustenance if I am to keep up my"—he gave her a wicked grin—"energy."

He sat up and Laurien moved to join him, but he tossed the blankets over her head. "Nay, keep warm. I will see what I can find."

Laurien curled up while he moved to where their garments lay drying. He stoked the fire, then pulled on his leggings and tunic, returning her brazen smile and daring her to watch, which she did.

He foraged about through the supply sacks, then returned to spread out their meal on one of the blankets. Rising, Laurien reached for her gown.

"Nay." Connor stopped her, grasping her arm. He could not stand the thought of seeing her in that gown again, the gown the Englishman had given her. Not yet, at least. He smiled to soften his overly harsh command. "I prefer you this way."

Laurien could feel a blush rising in her cheeks. It felt odd to be so vulnerable to his gaze when he was fully clothed. As if sensing her distress, Connor sighed in chagrin and slipped his tunic over his head. Laurien smiled at his thoughtfulness and put it on, rolling up the sleeves.

He settled himself against the hearth. She moved to sit beside him, but quickly found herself pulled into his arms instead. He nestled her against his chest and rested his chin on the top of her head, wrapping one arm about her waist.

" 'Tis warmer this way," he whispered, pulling a blanket over them again. He handed her some smoked fish and small cakes.

"Take care you do not get crumbs in my hair," Laurien said, giggling nervously. But she found to her surprise that her feeling of awkwardness melted away after a moment; she relaxed against him, liking the way she fit so snugly in his arms, reassured by the gentle strength of his hard muscles. It was indeed a most pleasant way to spend breakfast. Smiling, she gingerly sampled one of the cakes.

"They are oat cakes," Connor explained. "A favorite among we Scots."

Laurien found it quite tasty, and surprisingly familiar. "I remember eating these before, when I was very young. My mother made them."

Connor heard the wistfulness in her voice. "Tell me about your mother," he said impulsively.

Laurien was caught by surprise, finding it odd that he would ask, and odder still that she wanted to tell him. "I remember so little of her. I was about six years of age when she died. She was very beautiful—she had long black hair, and the most radiant smile . . ."

"And you loved her very much," Connor said gently when her voice trailed off. "Were you sent to the convent because your mother died?"

"Nay, that was later. It was Louis's doing," she said bitterly.

"Louis?"

Laurien hesitated, not wanting to tell him of Louis's mistreatment and her search for her real father; she feared it would lead to a discussion of her reasons for wanting to escape—and she did not want to think of that, not now, not when she felt so very comfortable in Connor's arms.

"Louis is m-my father," she said softly. "He sent me to the convent because he said I was becoming like a wild creature, growing up without learning any of the maidenly virtues."

"You are yet wild." Connor kissed the nape of her neck. "The nuns failed in their duty."

Laurien's voice lowered to a whisper. "They did not like me any better than he did. They said I was . . . unnatural."

"You are not unnatural." Connor gave her a squeeze, sensing how unhappy she had been. Her relationship with her father must be distant indeed if she called him by name. "Did you not tell me before that they banished you because you couldna keep to their rule of silence?"

"Aye, that and the fire I started."

"The fire?"

"It was a very small fire," Laurien protested, pinching his knee when she felt a chuckle rumbling through his chest. "I was late for vespers and I knocked over a sconce, and a tapestry caught fire. If the mother superior had a whit of sense and would have allowed me to put it out, instead of flapping about—"

By this point Connor had dissolved into laughter.

Laurien turned in his arms. "Do not laugh at me!"

Connor grinned at her mutinous expression. "I amna laughing at you, I am laughing at those poor nuns. They had no idea what they were getting themselves into when they agreed to take you on. I can well imagine their vexation."

"I suppose I did rather turn their convent upside down." Laurien smiled despite herself and returned to her meal, settling back against his chest. "But what of you? I am certain you have ruffled several feathers in your time."

Connor's laughter faded. He felt suddenly cautious, unsure he was ready to share the events of his past, uncertain how to put such painful memories into words. "What would you like to know?"

Laurien burned with curiosity to find out about Sibylla. She was still deeply puzzled about this name that he had called out in his fever. But Malcolm had warned her never to mention the name to Connor, and the one time she had said it, his reaction had been violent. Not wanting to destroy the blissful peace that had descended on them, she decided on a safer question. "Tell me about your mother."

"My mother?" Connor queried softly, indulging in a genuinely happy smile. "She was a Viking princess. Yseult of Norway, but they called her Yseult the Fair."

"I should have guessed as much." Laurien ran her

fingers over his well-muscled arm. "You look very much a Viking prince. But I thought the Norse and the Scots were enemies."

"We were, for many years. She came with her family to one of the peace celebrations, after the defeat of King Hakon's fleet. My father always told us he was determined to wed her the moment he laid eyes upon her. Mother always insisted it was her idea."

Laurien noted, with a pang of envy, the fondness in his voice, and the word "us." He must have been very happy, to grow up with parents who loved each other. "Have you many brothers and sisters?"

"Had," Connor said tersely. "My older brother, Duncan, died some years ago. My younger brother, Galen, was killed in an English ambush."

Laurien felt regret at having touched a painful memory. She thought of her brother, Henri, and how she would feel if he died. "But your parents—"

"Gone as well," he said gruffly. "Before I was twenty."

Laurien felt his muscles tense, and knew he was increasingly uncomfortable discussing his family. She asked naught more, feeling a wave of sadness that almost brought tears to her eyes. For him to have known the joy of a happy family, only to lose them all . . . Sweet Mary, he was so alone, more solitary than she could even imagine being. She did not know how to express her sadness to him. He would not want to hear her say that she was sorry, would not accept sympathy, would reject pity.

Finally she lay her hand, gently, hesitantly, on top of his.

Connor intertwined his fingers with hers, feeling the tension ebb from his body. She understood. For now, 'twas enough, enough that she was here, that she shared his pain and lightened the grip it had upon his heart. He wanted to tell her more, much more, but it was so difficult to find the right words. There was too much to say, and too little time. He knew Malcolm would return by the morrow . . . and then they must leave for Kincardine.

And so he neither said nor asked anything more, but was content to hold Laurien in silence, clinging to the hours that remained. And when holding her was no longer enough, they made love, then fell into a sleepy tangle of arms and legs and napped away the afternoon.

As evening descended, Laurien awoke to find Connor perched above her, gazing into her eyes with an expression that made her feel weak. He kissed her thoroughly and nuzzled her neck. *"Bon soir,"* he whispered.

He moved his hips against her ever so gently, and Laurien realized exactly what had awakened her. "And good evening to you, sly Scotsman—" The rest of her words were lost in a gasp of pleasure as he entered her completely, finishing what he had begun while she was asleep.

"What better way to greet the night?" he asked, nibbling her ear and teasing the sensitive skin of her jaw with lingering, moist kisses.

Smiling in agreement, Laurien curled her fingers in his hair and pulled his head down to hers. "What better way, indeed," she whispered, just before their lips met in a searing kiss.

And even as he fought not to think of the coming morn, Connor knew a fierce determination. If there were any justice, he would find some way to fulfill his duty *and* keep Laurien from de Villiers. He would fight for her to his last breath.

But he also knew, from hard experience, that the world was as short on justice as it was on happiness.

Chapter 16

~~~~~~~

C onnor heard the clatter of horses approaching and
was waiting outside when Malcolm rode up leading
two extra mounts.

"Good morn to you," Malcolm called out, swinging
down from the saddle. "I am pleased to see that you
and our lovely maiden havena torn one another to pieces
like dog and cat." He grinned. "Or mayhap you have.
Where is she?"

His smile faded at the look on Connor's face. "I dinna
believe I want to hear this—"

"Good, then I willna tell you." Connor took a deep
breath. "I asked Laurien to wait inside while we talked.
Malcolm I canna send her back—"

"Saints' breath, 'tis my fault." Malcolm groaned. "I
should have known this would happen if I left you alone
with her too long."

"I have a plan," Connor interrupted before Malcolm
could complain further.

"But there is no hope for it. Connor, the news from
Kincardine is not good. The English have begun raiding.
Three of the border castles have been attacked since we
have been gone. And the English king has demanded
Balliol's answer within a sennight. We must return the
girl and settle the alliance by then, else 'twill mean
war."

Connor listened patiently, but set his jaw in determination. "I willna sacrifice Laurien. In all honor and fairness, we must consider what will happen to her—"

" 'Tis too late. We canna consider it now!" Malcolm said in exasperation. "Whatever has happened, put an end to it, lad, before you interfere with our mission any further."

"God's teeth! Have I no say in this?"

"And what if you *do* manage to keep her from de Villiers?" Malcolm shot back. "You know you canna take her to wife. Do you think to keep her as a mistress? She wouldna stay with you. And if you forced her, she would only come to hate you."

It was a question Connor had avoided thinking about. He could offer Laurien his home and his bed, but not his name. Would she choose of her own will to stay with him on those terms? Or would she leave? And how could he ever bear to allow her the choice? She had told him time and again how much she treasured her freedom. He knew too well what her answer would be.

"I will set her free," he said at last, with more conviction than he felt. " 'Tis what she wants."

His eyes full of doubt, Malcolm considered his young friend. Women had always floated in and out of Connor's life like so much dust, settling for a while only to be swept off before they could work their way into the grain. Connor was alternately charmed, fascinated, infatuated, and disgusted with them.

But this woman seemed to have affected him deeply. Malcolm gave Connor a sly look. "You realize that Ceanna is in Kincardine."

"And what of it?" Connor replied, puzzled at the sudden change of subject. "I told her before I left, 'tis over between us."

"She seemed most eager to see you."

"And I dinna care if I see her or not. We were speaking of Laurien."

Malcolm sighed in exasperation. Never had he seen Connor so determined over a woman. The lad looked ready to stand rooted to this spot and defend the ruin and its contents against all comers.

"Do you think I dinna understand?" Malcolm said gently. "Do you think I dinna know what 'tis like, to long for a woman who can never be yours?"

Connor stared at the ground in silence. Aye, he knew Malcolm understood; Malcolm had fallen in love as a young man, only to have the girl die before they could marry. Connor knew that the years had not dulled his friend's pain, though Malcolm kept it well hidden.

"I willna send her back," Connor continued doggedly. "You can help me or you can oppose me, but I will carry out my plan."

"Stubborn, thickheaded—"

"Will you help me or nay?"

Malcolm sighed. Once Connor charted his course, there was no turning him. And though the lad would never admit as much, it was obvious his feelings for the girl ran much deeper than honor and fairness.

But some truths, Malcolm knew, 'twas best to let a man discover for himself.

And whatever his plan was, could it be any more foolishly desperate than kidnapping the girl in the first place?

"I am getting much too old for this." Malcolm shook his head, the beginnings of a smile tugging at his lips. "But I will listen to your plan."

Connor grinned and slapped his friend on the back in truce. " 'Tis quite simple . . ."

Laurien was growing impatient. She could see no reason not to get on with this. They were to leave for a town called Kincardine, she knew, somewhere to the north. What she did not know, what she wanted desperately to know, was what would happen once there. She hadn't been able to bring herself to ask the question.

Now that she was alone, and once again clad in the red velvet gown, the spell of tenderness had disappeared. The tiny chamber no longer felt safe and cozy, but cold and empty. The time had come to face the world, and she wasn't at all certain how her newly discovered love for Connor would bear up in the harsh light of day. But she held on to one thought: whatever lay ahead, they would face it together.

She could hear him talking to Sir Malcolm outside, and though she couldn't make out what was being said, she caught the occasional exclamation. Hearing a laugh, she decided to wait no longer. She stepped into the antechamber.

She froze upon hearing what Connor was saying.

" 'Tis best if I leave her in Kincardine," he said in a low, urgent tone. "She must suspect nothing."

"You will say not a word to the girl?" Sir Malcolm asked.

Connor chuckled. "She is stubborn, and reckless beyond reason. She would only insist on coming along, or find some way to follow me."

Their laughter knifed through her, and Laurien heard naught more but a stunned roar in her ears. *Leave her in Kincardine? Leave her!* After what they had shared in the past two days, he still planned to deliver her as he had been ordered—and discard her promptly.

She meant naught to him, no more than another conquest to laugh about with his friends. His only concern was that she would follow him! Laurien closed her eyes against the image of Connor laughing at her, mocking her for foolishly, innocently placing her trust and her heart in his hands. Nay, she could not bear that, nor would she grant him the enjoyment of her predicament.

She had already made one mistake too many by letting him into her heart. How could he do this to her?

The answer came from deep in her mind, out of countless years of pain and disappointment and mistreatment.

He was a man.

Smoothing her gown, she swallowed hard and raised her chin. She would not let him know that aught had changed. As she marched out to face Connor—*nay, her captor*—she set her mind to work. She would find some way to make good her own plan at last.

She was going to escape.

Connor turned, startled at Laurien's sudden appearance, then frowned as she strode toward them. Had she overheard? "I told you to wait inside."

Laurien forced a smile to her lips as she shrugged. "It sounded as if you were enjoying yourselves. I saw no reason not to join you. Greetings, Sir Malcolm." She nodded to the older man, then returned her gaze to Connor. She silently prayed that she had misjudged him, that he would have some explanation for his damning words. "I heard laughter. Tell me, what amusing subject were you discussing?"

Connor relaxed. She had not overheard. For her own safety, it was best. "News of Kincardine, naught of import," he said casually. As she walked toward him in the harsh morning light, clad in the ruined red velvet, wearing mud-caked boots, her hair in disarray, he thought she surpassed any dream of beauty.

He noted with chagrin that she had tried, unsuccessfully, to arrange her gown so that the tear would be less visible; the skirt's folds parted with her every step to reveal a teasing glimpse of her pale legs against the velvet. He swallowed hard. God's teeth, this was going to be torture. He wanted to take her in his arms, tell her all, and demand—nay, ask, he corrected himself—that she stay with him.

But until he had carried out his plan, until the alliance was won and she was free of de Villiers, that question would have to wait.

"We must be on our way," he said gruffly.

Laurien pierced him with a challenging stare but kept her tone light. "And what will happen once we arrive at our destination?"

Connor hesitated, then flashed her a grin and moved toward the shelter. "Most likely we will dismount from our horses. Then we will enjoy a hot meal and a good night's rest."

Laurien barely managed to keep from striking him as he walked past her. His teasing, evasive answer told her he was hiding the truth. How dare he make a jest of it!

While they awaited him, Sir Malcolm explained what would happen in Kincardine. Laurien seethed quietly and nodded acquiescently at his words. They would stay at the castle of Sir William of Lanark, leader of the Scots rebels. She would be introduced to visitors as Sir William's ward, a distant relative, recently bereft of family. She would enjoy his hospitality until . . . Here Sir Malcolm stopped suddenly.

"Aye? Until?" Laurien prompted.

"Uh, until, 'tis time to return you to the comte," Malcolm finished quickly.

"Very well," Laurien said, fuming as he confirmed her suspicions. *Nay. Until I escape,* she added to herself.

Connor reappeared, carrying his cloak and one of the fur throws.

"Are we not taking any of the food?" Malcolm grumbled.

"The journey is short. But," Connor said slowly, looking at Laurien, "I do not wish to listen to you complain all the way to Kincardine, Malcolm. Why not see what you can find?" He waved toward the shelter. Malcolm shot him an irritated glance, but went inside.

Laurien held Connor's gaze without blinking, and congratulated herself. She was carrying off an excellent imitation of a calm, unemotional woman. That was, until Connor led one of the horses over.

His hands closed about her waist, his touch so warm, so powerful, so sure that, despite herself, she trembled. Yet he did not lift her into the saddle. She looked up—a mistake, she realized too late.

His gaze was as soft as his hold on her was strong. His blue eyes sparkled with that odd, tender look she had seen so often the past two days. It made her shiver. Saints' breath, how she wanted to kiss him—nay, what was she thinking? Not kiss him—strangle him. That was what she had meant. She must not be taken in by a look as false as his words. She must not trust—

All hope of coherent thought fled as he kissed her. His mouth captured hers softly at first, then his kiss became hot, dangerous in its demand. Laurien found herself giving in without hesitation, spiraling downward with him into a sea of fire. Then the next instant she felt the cold breeze upon her moist lips, and Connor was lifting her into the saddle.

She blinked, half dazed by the sudden torrent of desire that had risen between them. He placed the robe over her.

"You will need this," he explained softly, tucking the fur about her legs, "lest you catch your death of cold."

Laurien looked down at him, at the crooked grin that made her heart skip a beat. She tried to catch her breath. She could not mistake the feelings that coursed through her so swiftly at his touch, the longing that made her tremble. Despite his betrayal, Sweet Mary help her, she still loved him.

Connor took her hand in his. "All will be well, Laurien. You must trust me."

Laurien could only nod, her throat feeling too tight to choke out a single word. *Nay, never,* her mind cried, *never trust him again!*

Connor released her hand and moved away when Malcolm came out of the shelter. The men fastened the supplies to their saddles and mounted their horses. Then the three of them turned their backs to the rising sun and set off toward the west, and Kincardine.

Chapter 17

The castle was at the edge of the city. They clattered over the drawbridge and into the bailey, where a servant took their horses. Sir William's home looked much like a French castle, Laurien thought as another servant led them into the great hall. Woolens dyed bright shades of scarlet and azure adorned the walls, and she could smell sweet grass and herbs mixed in with the rushes on the floor. The only thing missing, oddly enough, was a hearth; a large metal fire basket in the center of the hall supplied warmth instead.

A tall man with red-brown hair, dressed in bright red and blue, greeted them. He grasped Connor by the forearm, nodded to Malcolm, then turned to Laurien.

Malcolm cleared his throat. "Lady Laurien d'Amboise, allow me to present Sir William of Lanark."

"Welcome to my home, milady. I hope you have had a pleasant journey." Sir William bowed over her hand. From the gray in his hair and the deep lines on his face, Laurien guessed him to be about two score and ten years. His green eyes sparkled as he straightened and smiled down at her.

"And I hope you will excuse us," he said, signaling to a serving girl, "but I have much to discuss with these men. We shall see you again at dinner. Jane will show you to your chamber."

Laurien turned questioning eyes to Connor; his look

told her to do as she was told and make no trouble. Swallowing her irritation, Laurien decided she would, for now. Doubtless she could glean more useful information from Jane than she could from Sir William anyway. She followed the girl out of the hall and up the spiral stairs.

Connor, watching Laurien, didn't even realize William and Malcolm were walking toward the door until they called his name.

"Where are you off to?" he asked in surprise. "I thought we were to discuss what happened in France."

"Malcolm already told me most of it, when he was here two days ago," William replied. "The rest we can discuss outside."

Connor frowned, catching the slightest hint of a smile on William's face and wondering at the reason for it. He followed his friends out the door and through the bailey. When they reached the practice ground at the rear of the castle, the sight that met his eyes brought a soft exclamation of surprise from him, quickly followed by a rush of anger at William.

A group of a half-dozen young pages were practicing their swordplay under the watchful eye of one of William's knights. In the center of the group, apparently doing quite well for himself, was Aidan.

Connor almost turned and walked back into the keep. "Will," he ground out. "I thought your pages and squires would be away at one of the autumn tourneys."

"Most of them are, but the training master thought these younger boys needed more practice before they were ready for a tournament." William shrugged. "Besides, I thought you might enjoy a chance to see Aidan."

"Damn it, you know how I feel about seeing him," Connor said tightly. "I entrusted Aidan to your care because I knew he would be happy with you. I am pleased that he is well cared for here, but I dinna . . . You canna ask me to spend time with him. You *know* why.''

"But he has done so well,'' Malcolm interjected. ''Watch him, Connor. See how well he wields that sword.''

Despite himself, Connor could not help but feel a wave of pride at the lad's obvious skill. Aidan was indeed accomplished for his age, fast and strong. He held his own against a larger boy, then defeated him with a brilliant feint and parry. Still, Connor's feelings of admiration were matched by an equally strong, wrenching pain. The boy's features were so much like his own—and so much like Duncan's. Just looking at Aidan brought up images of his brother and Sibylla in bed together.

Before he had time to shake that vision from his mind, William called the lad over. Aidan came running, still holding his little training sword, his cheeks ruddy from exertion. Though it was William who had called, he came to stand in front of Connor. Aidan bowed quite formally, but a smile lit his features, reaching all the way to his blue eyes. "Father.''

The word went straight to Connor's heart, faster and sharper than an arrow. He started to speak, but found he had to clear his throat before he could get any words past it. "Hello . . . son.''

"If you will excuse me,'' William said with a grin, "I must speak with the training master. Mayhap you would accompany me, Malcolm. I am sure the lads could benefit from your experience and opinions.''

Connor shot William a black look.

"Father, are you angry with someone?'' Aidan asked. "You scowl so.''

"Nay, lad.'' Malcolm chuckled as he and William

walked away. "Of late, your father normally looks that way."

Connor turned his scowl on Malcolm.

"Father," the boy began again. "When Sir Malcolm was here two days past, he said he would be leaving soon on a journey. May I accompany him?"

Connor felt a stab of annoyance that Malcolm had known Aidan was here and had said naught about it. He shook his head. "Nay. You canna go."

At the disappointment on the boy's face, Connor regretted his brusque words. He sighed in vexation. If the truth were told, he felt a great deal of regret—and guilt—where Aidan was concerned. Connor had always kept his distance from the boy, to avoid reliving the events of that horrible November night, but at what cost? He did not want Aidan growing up feeling abandoned and bitter.

Was it selfish to keep secret the affection he felt? Of late he had begun to think that, mayhap, he had been thoughtless and selfish about many things—and many feelings.

He crouched down so he was closer to Aidan instead of towering over him. His action brought a puzzled look to the lad's face. Connor smiled. "I am sorry, I didna mean to be abrupt. It is just not possible for you to accompany Malcolm. He is traveling a great distance."

"But Sir William has taught me to ride better than even his squires. And I can already shoot a crossbow."

"A crossbow? You have done very well," Connor said, allowing his pride to show in his voice. "But there might be danger on this journey."

The boy's eyes lit with anticipation. "Then Sir Malcolm will need all the assistance he can muster."

Connor sighed, feeling admiration at Aidan's courage. "Your offer is most generous." He paused, thinking. He had denied the boy too much over the years;

surely he could grant this one small request in some way. "Sir Malcolm *will* be going past Castle Galbraith. Mayhap he could enlist your aid for the first part of the journey. Then you could spend some time at Galbraith with Sir Thomas and his pages."

Aidan responded with an eager nod and a broad, crooked grin. On a sudden impulse, Connor reached out and ruffled the boy's hair. "Go then, and tell Sir William he must make do without his favorite page for a few days."

"Thank you, Father."

Connor watched him run across the yard. *Father.* The word still brought a twinge of pain and bitterness, but this time it also filled him with a sense of determination, and a feeling that was stronger and deeper than mere affection. Aidan was his nephew in truth, but his son in every way that mattered. He had been a thickheaded fool about that for too long. He thanked God that, judging from the boy's manner, 'twas not too late to make amends.

Laurien paced up and down in the small but richly decorated chamber, impatient for Jane to leave so she could set about planning her escape. So far, she had learned naught of use from the girl. Jane bustled about, lighting a fire in the hearth and seeing that a washtub and towels were brought up and placed before it.

"Your castle is most strange to my eyes," Laurien said, trying to sound only casually interested. "Is there but the one stair that leads to these chambers?"

"Nay, milady, not one but two. We have a second stair to the *bouteillerie*," the girl replied. "I would show you about, but since you are Sir William's ward, I am sure milord would prefer that honor."

"Of course," Laurien murmured.

"I will leave you to rest now," Jane said, drawing

back the blue velvet bedcovers. "Pray call for me this evening when you are ready for your bath. I shall bring some gowns for you to choose from. Until then, milady." She curtsied and left.

As soon as the door closed behind Jane, Laurien went to the window. After pushing aside the velvet curtains, she opened the shutters and gazed out upon a sheer drop to the courtyard below. That, she grimaced, would not do as an exit.

Looking to her right, she saw a scene that made her blink in surprise. A group of pages was practicing in the bailey—and off to one side, Connor was engaged in conversation with one of them, a small boy of about ten years. The lad had a shock of blond hair that he kept pushing from his eyes. He held the Scotsman's complete attention, and Laurien watched in disbelief as Connor crouched down, smiling, and ruffled the boy's hair. Such public affection made her wonder if the man was Connor after all. And who could this boy possibly be? A young kinsman?

She closed the shutters, telling herself she did not care. She had more important matters to attend to. She crossed to the door and looked out, glancing in both directions, then started down the hall, opposite the way she had come with Jane. Reaching the second staircase, she tiptoed down to the *bouteillerie*, the dank, musty chamber where wine was stored. The sounds and scents of baking told her the kitchens lay beyond. It would be almost too easy to slip out this way, she thought with satisfaction. All she need do was wait for the cover of night, when all were asleep.

She hurried back to her chamber, making sure no one saw her. Closing the portal behind her, she paced about, then threw herself on the bed. With her escape route planned, she had naught to occupy her for several hours, but Laurien felt not the least bit sleepy. Her mind whirled. Sir William had taken no precautions to prevent her leaving. And Connor would not be expecting her to attempt escape. Not after she had been so completely seduced.

Laurien punched her fist into the pillow. How sweet, how deeply satisfying it was going to be to slip away without a word. She would never have to put up with another of his barked commands. Never hear his laughter. Never behold that piercing blue gaze, by turns shining with merriment and dark with desire. Never feel the easy strength of his arms pulling her near . . .

Saints' breath, she must stop thinking of him in this way! How could she care for him still? How could she possibly be in love? This was not the feeling the troubadors sang of. This was misery, this was torment.

But try as she might, she could find little joy in thoughts of finally making good her escape. The idea of never seeing Connor again made her feel as if something deep inside were being torn in two. And perversely, the thought of seeing him tonight at dinner, if only for a short while, made her pulse quicken.

If this be love, she thought, scowling and punching the pillow again, she would certainly be much happier without it.

Chapter 18

S tanding at the top of the stair, Laurien smoothed the skirt of her emerald gown and took a deep breath, inhaling the scent of spiced meats and buttery-fresh bread. The evening's feast would be a challenge; she must take care not to arouse the least suspicion about her plan to escape. As she descended, she heard the musical sound of feminine laughter amid the louder hum of masculine conversation. At least fifty guests sat at tables arranged about the sides of the hall, while a dais at one end of the chamber held a large trestle table for the lord and his entourage. The warm light of dozens of torches and candles glittered on the guests' gems and finery. Sir William appeared at her side as soon as she reached the bottom step.

"You are truly the jewel among us this evening, Lady Laurien," he said, escorting her through the crowd toward the head table.

"You are too kind, milord," Laurien mumbled, only half hearing his compliment, unconsciously already searching the unfamiliar faces, looking for a tousled blond head.

She had lingered over her bath, and nearly driven Jane mad by choosing and discarding one offered gown after another. Laurien managed to convince herself that her uncharacteristic primping came from a desire to postpone the coming evening—not from any wish to look her best for anyone in particular.

She had finally decided upon the gown of emerald velvet. A matching girdle tied about her waist, embroidered with gold and studded with tiny pearls, the tasseled ends falling almost to the hem. Jane had plaited her hair, weaving in emerald ribbons and golden threads with expert fingers.

Sir William seated Laurien in the place of honor at his right, and she responded politely when introduced as his ward to the knights and ladies at table. Three trumpeters sounded as the first course was served.

"I am certain you will find our repast to your liking," Sir William said.

Laurien only half listened to the rest of the dinner conversation, having spotted Connor. He sat only a few yards away, his back to her, dressed in finery that had made her mistake him for a nobleman upon first glance. But in truth, she reminded herself, the knave *was* a nobleman, though she rarely thought of him as such.

This night, he looked every inch a lord in his tunic of the finest linen and surcoat of white silk. His garments, she fumed silently, were, like hers, of emerald-green.

Laurien barely sipped at her barley broth and only nibbled on the ribs of mutton placed before her for the second course. She found something most disturbing about Connor tonight, and it was not his clothing, but his company.

A slim-hipped blond woman, a few years older than herself, sidled—nay, swayed—over to Connor and placed a hand upon his shoulder. Connor did not look up, in fact registered no surprise at all at her action. He motioned for a servant to fetch a flask of wine.

The servant hadn't moved two steps when the woman outpaced him and brought the requested wine herself.

Taking Connor's chalice, she poured a draught and handed it to him, a sweet smile enhancing her lovely features. Laurien felt a sudden tightness in her throat. She had the distinct feeling the pair knew each other exceedingly well.

Laurien did not notice that her fists were tightly clenched until she felt the pain of her nails digging into her palms. She turned to Sir William, suddenly aware that he had been speaking to her.

"Lady Laurien," he repeated patiently, "would you like me to introduce you to her?"

Laurien took a substantial swallow of wine before replying. "To whom?" she asked, embarrassed that her interest was so obvious.

"The lady you have been watching." Sir William nodded to the blond woman. "Lady Ceanna."

"Nay, milord," she said quickly, then realized she sounded terribly rude. "I . . . would not wish for you to interrupt your meal."

"Are you unwell, milady? You look a bit pale."

"Nay, I-I merely have little appetite tonight, Sir William."

Little was an understatement. Laurien felt her insides churning as she watched Lady Ceanna help herself to a seat at Connor's side. The woman listened, her head cocked like that of a trained dog, while Connor conversed with a man across the table. Laurien couldn't help thinking that this Ceanna seemed everything she herself was not—petite, quiet, sweet-tempered, obedient.

Most likely, Lady Ceanna was merely another of the churl's conquests. Well, Laurien sniffed to herself, she was more than welcome to have him back.

Sir William cleared his throat.

Laurien turned to him again. "I apologize, milord. You were saying?"

He laughed and helped her to her feet. "I merely asked, milady, whether you had finished. The servants would like to clear our table."

"Oh. Aye, I have finished," she said, belatedly noticing that the third course of roast fowl in a cinnamon sauce sat untouched upon her trencher. Sir William led her from the dais.

" 'Twould seem your thoughts are occupied this evening. I had hoped for a chance to come to know you better." They moved to one side as the tables were cleared. A group of musicians, seated in a gallery above the kitchens, struck up a lively tune, and a trio of jugglers entered, performing as they moved among the guests.

"My thoughts, Sir William, are occupied with my future," Laurien said, the music preventing her voice from reaching those about them. "And as for coming to know me better, we both know I shall not be your guest for long."

Sir William sighed. "I understand you are not eager to return to France."

"I have accepted my fate," Laurien lied. "Your men have made it clear to me I have no choice in the matter. But I have yet to hear precisely what that fate shall be. Tell me," she asked smoothly, "what will happen on the morrow?"

He smiled. "I have been told you can be a most inquisitive young lady."

"Aye, I can be," she said indignantly, "when my own future is kept a secret from me. I only wish to know when I am to be returned to the comte."

He hesitated a moment, then relented. "As soon as we receive the alliance bearing King Philippe's seal, we shall arrange your passage back to France."

Laurien listened in silence as he confirmed what she had overheard. "And Sir Connor will deliver me?"

"Nay, Sir Connor is to return home on the morrow. His part in this is done. I shall escort you."

Laurien felt as if her heart were splintering into a hundred anguished pieces. Connor was discarding her. Indeed, judging from the way he was ignoring her tonight, he already had. "I see," she said numbly.

The jugglers completed their performance, and the musicians began to play a lively carole. Sir William squired her over to the circle of dancers that was forming. "I will do my utmost to make your stay enjoyable, milady," he said, his tone indicating that he considered the subject closed. "Now, mayhap you would favor me with a dance?"

Laurien said nothing more as he held her hands and led her through the skipping movements of the carole. She glanced at the other dancers as they circled the room, twirling to the high-pitched notes of pipes and lutes and the regular beat of a tabor. She did not see Connor and Lady Ceanna. Mayhap, she thought irritably, dancing did not number among the woman's talents.

As the carole ended, a new musician appeared in the gallery, holding an instrument Laurien had never before seen. It appeared to be a large sack attached to an array of pipes. When the player blew into it, the bag puffed up and emitted a sound that was more screech than music to Laurien's ears. She turned to Sir William, thinking to claim a headache and retire to her chamber. But before she could speak, Connor appeared from out of the crowd and took her hand.

"You have kept your ward to yourself all evening, Will. 'Tis certain she is weary of your company by now." He gave his friend a grin and bowed over Laurien's hand quite formally. "May I have the next dance, Lady Laurien?"

A score of tart replies leaped to Laurien's tongue. She found herself unable to choose between "You may burn in hell'' and ''What befell your blond mistress?'' In the same instant she thought, oddly, that it was one of the few times he had *asked* her for anything; and all the while she was trying to ignore that he looked more handsome than she had ever seen him, with his hair freshly cropped, his face clean-shaven, and the white silk of his surcoat stark against his tan skin.

She held his gaze and managed to refrain from jerking her hand away and telling him exactly what she thought of him. ''I have never been an able dancer,'' she protested. ''I am certain you could find a more skilled partner.''

But Connor was already sweeping her off into the circle. ''You will find me an able instructor.''

Laurien understood quite well from the husky note in his voice that he referred to more than dancing. She felt like slapping him. It was bad enough that the cold hearted churl had seduced and discarded her; now she was going to have to suffer his taunts as well.

He held her right hand in his left as they fell in line, following the other knights and ladies in the gliding steps of an Italian *basse danze*. Laurien felt the heat of his skin upon hers, though only their fingertips touched as they moved. He looked straight ahead, barely acknowledging her presence. Why had he asked her to dance? Merely to torment her? Could he not, at least, speak to her?

''I find your choice of gown interesting,'' he said with a smile, as if reading her thought. ''I canna find words to describe your beauty tonight.'' He spoke quietly, so quietly she could barely hear him.

What was she to make of his comments? It was not like Connor to offer praise freely—mayhap he had consumed too much wine with his meal. Was he truly offering a compliment, or mocking her? Laurien did not trust herself to speak, afraid she would decry him as the lying knave she knew him to be.

When he spoke again, his voice was a notch above a whisper. "I believe I am going to kiss you."

The music ended a moment later, and a startled Laurien found herself maneuvered to the far end of the hall. Holding fast to her hand, Connor slipped away from the crowd and pulled her into the shadows at the foot of the spiral stair.

"Connor, nay. Wait a moment . . ." Laurien tensed, trying to think very quickly whether it would seem more suspicious if she allowed his kiss, or spurned him. Before she could make up her mind, she was closing her eyes and tilting her head up. His lips lowered to hers . . .

"There you are, my love!" Ceanna's voice shattered her dreamlike state. "I willna let you disappear from me once again."

Laurien's pounding heart stilled upon hearing the words "my love." She found herself suddenly released as Connor turned toward Ceanna. Anger pulsing through her veins, Laurien spun away and fled back into the crowd.

"Ceanna!" Connor rounded on the blond, torn between giving Ceanna the thrashing she so soundly deserved and starting after Laurien, who was scurrying to the far end of the hall.

"I have news of import I need tell you."

"I have already heard too much from you, Ceanna. I told you two months past, 'tis finished between us. How much more plainly need I put it?" He started after Laurien.

" 'Tis about this ward of William's," Ceanna called after him, deciding that mayhap a small helping of the truth, in this instance at least, would get her what she wanted.

She was rewarded when Connor turned back toward her.

"There were some men in the market square today," she continued quickly. "They were asking questions about a girl recently arrived from France—"

"And why did you wait until now to tell me of this?" Connor demanded, advancing toward her.

Pleased that she now had his full attention, Ceanna lowered her eyelashes. "I thought you were no longer interested in what I had to say, milord. After all, you didna come to find me when you arrived today. And you spoke mayhap three words to me at dinner."

"*Who* was asking questions?" Connor growled, not about to be dragged into one of Ceanna's games. "What did they look like?"

"Connor." She placed a hand on his chest. She was not about to answer any questions that did not pertain directly to her. At least, not yet. "You left no word when you went away. You disappeared for a fortnight, and tonight you reappeared with this—" she cast a frown in Laurien's direction—"this ward of William's. He never said aught to *me* of any relatives in France—"

"You are the orphaned daughter of one of his liegemen, Ceanna," Connor retorted. "That hardly makes you his confidante. You are fortunate he allows you to live here at all—"

"Let us not discuss *my* unfortunate situation." She used a pitiful tone that would have wrung sympathy from anyone else. "Why did you not tell me you were leaving?"

"Ceanna." Connor gritted his teeth. "*Who* was asking questions in the market square?"

"The worst part is"—Ceanna stuck to her subject like a mouse on a fresh cheese—"you spent all that time in France and didna bring me a single gift. I am told they have the most wonderful scented oils."

Connor was rapidly losing what was left of his temper. He wanted to shake the information out of her, but knew that would get him naught from Ceanna. And if there were danger for Laurien in Kincardine, he had to know of it. He knew the fastest way to get cooperation from Ceanna; he softened his voice. "You are right. My behavior has been remiss."

"It has." Ceanna sniffed, exchanging her pouting smile for her seductive smile. "However, I amna one to hold a grudge. I will tell you whatever you wish to know." She traced a finger across his chest. "But I do expect some small reward."

Connor felt sickened at her scheming and more sickened at himself for playing along. Ceanna was like most of the women he had long preferred: beautiful, quiet, attentive—a woman who aspired to naught more than a woman's place. True, she had a tendency to whining and deception, but that was to be expected.

So why was it that she paled in comparison to Laurien? Laurien, who was willful and demanding, who never missed an opportunity for an argument, who had only the vaguest idea of a woman's place, who had caused him no end of trouble.

Ceanna looked up at him, beckoning, familiar, alluring. She leaned closer until her small, high breasts pressed against him.

Yet all Connor could think of at the moment was finding Laurien and claiming the kiss he had been longing for all evening. It made no sense. He was helpless to explain it. He was honestly amazed that Ceanna's considerable charms left him cold. But if he was to glean the information from her quickly, he would have to convince her otherwise.

"As ever, you hold me victim to your charms," he said, offering her his arm.

He led her up the long spiral stair. As soon as they

had left the light and noise of the crowd behind, he pulled her to a halt. "Tell me about this man in the square, Ceanna. Now."

She looked at him in surprise. "I would have my reward first," she purred, pressing herself fully against him.

Connor took her by the shoulders. "Enough of your game. Tell me what you overheard in the square."

"But, milord, the game has yet to begin." She began tugging his surcoat over his head.

"Ceanna!" Connor finally lost his temper. Untangling himself, he pushed her away and flung the garment to one side. "Tell me this instant or, I swear to you, I will shake it out of you!"

Stung, Ceanna went to the top of the stairs and sat down as real tears sprang to her eyes. She knew Connor was not the brute he liked to pretend to be. She had seen his gentle side, indeed had been cultivating his feelings toward her for months.

As an orphan with no dowry, she had little hope of attracting a husband who possessed the wealth and power she longed for. Connor was the only nobleman who had ever shown more than a few nights' interest in her. She had expended a great deal of time and effort on him— and she would not let him go easily.

She crossed her arms, blinking to clear her eyes. "Very well." She sighed dramatically. "There were two men in the market square today, both Frenchmen, dressed in blue and gold silks. They said they were visiting all the towns near Strathfillan Abbey, asking about a girl newly arrived from France. They let it be known that they would pay handsomely for information about her."

"And?"

"What more?" Ceanna raised her hands in frustration. " 'Tis all I know."

She glared at him. Connor had been different, treating her gently, even taking her to his home at Glenshiel. True, he had offered no promises. But she had hoped . . . When he had broken off with her, she had been certain she could win him back. After all, there was no other woman in the Highlands more beautiful, more desirable than she.

And upon his return tonight, she had at last seen the look she longed to see in those blue eyes, the look that spoke of love and promises—except that he chose to bestow it upon another woman!

Ceanna rose, arching her back so that her breasts jutted forward. "My love, let us talk no more of this girl. Let us go to your chamber so that I may welcome you home properly."

Connor shook his head, wondering ruefully how he had let his liaison with Ceanna go on so long. "Save your efforts, Ceanna. 'Tis finished between us. I told you—"

"Aye, you told me before you left." Her irritation made her interrupt, a habit men disliked and, thus, one she normally avoided. She nudged off her slippers, bending over to pick them up, offering Connor a view of her cleavage. Straightening, she extended a hand toward him. "I know you too well, Connor. You canna resist me. You stayed with me a long time, longer than any of the others."

"I do not think five months an exceptionally long time. I am sorry, but you waste your efforts, Ceanna. I have important matters to attend to." He turned and bent down to pick up his surcoat. One of Ceanna's slippers hit him squarely in the back.

"Go, then!" she cried. "Turn from me and walk away, you bastard!"

"You know me too well." Connor tossed her slipper

back up to her. Pulling his surcoat over his head, he started down the steps.

Ceanna hurried after him, horrified that she had allowed her temper to show. "Connor, did I not please you?" she pleaded, grasping his arm. "Did I not make you happy?"

He stopped and gave her a humorless chuckle, matched by a wry twist to his lips. "I am afraid, milady, that some men are not meant to be happy."

Leaving her staring after him, he returned to the festivities below.

Connor found Malcolm seated at one of the trestle tables, gnawing on a leg of chicken, a full trencher before him.

"They do have food in Strathfillan, you realize." Connor sat across from him. "The monks willna starve you."

Malcolm grunted, giving Connor a dubious look. " 'Tis always wise to eat well before leaving on a journey."

Connor looked about the chamber, searching for a slender figure garbed in emerald velvet. The dancing had ended and many of the guests were taking their leave. He spotted Laurien among a small group gathered about a minstrel. The man was singing some nonsense about the constancy of a maiden's heart.

Malcolm drained his wine and nudged Connor in the shoulder with the empty cup. "I still say we should have told Will about this plan of yours."

"He would be bound by duty to try and stop us," Connor said. "And I have no wish to fight him about this.'Tis best if he thinks I've no interest in the girl."

"Aye, you were doing quite well convincing him of that. Until you danced with her."

" 'Twas only one dance."

"And did she like your newly cropped hair?"

Connor scowled at him. "That had naught to do with her. I needed to have it cut. And I only danced with her because Will was enjoying himself overmuch."

"Will is old enough to be her father." Malcolm smiled. "You realize he will be here with her, while I am at Strathfillan and you are at Glenshiel."

"She will be safer here than with either of us. And 'twill be but a few days," Connor said with more confidence than he felt. "But we must tell him to keep her from leaving the castle. I am told there are men asking questions in the villages."

Malcolm's humor faded quickly. "What kind of questions?"

"About a girl newly arrived from France. 'Twould seem, my friend, that we have yet to shake de Villiers's guards from our trail."

"Tell Will to keep a close eye on her, then," Malcolm said. "Although you seem to be attending to that quite thoroughly."

Malcolm's quip went unheeded. Connor was watching Laurien, who was now engaged in an animated conversation with a sizable group of knights and a few of the bolder squires. All were competing with one another for her attention. Connor had the most irritating urge to walk over and pull her away from her admirers. But, he decided, she must have seen him escorting Ceanna out of the hall; mayhap she was only exacting a small measure of revenge over what she had mistaken for a tryst. The thought that she was acting out of jealousy cheered him somewhat. But not much.

He turned as Malcolm finished his meal. "I will speak to Will before I leave on the morrow. Have you everything you need for your journey?"

"Aye." Malcolm pushed the trencher away and wiped his hands on the tablecloth. "I shall depart at dawn, take Aidan to Galbraith, then ride on to the abbey. There

I will await the message from our troublesome comte. But instead of delivering it here to Will, I shall send it to you at Glenshiel.''

"And instead of delivering Laurien to de Villiers,'' Connor finished, "we shall deliver a surprise.''

He heard a tinkling laugh and glanced over at the object of their conversation. Most of the guests had left by this point, but a persistent knot of men still lingered by Laurien's side. She was enjoying a jest told by one of her admirers, who had placed a too-familiar hand on her arm. Connor was halfway out of his seat before he realized it. Standing, he quelled the impulse to beat the man to a pulp. Instead he stretched and yawned lazily.

"I believe I have had my full measure of entertainment for one night. Have a safe and uneventful journey, my friend.''

"Retiring so early?'' Malcolm asked as Connor walked away. "But you have been such charming company all evening.''

Connor threw a parting scowl over his shoulder and stalked from the hall.

Opening the door to his chamber, he finally lost the very last of his temper.

Ceanna lay naked in his bed, arched into a practiced pose. "I knew you would return anon, my love,'' she purred.

She reached up to him as he strode purposefully toward the bed. He lifted her in his arms, blanket and all. "Oooh, gently, Connor, gently,'' she squealed.

Gritting his teeth to keep from venting his anger, Connor carried her to the door. He lowered her to her feet. Opening the door, he placed her outside and slammed the door behind her.

Ceanna stood speechless. As always, she recovered quickly. "How can you do this to me?'' she cried, knocking on the door. "How can you? Connor, open this door! Please?"

He opened it to toss out her clothes, slamming it again promptly.

Ceanna stared down at the pile of garments on her feet. Cheeks flaming, she dressed hastily. "I will leave the blanket here," she said venomously through the door. "I would not wish you to be any *colder* than you already are!"

By now she was seething with anger that fair brought steam from her ears, but Ceanna had never been one to vent such feelings on a man. Men, she had learned from hard experience, fought back.

Women, however, were another matter entirely. They made much better game. She hurried down the stairs to seek out Laurien.

The only ones left in the hall were the French girl and her admirers. Elbowing her way through the cluster of knights, Ceanna stood before Laurien, hands on hips. "I wish to speak with you, milady."

Laurien returned her cold look, surprised at Ceanna's sudden appearance. This entire evening had been one emotional blow after another. She had seen Connor leave with this woman on his arm; a short time later, he had returned, still adjusting his surcoat. Laurien could not believe the churl could ignore her all evening, then dance with her and try to kiss her, then bed his mistress moments later!

Laurien's emotions, like her stomach, were hopelessly tangled into a knot. And now what did Ceanna want?

The woman at least provided Laurien with an excuse to free herself from the group of persistent knights. Taking her leave of them, she started after the blond's retreating form.

Ceanna moved with practiced grace to a corner of the room. She turned, arms crossed below her small breasts, and watched Laurien's approach. The girl was far too tall, Ceanna noted with pleasure. And her nose was too large. And judging from her conversation, she had intelligence too, not a trait highly valued by men. Truly, Ceanna could see no sense in Connor choosing this woman over herself. She decided she could hate Laurien very easily.

"And what requires my attention?" Laurien asked, putting every haughty note she could into her voice. She looked down at the woman, glad for once that her physical size put her several inches above others of her sex.

"I only felt it fair, milady," Ceanna replied, "that you be fully informed."

"I believe I understand completely." Laurien smiled and shrugged her shoulders. "You wish to tell me to stay away from Connor. I shall. Is that all?"

Ceanna was not taken in for a moment. The girl was hiding her feelings admirably. But Ceanna had watched them dance together, had seen them sneaking glances at each other—and she was a scholar when it came to the unspoken messages that pass between intimates. This girl was clearly in love with Connor. Ceanna meant to put an end to it. She was not ready to give him up; there were not that many wealthy, powerful men about to choose from.

She launched her first volley. "Do you know that he has a son?"

Laurien's smile twitched ever so slightly as she remembered the blond boy she had seen earlier. "By you?" she asked boldly.

"Nay." Ceanna smiled at this intruder who had stolen Connor's affection, feeling the sweet joy of knowing she was about to break Laurien's heart. She spoke slowly, savoring the next blow. "By his wife, Lady Sibylla of Glenshiel."

Sibylla. Laurien felt a rush of cold shiver through her,

ut her first reaction was denial. It could not be true. This woman was the sort who would use any means to get what she wanted. "Why"—she managed to force words from her suddenly dry throat—"should I believe what you say?"

A grin curved Ceanna's mouth. "It is the truth. He has a son named Aidan and a wife named Sibylla. Ask anyone."

Only the practice of years of lying got Laurien through the next moment. She managed to keep her voice steady, her tone light. "What is that to me? Now you must excuse me. I find myself most fatigued. I wish to thank our host and retire for the evening."

Laurien turned away with as much calm as she could muster, walking directly toward Sir William, who was speaking with one of his knights. Painful images kept flashing through her mind: Connor and the boy talking together, smiling at one another, the affectionate way Connor had ruffled the lad's hair. She felt her heart turn over.

Laurien interrupted Sir William's conversation, unable to speak even a word of pardon or greeting. The question tumbled out. "Tell me, Sir William, does Sir Connor have a son?"

"Pardon me, milady?"

She forced her mouth to form the words a second time. "Does Connor have a son named Aidan?"

The other knight politely answered when Sir William did not. "Why, aye, he does."

William cleared his throat. "Lady Laurien, have you met Sir Richard? He is the training master for my pages and squires."

Laurien barely gave the man a nod, not allowing William to change the subject. Her heart was beating so hard it hurt. "Tell me, Sir William, what became of Connor's wife?"

This time he replied, slowly, "What became of her?"

Laurien licked her dry lips and, to her own amazement, managed to speak without a stammer. "Aye, where is his wife, the Lady Sibylla? Did she die in childbirth?"

"Nay," Sir William said quickly. "She didna die. Now you must excuse us, milady, there are important matters which require our attention. Good evening and sleep well."

Laurien stood frozen in place as they walked away. She could not think, could not move, could not breathe, could not remember who she was, or where she was, or why. Her mind had gone completely blank. Ceanna had spoken the truth. She could hear the woman's voice ringing out over and over in a numbing echo. *Aidan . . . Lady Sibylla of Glenshiel . . . Connor . . . Aidan . . . Sibylla.*

His son.

His wife.

Lies, lies, lies—his whispered endearments, his tender caresses, his promise that all would be well, all of it. Little wonder that he could discard her so easily—from the very first, he had intended nothing more than bedding her, keeping her quiet and cooperative.

He despised her as a liar, and all the while hid his own truth from her with astonishing ease. Even the two nights they had spent alone, the magic he had woven about her, must have meant naught to him but physical pleasure and a means to an end. She had allowed herself to be used, repeatedly, thoroughly. Laurien felt her stomach lurch and knew she was about to be sick. Blindly, she turned and walked toward the stairs.

Ceanna watched her go. Laurien moved with her back straight and her head held high, but Ceanna had not missed the pain-glazed eyes, nor did she miss the trem ling hand Laurien placed against the wall to steady herself.

Laurien had not delivered the emotional scene Ceanna had hoped for, but the surprise attack had at least managed to wound Connor's beloved. That would have to do. For now.

Satisfied, she left the hall, snatched a torch from a wall sconce, and went outside. She headed for the stable, looking for James. Aye, he would cool her blood. The stableman was a skilled lover, and he had kept her amply amused in Connor's absence. And Ceanna felt like celebrating.

Many women would like to replace her in Connor's life: women attracted by his handsome looks and his wealth; women attracted by the challenge of piercing the nearly legendary armor of cool control that surrounded his heart. Ceanna had fought them all off.

She had even managed to keep Connor's wife from coming back into his life. Ceanna—and Ceanna alone—knew the truth about Sibylla. And as soon as she could devise a way to turn the information to her advantage, she would reveal it to Connor.

Surely, this French girl would not prove a difficult challenge. Ceanna would find a way to be rid of the wench. And then Connor would turn back to her. She was, after all, the most attractive woman in the Highlands. A dove among crows, one might say.

Giggling with delight at her own wit, Ceanna did not notice the shadow that rose out of the darkness near the tables.

"Pardon, *ma demoiselle,* but I am in need of assistance," a low, masculine voice called.

Ceanna stopped, making no move to go closer. "Who is there? Who are you?"

"I am seeking a girl recently arrived from France. Your friend James told my men she is here." He moved into the circle of torchlight. "And he also told them you may be of some assistance."

Before Ceanna could recover from her revulsion at the man's ugliness, he grabbed her arm. Taking her hand, he pressed something into her palm.

Ceanna stared down at an enormous emerald. Her fingers curled around it instantly and she looked up, smiling her enticing smile. "Mayhap we *can* help one another, Sir . . . ?"

"Comte," the grotesquely fat man corrected. "Comte Jacques de Villiers."

Chapter 19

Stumbling to her chamber, Laurien closed the door behind her and leaned against it, gasping for breath. She felt as if she were suffocating, caught in a tempest created by her own emotions. She pressed her hands against her eyes, blocking out the horrible truth, holding back the tears that threatened to fall in an unstoppable torrent any moment.

Sibylla. The name Connor had called out in his fever, the one he had reacted to so violently, the one Sir Malcolm had warned her not to question—the name was that of his wife!

Laurien groaned with the hurt of it. She had always scorned the naive maidens who swooned at a man's flattery and handsome smiles. Not her, never her; she had held herself apart from such foolishness, too wary, too intelligent to be misled so easily.

She laughed, but the sound came out as a choked sob. How those maidens would love to see her now! She had surrendered—body, heart, and soul—to a man for whom love was an illusion, and lovemaking a weapon to be wielded like any other, skillfully and ruthlessly. He had betrayed her, as men had always betrayed her. How many times did it have to happen? How many lessons would it take to open her eyes? Men were not capable of love.

A soft rap on the door startled her. She backed away

until she collided with the edge of the bed. Was it Ceanna, come for another friendly conversation? "I have retired for the night," she said. "Leave me be."

But the door opened even as she spoke. To her amazement, to her utter outrage, Connor stepped inside.

"How dare you," she said in a low, tight voice. "Begone. Leave me in peace."

Connor smiled slightly, amused at her ire and more than a little pleased that Laurien could be so jealous over Ceanna. He had decided, after tossing restlessly in his bed for half an hour, that he could not let Laurien stew in her jealousy all night. And, besides, he had not yet claimed his kiss.

But by the look of her, she was more of a mind to kill him than kiss him. She was so tense she trembled, and she glared at him, her eyes like twin emerald flames. Still, he might yet bring about a pleasant ending to this night, he mused, if he quieted her fury with a gentle but firm hand.

He reached out for her. "Laurien, you are upset about my leaving with Ceanna. I know what you must think but—"

"Let go of me!" Laurien tried to shake him off but he pulled her into his embrace. "Damn you to hell! I care not if you have a score of concubines!"

"What say we agree to discuss it later?" Connor said huskily, lowering his head to hers.

Laurien shook her head furiously, avoiding his kiss. "Is he yours?" she blurted out. "The boy, Aidan, is he your son?"

Connor froze.

Laurien broke free, stumbled back a pace, waited for him to confirm it. He might lie easily to her about Sibylla, but a man would not deny his own son.

Connor stared at her, a thousand thoughts tumbling through his mind. God's teeth, how could he explain this

to her? And why did it have to come out now? He had
come here to reassure her about Ceanna, not to reveal
the intimate details of his past.

"Is . . . he . . . your . . . *son?*" Laurien demanded.

"Aye," Connor snapped at last. "Nay . . . aye!" He
shook his head in frustration and turned away from her.
He could not decide what to tell her—the story he had
lived with for years, or the real truth about his brother
and Sibylla. He felt his temper beginning to rise. Saints'
blood, why must Laurien always be so damned determined? And why did she have to demand *this* of him?
He was not ready to share such pain with her.

"Which is it?" she spat. "Or do you not know?"

He spun about and returned her glare. "He is my
son." He said each word distinctly.

Laurien chose to ignore the dangerously flat tone of
his voice. Her hurt came out in a rush of hysterical words
before she could stop herself. "Tell me more. Tell me
what became of the boy while you were whoring your
way across the continent with your friend Gaston. Tell
me how you left the lad to fend for himself."

"Laurien," Connor growled, his anger rising sharply
as she put his own guilt into words. "Enough."

"You coldhearted bastard, you deserted him! You deserted them both. You have a son and a wife, *Sibylla!*"

Connor almost exploded. It was bad enough that she
knew about Aidan, now this! How could he ever hope
to explain the tangled mess Sibylla had made of his life?
He caught Laurien by the shoulders. "Nay, you dinna
understand.'Tis not true—"

"Do not dare deny it! Everyone else knew about them.
Everyone but me." Laurien put her hands against his
chest to push him away. Instead she found herself grasping his tunic. Her voice dissolved into accusing sobs.
"You have lied to me all along. Tell me the truth for
once, burn you!"

"Be silent and listen to me!"

"One word will do. Sibylla is your *wife*, aye or nay?"

His control finally snapped. "Aye!" he yelled. "Aye, she is my wife!"

As the booming echo of his voice faded, they glared at each other, their hands locked upon each other, neither willing to move closer, neither willing to let go.

They stood thus until Laurien, suddenly aware that she had been holding her breath, exhaled shakily. What had she expected to hear? Had she thought he would deny the truth once more? Nay, she admitted to herself, but she had *wanted* him to.

Time seemed to stop as the fragile threads that had bound her to Connor unraveled.

She released her grip on his tunic. She stared at the two rumpled spots on the fabric, where her fingers had clung so tightly. How out of place the delicate wrinkles appeared on his hard-muscled frame. She held her hands awkwardly in front of her, unable to bear the thought of touching him again, unable to lower her arms because Connor still held her roughly by the shoulders.

She was surprised to find that having his hands upon her did not sicken her. She felt no shock, no outrage, no pain at his admission. Her wound was already so deep, she thought dazedly, it could be made no deeper. She felt naught but a numbness that settled over her heart.

Her voice was a whisper when she spoke at last. "Release me. Leave me alone."

Connor could feel the wave of emotions rushing through him—anger at whoever had told Laurien this, vexation with Laurien for pushing him into answering, frustration at his own inability to share his feelings with her. His wrath was building so quickly, he feared what he might do next. She had caught him unawares, forced him into a corner. How could he ever *begin* to explain?

Ceanna was a problem easily solved; Sibylla was not. And the secret was not entirely his to tell. If Aidan should find out the vile truth about his birth, it would be a terrible blow for the boy.

'Twould be better to leave Laurien angry, for now, safer for her. He would no longer have to worry about her following him when he left. And when he returned, he would explain everything. He would ask Will to keep a close eye on her until then. For tonight, she would not be able to leave the castle even if she tried; the drawbridge would be raised by this late hour.

"I need time," he said tightly, struggling to speak past the emotions that raged inside him. "I can offer you naught at the moment but another argument."

"Leave, then." She squeezed her eyes shut. "Please, just leave me alone."

It took every ounce of will he had, but Connor complied with Laurien's request. He released her. Then, without another word, he turned and walked away, closing the door behind him.

Laurien stood where he had left her. She wrapped her arms about herself to still her shaking, feeling suddenly more alone than she had ever felt in her life. Her knees gave way, and she slumped to the floor. An image flashed into her mind of herself in a very like situation— that night when she was but six years old, discovering the truth about her real father, losing her mother an instant later . . . running to Louis, who unwrapped her tiny arms from around his neck and left her alone and sobbing.

Deserted, once again. She shivered as the image of Louis's retreating back became Connor's. Tears welled in her eyes, a child's tears. She pressed her palms against her eyes to hold them back. *Fool, fool,* she berated herself, *hundred kinds of a fool! A man will ever leave you unless you leave him first!*

She looked up, glaring at the door, hot fury replacing the frigid numbness in her heart.

Never again. Never again would she be so betrayed by a man. She had made the mistake of trusting a man for the last time.

And there was still time to steal the triumphant laughter from Connor's lips, time to make good her escape.

She got to her feet and walked purposefully to the foot of the bed, where her cloak lay. Wrapping it about her, she opened the door and peered into the darkness of the hallway, seeing no one. Quiet, hurried steps carried her down the back stair to the *bouteillerie,* then through the deserted kitchens. Her heart beat louder than the tabor she had danced to earlier; she took a deep breath, and stepped into the silent great hall. A dash to the portal, then she was down the stairs and outside, the night wind cold upon her cheeks.

She gulped in bracing gasps of the autumn air, forcing her trembling legs to assume a casual pace as she passed the brewery, mill, and granary. Nearing the castle gates, she wondered how she was going to convince the guard to lower the drawbridge for her.

She stopped when she arrived at the curtain wall, surprised to find the drawbridge already lowered.

Looking at the tower above, she saw that the guard had left his post.

She thought it odd but was not about to stop and ponder a scrap of luck thrown in her path. She hastened across, darting a glance behind her, half afraid this was some sort of trap.

The road curved away toward the south. She pondered a moment what direction she should take, then started toward the twinkling lights of Kincardine.

When she was well clear of the castle, she turned about. The fortress was now no more than an enormous shadow against the darker black of night. No one had followed her, watched her, noticed her.

She was completely alone.

"Adieu," she said with quiet determination, turning back toward the village. "Farewell, forever."

Then her tears began at last to fall, and she broke into a run.

The darkened chamber was stuffy with the odors of sweat and hearth smoke and the half-rotted rushes on the floor. Ceanna lay on the bed, trying to catch a breath of the fetid air. Her body ached from a score of bruises, delivered by the comte, who had finally heaved himself off her. This was not what she had had in mind when she had agreed to accompany him to the Bear's Head Inn in Kincardine.

De Villiers sat on the edge of the bed, a goblet of wine clutched in his fat white hand. He grinned down at her, and she smiled, her carefully practiced, enticing smile wavering ever so slightly. Despite her distaste for his appearance, she had accepted his advances; one did not spurn a man who could hand out egg-sized gems as if they were sweetmeats. But never had she been handled so roughly.

"It is important," he purred, wrapping his whip around her throat, "that you relate naught of what I have told you to anyone."

Ceanna could barely nod. He unwrapped the whip and ran a hand down her throat and over her breasts.

She felt a chill at his touch, but it was accompanied by a warm thrill of admiration for him. Here was a man who would not be trifled with, a man who would not be weakened by an emotion so foolish as love. And he would soon sit on the thrones of both France and Scotland—if he could indeed carry out the plans he had described. "Y-you have not yet told me, milord, how I may assist you in this."

"Aye, we must speak of that," de Villiers replied, heaving himself up from the bed and squeezing his oversized body back into his silk garments. "You will bring her to me, tonight. My man Balafre is taking care of the gate sentry and the drawbridge. Enter her chamber and use this."

He plunked a small sack onto the bed beside her. Ceanna opened the drawstrings to find a fine white powder inside. "I dinna understand."

"It is a drug." De Villiers smirked. "It will benumb her sufficiently so that you may lead her from the castle and bring her to me here."

"But, milord, why do you not simply go in yourself and take her? If, as you say, she is your betrothed, do you not have the right to do so?"

De Villiers shook his head. "Nay, they would fight to protect her, and I will not risk my life for her. I simply need her to become my wife, quickly. Once I have the d'Amboise lands, I can pay my mercenaries and take the French throne."

"And once you have the French throne you will use the alliance to take the Scottish throne," Ceanna finished. "And what," she urged softly, "shall be my reward if I assist you? If you are to become king of France, I imagine 'twould be within your power to grant a great many things."

De Villiers caught her chin in his hand. "How would it please you to be my queen?"

Ceanna gaped at him. A queen! To think that she had been ready to settle for a mere knight. Aye, 'twould be satisfying to look down upon those who once spurned her. Wealth, power, servants . . . A sudden thought interrupted her glee. "But, milord, what of your new wife? What of Laurien?"

De Villiers's smile broadened. "My man Balafre had given many years of loyal service. It is past time he had a reward. As soon as I tire of Laurien, I shall turn her over to him." He ran a finger along the bruises on Ceanna's throat. "Balafre is not so gentle as I. I do not believe she will live long under his hand."

Ceanna licked her lips. How utterly perfect. She herself would be wed to one of the most powerful men in the land, after Laurien suffered endless degradation and death at the hands of her husband's servant. Ceanna would love to have Connor see that.

"For now," de Villiers continued, "the only Scots who will know I am here shall be the two who kidnapped my betrothed. And I have already made arrangements for them." He stood and offered her his hand to help her to her feet.

Ceanna looked up, hesitating. He would kill them. She could feel it in the cold tone of his voice. Connor was going to die. She thought a moment of the kindnesses Connor had shown her. But the painfully fresh memory of a door slamming in her face blotted out the gentler thoughts. She did not allow herself to think further on his fate.

She smiled up at the comte and placed her hand in his. "Let us proceed, milord, without delay."

Dawn was only a wisp of pale gray along the horizon as Aidan hurried toward the stable, his breath rising in puffs of steam against the darkness. He noted that he and Sir Malcolm were awake even before the stablehands; 'twas a fitting time of day to begin an adventure. He felt a bit disappointed when he saw that Sir Malcolm had saddled a small bay horse for him, rather than a destrier. But he was not about to let it dampen his spirits.

"There you are, lad." Malcolm returned the boy's

smile. "I had begun to think mayhap you changed your mind. We have no time to tarry." He finished securing his saddle and nodded to the boy to mount.

"Nay, Sir Malcolm." Aidan fastened his pack and his small crossbow to the horse's saddle. "But I didna wish to leave without securing a weapon from Sir William's guardroom"

Malcolm eyed the little crossbow dubiously. At most, it would be useful in hunting grouse. "A fine idea, Aidan. I am glad to have a well-armed traveling companion."

Aidan looked up to offer thanks for the compliment, only to be startled into silence. A figure loomed out of the darkness from behind the stable—an enormous man, his face wreathed in shaggy hair. The stranger suddenly raised a club behind Sir Malcolm's head.

Aidan shouted, "Sir Mal—"

But Malcolm saw the danger an instant too late. The blow knocked him to the ground. A flash of white-hot pain lanced through his head, followed by a darkness that engulfed him completely.

Aidan never had a chance to cry out a second time. A large gloved hand closed over his mouth, cutting off his scream before he could even draw the breath.

Chapter 20

D awn wore on into morning and Connor tarried abed, still wearing the tunic and leggings he had donned before going to Laurien's chamber. With his arms folded over his chest, he slouched against the pillows, watching the last of the fire on the hearth burn out. Bitter thoughts vexed him, as black as the smoke that choked the flue.

He had allowed the morning to slip past, telling himself he should wait until a decent hour before returning to her chamber. In truth, he could not bring himself to walk those few short steps, for a sleepless night had brought him to two inescapable conclusions.

First, he cared for Laurien—more deeply than he wanted to admit.

Second, even if he explained everything to her, even if she believed him, they could have no future together. He could not take a wife, and he would not ask her to live as his mistress. To do so would be to abuse her honor and selflessness, the very qualities that made her so special to him.

With a growl of frustration, Connor threw himself from the bed and paced to the window. He threw open the shutters, and a trio of pigeons burst from the ledge, squawking at him as they flew away. In the distance, the sun warmed the thatched rooftops of Kincardine.

Sibylla had again risen up to ravage his life and lay

waste to any hopes of future peace or joy. He had dared think Laurien cared for him, that she might even . . . love him, just a bit. She had at least begun to trust him; now even that tiny spark had been snuffed out.

He slammed a fist against the sill. Nay, he could not stand the thought of losing her. Regardless of how much Laurien now despised him, he cared for her, and he owed her an explanation. 'Twas naught but cowardice to put it off until he returned from his journey. Will was certainly capable of preventing Laurien from following along.

He strode to the bed, snatched up his surcoat, and jerked it on over his head. Running a hand through his freshly cropped hair, he left his chamber and went to seek her.

He knocked on her door. There was no reply.

He knocked louder, and again received no answer.

A twinge of foreboding tickled at his mind even before he opened the portal. Throwing the door wide, he looked about in disbelief. The chamber was empty, the bed not slept in.

One heartbeat passed. Two.

"Sweet Christ!" he yelled, then spun from the room, not pausing to close the door. Even as he ran down the stairs, he somehow knew he would not find her at breakfast, or in the great hall.

Nay, in the middle of Scotland, with her home far away, the reckless little fool had run off. How could she have gotten past the drawbridge? Where would she have—

Kincardine, he knew in an instant, the only village for miles. Where de Villiers's men had been asking questions about her only yesterday—

He swore savagely and raced down the last few steps, yelling for Will to gather his men.

* * *

This was not, mayhap, the most intelligent thing she had ever done.

That was Laurien's first thought upon awakening behind a stable in Kincardine. She stood and stretched, her muscles stiff from a night spent curled upon a pile of hay. She picked bits of straw from her hair and brushed in vain at the mud on her green velvet skirt, then cast another heartfelt oath upon the name of Sir Connor of Glenshiel.

She gathered her cloak more tightly about her, finding no warmth within it. The cold seemed to have soaked into her bones. Her stomach growled, and she wished fervently that she had eaten more at the feast last night. Or that she had thought to take some food as she ran through the kitchens. Or that she possessed a single coin to her name. Had she not been so upset, she thought irritably, she would have considered such practical matters. Now it was too late.

She cautiously stepped around the corner of the stable and into the street. Without money, without any way of reaching the coast or securing passage on a ship, how was she ever to get back to France? Laurien felt so frustrated, she wanted to scream. She was determined not to cry, having already spent the better part of the night at that. Squaring her shoulders, she started down the street. She had succeeded in escaping the Scotsman; she would succeed in finding a way home.

Laurien wandered down one street of stalls after another, trying to decide what she should do, hoping some idea would strike her. Kincardine's shopkeepers were already prepared for the day's business, their shutters folded upward to form awnings and downward to provide display counters. Inside, they and their apprentices bent over their tasks, leaving their work the instant a customer approached.

She walked and thought, finally arriving at the village's main square. A peddler stepped into her path.

"A pork pie, milady?" He waved the golden-brown pastry under her nose. "They are still warm."

"No, thank you." Laurien shook her head in regret, her mouth watering at the spicy steam. She moved on quickly before the scent could torture her further.

Looking at the crowd of servants, peasant women, vendors, and artisans, she wished she had changed clothes before fleeing the castle. Her emerald velvet garments could not help but attract attention; unescorted and unarmed, she could fall prey to all manner of knaves.

She edged toward a shadowed corner of the square and settled herself upon an upturned cart, trying to think despite the noise. The peddlers kept up a steady din, calling out the merits of their wares, while women's voices sounded strident objections to milk thinned with water, or too-yeasty bread.

She had, she decided, two choices. She could walk to the coast or she could steal a horse. Neither thought appealed to her. She sighed in frustration, watching women bustle about the marketplace, their baskets laden with a tempting array of cheeses, wine, bread, and tarts. Her stomach growled again, and at last she stood, having decided upon walking.

As she moved, a large figure across the square caught her eye, for he was matching her pace step for step. Though a deep hood concealed the face, Laurien felt the uncomfortable sensation of eyes trained intently upon her. The person was tall, but garbed in a cloak so voluminous Laurien could scarce tell whether its folds covered a man or a woman.

Her first thought, accompanied by an oath, was that Connor had found her. But what reason, she wondered, would he have for so concealing himself? And Connor would not observe her thus—he would seize her in an instant and drag her back to the castle. No sooner had she begun to wonder at the person's identity, than the mysterious cloak disappeared into the crowd.

Laurien swallowed, finding that her throat had suddenly gone dry. Feeling ill at ease, she moved quickly along, trying to lose herself in the crowd.

She stopped upon reaching the edge of the market square. Some impulse made her turn her head to look behind her. Her heart took a nervous skip; she saw the hooded figure, once more directly across from her. Keeping her eyes on him—or her, for she truly could not tell which—Laurien moved warily along. Like a shadow, the figure moved with her, step for step. A chill ran down Laurien's back, like a rain of icy pinpricks. He—she?—*was* following her.

Who could it be? One of Sir William's men? Someone she had met at the feast the night before? Or could de Villiers's guards somehow have tracked her down? Close on the heels of her initial fear came the disturbing feeling that she had seen this person before. She came to a halt again, to study her pursuer in greater detail. It must be a man. The figure was too tall for a woman, and quite broad of shoulder. The thought struck her that anyone who would disguise himself thusly was more likely foe than friend.

As she stood watching, he started across the square toward her. Not of a mind to make the man's acquaintance, she turned and ducked down the nearest alleyway. Without looking back, she dashed past a long line of shops, then quickly turned a corner into another street.

She waited the span of a few nervous breaths, then chanced a look around the corner.

The figure was there, at the head of the street. And she knew at once it was indeed a man, for she could see the point of a sword's scabbard extending below the cloak's hem. Laurien's heart doubled its pace. She hurried down the street, turned a corner, then another. Throwing a glance over her shoulder, she saw that he followed her still. She broke into a run.

A commanding masculine voice rang out behind her. "Nay, stop!"

Instead she ran faster, racing blindly away from him, the cold air burning her throat and lungs. She only held the lead for a few paces before he caught up with her. He reached out to grab her cloak. Tripping on her heavy skirts, she fell. She screamed and came up fighting as he grasped her arm and pulled her to her feet. She tore at the man's hood with her free hand.

He fended off her attack. "Laurien—damn it—enough!"

The familiar voice shocked Laurien into silence, but even as he lowered the hood himself, her eyes could barely accept the evidence before her. The man had dark hair, pale blue eyes, and a decidedly irritated mien.

She was staring up at her brother.

"Henri!" It was all she could think of to say.

"God's breath, Laurien, that is some poor greeting after what I have been through to find you." He held her by the shoulders and looked her up and down as if surveying her for damage.

Then he continued in the same half-growling tone. "I have come to take you back to France."

Chapter 21

Laurien could only stare at her brother in disbelief. "B-but what," she sputtered, "how—"

"You are alone? What became of your captors?"

"I escaped," she said simply. "Now tell me—"

"And you are unharmed?" he interrupted again, then softened his voice as he looked at her with concern. "They did not . . . harm you, did they?"

Laurien looked away, feeling a blush warm her cheeks. She knew what he meant, but was unsure how to answer truthfully. "Nay, they did not . . . He . . . I have not been abused."

"Thank God." Henri enfolded her in a hug. "I would never have forgiven myself had you come to harm."

Laurien returned his embrace and lay her head against his chest. Though Henri was a year younger than she, he was a good head taller. The cloth of his brown homespun garments felt rough beneath her cheek, his arms safe and welcoming.

Just as quickly, she withdrew and looked up at him in irritation. She could think of a great deal of harm she might have avoided—if only Henri had not stopped her from escaping to Tours and evading her betrothal in the first place!

"Henri, how came you to be in Kincardine? What do you mean you have come to take me home? And why are you so strangely garbed?" She tugged at his enormous cloak.

"It is best that we not speak of it here," he replied, already taking her by the elbow and escorting her along the street. "I have seen de Villiers's men about."

"De Villiers's men! But how did they find me? Henri, how did *you* find me? For that matter," she snapped, "why did you come after me at all?"

He grinned at her onslaught of questions. "It would appear, my dear sister, that the past fortnight has not tamed your temper a whit." Before she could utter a sharp reply, he hurried to explain. "I have a horse in the stables nearby. We should leave as quickly as possible. I will tell you all as soon as we are on our way to the coast." He tightened his grip on her arm and propelled her in front of him.

She shot him a sidelong glare. "You do not plan to return me to de Villiers?"

"For what reason would I spend all this time following de Villiers's guards, disguise myself so that they would not recognize me, and track you all the way to Scotland only to hand you over to him again?"

"Because you are a *man*," she snapped.

He looked at the heavens in supplication. "Sweet Mary, save me from feminine logic."

"And save me from masculine loyalty," she retorted, trying to free her elbow from his hand. "I trusted you before and you betrayed me."

"Laurien, if a bit of gratitude is too much to ask, at least save your accusations for later." They had reached the stable, and Henri spoke briefly with the stableboy. As soon as his dappled horse was saddled, he gave the lad a coin and mounted. He held out a hand to help Laurien up. His silver and emerald ring—the token of love and loyalty she had given him years ago—flashed in the sunlight. "Trust me, I have no dire intentions."

She sighed in exasperation but decided it was best to keep her temper in check for the moment. She reached up and allowed him to pull her into the saddle behind him. Henri nudged the stallion into a trot. As soon as they passed beneath the east gate, he urged the horse into a gallop that quickly carried them far into the forests that surrounded the village.

Laurien held on to his waist and remembered all the times they had ridden thus at home in Amboise. She realized, reluctantly, that she found Henri's presence comforting; he at least offered her escape from the maelstrom she found herself trapped in. Still, she was not at all sure she could forgive what he had done.

She frowned at his back and tried to focus on the beautiful scenery rather than the angry accusations in her mind. The day had turned unseasonably warm, and although it was autumn, summer-green grasses blended with the darker hues of moss and ivy. Pines, oaks and elms spread eager branches toward the sun, and thickets and weeds clogged the road at every turn. Only patches of stone and white-blue streams broke through the emerald landscape.

When they had been riding for some time, she realized he was not going to offer an explanation unless she prodded him. "Henri, have we come far enough for you to explain yet?" she asked tartly.

He relented and reined in alongside a brook. "Aye, I suppose we merit a rest."

Laurien slid to the ground and waited while Henri removed the horse's saddle and bridle and set the animal free to graze. That done, he slung the saddle and his pack beneath a tree, then plunked himself down beside them. "First, Laurien, about the way we parted," he began slowly. "You had every right to be angry with me—"

"I should certainly say I did." Laurien glowered at

him and remained standing. "Burn you, Henri, if not for you, none of this ever would have happened! Why did you stop me from going to Sister Katherine? You know how much finding my father means to me. How could you do that, Henri?"

He looked at the ground, his expression doleful. "You have been searching for years to no avail. I thought it was time for you to put away your childhood hopes and start a family of your own."

"And you decided you had the right to make that decision for me."

"Someone had to. It is long past time for you to marry, Laurien. If it were left up to you, you would never choose a husband. I thought you were simply being your usual stubborn self in refusing de Villiers. Louis had already signed the betrothal papers, and I thought it your duty to accept the match—"

"My *duty,*" she bit out. "Why is it that men always seem to have the rights and women the duties?"

He glanced down again, not quite succeeding in hiding his grin. "You do need a husband, Laurien, one who can keep a short rein on that temper of yours."

She frowned at him and looked away, watching the water gurgling along the banks of the stream. The breeze was soft against her cheek. "You have no idea how much you hurt me," she said quietly.

"I am sorry, Laurien." His voice was full of pain and regret. "I realized what a mistake I had made, once I met de Villiers. I could not see you spending your life under the hand of one so brutal."

"Your change of heart arrived a bit late to help me."

"Not quite. I felt terrible that I had helped condemn you to such a fate, and when you were abducted, I was nearly frantic with worry. I knew I had to help you, and to try and make all this up to you. I went to see Sister Katherine before I left France."

Laurien looked at him in surprise, her heart leaping with a surge of anticipation and apprehension. "What did Sister Katherine say? Did she tell you my father's name?" She knelt beside him on the grass. "Come, Henri, do not keep me guessing!"

"She wanted to speak with you herself," he said, turning to rummage about through his pack. "But when I explained what had happened, she gave me this." He pulled out a folded piece of parchment and handed it to her.

"Oh, Henri," Laurien breathed as she accepted the missive. The parchment was bound with ribbon and sealed with wax, and she recognized the mark as Katherine's. She stared down at it in amazement, knowing she held in her hand the answer to thirteen years of questions. Her fingers trembled. She had at last reached the end of her quest.

She held the paper in her lap and looked up at her brother. "Henri, what if—"

"Nay, torture yourself no more, Laurien. Open it."

Biting her bottom lip to keep it from trembling, she broke the seal. Her eyes skimmed quickly over the lines, looking for a name . . . and found none.

She went back to the beginning and began to read, feeling her spirits fall even before she finished the first sentence.

My dearest Laurien, the note began in Sister Katherine's neat hand. *It is with no small regret that I must tell you I have not been able to discover the name, or the whereabouts, of your father.*

Laurien groaned, squeezing her eyes shut against the tears that suddenly blurred her vision. She swallowed hard and forced herself to read on.

You must be strong, my child, for I do have some tidings of him. I was able to locate a nun, one Sister Marguerite, formerly of Evreux, the town where your mother grew up. This dear lady is quite old and hard of hearing, but she knew your mother well. She remembers clearly that your mother was often seen in the company of a handsome young man during the summer of her seventeenth year, just before she left for Amboise to marry Louis. She does not recall the man's name, but she assures me that he was not a Dane.

"Impossible!" Laurien said aloud.

"What is impossible?"

Laurien barely heard her brother's query, as she was devouring the rest of the letter.

Sister Marguerite recalls that he spoke French quite well, and believes he had come to France to take part in the Crusade of 1275, though she cannot be certain on that point. She cannot remember what country he said he was from, but she was most certain that it was not Denmark.

Sister Marguerite would like to speak to you personally, but her health is quite fragile, and that is why I wish for you to come to Tours as soon as you can. Mayhap you will be better able to make sense of her recollections than I. My dear, I know this news will be hard for you. It seems I was wrong about the markings on your knife. Mayhap they are not Danish after all, or mayhap you were mistaken in thinking the knife came from your father's homeland.

I wish I could be with you in this difficult time, and I pray that you will find guidance. Your brother tells me that he intends to help you evade marriage to this comte. If you can, my dear, come to Tours, and we will speak further with Sister Marguerite. I will do all I can to help you to find your father.

Remember what I have ever told you, that through love you will find the strength to rise above all limitations. Do not squander your time in useless lamentations, rather seek that love and that strength. I am

*certain, my Laurien, that one day you will find all you
search for. Yours, Katherine.*

The missive fluttered from Laurien's numb fingers and
she gazed at her brother, her eyes misting with tears.

"Henri, how can this be? Mother said . . . And Sister
Katherine was so certain the runes on my knife were
Danish. . . . I have wasted all these years looking in the
wrong place!" Then her throat went dry and she could
hardly speak. "How will I *ever* find him now? And what
shall become of me if I cannot?"

Henri picked up the letter and read it quickly. "Laurien, I am so sorry." He wrapped her in a hug, and this
time Laurien did not pull away. "I thought I carried the
answer you have been seeking. It is bad enough that I
embroiled you in this trouble, and now I have only made
you feel worse."

"Nay, do not blame yourself, Henri." She wiped at
her eyes. "Sister Katherine was right. I will not squander my time in useless lamentations. Blaming you made
it easier for me to bear this, but I was wrong. You were
only doing what you thought best for me. And you were
very brave to come all this way to rescue me. I am sorry
for chastising you so. Can you forgive me?"

Henri grinned. "If you can forgive me, Featherwit, I
can certainly forgive you."

The familiar nickname wrung a smile from Laurien.
"Then count yourself forgiven, Thickhead." She
punched him with mock ire. "Now then," she said,
sitting up and lifting her chin in determination, "tell me
how you found me in Kincardine. Then . . . then we
must decide how we shall make our way back to
France."

Henri sighed, as if only now feeling how arduous his
journey had been. "I trailed de Villiers's guards to England, bought one of them too many drinks, and persuaded him to tell me where his lord had gone. He told

me there had been news of you in the Highlands, and that de Villiers was searching for you in a village by the name of Kincardine. I arrived there yesterday, and this morn I went to the market square to buy some food—''

''And proceeded to scare the wits from me.''

''At first I could not believe it was you!'' he exclaimed. ''Then I could not believe you were alone. I did not wish to call out to you or reveal myself to you, for fear of bringing down either your captors or de Villiers's men upon us. It was not my intention to frighten you.''

''It is all right, Henri. By this morn, one ordeal more or less could do me no harm.'' Laurien gave him a wry grin. ''Sweet Mary, I still cannot believe you would go to all this trouble for me.''

Henri took her hand and squeezed it tightly. ''Of course I would, Laurien. You are my sister. I love you.''

Laurien's grin gave way as her lower lip trembled, and she again found tears in her eyes. ''I love you too, Henri.''

He hugged her. ''I am so glad I found you. If your captors had hurt you—''

''Please, do not vex yourself with such fears any longer,'' she said, a bit too brightly. ''As you can see, I am quite fit.''

He sat back and gave her a long, doubtful look before he spoke again. ''I will understand if you do not wish to speak of it, but would you tell me . . . what happened?''

She gazed into the distance, where mountains stood out in pale contrast against the dark foothills of the Highlands. ''Mayhap, some day. For now, I would prefer to let it remain in the past, Henri.''

He nodded and rose. After picking up the saddle, he walked over to the dappled stallion. ''We had best ride on. It is a long way to the coast.''

As soon as he had the horse saddled, they moved on, keeping to the southeast road. When night fell, they camped in a small clearing, sleeping side by side, not daring to light a fire for fear of offering a signal to any searching for them.

Long after her brother fell into an exhausted sleep, Laurien lay awake, her thoughts not of her elusive father, but of a blond Scotsman who was half Viking prince, and of a crooked grin and indigo blue eyes that haunted even her dreams.

Laurien awoke, some instinct sending a tickle of warning down her neck. Moonlight had transformed the dark clearing into a pool of speckled shadows that shifted and danced. Moving only her eyes, she glanced about, not daring even to roll over. She felt certain that she and Henri were no longer alone, yet she could hear no footfall, see no movement.

She raised herself to her elbows, very slowly, and was about to awaken Henri when a gloved hand clamped over her mouth.

"How charming a scene," an angry masculine voice growled in her ear. "I regret that I must interrupt."

With a jolt of surprise followed by a quick rush of anger, Laurien recognized Connor's voice. She struggled against him, flailing out as he jerked her to her feet. His free arm quickly encircled her, holding her still against him.

"I will give you until the count of three to explain," he said tightly, "before your lover meets his end on my sword! One—" He released her mouth, but before she could speak, Henri was awake and reaching for his own weapon.

"Laurien? Who is there? Release her, knave!" He jumped to his feet, brandishing the sword.

"You should choose your champions with greater

care, milady," Connor snapped. "Not only does this *boy* take the most obvious road to the coast, he is a fool as well if he thinks to best me!"

"Cease this, both of you!" Laurien cried. "Henri is—"

"Come taste a fool's steel!" Henri shouted at Connor, already dropping into a fighting stance. Connor thrust Laurien behind him and drew his weapon. Their male minds were intent on combat, and they paid her no heed.

"Henri is my *brother!*" Laurien shouted, grabbing Connor's sword arm in a vain effort to hold him back.

Connor turned to her with a look of astonishment just as Henri lunged. Laurien saw her brother coming and leaped forward, holding up her hands. "Henri, nay! Do not hurt him!"

Henri pulled up a hair's breadth from wounding her, his face a mask of surprise at her action. The three stood in stunned silence a moment, then Connor took the advantage. He spun and hit Henri, landing a blow to the chin that knocked the younger man out. Before Laurien had a chance to react, she found herself scooped up and tossed over Connor's shoulder.

"You bastard!" She pounded on his back as he carried her toward the road. "You have hurt him. We cannot just leave him!"

Connor did not slow his steps. "Were I you, I would be more fearful of my own fate," he growled.

"Where do you think you are taking me?" she demanded, kicking and squirming to no avail.

"Home," he said cryptically.

When they reached the edge of the road, he led his horse from the shadows. He mounted, seating Laurien across his knees while she cursed him with all manner of oaths. He kicked the stallion into a gallop—not back up the road, Laurien noted with surprise, but into the forest on the other side.

"Where are we going?" she cried. When he did not answer, she twisted in his grip, frustrated when he only held her tighter. "Damn you to hell, I hate you! Do you hear me? I hate you!"

She grabbed one of the reins and jerked it, intending to slow the horse. Instead the stallion reared, its wild neighing shattering the night. Connor fought to control the panicked animal but lost his hold on Laurien. She twisted free, tumbling from the horse's back, and barely missed being struck by one of its hooves. She landed with a yelp of pain as the breath was knocked from her.

"Laurien!" Connor managed to control the horse and leaped to her side. He pulled her to her feet, anger and concern in his voice. "You have done many a foolish thing, but that was stupid beyond reason!"

Laurien tried to fight him off. "I loathe you! I despise you!"

"Truly?" he mocked her, pulling her into his arms, relieved upon finding she had not caused herself serious damage. "Then why did you not allow your brother to run me through?"

"I wish I had! Then I would be rid of you at last!"

In response he crushed her against him, one arm about her waist, the other about her shoulders, forcing her to tilt her head back.

Though she could not make out his expression in the darkness, Laurien glared at him, fighting the all too familiar urge to melt in his arms. Suddenly she was aware he had said "your brother" and not "your lover." "You have never trusted me before. How is it you believe me about Henri?"

"I thought the worst when I saw you beside him," he said, his voice husky, "but now I know better. You wouldna lay with any man but me."

His smug declaration nearly struck Laurien speechless. "Only moments ago you accused me of exactly that! How can you now be so sure?"

"Because you love me," he said quickly. "That is why you would not allow him to hurt me. You love me."

Laurien felt a tremor deep inside at hearing it spoken aloud. *Nay, you arrogant knave, I love you not,* she wanted to scream, but somehow she could not force her lips to form the words. When she remained silent, Connor tightened his hold on her until she could scarcely breathe. His voice was taut with emotion when he spoke again.

"Deny it," he dared her.

"H-how could I love you? After all you have done to me! After you have used me, lied to me, and all along you were married—"

"I mean to explain that—"

"I will not listen to your excuses!" She shook her head, wanting desperately to escape his arms before he forced her to admit the truth, to say words of love she would surely live to regret.

"Last night you were so damned impatient for answers—and now you willna listen?" he bellowed. "Well, by nails and blood, woman, you *will* listen to me! I should have told you last night. When I found you missing, I finally realized I—" He stopped suddenly.

"Realized what?" she demanded.

He was nearly shaking with the force of feelings so strong he did not know how to control them. *Realized how much it would hurt if I lost you. Realized just how deeply I care for you,* he had almost blurted. God's teeth, 'twas agony worse than hell's fire to feel so strongly about her when she could only shout words of loathing at him. He could stand it no longer. He must hear from her own lips that she loved him, and he must begin by telling her the truth.

"I realized 'tis madness to brook any more of your foolishness," he said gruffly, taking her hand. "You wanted the truth, and you shall have it. You are going to listen to me, Laurien, and you are going to listen right now."

He sat down beneath a tree and pulled her down beside him. She tried to jerk free, calling him every name she could think of. He ignored her protests and held fast to her hand.

"What I am about to tell you, 'twas not a problem to me before—before I met you. But it *is* now. Do you understand what I am saying? I dinna have an answer to it, but I wish I did, because it *matters* now."

Determined not to listen, Laurien turned her back on him, not caring that this stretched her arm into an uncomfortably awkward position.

Connor leaned back against the tree. "Have you never done aught you regret? Aught you are ashamed of?"

Laurien ignored him.

"I have," he continued. "And 'tis not a thing I have spoken of to many. You know it isna easy for me to talk about my past. I wasna ready to tell you last night, but I willna allow secrets to divide us any longer. If you are going to hate me, at least hate me for the truth."

Laurien was looking up at the night sky, at the stars and a sliver of moonlight that peeked through the thatch of leaves over their heads. Her heart gave a funny little skip when he said he did not wish secrets to divide them. But then, was he not a master at using her emotions for his own gain?

Half hopeful, half skeptical, she waited for him to explain.

He remained silent a long moment, and when he finally started, he spoke quickly, the words spilling out in a torrent. "It all began on a night nine years past. Sibylla,"—he said the name as if it were a curse—"had been my wife for only a year then. I was gone for most of that time, trying to win my knighthood. During the summer tournaments at Edinburgh, I acted like the young fool I was, and challenged a man twice my age and twice my size. He not only unhorsed me, he nearly killed me. That whole summer, I lay fighting for my life, and she never once came to me.''

He paused, and his voice lowered to a harsh growl. '' 'Twas only after I won my spurs and returned home that I discovered she had been bedding my brother Duncan the entire time.''

Laurien, despite herself, began to listen intently. His own *brother!*

''By then, she was fat with Duncan's child,'' Connor said, his voice choked with bitterness. ''I nearly killed him when he confirmed the babe was his. And then I only wanted to get away, to run from them. That was when I decided to leave for the continent. When I went to tell Sibylla, she was already gone. But she left the baby behind. I claimed him as my own, because without me he would have had no one. I named him after my grandfather, Aidan.''

Laurien's earlier shock gave way to understanding, and she found herself burning with outrage and aching with hurt at what Connor had suffered. Was it any wonder that he had kept such secrets locked away from her—from everyone, she sensed—or that he had treated her with such wariness and distrust? Nay, what was surprising was that he had any finer qualities at all, after the blow life had dealt him.

He paused, and Laurien could hear in the stillness of the night that his breathing was strangely harsh. He cleared his throat and continued. ''In truth, Aidan is my nephew. But everyone believes him to be my son, and in . . . in my heart, that is how I think of him now.'' His voice broke, and it was a moment before he could continue. "He is all I have left. Duncan and Eda are gone, and my parents, and . . . and my younger brother, Galen."

Laurien heard the anguish in his voice, the loneliness and grief spilling out, and she felt tears welling up in her eyes. It was like watching Connor shed his armor of control, piece by piece, until there was nothing left of it.

"And Aidan is all the family I shall *ever* have," he said more forcefully. "I have never been able to find any trace of Sibylla. And unless I can prove she no longer lives, the Church considers me married." He made a sound that started out like a cynical chuckle but ended up a groan. "Some would find this humorous, I suppose. I have a wife, but I dinna have a wife. I dinna have a son, yet I have a son."

He stopped again, and Laurien turned to look at him. He had released her hand at some point, and now he was staring at the ground, his fists clenched against the grass, his features a blank, numb mask.

As she gazed at him, the last of her anger and feelings of betrayal disappeared, like fog burned away by the morning sun. Before her she saw not a coldhearted warrior who had carelessly deserted his family, nor a liar who had ruthlessly used her. She saw a man harshly buffeted by the winds of fate, a man who wanted naught so much as the two things life had always taken from him: love and family.

"I never meant to mislead you," Connor said finally, his voice hoarse by now. "At first I didna tell you any of this because you were of no consequence to me . . ." He kept staring at the ground, not wanting to look at Laurien, dreading the loathing he knew he would find in her eyes. "And later I didna tell you because . . . I couldna bear for you to hate me as you do now. So that is—"

He forced himself to look up, and the expression on Laurien's face stole the words and the breath from his lips.

Her features were etched in compassion, her eyes shining with understanding, her cheeks wet with tears.

He never finished the rest of his sentence. In the span of a heartbeat, he pulled her into his arms and held her to his chest as she sobbed out all the hurt he could never put tears to.

"Shhh," he soothed, utterly astonished that she could feel his pain so forcefully. Her silent acceptance of all he had said—of *him*—touched Connor more powerfully than any words she could have spoken.

He cupped her face in his hands and tilted her head back, his thumbs wiping away her tears; at the first touch of his mouth, her lips parted beneath his. He had thought he remembered how sweet her kiss could be, but reality far surpassed his most vivid memories. His tongue probed her softness, and his body tensed with desire.

Connor broke the kiss quickly. He could not take her, not now, not ever again. 'Twas not right. He had already hurt her too many times—he was not going to treat her as if she meant no more to him than a pleasant tumble.

For he knew, with a certainty that was growing stronger every minute, that she meant far more than that. He could not bear to let her go.

" 'Tis late, and we should find shelter," he said tersely, afraid that if he did not gain a bit of distance from her, he would take her right here on the forest floor. He stood and helped her to her feet. "We have a long journey on the morrow."

"Aye," Laurien said, puzzled by the way he had broken away from her so suddenly. "And we have to go back for Henri."

Connor shook his head as he led her to his horse. "Your brother isna hurt. He will have a sore jaw and a

oul temper for a few days, no more. Like as not, he
vill be downing ales in an inn before we are halfway to
ur destination.''

"Not Henri. He will come after us."

"I am not easily followed."

"Henri is very persistent."

"Let him come." Connor turned toward her, frown-
ng.

Laurien felt confused at his vehemence. "Connor, you
vould not harm him—"

"I wish him no ill." He mounted his horse, hesitated,
hen reached down to lift her onto his lap. "But no man
vill take you from me again. Not even your brother."

Laurien knew from experience it was impossible to
way Connor when he used that tone. She sighed, half
xasperated at his commanding attitude, half pleased at
iis possessiveness. "We are not going back for Henri?"

"Nay," he said flatly.

They silently resumed their journey through the for-
st, Connor trying to ignore the very pleasant sensation
f having Laurien's body pressed against him, Laurien
ost in troubled thoughts.

She prayed Henri would be all right. Then she began
o worry about Connor. He had said naught of their
uture together. Mayhap, she thought with a wave of
urt, mayhap he did not *want* her to be part of his life
eyond these short weeks. Could he ever form a bond
vith another woman, after what Sibylla had done to him?

A short time later, they came to a ramshackle group
f cottages scattered about a clearing. At Connor's sum-
nons, an elderly man trudged out of one of the hovels,
ubbing the sleep from his eyes. Connor exchanged a
ew words with him in Gaelic, then tossed him a gen-
rous sack of coins. Riding to a shack that served as a
table, Connor stopped and lowered Laurien to the

ground. She waited, feeling uneasy, wanting to ask a score of questions, while he stabled the horse.

When he came back to her, she reached out to touch him. "What did you mean, when you said you were talking me home?" she queried softly.

"I am taking you to my home, to Castle Glenshiel."

She frowned up at him, feeling a spark of her former vexation. *"Your* home—"

"I amna taking you back in order to give you to de Villiers." He smiled at how quickly her spirit returned. "I have a plan to secure the alliance without turning you over to him."

"What kind of a plan? How—"

"Shhh," he said, placing a finger on her lips. "If you dinna know, you canna follow me. I have put you in too much danger already, Laurien. I want you safe when I return." He took her by the elbow and led her around to the back of the stable, where a ladder led to the hay loft above.

"But, Connor, if your plan works, what then? What will happen . . . to us?"

He took her by the shoulders, desperately wanting to take her in his arms, to tell her how he felt. But it would be senseless cruelty to torture her with words of love when she could not be his. With bitter resignation, he settled instead for calmly telling her the truth.

"Laurien, I canna tell you what the future holds, but I canna marry you and I willna dishonor you by keeping you as my mistress. I mean to set you free. When all this is untangled—de Villiers and the alliance—I will return you to France."

Laurien gaped at him.

"Promise me," he asked before she could reply, "promise me that . . ." And for an instant, he thought of throwing honor to the wind and asking her to stay with him, to give him all her tomorrows. He just a quickly abandoned the idea, for he had no right to ask such a commitment of her when he could offer none in return. "Promise me that you willna interfere."

Laurien lowered her eyes, feeling a stab of disappointment. She knew better than to expect soft words from him. And he was right. They could have no life together. He could never truly be hers, for he was married. He would return her to France, and she would be able to continue her search for her father. It was what she wanted, was it not?

Was it not?

How noble of Connor to think of her feelings, to grant her freedom, instead of asking her to be his mistress.

It only made her love him all the more.

It only made her want to stay with him all the more.

If he asked her, she knew what her answer would be, and honor be damned.

She felt like crying. She had only just learned to love Connor, and now she was losing him.

Connor placed a finger beneath her chin and tipped her head up. She saw the concern in his gaze, and it made her feel even worse. He did care for her, mayhap it was not love, but he cared.

She would do as he asked. For love, she could at least do that.

"Aye," she breathed softly, thinking it the hardest promise she had ever made. "I promise I will not interfere with your plan."

Connor lowered his head to hers and kissed her, the briefest sharing of breath to seal her vow. Even that chaste joining sent passion blazing through his body. To be near her at all was pure torture. He stepped away, turning his back and gazing up at the starlit sky.

He shrugged in the general direction of the loft. "You should sleep. I will stay out here."

Laurien realized what he was trying to do, and she

thought her heart would burst with longing. In that moment, she knew more clearly what she wanted than she
ever had in her life. She wanted to be his, body and
spirit, forever. Let the world call it wrong, let the Church
call it sin.

Her heart called it love, true and glorious.

"Connor, I . . ." She touched his shoulder and felt
a tremor shudder through his entire body. "I want—"

"Laurien," he rasped, his voice deep with longing,
his body taut. "God's teeth, you know that I want you,
but I willna hurt you—"

"The only thing that can hurt me is to never know
this feeling again. To never be able to touch you again."
Her other hand came up to stroke his shoulder. "If we
cannot have forever, let us have tonight. Let us share
one last time together that I may hold you forever in my
heart. Love me, Connor, please *love me.*"

The next instant he captured her in a fierce embrace,
and they were in the loft before she knew whether she
had climbed the ladder or he had carried her. With a
groan that came from deep in his throat, he slowly,
slowly fell with her to the hay. She could see little by
the slim shaft of moonlight that pierced the darkness.
The loft smelled surprisingly sweet, filled with the scent
of fresh hay and bunches of herbs that hung drying from
the rafters just above their heads. Connor kissed her with
an urgency that set her senses afire.

Laurien felt a shiver, part apprehension, part excitement, when Connor stretched out beside her and raised
her hands above her head. His eyes never leaving hers,
he unfastened her cloak with his free hand.

She trembled when he feathered kisses down her bare
neck.

"Tell me you want me," he said huskily, nipping the
delicate skin of her throat.

Laurien knew a flare of heat at his bold demand and ungentle kisses. "I do."

He tugged at her bodice with his teeth, pulling it lower to expose more of her skin to his kisses. "Nay, play not the shy maiden." His voice was suddenly fierce, and he lifted his head to gaze at her intently. "Say it, my fiery *demoiselle*."

The desire in his eyes warmed her even more than his touch, and when she answered it was with a passion equal to his own. "I want you."

Keeping her pinned, he swiftly shed his own garments. Then he pulled her bodice lower, freeing her breasts. She gasped at the touch of the cold air upon her skin, quickly replaced by the warmth of his hand closing over one soft mound. He nuzzled her neck, whispering in her ear.

"Tell me you belong to me."

Laurien hesitated, part of her wanting to give in, part of her needing to hear words of love from him first. Connor's free hand left her breast to slowly, slowly pull her skirt above her knees, and her pulse began to race.

When she still did not respond, he teased a path up her leg, resting his fingers ever so lightly upon the dark curls below her belly.

"Connor . . ." Laurien challenged weakly, her eyes half closed.

"Tell me you are mine."

She shook her head very slowly. His lips came down upon hers in a feverish kiss, his tongue plunging into her mouth. His thumb found the delicate nub of her pleasure and flicked it gently. He eased a finger inside her.

Laurien moaned softly at his possession, knowing she was utterly his, but not yet willing to admit it to him. He pressed his hand against her, sending exquisite sensations rippling through her.

"Say it," he murmured against her lips.

"Nay," she breathed, barely completing the word when his tongue again plundered her mouth. Her senses reeled as he began to stroke her, his finger moving in and out of her dampness. His tongue mimicked the thrusting of his finger, gently at first, then harder, deeper, demanding a response.

Held motionless beneath him, Laurien thought she would go mad at this double onslaught. His thumb began to move in a tight, circular pattern, faster and faster. He fired the tension within her until she arched helplessly against his hand, crying out for release.

He shifted quickly so that he was poised to enter her. She tried to tilt her hips upward, but he held her still.

"You belong to me," he urged, touching his tongue to the corner of her mouth.

Laurien closed her eyes, moaning with frustration as he teased her, pressing just the tip of his manhood against her. She trembled with anticipation, with her need of him, and finally surrendered.

"I belong to you," she said breathlessly.

He let go of her hands at last, and she wrapped her arms about his shoulders, pulling him closer. Connor slid inside her with a single thrust.

He groaned as she opened to him, his joy at her words doubling his pleasure at her sensual response. Tonight he needed Laurien as he had never needed or wanted anything in his life. If only for this one last time, he would make her utterly and completely his. He probed the deepest length of her silken sheath, and she tightened herself around him, as if she wanted to hold him inside her forever. He watched her eyes darken with rapture until they were the color of Highland hills warmed by the summer sun.

He claimed the sweetness of her mouth, and she caught his bottom lip between her teeth, nibbling i gently. Shuddering, he varied the rhythm of his thrusts, plunging into her wildly only to slow down and tease her, withdrawing almost completely. Fiery tension coiled at the very center of his being, tighter, stronger, pulsing with the need for release. He gathered her to him and moved against her, harder now, faster, intent on carrying them both to the untamed heights of ecstasy.

Laurien clung to him, gasping with the mindless, heart-stirring joy of being one with him. He surged within her, and a shock of pleasure exploded through her, stronger than anything she had felt before. She felt hot and cold and breathless and brilliantly alive, all at once. Her nails marked his hard-muscled back, and he called out her name in a hoarse shout of release.

He lowered himself atop her, pressing her down into the hay, and traced a path of wet kisses along her glistening skin. Laurien stroked his back and pressed her lips to his shoulder, his neck, his chin, relishing his weight, his strength.

"If a few words be the price for such bliss," she murmured against his warm skin, "I pay it gladly."

Connor lifted himself to his elbows and cupped her face between his hands. He looked down at her intently. "Then give me another few words. Tell me that you love me."

She raised a hand to his cheek, her throat feeling tight at the vulnerability she saw so clearly in his eyes for the first time.

"You do love me," he murmured, pressing a kiss against her palm. "I know you love me. Let me hear the words, Laurien."

Her world was still spinning from their lovemaking, all the reasons she should give in clashing with all the reasons she should not. She could think of any number of ways to say she loved him without truly saying it.

Chapter 22

Malcolm tried to awaken, but heavy, enveloping waves of sleep kept fogging his senses. When at last he fought his way upward from the numbing darkness, the pain in his head nearly sent him under again. It felt as if he had been kicked—twice—by a destrier with a grudge to resolve. As he struggled against the layers of shadows, he heard a man's voice, somehow familiar.

"I waited until guests began departing, then crossed the drawbridge and knocked out the guard. But in the morn came only this one and a boy . . ."

A boy? Aidan! Malcolm tried to open his eyes, but found the effort too great, his eyelids weightier than iron. He took a breath to clear his head but was rewarded only with a draught of smoky, fetid air.

He could feel brittle rushes beneath his cheek, the warmth of a fire at his back. He could also feel his own dried blood on his face. Where was he? How much time had passed since he and Aidan had been attacked? He tried to make sense of what was being said.

"I did exactly as you told me. She wasna in her chamber and I couldna find her anywhere . . ." This was a woman's voice. Ceanna? The shrill sound lanced through his head, and Malcolm sank into blissful oblivion again, only to float upward once more moments later. Now a man's voice was shouting.

"By Christ, I was to have the girl *and* both of her accursed abductors by now!" Malcolm recognized that bellow instantly. It was de Villiers. "Instead you bring me only one man and a boy! Where is Glenshiel? And what in the name of Christ do you mean, my betrothed has disappeared?"

"Obtaining Connor's son was a stroke of luck," Ceanna replied in a placating tone. " 'Twill work to our advantage—"

"Enough about the brat! He is of no use to me if we cannot locate the girl."

Malcolm fought again to open his eyes and succeeded just long enough to glimpse a darkened chamber, the edge of a bed, two pairs of legs standing a few paces away, and the skirt of a woman's dress. But even the small amount of light in the room sent stars exploding through his head, and he closed his eyes against the pain.

What had they done with Aidan? And what had de Villiers said? Laurien had disappeared?

He waited for the savage ache to dull a bit, then attempted to move. He was not surprised to find his hands bound behind his back. An attempt to move his feet met the same result. He heard de Villiers's voice draw nearer.

"You hit him too hard, idiot! You were only to subdue him and bring him here, not render him senseless."

This time the second man defended himself. "We have MacLennan. That is more than we had two days past. I have the men out searching for Glenshiel and the girl."

"Well, I have suffered enough delays. We must find Laurien, and we must find her now! Awaken, damn you!"

Malcolm was grabbed by his tunic and jerked to a sitting position. The sudden movement sent cramps stabbing up his legs. A stinging slap landed on his cheek and brought him fully awake.

This time when he opened his eyes, he saw de Villiers's bloated face only inches away, reddened with rage.

"I want answers and I shall have them!" De Villiers released his tunic, and Malcolm fell helplessly back against the edge of the hearth, the impact sending a fresh bolt of anguish through his head.

Squinting against the light, he quickly identified the others. He recognized the man as de Villiers's assassin, Balafre. The woman, he saw with disbelief, was indeed Ceanna. The tiny chamber was evidently in an inn, for it held naught but the bed and a richly decorated traveling chest in one corner.

Aidan was nowhere to be seen.

"Where is your friend, and where is the girl?" de Villiers snarled down at him.

His question sparked an uneasiness in Malcolm that quickly deepened to worry. Laurien was supposed to have remained safe with William. If she was missing, something had gone terribly wrong.

Instead of answering de Villiers, Malcolm locked his gaze on Ceanna. "How could you take part in . . ." The rest dissolved in a cough. His mouth was so dry he could barely speak. "T-tell me what they have done with Aidan."

"The boy is not my responsibility." Ceanna glanced away. "And I owe you and the others naught. Connor never recognized my worth, but the comte is willing to reward me as I deserve—"

"Silence!" de Villiers shouted at her over his shoulder. He glared down at Malcolm. "*Where* is Laurien?"

Malcolm started to shake his head, but decided that speaking, though equally difficult, was less painful. "I dinna know."

Balafre stepped forward at a signal from de Villiers.

The grizzled giant was like a child's nightmare come to life, the necklace of white teeth gleaming about his neck. Malcolm bit back a groan as Balafre grabbed him by the shoulders and slammed him up against the wall.

"Torture has its attraction," de Villiers said in a tight voice. "But it is, unfortunately, quite time consuming. I suggest you save us both the trouble and simply tell me where Glenshiel has taken my betrothed."

Malcolm's only reply was a silent stare. Balafre hit him, a blow to the stomach that knocked Malcolm's breath from him and wrenched a groan from his lips.

De Villiers repeated his question. "Where are they?"

Malcolm glared up at him, gasping for air. Despite the agony throbbing through his body, he could not suppress a chuckle. "You willna believe this, but I have no idea. Do what you will, I shall only tell you the same. I dinna know where they are."

Balafre hit him a second time and Malcolm doubled over, falling to the floor, when de Villiers suddenly ordered Balafre to release him.

"I shall waste no more time on this," de Villiers spat. He turned to Balafre and jerked a thumb toward the door. "Bring me the boy."

Malcolm lay where he had fallen, gulping tortured breaths of the rank air, watching helplessly as the assassin left the chamber. Anger coursed through him when Balafre returned moments later, pushing Aidan in front of him. The boy was gagged, his hands tied. He started to run toward Malcolm, but Balafre grasped the lad's collar and jerked him backward.

"Harming the boy will avail you naught!" Malcolm choked out.

"You chose to make this difficult, not I," de Villiers returned smoothly. "I ask you for the last time, where are they?"

Anguished, Malcolm looked at Aidan, then turned a

hate-filled gaze on de Villiers. "I canna tell you what I dinna know!"

"I warned you, my patience is at an end." De Villiers stalked over to Balafre and slapped Aidan across the face, so hard the lad tumbled to the floor with a muffled cry. Towering over the boy's prone form, the comte withdrew his whip from his belt.

"Nay!" Malcolm shouted, struggling to rise to his knees. "I dinna know where they are! Connor was to await my message at Glenshiel, and Laurien is supposed to be at William's castle.'Tis all I know, damn you! Leave the boy alone."

The whip still coiled in his hand, de Villiers turned slowly to look at Malcolm.

"Milord." Ceanna sidled over to the comte and lay a hand upon his arm. "If the girl is missing, she is with Connor."

De Villiers kept his gaze on Malcolm. "How can you be certain?"

Ceanna's features twisted into a mask of hatred. "Because he is in love with her—"

"Ceanna—" Malcolm tried to stop her.

"If she left him, he would not rest until he found her," Ceanna hurriedly continued when de Villiers gave her his full attention. "If Connor is at Castle Glenshiel, you can be certain she is there with him."

The comte looked down at Malcolm, who tried to mask his reaction to Ceanna's words. With a sinking feeling of frustration, Malcolm knew she was right. Connor would search for Laurien until he found her or dropped from exhaustion. And once he found her, he would not allow her to leave his side again. Damn Ceanna for helping them!

A slow smile curved de Villiers's thick lips, and he stuffed the whip back into his belt. "I believe that you might be correct, my dear. Tell me, how far is it to Castle Glenshiel?''

"Less than a day's ride," Ceanna supplied, beaming with self-importance. "I know the way. And I know the guards quite well. It shouldna be too difficult to convince them to let me in." She nodded toward Aidan. "The boy will also prove useful."

"Very good." De Villiers nodded, his smile giving way to a laugh. "In fact, this could work to our favor."

Leaving Aidan where he lay, de Villiers went to the trunk in the corner. He lifted the lid and searched through the contents. One by one, he withdrew a sheet of parchment, a plume, and a container of ink. And a knife.

He walked back to Malcolm. "I shall need further assistance from you," he said, bending down and placing the writing implements on the floor. "And do not insult my intelligence by trying to tell me you do not know how to write."

Taking the knife, he sliced through the ropes that bound Malcolm's wrists. Malcolm had to stifle a groan as the blood rushed back to his fingers. It felt like shards of glass raining along his skin. De Villiers wrenched Malcolm into a sitting position against the wall, then held out the parchment and plume.

"You will write a letter to this Glenshiel. Tell him a problem has arisen, and you must discuss the situation with him in secret. Tell him to ride with all haste and meet you at Strathfillan Abbey, alone."

"Go to hell," Malcolm ground out.

De Villiers shook his head, the rolls of fat beneath his chin wobbling. "Your refusal will bring your young friend to great harm."

At a flick of de Villiers's hand, Balafre jerked Aidan to his feet. The assassin whipped out his own knife and placed it against the lad's throat. Aidan went pale, his blue eyes wide in an expression of mute terror.

"Nay!" Malcolm's heart pounded. What was he to do? Send Connor into a trap, where all of de Villiers's guards would be awaiting him? He would not stand a chance. Malcolm tried to think clearly despite the throbbing in his head. He knew that regardless of what he did, de Villiers did not plan to let him leave here alive.

Malcolm eyed the knife that the comte still held. One lunge and he might wrest it from him—but in that same moment Balafre could harm the boy. He must try to think of something. For now he would have to bide his time, he decided. And 'twould be best if they thought him weaker than he actually was.

He rubbed his wrists, glaring up at the comte, then slowly took the plume and paper.

"I warn you," de Villiers threatened, "write exactly what I tell you. One misplaced word, even one stray blot of ink, and you shall watch the boy's blood flow."

De Villiers dictated the short message, fingering his knife in impatience while Malcolm wrote with maddening slowness. When Malcolm finished, de Villiers snatched the parchment from him and looked it over intently. Then he folded it and tucked it inside his tunic.

"Ceanna, my dear." He stood and turned toward her. "Bring the boy along. It is time for us to go."

Hurrying to obey, Ceanna took Aidan by the arm and swept from the room without a backward glance. Malcolm felt relief that the boy was unharmed, at least for the moment. Now if only he could get his hands on that knife . . .

"As for you." The comte turned his cold, gray gaze back to Malcolm. "You are about to learn the cost of incurring my wrath." Crossing the chamber, he picked up his ermine-lined silk cloak from atop the trunk. "I had planned to enjoy this, but unfortunately the matter of my marriage requires my immediate attention.''

"I wouldna celebrate yet, de Villiers," Malcolm said, letting his arms rest limply at his sides. "Had I the strength, I would fasten my hands around that flabby throat of yours and choke the last breath from it.''

De Villiers only smiled down at Malcolm, his eyes glittering with satisfaction and triumph. He fastened the jeweled clasp of his mantle and handed his knife to Balafre. "Amuse yourself, Balafre, but do not tarry overlong. Ride to Strathfillan as soon as you can gather our men together.''

"Connor will kill you," Malcolm said flatly. "And if any harm comes to him, or to Laurien or the boy, I shall kill you myself—''

"It will be most difficult for you to carry out such vengeance, *mon ami.*" De Villiers chuckled. "Unless of course, you plan upon returning to haunt me. *Adieu.*" In a swirl of silk, he left, his self-amused laughter echoing in the hallway.

Malcolm stared up at Balafre, who stood only a few feet away, a knife gleaming in each hand.

Balafre looked like some barbarous lord preparing to carve the main course at a feast. An ugly half smile curled the edges of his lips, and he began to pace slowly back and forth, his gaze never leaving Malcolm's.

Malcolm lay completely still, his muscles tensing. Balafre continued to move in a half circle, taunting him, playing with him. He began sharpening the blades against each other. The sound of metal scraping upon metal was shrill in the stifling silence. The assassin edged forward. One step closer. Two. Malcolm swallowed hard, uttering a silent prayer that his legs would not fail him.

The steel blades glimmered in the firelight.

Balafre took another step closer.

With a wild battle cry, Malcolm launched himself forward. He pushed off from the wall, driving upward. His head collided with Balafre's midsection. One of the knives flew from Balafre's hand and skidded away into the rushes. The other blade came slashing down toward Malcolm's face as the two men landed in a tangle.

Malcolm dodged, grabbing Balafre's wrist, and brought both his knees up sharply into his opponent's groin. Balafre bellowed in pain but managed to hold fast to the weapon. Malcolm twisted his legs about, pulling on Balafre's arm to angle the knife downward. He managed to cut partway through the ropes about his ankles before Balafre regained control enough to pull back.

The assassin landed a punch to Malcolm's ribs, then another. They rose to their knees, Malcolm struggling to wrest the knife away. He tried to kick free of the bindings on his legs. He succeeded just as Balafre suddenly wrenched sideways and jabbed an elbow into his chest. For barely an instant, Malcolm's grip faltered. Balafre jerked his wrist free and slashed out.

The knife plunged into Malcolm's side right below his ribs.

Shock and pain wrenched a cry of agony from Malcolm's lips when Balafre pulled the knife free. He could feel blood seeping down his side, could smell its metallic scent heavy in the thick air. Only years of battle experience brought him through the next few moments. Balafre came at him again, and Malcolm deliberately fell onto his back, kicking upward as he rolled. His feet smashed into Balafre's midsection, sending the assassin sprawling into the hearth. Balafre's head struck the edge of the stone, and he fell to the floor, dazed.

Malcolm struggled to his feet. But before he could make a grab for the knife, Balafre was coming around, already on his knees. Malcolm ran for the door, his half-numb feet in agony, his left arm clutched against his blood-soaked side.

Once in the hall, he recognized the inn—the Bear's Head, not one of Kincardine's more respectable establishments. He staggered along the hall and down the stairs to the inn's tavern. It was almost deserted; only a handful of local crofters huddled together over their cups.

"A weapon," he called in Gaelic as he half fell down the stairs. "Give me a weapon!"

The inn's startled patrons looked up, the few women in the place screaming at the sight of the bloodied man rushing toward them. "I am Sir Malcolm MacLennan," Malcolm shouted, hoping some of the men might recognize him. "I need aid."

Before the startled cofters could reply, Balafre appeared at the top of the stairs, roaring in rage. With an oath, Malcolm turned and ran for the back of the inn. Saints' blood, he needed a weapon! He looked madly about as he stumbled down the hall toward the back door. He could spy naught but a tall iron candle stand against one wall. Swearing, he grabbed it and tore open the back door, throwing himself to one side.

Balafre appeared an instant later, and Malcolm struck, hitting him across the shoulders with all the force he could manage. Balafre staggered, but the blow only slowed him. He spun and came at Malcolm, his knife raised to strike. Malcolm lifted the iron pole again and swung upward this time. He caught Balafre across the arm with a resounding crack, sending the knife flying. Before he could strike a third time, Balafre grabbed the end of the stand. He attempted to jerk Malcolm off his feet, but Malcolm suddenly let go. Balafre's momentum sent him tumbling backward.

Unarmed once more, Malcolm forced himself into a run, heading toward the stables. The sorry-looking lean-to offered an even sorrier group of mounts: an emaciated gray horse, a mare in foal, Aidan's little bay. Malcolm looked desperately about for a weapon, seeing naught but Aidan's saddle—and the tiny hunting crossbow the boy had insisted on bringing along.

Malcolm snatched the crossbow from the saddle and loaded it, dropping to his knees. What should have been an effortless task left him weak. Sweat trickled down his forehead and into his eyes. Balafre charged toward him.

Malcolm spun, raising the weapon as he turned, and fired.

And missed.

The slim bolt flew wide and struck Balafre in the arm. With a grunt that sounded more like annoyance than pain, Balafre dropped, rolled, ar.d then dove at Malcolm. Malcolm struck out with the crossbow, using what he knew was the last of his strength, and landed a numbing blow to Balafre's head.

Malcolm lurched to his feet. Balafre tripped him, and he fell on his wounded side with a shout of pain. Before he could move, Balafre's hands were around his throat, squeezing with killing force.

Malcolm grasped the assassin's wrists, trying in vain to break his hold. He fought for air, for life, even as he felt both ebbing from him. His side felt as if it were on fire. Dizziness and nausea assailed him, and he knew he was about to pass out. His fingers grew weaker. The world fogged and began to fade.

"You there! Stop at once!" a voice shouted in Gaelic.

Balafre's grip loosened enough for Malcolm to break free. Coughing and choking, he rolled away, gulping air into his starved lungs.

Looking up, he saw the crofters from the tavern, armed now with a variety of scythes and rusted swords. They quickly surrounded him, placing themselves between him and Balafre.

"This man is known to me," one of them said, kneeling by Malcolm's side. "Sir Malcolm, who is this? Why has he attacked you?"

Malcolm tried to speak, but at first could only make rasping sounds. "H-hired to kill me," he managed at last, closing his eyes when the sky and the ground began tilting and spinning.

This brought a murmur from the group. They moved toward Balafre, brandishing their weapons.

Balafre backed away, yelling at them in French. Before they could corner him, he grabbed for one of the horses. He heaved himself onto Aidan's little bay with surprising agility. Not giving the crofters time to react, he wheeled the animal, digging his heels into its sides, and sent it away at a gallop.

"Nay! Stop him," Malcolm said weakly, struggling to rise. "Bring him back. They mean to kill Connor . . ."

But before Malcolm could even begin to explain, darkness engulfed him once again.

Chapter 23

❧⟋⟍❧

It was late afternoon before Connor and Laurien neared the rocky coast and Castle Glenshiel. Laurien tried unsuccessfully to relax in Connor's arms. After several attempts at conversation, they had lapsed into silence, neither of them able to pretend good cheer. Both were tense with thoughts of Connor's plan, and with the awareness that they must soon part.

Their horse picked its way through the boulder-strewn banks of a river, slipping on the stones and gravel. The river was called the Linnhe, Connor said. He had told Laurien the various place names as they rode, but her usual ease with language failed her as she struggled to repeat the words: Argyll, Strathclyde, Dalness Forest, and Rannoch Moor. The Gaelic tongue had always troubled her, and she wondered if she could ever master it.

But then, she thought with a pang of despair, she would never need to master it. If Connor's plan failed, she would be returning to France with de Villiers; if he succeeded, she would be returning to France alone.

She tried unsuccessfully not to think of the future as they rode on. Connor urged the horse to a faster pace when they reached the shores of Loch Shiel. The lake, Connor explained, wasn't truly a lake, for its distant western end was open to the sea. They passed a sprawling ruin of a castle, and she heard a wistful note in his

voice when he recalled the hours spent exploring its secret passages with his brothers.

As the afternoon sun sparkled on the water, Laurien
caught her first glimpse of Connor's home. Hidden in
this maze of water and mountains, Castle Glenshie
perched on an island in the middle of the loch.

Isolated was the first word that came to her mind as
they approached the fortress of stone. A slim causeway
offered the only access to the island. They cantered down
the slope that led to the ribbon of land, then crossed it.
This place suited him, Laurien thought with a twinge of
sadness. The castle was solitary, rugged, impervious to
storms, to time—a place where a man could live very
much apart from the world.

White swans floated past, rippling the castle's reflec-
tion in the water. Even before the horse reached the
castle's outer wall, Connor's guards hailed him and
opened the gates.

A riot of color met Laurien's startled eyes on the other
side. What should have been a practice ground was instead a garden gone wild. Flowers grew in a thicket of
color, vibrant reds, luminous violets, cool blue and saf-
fron yellow. As they passed through the bailey, she could
see that the flowers grew in an irregular strip, several
feet wide, all along the inside of the wall. It was the last
thing she would expect to find in Connor's home.

They came to a halt at the foot of the steep stairs that
led to the main entrance. One of the guards, a tall man
with red-blond hair, came forth to take their horse.

" 'Tis good to have you home, Sir Connor!'' He nodded to Laurien, showing no surprise at her presence.
"Milady."

"Thank you, Ranald." Connor leaped down, then
lifted Laurien from the saddle. One of his hands strayed
to her waist. "Laurien, this is my steward. Ranald, this

is Lady Laurien d'Amboise. She will be staying with me . . ." He paused, then added, "For a time."

The guard bowed to Laurien. "Welcome, milady. If you have need of anything, please ask for it."

Laurien returned the man's polite greeting with a curtsy. He had a ruddy complexion and gray eyes that conveyed a sparkle of curiosity held in check. He also had the slight squint and inkstained fingers common to stewards, who spent most of their days bent over their lords' accounts.

Before Ranald and Laurien had time to exchange any more pleasantries, Connor started for the castle's entrance. "Has Sir Malcolm's message arrived yet?"

Ranald gave him a perplexed look. "You were *expecting* a messenger?"

"Aye. He is here, then?"

"She is in the solar."

"She?" Connor stopped suddenly, and Laurien nearly collided with his back.

"A nun. She has come every day for the past sennight—"

"What do you mean, a nun? Malcolm wouldna send a—and he couldna possibly have sent a message that many days ago." Connor strode through the massive entry doors and into the great hall.

"I told the woman we didna know when to expect your return. She wouldna believe me," the steward explained as he followed them.

Laurien glanced about her as they hurried through the hall. It was empty save for a single trestle table before the hearth and a few ancient weapons scattered about the walls as decoration. When she gave Connor a curious look, he shrugged.

"I spend little time here," he said by way of explanation before continuing his questioning of Ranald. "What is this nun's name?"

"She wouldna tell us her name. She simply returned
every day, and when she kept coming back, Mara and
Aileen insisted on allowing her to stay. She said she will
speak only to you, alone."

The three of them stopped outside the solar. Connor
paused with his hand on the door, a worried frown
creasing his brow. He looked at Laurien, who gave him
a reassuring smile that neither of them found reassuring.
If the message was not from Sir Malcolm, Laurien
thought, she could take some comfort from the fact that
Connor would not be leaving immediately. But what kind
of message could a nun be bringing, what news so dire
that she would speak only to Connor?

"Have Mara and Aileen prepare a meal for Lady Laurien," Connor told the steward. "Then have them make
one of the upstairs chambers presentable for her. Mara
and Aileen are the kitchen servants," he explained to
Laurien. "They have been here since I was a lad." He
gave Ranald a wry look. "And I have been away too
long if they have started issuing orders."

Laurien followed Ranald across the hall, and Connor
watched her go, not liking the feeling of being parted
from her for even a short time. God's teeth, if a brief
separation was difficult, how was he to survive after
sending her back to France?

Gritting his teeth, he entered the solar. The chamber
was like the others in his home, austere and lacking in
decoration. The solar held a table, candle sconces, and
a pair of high-backed chairs lined with red velvet, the
only spot of color in the room. Shutting the portal behind him, he looked in puzzlement at the tiny form
across the chamber, sitting in his favorite chair.

She sat before the window, her back to him, humming
softly in the sunlight that streamed through the glass.
She was a small woman, garbed in the simple, flowing
black robes of a novice. She was apparently huddled

over a piece of needlework, for long strands of floss trailed over her skirt. The woman did not even turn at his presence, so absorbed was she in her task.

Connor cleared his throat and spoke quietly. "I am told you are anxious to speak with me."

The little woman nearly jumped out of her chair, then sat frozen in place for a moment. Then, very slowly, she put her needlework on the floor and turned to face him.

As she turned, a single word escaped Connor's lips, an oath choked with amazement, fury, and the bitterness of uncountable angry days and nights.

"Sibylla!"

If not for her eyes, he might never have recognized her. Those shining blue eyes were just as he remembered, but all else about her had changed. Her luxuriant hair was hidden beneath a tightly wrapped wimple. Her flawless complexion had been marred by wrinkles that bespoke days spent in worry, and darkened by too much time in the sun. When she smiled at him, tremulously, hesitantly, he could see that her teeth were no longer brilliantly white. And when she spoke, her voice held only a wisp of its former grace and strength.

"I-I have finally gathered enough courage to face you myself."

Connor snapped out of his amazed stupor. "Courage?" he snarled. "How dare you taint that word by even uttering it. How dare you come here after nine years and speak to me of courage!" He crossed the chamber in two strides, and his hands very nearly found her throat. Only the fact that she fled to a far corner saved her. His fingers dug into the back of the chair, and he sent it tumbling across the floor. *"Nine years, damn you to hell!"*

"I explained all. In the missives I sent—"

"I received no missives from you! Not a word! I thought you were dead. I *hoped* you were dead."

She frowned in what appeared to be genuine confusion, and edged away when he came closer. "But I have been sending messages to you for months now. When you wouldna respond, I knew I must come and face you—"

"I willna stand here and listen to your lies. I have received no messages. I have rarely even been here these past months. There has been no one here at all but the guards and servants and—" He stopped suddenly in his pursuit of her.

Ceanna had been here when he was away negotiating for the French alliance. She would have had ample opportunity to sneak a look at any messages. And she would have felt no qualms about concealing missives from Sibylla—if they contained information Ceanna wanted to keep to herself.

His anger cooling to only a slightly less violent boil, he stalked across the chamber and righted the chair, then curtly motioned for Sibylla to take the seat.

When she had complied, he paced in front of her, trying to get his temper under control. "Tell me," he growled, "what is it you explained in these messages? How could you *possibly* have an explanation for deserting your own child? How can you explain the nine years of torment you have inflicted on me?"

Sibylla stared at her hands, clutched in the folds of her robes. "I-I knew you would be like this," she began, her voice so soft he had to strain to hear her. "That is why I tried to explain by writing to you—"

"Explain what?"

"That we are not married."

"*What?*" Connor roared. Unable to restrain himself this time, he grabbed her by the arm and pulled her out of the chair. "What did you say?"

Sibylla cringed away from him, one hand raised to protect herself from his rage. "Please, Connor, I know I have done a terrible thing, but please allow me to explain. We are not married. We were never married."

The room seemed to tilt crazily before Connor's eyes, and for a moment he had the most disturbing sensation that this was a dream and he was being dragged deeper and deeper into it, never to awaken. He seemed to be going numb. He released Sibylla, and she slumped into the chair.

He shook his head to clear it. "We were *never married?*" He stared down at her, thinking she must have lost her mind, along with her youth. "Have you taken leave of your senses, woman? I was there. I spoke the words before the priest. We took vows—"

"But they were not binding. You see, Connor, wh-when we took those vows, I-I was already wed to another."

At this, Connor could only gape at her, his mind reeling. "Who?" he choked out at last, the answer already half clear to him.

Sibylla swallowed hard and stared at her hands again. "Duncan."

Connor felt such a torrent of anger and hurt that he nearly struck her. He forced himself to stay where he was, quite certain that if he took one step toward her, nothing could stop him from beating her.

"I was but five-and-ten, and I was in love with Duncan, and I thought he loved me," Sibylla explained. "I knew my father would oppose the match, for he had already told me of his plans to betroth me to a wealthy merchant from Edinburgh. But I knew that if . . . if Duncan and I lay together, Duncan would have to marry me. We rode to Kilwinning and found a priest willing to marry us in secret. It was only after, when we went to face my father, that the trouble began."

Connor sank into the chair across from her, numbly taking it all in, his fists still clenched.

"I couldna face my father's wrath, so I sent Duncan alone to tell him the news. But Duncan was no braver than I. Instead of telling him of our marriage, he asked for my hand. Father refused, for he had just signed my betrothal papers. But he wasna about to let so wealthy a lord as Sir Duncan of Glenshiel get away easily," she said bitterly. "He offered Duncan the hand of my sister, Eda, along with a generous dowry of lands."

"Sweet Christ," Connor said. "And Duncan, being the greedy sot he was, accepted without saying a word about you."

Sibylla nodded, her eyes shining with unshed tears. "I was furious when I found out. Duncan didna come to face me. He came straight back here and began to make plans for his wedding."

"Sibylla, you could have stopped it! One word from you would have ended his betrothal to Eda."

She shook her head. "I was so angry I wasna able to think. When I saw that he could hurt me so easily, that he could abandon me without a word, I no longer wanted him. I set my mind to making him pay, and I kept my secret to myself. I went to the wedding, appeared to be the good sister, happy for the new couple. And there I met Duncan's brother." She looked up at him, tears falling now. "Young Connor, so sweet, so young—"

"So gullible," Connor finished for her.

"Nay, you were very chivalrous. When you fell on your knee and proposed, 'twas just the excuse I was looking for. You gave me the reason I needed to stay near Duncan and have my revenge."

"And how did you convince your father to allow us to marry? What became of your betrothal?"

She chewed at her bottom lip. "I told Father that you

and I had been trysting in secret for months and I was already carrying your child.''

"God's teeth, you planned all of it.'' Connor felt such a surge of disgust, it overwhelmed even his anger. ''That was why you wouldna lay with me after our one time together on our wedding night. You *planned* to lure Duncan to your bed when I was gone, so he would get you with child and I would know it was his.''

She nodded. ''I knew you would be angry enough to kill him. I never wanted Duncan's child—''

"Aidan,'' Connor said. ''Your son's name is Aidan.''

Sibylla winced, closing her eyes, her face etched with pain. She said the name softly. ''Aidan. The night he was born, and you came to my chamber . . . 'Twas the first time that I saw what I had done, that I realized I was hurting others as well as Duncan. It was like waking up from a nightmare. I have never been brave, Connor. You were angry enough to kill Duncan, and angry enough to kill me. I did the only thing I could think of. I fled.''

"If you regretted what you did, why did you not confess *then?*'' Connor's voice was filled with contempt for her cowardice. ''How could you keep silent for so long?''

"I was in fear for my life. I thought you would hunt me down and kill me, so I took refuge in an abbey under a false name.'' She wiped her eyes with the edge of her sleeve. ''It may make you feel better to know I have been in torment these nine years, Connor. Every morning I awoke certain that this would be the day you would find me and kill me for what I had done. I had naught but time upon my hands. Time to think, to relive every one of my sins over and over. Time to be haunted by nightmares . . . horrible nightmares.''

"And now you have come seeking forgiveness.'' He said it with deceptive softness. Her vengeance and cowardice and silence had cost him dearly the past nine years. He did not believe himself capable of granting her any favor.

Sibylla shook her head. "I dinna expect you to forgive me. I deserve naught but your scorn. I only wanted . . . I needed to at least *try* and set things aright. The sisters have at last accepted that my repentance is true. They have agreed to let me join them as a novice. But I couldna withdraw from the world with this upon my conscience. Now that I have told you the truth, I-I hope my nightmares will cease. I seek only peace now. I canna ask for more."

She rose, trembling, as if she would flee the chamber. "The mother superior at the abbey spoke with the priest who married . . . who thought he married us. He asked to hear my confession." She reached into her voluminous robes with shaking fingers and pulled out a roll of parchment, which she handed to Connor. "This is for you. 'Tis proof of our annulment."

He unrolled the paper, looked at the illuminated lettering and elaborate signatures. It was real. She spoke the truth.

"And what of Aidan?" he asked tightly.

"I-I dinna wish to cause any more pain than I already have. I am certain he is much better off with you than he ever could have been with me. When he is old enough to understand, explain it to him. Tell him that . . ." Her voice faltered. "Tell him to try not to hate me."

She moved to the door and stopped, waiting, wanting, he knew, some kind of absolution from him.

He had hated her all these years, and now he had been denied even his hate. How could he despise this pitiful woman? 'Twas all so senseless—the suffering she had inflicted, the fear that had kept her from coming forth with the truth. Time had punished her more severely than he ever could; years of worry and regret had crushed the once-regal Sibylla into a trembling, beggarly shadow of herself.

He knew she thought him threatening, terrifying, piti-less. Was she right? Could he find no scrap of mercy in his heart? She *had* gone to great effort to right the wrong she had done him. And she had shown courage in facing the one thing she feared most in the world—him.

'Twas time to let go of his bitterness and anger before it consumed any more of his life.

"Dinna fear me any longer, Sibylla," he said quietly. "I feel naught but pity for you. And I grant you my forgiveness."

She smiled, her expression filled with sadness and gratitude, then opened the door. "I wish you only hap-piness," she whispered over her shoulder. "Please be-lieve me."

And with that she fled from the chamber.

Connor sat for a long moment, gripping the chair arms so tightly his fingers began to go numb. His mind was still reeling from the shock of what he had just learned, and his heart was pounding with a storm of emotions. At first only anger and bitterness choked him, mixed after a moment with relief and wonderment. Then, stronger than all the others, unnerving in the way it swept over him, came hope.

He needed to sort this all out, to think of what it meant to his future. In a sudden movement, he flung himself out of the chair and left the solar.

The great hall was empty but for Ranald, who gave him a curious look. "I will be outside," Connor said without breaking his stride.

Ranald knew from Connor's intent expression that his lord wished to be left alone.

Laurien found Connor hours later, in a thicket at the edge of the lake. Sunset ran golden fingers along the loch, bringing the water alive with color while leaving the trees and hills beyond in dusky shadow. He stood staring out across the still waters, his back rigid.

After the strange nun had gone, Connor had stormed out of the castle without pausing to explain the woman's message. Laurien had somehow felt his need to be alone. Even as she burned with curiosity, she had spent the afternoon patiently eating and bathing, listening to Mara and Aileen tell tales of Connor's childhood. But he had been out here for hours now, and the evening was growing cold. Though she respected his need for privacy, she felt a stronger need to offer comfort, to share whatever burden had befallen him.

As she approached along the water's edge, he seemed unaware of her presence. Never had she seen him so completely absorbed.

"Connor?" she asked softly.

He turned suddenly, and Laurien froze, thinking she had made a mistake in interrupting him. But as he recognized her in the day's last light, his hard expression softened to a look she could not describe. It was almost the way he looked just before they made love—full of longing and a fire that threatened to consume her. But this time his gaze held something else, an emotion so strong it almost frightened her. She could feel the warmth of a blush rising in her cheeks.

When she did not move, he opened his arms in invitation. She crossed the distance slowly, cautiously. He met her halfway, pulling her close, enfolding her in the warmth of his cloak and his embrace. She slipped her arms about his back and gingerly rested her head against his chest.

She quelled the impulse to deluge him with questions, knowing how difficult it was for him to reveal even the smallest scrap of personal information. She simply held him, the thrumming of his heartbeat and the gentle waves of the loch the only sounds in the silence.

"It was Sibylla," he declared.

Laurien felt her heart thud. Shock overwhelmed her, then an unreasoning terror that she had just lost something more precious than her own life. She unlocked her arms from about him and looked up at his unreadable gaze, feeling desperate, unable to think of aught to say. "What . . . ," she mumbled. "What did she . . . How . . ."

Connor suddenly raised his hands to her face, holding her still, and kissed her before she could put her fear into words. Surprised, Laurien stiffened at first, then slowly relaxed against him. His lips moved gently over hers, questing, possessive, and Laurien's doubts faded under the warmth of his passion. She responded with all the love she felt for him, leaning into his chest, her arms circling his neck. It was so like him, she mused when his lips finally left hers, to reassure her with a kiss rather than words. It was his way of telling her, swiftly and convincingly, that she had not lost him at all.

Wrapping an arm about her shoulders, Connor led her to a grassy area near the shore. They sat side by side, and he told her, in a voice still fraught with disbelief, all that Sibylla had said.

When he had finished, Laurien felt such a confusing knot of emotions that she could barely think. Her first feeling was elation at the thought that he was at last free, quickly followed by fear that he might never overcome his bitterness—that he might never make room for another woman in his life.

"Saints' breath, can you ever forgive her?" she asked finally.

"I already have. I wasna sure I had it within me, but I *had* to grant her forgiveness."

"Why?"

"Because I amna guiltless in this. Duncan started all of it with his greed, and Sibylla continued it with her revenge. But I allowed the . . . pain I felt to consume nine years of my life. If I call Sibylla coward for hiding all this time, I must call myself coward as well."

"Nay, Connor, that is the last word one would use to describe you—"

"I fled from what I feared, just as she did," he insisted. "I have been in hiding, just as surely as if I had the walls of a cloister about me. I have shut myself away from everyone rather than risk such betrayal again."

"And that is what made you angry—not Sibylla, but yourself for feeling fear."

They sat in silence for a time, gazing out across the loch as day passed into night. Red-brown rock formations towered out of the waters, their dark shadows stealing across the loch's glassy surface.

"How is it," Connor said softly, "that you know exactly what I feel before I am even able to put a name to it?"

"Because I have felt the same," she said, almost to herself. "Better to be alone, than to risk being *left* alone."

Connor tightened his arm about her, drawing her to his chest again. "And what else can you tell me of myself, my learned *demoiselle?*"

She fingered the fastenings on his tunic, brushing her fingers over the bristle of hair that peeked over the opening. "I can tell you that it is not bravery to be fearless. Rather it is bravery to feel fear, and do what you must nonetheless."

She slowly raised her eyes to his. That devouring, urgent, almost frighteningly possessive look had returned. So strong was the emotion in his gaze, she could feel it like a physical touch, a heat that warmed her to the depths of her soul.

"I have so much I want to tell you," he said at last. "God's breath, I have so much I need to ask you, I dinna know where to begin."

Laurien felt her pulse quicken. She rested her head against his shoulder, unable to bear the waiting for the words she so longed to hear. "You do not have to tell me, if you do not want to."

He brushed his lips against her hair. "But I want to. I have spent too long keeping this locked inside. I feel as if I . . . as if I have to let it out or go mad with it."

"Then tell me," she urged gently.

"Laurien, if the choice were yours . . ." Connor hesitated. What if she refused him? How could he bear going back to his solitary existence after knowing the joy of having Laurien in his life? Steeling himself for her answer, he finished his question quickly. "If 'twere your choice, between having your freedom and staying with me, here, which would you choose?"

Laurien remained silent a long moment, surprised at his question. He was asking her to stay with him, yet he said naught of love, or marriage.

But mayhap he needed time to adjust to those ideas; for so many years now, love and marriage had meant only bitterness and betrayal to Connor.

Would she be willing to stay, to give him the time he needed? She thought about Sister Katherine, about her search for her real father, about her knife and the strange runes upon it—a trail that had only led her in circles.

All the unanswered questions that had rung in her head for thirteen years echoed in her mind. *Who is my father? Where is he? Why did he leave my mother? Was it my fault? Why has he not tried to find me?*

Could she *ever* find him, or was it truly time to put away her childhood dreams?

In the end, she decided, the choice was a simple one.

Far better to live with unanswered questions than to try to live without her love by her side.

For that would be no life at all.

"I would stay here with you," Laurien replied, and knew that she spoke her heart's truth.

"Nay, Laurien, take time to consider—"

She sat up and placed her fingers upon his lips. "I would stay here with you," she repeated. "Without you, I have no freedom."

He started to say something else, then nipped at her fingers and smiled suddenly, masking his feelings as he always did. Laurien felt a tug of disappointment. Connor might be free of his past, but he was not yet free of himself, not yet sure enough of her love that he could allow himself to voice his own feelings.

But she must be reasonable, she told herself. He had been hurt very badly and had spent the last nine years avoiding emotional risks; it would take time for him to change. She would have to be—nay she *would* be—patient.

"I am willing to guess," he murmured, "that there was one part of the castle that was left out of your tour today."

"And what is that?"

"The master's bedchamber."

Laurien sighed and returned his smile. If she could not hear of his love, she would happily settle for a demonstration. She let the full force of her love and passion and longing show through her gaze. "Aye, milord."

"Well then, milady." He lifted her in his arms. "Let us remedy that oversight without delay."

Chapter 24

Connor and Laurien lay side by side in his bed, their bodies pressed together in warm union amid a tangle of sheets and blankets. Connor watched rays of morning light shimmer through a crack in the shutters and dance along the floor of his chamber. He felt pleasantly exhausted, the kind of sleepy half awareness that told him the night was spent and the day fast approaching. One of his legs was draped over Laurien's, his arm tight about her waist.

In the tentative sunlight, her skin looked very pale against his. She felt so soft and feminine and vulnerable, it made him ache. They had kept each other awake most of the night, giving themselves to one another again and again. Laurien had surrendered to him completely, holding back nothing, by turns crying out his name and whispering words of love.

Have we been together so short a time? he thought in wonder. Laurien fit beside him so perfectly, fit his life so perfectly, filling all the empty spaces within him. It was hard to imagine a time without her; yet only a few weeks before, he'd been utterly alone. It was like falling asleep in a desert and awakening in an oasis. Laurien was the water his parched spirit had thirsted for, the gentle rain that cooled the fires of longing within him.

He accepted all she could give, and marveled that she gave without demanding aught in return. What aston-

341

ished him even more was the fact that he *wanted* to share
so much with her—his secrets, his past, his future. He
would give his very life for her, if that was what love
demanded.

Love. The thought should have shocked him, but it
did not. He was not sure when he had first known the
name for this feeling that overpowered him, he had been
fighting it so long. But in the dawn's light, he found
himself calmly accepting it as fact, yielding to it without
a struggle. This love for Laurien had quietly become a
part of him, until it was no more changeable than the
beating of his heart or the color of his eyes. To fight it
now would be to fight himself. Instead he chose to revel
in his own surrender.

He brushed his lips through her hair, thinking *I love
you,* wanting to say it, but finding the words still caught
in his throat. Frustrated, he planted a kiss on her shoulder, then rubbed his chin lightly against her back, tickling her with the stubble of his beard. She moaned softly
in protest and tried to roll over, but he held her still.

Laurien sighed, enjoying his hard-muscled strength
surrounding her. Her body felt deliciously weary, tender
in all her most sensitive places. Part of her wanted to
savor the only hours of rest she had had this night, part
did not want to be separated from Connor even by sleep.
As always, he was trying to make the choice for her,
nibbling the nape of her neck.

She really should awaken so they could talk, she
thought fleetingly. In fact, she should insist that they
talk. He had yet to say more than a few vague words
about his plan to outwit de Villiers, and she wanted to
help him.

He also had yet to say what she most longed to hear.

His eyes, his hands, his body had spoken eloquently
of his love all night, but he could not seem to say the
words. She knew how difficult it was for him, but she

needed to hear him say it. Only then could she hold him in her heart with a woman's certainty.

He feathered an exquisitely arousing path of kisses over her shoulder, then began suggestively pressing his hips against her. Laurien shivered, feeling the evidence of his arousal and smiling at the thought that he could desire her so, after the long and passionate night they had just shared.

She moaned when his tongue found her ear and flicked teasingly at the lobe. The man would be impossible if she kept giving in to him so easily.

"Saints' breath, if you make love to me again I shall faint," she whispered. "Connor, we must talk." Despite herself, she tilted her head back, baring her neck to his kisses.

"Later," he commanded softly, nuzzling the tender skin of her jaw. Connor did not want to spend the morning talking, questioning, wondering what this day or the next would bring. He wanted to feel, to glory in the way Laurien responded to him, to know again the joy of her body and spirit blending with his. Holding her tightly against him, he nudged her thighs apart with his knee.

"Connor . . ." Laurien protested weakly. "I am serious. We need to—" She cried out softly when his hand suddenly left her waist to find the moist core of her desire. She was already so sensitive that his lightest touch nearly sent her into madness.

His fingers, exquisitely gentle, grazed her delicate bud. He explored her, opened her, until Laurien lost all memory of what she had been about to say, lost capacity for speech of any kind. When her lips parted, she uttered not a protest but a gasp of sweet longing. Even as her pulse quickened, her limbs felt heavy, powerless.

She felt terribly vulnerable in this position, but any uncertainty she felt was drowned in the liquid fire that Connor's touch sent flashing through her. She could summon no urge to even try and pull away. She trusted him completely, and knew that he alone held such absolute power over her. Only Connor could take her to the heights where they soared as one.

His fingers parted her soft folds, and she could feel the blunt, heavy hardness of him pressing insistently against her. He slowly, slowly began to ease himself inside her, his fingers returning to stroke her tender nubbin of desire. Her body tensed instantly as a riot of sensations overwhelmed her, pleasure on the very edge of pain.

"Nay, be calm," Connor ordered in an urgent whisper. "I am here, and you are safe with me."

His words worked like a spell, weaving around her to soothe her. Laurien opened to him, her softness yielding to his steely hardness. He thrust forward, gently filling her until he possessed her completely. She uttered a soft moan of satisfaction and joy at feeling him so deep inside her, then cried out in protest when he withdrew. Her body tightened around him, trying to hold him within as he began to move slowly.

His fingers returned to work their magic in the damp curls between her legs. She arched against him, her lips parting in a soundless expression of pleasure. She felt an exquisite sense of feminine power, knowing she was the sole focus of all his passions. At the same time, she was almost faint with awareness of the masculine power he wielded over her, a fierce, demanding forcefulness; yet she did not fear it even as it threatened to overwhelm her.

She felt utterly alive with awareness of him, the heat of his body, his solid muscles flexing and straining against her back as he moved within her. She need not fear losing herself to his power, she knew, for her strengths balanced and nourished his. To be complete, to be whole, they needed each other. Only together could they create a new and undefeatable power that began and ended with love.

They moved together like two waves upon the sea, ebbing and flowing one into the other. Laurien was nearly dazed with the hypnotic, undulating motion of his hips against her, with the unbearably sweet sensation of his manhood caressing the depths of her femininity. When she thought her body would shatter with the tension, her release at last blazed through her, shimmering with such intensity it left her trembling in Connor's arms. He joined her an instant later, embedded deep within her, filling her with life. His hoarse shout of exultation rang out, and then he lay beside her utterly spent, his breath hot and moist against her neck.

Incapable of movement and unwilling even to contemplate leaving the bed, Laurien offered no resistance when he eased out of her and turned her in his arms. She had time only to place one light, damp kiss in the thatch of hair on his chest before sleep claimed her.

She awoke sometime later, noticing that Connor's warmth no longer surrounded her. He was up and beginning to dress.

Laurien could barely raise her head from the pillows. "Where do you go?" she objected sleepily.

"To see if Malcolm's message has arrived yet. Stay here and sleep," he whispered, as if afraid to disturb the gentle feelings that still swirled about the room. He bent over her for a kiss, smiling down at her, his eyes still passion-dark. "You look beautiful in my bed."

As he left, Laurien started to snuggle back down into the sheets, still half asleep, then sat up suddenly in vexation. He had done it again! She had been certain he was ready to declare his love for her, and he had neatly managed to distract her and get away without saying a word.

Throwing the sheets aside, she got out of bed and

began to dress. This new tendency she had developed toward following Connor's orders—without even thinking twice—was most disturbing. She had best stop being so obedient, lest the man become insufferably pleased with himself.

She found him in the great hall, alone before the hearth. Connor was studying a piece of parchment, his features cast into a frown.

"It is not what you expected?" Laurien asked, worry edging into her voice as she descended the stair.

Connor looked up as she approached and gave her a chagrined half smile. "And I thought I could keep you abed all day. Foolish of me to think I had you in hand at last."

Laurien ignored his attempt at humor. "Is it the message from Sir Malcolm?"

Connor nodded his head. "Aye, 'tis from him. I recognize Malcolm's hand."

Laurien could tell that something was wrong, and that he was trying not to let her see his concern.

Connor silently read the missive again. *A problem has arisen. I must discuss the situation with you in secret. Ride with all haste and meet me at Strathfillan, alone.* Why did he supply no details? Connor and Malcolm had planned to deliver a surprise in place of Laurien: the ten thousand in silver that de Villiers had originally demanded. 'Twould mean giving up every last coin they had between them—funds they had intended to use to help the Scottish cause—but 'twas worth it to save Laurien. Once allied with France, Scotland would be powerful enough to fend off the English.

Why did Malcolm make no mention of bringing the money? Had de Villiers not secured the alliance? Saints' blood, he did not want to think of what that would mean for Scotland.

The only way to find out was to ride to Strathfillan as

Malcolm instructed. Filled with a sense of foreboding, Connor folded the paper and tucked it into his tunic.

Laurien touched his sleeve. "Connor, what is it? What has happened?"

He tipped her chin up, smiling at her reassuringly. "Naught for you to be concerned about."

Laurien knew he was trying to protect her, a very noble and very male impulse that she did not care for one bit. If he was going to be in danger, she wanted to know every detail of his plans and how she could help. But she could tell his mind was made up—and knew from past experience it was pointless to argue with him. "You are leaving," she said flatly. "And I am to stay here."

"I have ever admired your quick mind, Laurien," he said, his tone light and teasing. "I must go and meet Malcolm. Ranald is already having my horse saddled."

He put an arm about her shoulders. Laurien tried to push him away, feeling unreasonably angry with him. He was shutting himself off from her again, when he had only just begun to open his life to her. She did not want to be treated like a fragile creature in need of his protection; she wanted to share every part of his life, the danger as well as the laughter and joy.

Connor did not allow her to leave his embrace. "Laurien, 'tis for your—"

"I do not *care* if it is for my own good!" She glared at him, frustrated at being made to feel helpless. "What about *your* good? Am I not allowed to care about you?"

"Aye, that you are." He kissed her tenderly. "But we willna be able to discuss that now. 'Tis time for me to leave."

Giving her no chance for further questions or objections, he led her from the hall, one arm still about her shoulders. Outside in the bailey, a stableboy stood beside Connor's horse and Ranald waited with his cloak and sword.

Connor quickly donned both, looking at Laurien. "You willna follow," he said, gently but sternly. "You willna leave here."

"You will try to remember you are not made of steel," she said in the same tone. She felt a pain in the pit of her stomach as she watched him strap the scabbard about his waist.

"And your promise?" he insisted.

"I give you my solemn word, I will be here when you return . . . if you promise to return to me safe and whole."

A spark of humor still lighting his eyes, he caught her about the waist. "Demanding wench." He kissed her a hard, possessive kiss that was over too soon, leaving her feeling as if she might sink to her knees. "Aye, I promise," he whispered for her alone. Still gazing down at her, he spoke to his steward. "I leave her in your care, Ranald. If aught befalls her, you shall answer to me."

"She shall have the protection of this keep and every last man in it, sir." Ranald saluted smartly, then motioned for the stableboy to join him. They walked back toward the keep, discreetly giving Connor and Laurien privacy to say farewell.

As the steward left, Connor started to say something to Laurien, then seemed to reconsider. With one last hug, he silently released her and started toward his horse. Laurien wrapped her arms about herself, noticing for the first time the biting cold of the autumn wind. Her eyes burned with unshed tears, but she blinked rapidly, not allowing herself to give in to the worry she felt.

Connor was beside his stallion now, one hand on the bridle, the other on the saddle. Suddenly he stopped, stood still a moment, then turned around. Striding back to a surprised Laurien, he pulled her into his arms and held her tightly.

He said nothing, simply held her against him, one hand reaching up to tangle in her hair. Laurien could feel his chest rising and falling rapidly, his heart pounding as if he were running a race. Then he brushed his lips against her cheek and spoke in a voice that was somewhere between a whisper and a growl.

"I love you."

For a moment, Laurien could not believe what she had heard. The next instant she felt as if she were soaring on the wind. His words sang in her heart and she looked up at him, the tears spilling onto her cheeks.

"You already knew that," he said, his tone gently accusing as he kissed her tears away.

"Nay." She leaned into his embrace and held him to her with a fierce strength she had not known she possessed. "I hoped."

"Now you know," he said gruffly. As if to ward off any further discussion or doubts on the subject, his lips lowered to hers, capturing her in a kiss as sweet as it was brief, like a flame flaring to life, only to be suddenly extinguished.

He crossed the bailey again, this time mounting his horse. He turned toward her one last time, and their gazes locked across the distance. The wind whipped his pale hair, tossing it over his dark eyes, which shone with determination, with passion. Holding the stallion in check, he looked so powerful, invincible, every inch the warrior. The flame in his gaze was stronger than a physical touch, and she knew that he was capturing her image just as she was etching his into her mind and heart. *Please, God,* she begged silently, *bring him back to me.*

Then suddenly the contact was broken. He wheeled his mount and galloped over the drawbridge, across the causeway, and into the fields beyond. Laurien watched until he was a shadow against the hills.

And when she could see him no more, she had a sudden, unreasoning feeling that she would never see him again.

It very nearly made her toss her vow to the wind and ride after him. She steeled herself against the reckless impulse. She *must* prove herself worthy of Connor's trust. She forced herself to turn away from the bailey and walk back toward the castle.

Her thoughts were so filled with love and hope and worry for Connor, she never considered the possibility that she herself might be in danger.

Malcolm only made it halfway to Castle Glenshiel before he collapsed again. He managed to slip from his horse, realizing that, had he fallen, he would likely have reopened the wound that the crofters had stitched and bandaged for him only hours before. Anxiety seized him. He had to warn Connor and Laurien before Balafre and de Villiers reached them. Perhaps if he were to rest . . . He stumbled into a thicket by the side of the road before he passed out completely.

He did not awaken until he felt someone shaking him by the shoulder. Opening his eyes, he saw that the sun hung low in the sky and a man was hovering over him. The man's image doubled, tripled, then resolved into a single face that made Malcolm shut his eyes tightly.

"Holy Mary, Mother of God," he groaned. "The angels have come for me. I *am* dead."

This was met with a chuckle. "Nay, sir, I am no angel," the young man's voice said in French. "And I assure you, you are alive. It seems you have taken a fall from your horse. Are you unwell?"

Malcolm opened his eyes experimentally, but could not speak, so great was his amazement. If he was neither dead nor delirious, where could this visage have come from? He blinked, and the image did not disappear, but seemed quite solid and real. It was the face that had taunted him in dreams for twenty years. All the features were as he rememberd—the dark hair, high cheekbones, and pale blue eyes, the color of the eggshells of some rare bird—yet recast in masculine form.

If this was not the ghost of his beloved Adelle, then who in God's name could it be?

The lad impatiently rubbed a large bruise on his chin, and a ring upon his hand flashed in the late afternoon sun. Malcolm stared at the gem—a small emerald set in a broad silver band. 'Twas exactly like the ring he had given Adelle before leaving on Crusade!

"I would offer you assistance, sir, but I am in a hurry," the stranger said. "Allow me to help you onto your horse and I will be on my way."

"Nay, wait," Malcolm said urgently, grasping him by the arm. "That ring, where did you get it? What is your name, lad?"

The masculine version of Adelle's face frowned at him. "It was given me by my sister. Really, sir, I am not in the habit of conversing with strangers—"

"Your parents," Malcolm choked out. "What was your mother's name?"

"What difference in that?" The lad shook his head, looking down at Malcolm as if he thought the older man delirious. "Mayhap you should see a physician—"

"Your mother's name," Malcolm insisted, grabbing the boy's tunic to restrain him from rising.

The lad seemed puzzled a moment. "Mayhap we can be of assistance to one another. I have been traveling this road all day, but I seem to have become lost. I will tell you what you wish to know if you can direct me to a place called Glenshiel—"

"Aye," Malcolm cried, his mind racing ahead, "Sweet Christ, what is your name?"

"I am Henri d'Amboise, son of Louis d'Amboise. My mother was Adelle d'Evreux," the boy responded.

At this Malcolm released Henri's tunic and fell back upon the grass, convinced he had lost his mind. "This canna be." He closed his eyes, shaking his head.

"I assure you sir, I speak the truth," the lad said in irritation. "Had I known I was to be insulted, I would not have stopped to play Samaritan. Now if you would do me the favor of telling me who you are—"

"I am Sir Malcolm MacLennan." Malcolm raised himself to his elbows, staring at Henri and trying to sort through the maze of facts assaulting him. "D'Amboise, you said. That would make you . . . Lady Laurien's brother? But they told me Adelle was *dead* . . ."

"She died many years ago. Did you know my mother? And how is it that you know my sister?" Henri's gaze darkened.

Malcolm absorbed the news that his Adelle was dead, but strangely felt no new surge of grief. For twenty years, he had believed her lost. Even as his mind was reeling, his heart was gladdened to find some part of her still alive, in Henri . . . and in Laurien. "How old is your sister?" he asked suddenly.

Mayhap it was the urgency in Malcolm's voice, for Henri answered quickly, his own eyes lighting with realization as he looked at Malcolm more closely. "Twenty, come spring. God's breath—your eyes are the right shade, and if your hair had less gray—"

"Had your mother a knife? A silver blade with an emerald in the hilt, and an inscription in Norse runes?"

"*Norse* runes? Aye." Henri nodded. "Mother gave Laurien the knife and this ring before she died. Laurien gave the ring to me and carries the knife with her always—"

Malcolm's cry of joy and shock interrupted him. "It must be true. She is my child, my own daughter!" He was overcome by such a mixture of emotions that he would have leaped to his feet and danced had he the strength. Sweet, beautiful Adelle had given him a daughter. He wanted to laugh and cry and shout his pride to the sky all at once. "They told me Adelle had died bearing our child. But they lied to me. They sent her to marry another—and the child lived!"

"But how do you know Laurien?" Henri shouted.

A sudden, urgent fear stifled the other emotions Malcolm felt. He hesitated, then rose painfully to his feet, deciding honesty would be best at the moment. "I helped to abduct her from de Villiers. 'Tis a very long story and I havena the time to explain it all to you. She is in very great danger."

"From the man who kidnapped her?"

"Nay." Malcolm shook his head impatiently. "She is with him, but believe me when I tell you he is no threat to her. He loves her."

Instead of arguing as Malcolm had expected, Henri nodded, smiling. "My sister may be able to hide many things, but she has never been able to hide her feelings from me. I do not know how it came about, but she is in love with this man who abducted her. If you say he loves her as well, then I believe you."

"They are both in danger. De Villiers means to lure Connor to his death and take Laurien from Castle Glenshiel." Malcolm looked at the sun hanging low on the horizon. "And 'tis too late to get to the castle in time to stop Connor. I must ride to Strathfillan before he reaches it—"

"Nay, Sir Malcolm. You are in no condition for a hard ride. Tell me the way and I shall go."

Malcolm started to protest, then gave Henri a considering glance. The lad was young, but had the same fire and stubbornness as his sister—as Adelle. Nodding, Malcolm knelt in the road. While he drew Henri a map in the dirt, he quickly explained how he and Aidan had been captured, and told Henri about the note and the trap de Villiers planned for Connor.

"Follow this road until you come to another that forks to the south, thus." Malcolm pointed. "Ride south until you come to Strathfillan Abbey. But be wary, for de Villiers's men will be there in hiding. If you dinna come upon Connor along this south stretch of road, ride back toward the north until you find him."

Henri studied the map, then rose. "Are you sure you will be all right?"

"Dinna worry about me. Find Connor and tell him what has happened. Then ride back to Glenshiel as fast as you can. I will try to get there anon."

Henri paused, again rubbing his bruised chin. "I have already met this Sir Connor, and we did not part on the best terms. How can I be sure he will trust that the message I bring is from you?"

Malcolm paused, thinking quickly. "Do as I do." He placed two fingers in his mouth and demonstrated the falconer's whistle. "He will know by that signal that I have sent you."

Henri imitated him, then mounted his horse and sent it away at a gallop. Malcolm managed to pull himself back into his own saddle, setting off at a pace that jarred his wounded side relentlessly. He hardly felt the pain, so concerned was he about Laurien, his *daughter*. He must get to Glenshiel before de Villiers.

The very last light of day gave way to darkness as the two horses cantered around the edge of the loch. Ceanna felt her heart begin to beat faster as they came within sight of Castle Glenshiel. She pulled her mount to a stop and turned to de Villiers's guard.

"Do you remember the directions I gave you?"

The man nodded, dismounting to remove his cloak and boots.

"Good," Ceanna continued imperiously. "Ready one of the boats you will find at the edge of the loch, then make your way to the back stair and await my summons. I dinna know how long I shall be."

"Aye, milady." He led his horse into the thicket at the edge of the lake. A moment later, Ceanna heard a soft splash as the guard dove into the freezing water and began to swim toward the island.

Smiling with satisfaction, she rode on. She liked giving orders and having them so quickly obeyed. Soon, as de Villiers's queen, she would be able to experience the feeling all the time. Pleased beyond measure by that thought, she guided her horse onto the causeway that led to the castle's main entrance, one hand wrapped around the tiny flask hidden deep in the folds of her cloak. She hoped she could remember all the comte's directions about how to use the drug.

Too much could be deadly, and 'twould be *such* a shame for Laurien to die too quickly.

It was long past midnight by the time Malcolm arrived. The guards greeted him as he reached the end of the causeway and rode beneath the gates. He dismounted awkwardly, feeling a stab of pain in his side as he did so. Touching his wound, he felt fresh blood seeping through his tunic. He swore, pressing his arm to the cut, and started up the stairs into the keep.

Ranald came down to greet him. "Hail, Sir Malcolm." His smile faded. "You are wounded. What hap—"

"Never mind that. Rouse the guards. Has anyone attempted to enter the castle? Is the Lady Laurien within?"

"She is asleep upstairs," Ranald responded quickly,

alarmed by Sir Malcolm's appearance and agitation, following him into the great hall. "I have seen no strangers enter or leave since Sir Connor rode out this morn."

Malcolm digested this news with some relief, saying a silent prayer of thanks that Laurien, at least, was safe. Now if only Henri could get to Connor in time . . .

"Let me help you, sir." Ranald tried to support Malcolm as he started up the steps to the upper floors.

"I am fine," Malcolm insisted, shaking him off. "Show me to Lady Laurien's chamber. I will rest after I see her."

Frowning, Ranald led him down the hall. Malcolm knocked hesitantly at Laurien's door, knowing he had much to discuss with her and not at all sure how to even begin.

There was no reply. He knocked again. When there was still no response, he opened the door to find an empty chamber.

"Where is she, Ranald?"

"But, sir, she was here," the steward replied, his voice concerned. "She dined with me and Mara and Aileen in the hall, then retired early. The Lady Ceanna arrived shortly after and asked to speak with her—"

Malcolm swore and hurried back toward the stairs. "Summon the women, and rouse the guards! Ask if anyone has seen her."

They quickly began a search, but an hour later one thing was clear.

Laurien was nowhere to be found.

Chapter 25

Something had gone terribly wrong. Laurien knew that with certainty as she fought against the grogginess that clouded her mind. Even through her fogged senses, her knowledge of healing told her what the problem was. Someone had drugged her.

She could feel the motion of waves beneath her and suddenly realized what had brought her awake. Her hand was trailing in water that was wintry cold. She tried to pull it away and found she could not. Opening her eyes, she discovered that she was lying on her back, the blackness of night surrounding her, tiny pinpricks of light shining above . . . stars. She was in a small boat, upon the loch. She struggled to sit up and instead lurched sideways, her arms and legs refusing to respond to her mind's orders.

Her heart began beating wildly, and beads of perspiration broke out on her forehead. She fought back waves of dizziness and panic. What kind of strange drug was this, that made her muscles limp but left her mind keen and clear?

"Sit still, you fool, or you shall tip the boat!"

Laurien blinked into the darkness and felt a surge of anger as she saw who shared the boat with her. Ceanna! Laurien could not make her lips form the sharp reply that came to mind. The only sound she made was a babbling that seemed more like a piteous moan. Ceanna laughed and turned her back.

What in God's name was happening? As Laurien's eyes adjusted to the gloom, she could make out the figure of a man at the prow, pulling steadily at the oars. Though she could not see the color of his garments, the pattern and style were familiar to her. It was one of de Villiers's guards!

A frisson of fear shot through her half-numbed body. She had no idea how Ceanna had come to be in league with de Villiers's men, but she knew it boded ill. She tried unsuccessfully to sit up, but did manage to raise her head to look about. They were in the middle of the loch, quickly approaching the far shore and the abandoned castle Connor had pointed out to her earlier. Laurien wanted to scream in frustration. She was being taken away from Connor, and was helpless to stop it. For once she had obeyed him and stayed put—and still she would be gone when he returned! The irony of it nearly wrung a hysterical laugh from her lips.

She must find a way back to Castle Glenshiel. She peered over the edge of the boat, briefly toying with the thought of throwing herself over the side and swimming to shore. She just as quickly discarded the idea. In her muddled condition, she would surely drown.

She tried again to speak to Ceanna. "Wh-where . . ." was all she could manage.

"Where are we taking you?" Ceanna smiled over her shoulder, a cruel leer that gleamed in the starlight. "Why, to your wedding, of course. You are several weeks late for the ceremony, *milady,* and your groom has become most impatient."

Laurien's eyes widened, and she felt a nausea that had naught to do with the drug or the choppy current.

Ceanna continued, seeming quite happy to carry on a one-sided conversation. " 'Twas ridiculously easy to get inside the castle. Ranald knows me quite well, and he had no reason to suspect my real purpose. Not after I told him I had traveled *such* a long way to visit with my *dear* friend Laurien. I told him not to announce me because I wanted to surprise you. Did you not enjoy your surprise?'' She laughed and turned her back again. ''Once I was inside, 'twas not difficult to conceal myself in your chamber and wait for you to retire.''

Laurien knew the rest. Exhausted from her near-sleepless night and a day spent worrying about Connor, she had fallen asleep quickly, only to awaken upon feeling hands about her throat. She had started to cry out, but someone—obviously Ceanna—had forced a burning, bitter liquid past her lips. She'd had only an instant to struggle before losing consciousness.

Laurien tried to gather her wits about her. How had Ceanna gotten her out of the castle? De Villiers's guard had probably helped Ceanna carry her. If they had snuck down the back stair and out to the loch, they would not have aroused the slightest alarm, and no one would know Laurien was gone until morn.

By then, Ceanna and the guard could have her on a ship bound for France. Bound for de Villiers.

Laurien steeled herself against that thought. She had made her choice, and that choice was to stay with Connor. She was not going back to France and, by Blessed Mary, she was *not* going to marry the comte! They could not keep her drugged all the way to the coast, lest they risk killing her. She would find some way to slow their journey, and pray that help would arrive.

The tiny craft was drawing closer to the far shore. Laurien could see a ribbon of sand, glowing eerily in the moonlight, and the craggy outline of the ruined castle just beyond. A figure came forth from the shadows of the abandoned fortress.

De Villiers!

Had she been capable of screaming, Laurien would have rent the night with her cry of anguish. There was no mistaking that enormous form. She could almost feel his anger and hatred radiating toward her.

In the same instant, she knew with certainty what his plan for her would be. He would not give her another chance for escape. He would not wait to return to France. He meant to perform the ceremony here! She felt the bitter stab of an emotion she had never before known.

Despair.

The boat came within a few feet of the shore and the guard leaped out, splashing into the shallows and dragging the small craft forward until it ground upon the sand. De Villiers approached, ignoring Ceanna's outstretched hand. "You middling wench, what took you so long? I've roamed that rotting castle until I was blue with boredom."

He reached for Laurien. She cringed when she felt his cold, damp fingers close about her wrist. She struggled helplessly, her arms and legs flailing as he hauled her from the boat and onto the shore.

"Are you not glad to see me, sweet?" he said in a soft, taut voice. "I have rescued you from your captors. Haven't you a kiss for your champion?"

His mouth came down on hers, and Laurien thought she would choke with revulsion. His hands gripped her painfully by the shoulder while his soft, thick lips pressed against her mouth. He tried to force her lips apart, but Laurien kept her teeth clamped shut. Suddenly he released her, shoving her away. Laurien staggered, but her legs would not support her, and she fell to the sand at his feet.

"This is how I have longed to see you. Upon the ground before me, begging forgiveness for all the trouble you have caused me. It is how you will spend what is left of your life,'' de Villiers growled in the darkness above her. ''Ceanna has told me the truth about you, you little whore. How dare you throw yourself at that thieving Scotsman after you rejected *me!* You will regret it, I promise you that.''

Laurien glared up at him, telling him with her eyes what she could not force her tongue to say. She was not beaten, would never beg, would never submit to him. Not as long as she lived. She loved Connor. De Villiers was *not* going to force her into marriage.

De Villiers clucked his tongue. ''I can see by your expression that you have yet to accept your fate. You still hold some hope of rescue. I am afraid I must be the one to dash those hopes. Ceanna wanted to tell you, but I reserved this pleasure for myself.''

He bent down so that his face was only inches from hers. ''They are dead, milady. Both men who abducted you are dead. My man Balafre killed MacLennan this morning. And your Connor has been cut to pieces by now.''

Laurien felt her heart pounding against her ribs, her blood surging through her veins. It could not be true! De Villiers was lying to make her give in to him. She at last found her voice. ''N-nay. You lie!''

De Villiers laughed. ''It is the truth, I assure you. The message your lover received this morning was no more than a lure that drew him to his death. Twenty of my men were waiting for him. They killed him slowly and trampled what was left into the ground.''

Laurien was shaking now as the pounding of her heart sent the last of the drug through her. The note! She had known there was something wrong about the note. Connor had ridden straight into de Villiers's trap.

Her anguish came out in a scream, a primitive, wordless cry, shrill with the depth of her pain and the loathing she felt for de Villiers.

"You hateful, murdering bastard!" She struck desperately at him, her nails aiming for his eyes, and managed to draw blood upon his cheek before he caught her arms and jerked her to her feet.

"Do you not understand?" He shook her roughly. "I have won. It is time you accepted your fate."

"My fate is to be with Connor."

"I shall grant that wish, as soon as I grow tired of you," he growled. "And I am glad you have found your voice. You will need it to say your vows and become my wife!"

"You will grow old and *die* before you hear me say the words!"

"We shall see, milady."

He half dragged, half carried her toward the ruined castle, Ceanna and the guard trailing behind. Though the outer walls had long since tumbled into ruin, a few of the castle's chambers and one of the towers were still standing. They entered the great hall, nearly intact but for a gaping hole high in one wall. Laurien saw that one more shock waited for her inside.

Aidan, his hands tied and his mouth bound, sat before the hearth.

"We captured the boy when we killed MacLennan," de Villiers informed her with relish. "So if you have any hopes left that my words are false, I suggest you give them up."

"By God's truth," Laurien cried, "I shall *kill* you for what you have done—"

"If you want to see this child live," he replied coldly, "you will stand before a priest and say your vows without protest."

Laurien realized then just how empty her threat was. She felt an icy shiver of frustration and anger knife through her. She was powerless, trapped, utterly alone. She squeezed her eyes shut, Connor's face and voice and every cherished moment they had shared flashing through her mind. The words he had whispered only this morning haunted her. *"I love you . . . love you . . . love—"*

He was lost to her forever.

A wrenching sense of loss and helplessness drowned the last of her defiance. She stared at the floor, blinking back tears she would not allow de Villiers to see. Whatever dreams of happiness she had dared allow herself were shattered.

Her shoulders slumped. She shook her head in disbelief. "Why? Why have you done this? Are my lands so important that you would kill to make me your wife?"

"Aye," he said quickly, that single word filled with a lifetime of viciousness and greed and longing.

Laurien glared at him. She had but one thing left to live for—to save Connor's son.

And she had one thing left to offer in trade. "You will let Aidan go free," she choked out, "as soon as . . . we are wed."

De Villiers shrugged. "Once you are my wife, you may escort him home yourself."

"Then I will do as you wish."

De Villiers broke into a grin that was nearly ecstatic with satisfaction and triumph. "Then let us prepare for the ceremony."

He led her into what must have been the castle's solar. There, lying across de Villiers's traveling trunk, was a satin gown—not simply a gown, but a precise replica of the wedding garb Laurien had donned on that fateful day that seemed so long ago in Chartres. It was of de Villiers's blue and gold, with a long, trailing train and tight, fitted sleeves. Even the slippers, the veil, the wimple were the same.

"No one bests Jacques de Villiers." He smiled at her. "No one denies me what I want. I mean for you to remember that. You shall wed me precisely as I intended, and if ever again you feel the urge to make trouble for me, remember this day.'' De Villiers shoved her inside the chamber. ''I will allow you a few moments to dress. Do not make me come back to fetch you.''

As he slammed the door, Laurien wanted to rage and cry and scream, all at the same time. She was trapped in an elaborate, cruel jest, a nightmare she was doomed to live over and over until the ending satisfied de Villiers. He saw all of this as some kind of twisted game—a game he had begun losing that day in Chartres. Like a child in a tantrum, he had overturned the playing table and rearranged the pieces so this time, he would emerge the winner.

Except this time, two of the game pieces were missing.

Connor and Malcolm were dead.

Laurien threw herself upon the trunk, her fists pummeling the hated gown as tears streamed down her cheeks. She gave herself over to her grief, sobbing. A low moan of agony and emptiness tore from her throat, and she cried until she no longer had the strength to wipe her tears away.

But as the minutes slipped past, she knew she must think of Aidan. She sat up and pushed her tangled hair from her eyes. This time there would be no last-minute rescue, no flight to freedom. She had only herself to depend on. Aidan yet lived, and his fragile life lay in her hands.

Very slowly, she stood and slipped her garments from her shoulders, picked up the despised wedding gown, and began to dress. She plaited her hair, covering it with the veil and wimple, exactly as it had been before. And when she was finished, she went out into the hall, feeling too numb for terror, grief, or even anger. She felt as if her life were ending.

De Villiers waited before the hearth, dressed in the same blue and gold tunic and leggings he had worn that other wedding day, weeks ago. A priest stood beside him, and, to one side, Ceanna and the guard. Aidan stood between them, no longer bound and gagged, but held firmly by the guard. Every member of the little assembly—all but Aidan—had broad, cheerful, utterly false smiles upon their lips.

Laurien walked toward the group, her legs stiff as wood, her slippers soundless upon the cold stone floor. She stopped at de Villiers's side. He took her hand in a painful grasp. Laurien looked out at the night sky through the hole in the castle wall. She stared at the tiny points of starlight. The priest began speaking in Latin.

Her mind drifted as the priest hurried through the ceremony. And then he spoke to her, asking if she accepted de Villiers as her husband.

Her eyes upon Aidan, she heard herself saying yes.

De Villiers took her left hand. He thrust a band of gold upon her finger. Then Laurien heard the words she had been running from, the words she had been sure she would never hear—not while standing beside de Villiers.

"I now pronounce you man and wife."

Chapter 26

No sooner had de Villiers thrust the ring on her finger than he was dismissing the priest. The cleric gratefully accepted the sack of coins de Villiers handed him, and headed for the exit.

As Laurien turned to watch him leave, she saw a man standing at the door. Her gasp of surprise drew de Villiers's attention.

"I have returned to haunt you, precisely as you predicted," the stocky figure said, walking closer to the hearth and into the light. He appeared tired, almost ragged, and he had blood on the left side of his tunic, but oddly enough he was smiling.

"Sir Malcolm!" Laurien cried.

"You!" de Villiers roared at the same time. "How did you find us?"

"The Lady Ceanna was so kind as to steal a boat, which narrowed the search." Malcolm raised his hands. "As you can see, I have come unarmed. I bring a message for your bride." He turned to Laurien, who for once was rendered speechless. "Dinna despair, milady. Connor isn't dead. He should, in fact, be arriving shortly."

De Villiers shouted at the guard. "Kill him!"

"I wouldna do that," Malcolm said. "I have a sizable contingent of Connor's men outside, and if I dinna re-

urn to them within the half hour, they will come in after
ne. And I have ordered them to take no prisoners.''

"You are a fool," de Villiers snarled. "*My* men killed
our friend at Strathfillan. They shall arrive here any
moment and finish you as well!''

"Do you think so?" Malcolm said, still appearing
quite calm and confident. "Do you not wonder why they
have been delayed? Mayhap their prey never arrived and
they are waiting for him still.''

Laurien's heart beat wildly with hope that Malcolm
was right. She saw a rare glimmer of doubt pass over
de Villiers's features. It was quickly replaced by a sneer.
The next instant, he grabbed her by the arm and dragged
her toward the stair at the rear of the hall. She struggled
against him with renewed spirit.

"Enough," he shouted at her, shaking her roughly
before he turned toward his guard. "Bring that overcon-
fident fool and the boy. We shall imprison them below!''

The man hastened to obey. Ceanna, who had stood
clinging to the guard's arm throughout all this, trailed
along behind. De Villiers snatched a torch from a wall
sconce and led them down the stairs. He nearly yanked
Laurien off her feet when she tried again to fight him.

They passed floor after floor until they reached the
very bowels of the ruined castle, a dank chamber
cloaked in darkness and cold with moisture. Laurien
could hear the steady drip of water over the pounding of
her heart. In the center of the dirt floor, she saw a square
of wood with an iron ring in the top, like a door of some
kind. After releasing her, de Villiers crossed to it and
pulled on the ring.

The trapdoor opened to reveal an even smaller chamber below—a prison cell, Laurien realized. An ancient
wooden ladder led into the musty darkness.

"Inside," de Villiers snapped, pushing her forward.
Laurien looked at Sir Malcolm, who was holding

Aidan's hand and still showing no sign of worry. He nodded imperceptibly. Taking strength from his courage, Laurien swallowed her fear and slowly went down the ladder. The guard sent Malcolm and Aidan down after her, then lifted the ladder up. Laurien glared up at de Villiers's pale moon-face, ghostlike in the torchlight.

"You shall stay in there until Balafre and my guards arrive, and then, my bride, we can at last leave this accursed country." De Villiers looked at Malcolm with a mocking smile. "And even if your men do come in, you fool, they will never find you in there."

With that he kicked the door shut, leaving the three of them alone in utter darkness. Laurien could see nothing, could hardly breathe in the humid, stale air. Sir Malcolm touched her shoulder, and she gave in to the worry she felt and hugged him. "I am so glad you are safe, Sir Malcolm. They said you were dead. But Connor—is he truly unhurt?"

"Sir Malcolm, is my father all right?" Aidan chimed in, his voice calm despite all he had been through.

"Aye. Now listen to me, both of you. I have only half a dozen of Connor's guards outside. There is a way out of here and we must find it before de Villiers returns." He gave Laurien a hard squeeze before releasing her. "Look along the walls. If I remember correctly, there should be a latch of some sort."

"How can you be certain that Connor escaped harm?" Laurien asked as they began to search in the darkness.

"Your brother, Henri, has gone to tell him that the rendezvous is a trap—"

She spun about in surprise. "Henri? You saw Henri? When—"

"I was on the road to Glenshiel and he stopped to help me. I sent him on to Strathfillan, and the rest of Connor's men are on their way there now, in case Connor and Henri run into trouble. I told the guards to bring

Connor back here straightaway. Dinna despair, lass. We willna allow de Villiers to take you anywhere."

"But I have *married* him," Laurien cried. "He would have killed Aidan! Sir Malcolm, you are very brave to try and protect me. But I am afraid I cannot escape de Villiers this time. Your efforts are for naught."

"Nay, dinna give up now, lass! Not when I have just found you." His voice was taut with an emotion so intense it startled her. Malcolm started to say something else, then hesitated. She could feel his hand groping for hers in the darkness. She reached out and felt his broad, callused fingers close about her own.

"Laurien, if aught should happen to me," he said haltingly, squeezing her hand, "I want you to know . . . God's breath, I wish I could think of a gentle way to tell you this, but I canna. Laurien, I am your father."

A heartbeat passed, then another. She was not sure she had heard him right. Laurien blinked, struggling to see in the gloom and make sense of Malcolm's words at the same time.

"What do you mean? How can you possibly—"

"You must believe me, Laurien. I loved your mother very much. We met when I came to Evreux on my way to join the Crusade in 1275. By the time I had to leave, we were in love."

"But . . . why did you not return for her, for *me?*" Laurien's voice rose as thirteen years of searching and bitterness and unanswered questions chased through her mind. "I do not understand."

Malcolm's hands rose to her shoulders. "I *did* come back. Her parents told me that she had died bearing my child, and the babe as well."

The truth began to dawn on Laurien. "When they discovered that my mother was with child, they would have been desperate to find her a husband. And what man would be willing to accept a pregnant woman as bride, except a provincial lord desperate for the dower lands she brought? She must have been forced to marry Louis.''

"Laurien, please believe me, if I had thought there was any chance she was alive, I would have searched for her, for you, to the end of my days.''

Tears welled in Laurien's eyes. She shook her head at the cruelty of it—she and her mother and Malcolm torn apart by lies, all living in loneliness.

For thirteen years she had been searching, and only now did she know exactly what it was she sought. It was not answers to questions, or freedom. "All these years,'' she said in wonder, "I have been so bitter, because Louis despised me, and Mother was gone, and I felt so alone. All I ever really wanted was . . . love.''

Malcolm pulled her into his arms. "You have that, lass.''

Laurien could hear the emotion in his voice, the strain, the guilt he felt over her unhappiness.

And she embraced her father for the first time.

"Nay, Sir Mal—Father,'' Laurien struggled with the word, but decided she liked the sound of it when applied to Malcolm. She felt her anger and bitterness floating away like dried autumn leaves on a brisk wind. "Please, Father. Do not feel badly for me. The past is over now. I am only grateful that I have found you.''

Malcolm gave her one more squeeze, then cleared his throat and let go of her at last. " 'Twas a brave thing you did, daughter, marrying de Villiers to save Aidan.''

"Brave?'' Laurien smiled and wiped at the tears that had spilled onto her cheeks.

"Well, foolish and brave,'' Malcolm chuckled. "But the line 'tween the two is often hard to find. Especially for a Scot, and a Scot of MacLennan blood at that.''

He hugged her again, then quickly resumed his search for an exit. Laurien started to ask one of the dozen questions whirling in her mind, but at that moment the door above them was thrown open. She put a hand over her eyes, dazed by the sudden light of several torches blazing into the darkness.

When she could finally see well enough to make out the faces looming above, she choked back a scream of fear. It was not Connor and Henri, but de Villiers and Balafre. Ceanna smiled down at them as well.

"As you can see," de Villiers said, a sneer curling his thick lips, "my men have been delayed no longer. Your paltry force is even now going down to defeat outside." He thrust the ladder through the entry. "Up. Now. My *wife* first."

For an instant Laurien froze. What had happened to Connor? She thought of refusing de Villiers's order, but she realized any struggle would be futile against Balafre. She climbed the ladder. De Villiers jerked her aside as soon as she had cleared the doorway.

Reaching down, he slammed the trapdoor shut.

"What are you doing?" Laurien cried, whirling to stop him. Before she could touch him, Balafre caught her arms and held her fast. De Villiers tossed one of the torches on the wooden door.

"Nay!" she screamed, reeling with a wave of shock and horror.

He threw another in a corner, where a pile of ancient barrels and empty sacks went up like tinder.

"Your friends are no longer of use to me," he said flatly. He held out his elbow, and Ceanna came forward to slip her hand possessively about his arm, flashing Laurien a smug, victorious grin. They hastened toward the stairs, Balafre dragging Laurien behind.

The crackle of the flames devouring the chamber drowned out her screams.

* * *

Connor had pushed his stallion to the very limit of its speed and endurance. The poor animal was lathered by the time he and a dozen of his men thundered into the bailey of the ruined castle. Henri rode beside him, having insisted on coming along when Connor's men intercepted them on the road and explained that Laurien had been taken.

With a practiced eye, Connor took in the battle scene in an instant. Six of his men were struggling valiantly against a score of de Villiers's guards. It was going badly for his side—until his reinforcements plunged into the melee. Connor's heart leaped into his throat when he saw smoke pouring from one side of the castle. He spotted Ranald and galloped through the fighting until he reached his steward's side.

"Where are Laurien and Aidan?" he cried hoarsely.

"The Frenchmen have them inside," Ranald called back. "And Sir Malcolm as well, sir—"

Without waiting for further explanation, Connor spurred his horse toward the keep and up the stairs, Henri right behind him. They threw themselves from their saddles, already drawing their swords. Side by side, they ran into the great hall, coughing on the acrid, bitter smoke that poured up the stairwell at the far end of the chamber.

De Villiers had just come to the top of the stairs, hunched over against the smoke that billowed above his head. Connor felt a wave of rage as he spotted Ceanna, and behind her the grizzled assassin, Balafre, dragging Laurien.

"Connor!" Laurien cried. He could hear the relief, joy, and terror all mingled in her voice. She struggled desperately against Balafre, who drew his weapon. De Villiers stood frozen in indecision.

"Release her!" Connor dropped into a fighting stance. "Your men are defeated, de Villiers. You canna get away. Let her go now or die!"

De Villiers glanced frantically from the two armed men before him to the flames licking up the walls behind him. "Never!" he shouted. "You will never take what is mine!"

Pushing Ceanna away, he grabbed Laurien and ran, back into the burning castle, running for the stairs that led to the upper floors. "Quickly Balafre, there must be another way out!" The assassin followed instantly.

Henri spat an oath and sprang after them.

"Nay, wait." Connor stopped him, running toward Ceanna, who had crumpled to the floor and was in tears now. He knelt beside her, grabbed her by the shoulders, and shook her. "Where are Aidan and Malcolm? Damn you, Ceanna, answer me!"

"B-below," Ceanna sobbed. "He left them in the pit prison. But you canna save them. 'Tis where he started the fire!"

"Sweet Christ!" Connor pulled her to her feet and shoved her in the direction of the door. "Get out of here. Run, before this entire castle burns to a cinder!"

Ceanna needed no urging. Smoke already choked the air, and they could feel the heat of the flames that were hungrily devouring every scrap of wood in their path—including the ancient beams that held the floors and ceilings in place.

Connor stared at Henri for a desperate moment, torn. Should he go after Aidan or Laurien? Love and anguish warred within him. He could not be in two places at once. Reason finally made the decision for him. He knew Henri would not stand a chance against Balafre.

"Listen to me, Henri. There is a secret passage that leads to the pit prison. You will find the entrance outside beneath the south tower. Find my son and Sir Malcolm!"

Henri was already moving as Connor finished the order. Connor turned in the direction de Villiers had fled, taking the stairs two at a time. The air in the tight passage nearly choked him, burning his throat and stinging his eyes. It only worsened as he reached the upper floor, where wooden doors and the remnants of timeworn tapestries were ablaze.

Where was she? What chamber might they be in? Had they gone to the left or the right? He had only moments to find her before the fire would make any search impossible. They would all be trapped.

"Laurien!" he shouted.

A moment later he was rewarded. He heard a whistle coming from one of the chambers to the right, cutting clearly through the smoke-clogged air. The falconer's whistle! He dashed toward it.

He threw himself against the door, and it gave way beneath his shoulder. He rolled into the chamber, coming up in a crouch. The room glowed, an angry red color made of bright flames and dark smoke. De Villiers was in one corner, tugging madly at something on the wall.

"You are finished!" Connor yelled hoarsely. "There is no further place to run to! Give up before we are all killed!"

De Villiers spun about, pulling Laurien in front of him with one arm while he shouted at Balafre. "Take him!"

Then the comte disappeared into the shadows, seeming to melt into the wall, pulling Laurien with him.

Balafre turned to face Connor. The assassin drew his sword with one hand, his knife with the other.

Connor did the same, and without preamble, they launched themselves at each other. They fought without grace, without style, with naught but a silent desperation to finish each other before the fire could finish them both. Connor forgot about the tricks he had learned as a mercenary. There were no taunts, no talking, no oaths.

They made no sound save the rasping of their breath and tight-lipped snarls of effort as muscle and sinew and bone and steel fought for supremacy.

Connor's arm began to ache as he warded off blow after ringing blow. Balafre tried to back him toward the door, to force him into the flames in the hallway beyond. Connor stood his ground, struggling forward a step for every step he was pushed back.

The roar of the flames drowned out even the ring of steel against steel. The heat was unbearable. Sweat dampened Connor's hair and made his garments stick to his body. His hands became slick on the pommel of his sword, and he could feel his grip slipping. With a lightning-fast feint, Balafre slashed in with his knife. Connor felt a hot stab of pain along his ribs. Ignoring it, he danced away, then came in again.

Both had the disadvantage of breathing cinder and ash, and they were well matched in experience, size, and weapons. The fight might have gone on interminably, save for Balafre's one weakness.

Connor understood that weakness with sudden insight, then wondered why it had taken him so long to recognize it.

From the moment Connor had entered the castle, he had been thinking of naught but Laurien and the need to get her out before the flames brought the keep down around their heads.

But Balafre was not truly thinking at all. He was utterly focused on this fight; his mind was filled with this moment, this opponent. The man was a killer, trained and paid to deliver death. And that was his weakness. Connor could see it in his eyes—Balafre *craved* death, like a thirsty man craves water. At the moment, Connor's death was the one thing Balafre wanted most in the world.

So Connor decided to give it to him.

He returned the blows more slowly, purposely warding off Balafre's attack with less and less force. He breathed harder, for all the world looking as if he were tiring. He let Balafre start to back him toward the doorway, and the hall of fire beyond.

Balafre took the lure, fought harder, his eyes gleaming with confidence that a victory was close at hand. He threw everything he had into the battle.

Looking exhausted, Connor dropped his knife so that he could use both hands on the sword.

Smiling a smug, self-satisfied smile, Balafre did the same.

And then Connor made his last move. He stumbled and fell, flat on his back, leaving himself wide open.

Balafre closed in for the kill.

And in that instant Connor's hand shot out. In one swift movement, he snatched up his knife from the floor. A flick of his wrist sent it straight into Balafre's neck.

Balafre, his sword raised in both hands above his head, staggered.

Connor was on his feet in a heartbeat, leaping forward as Balafre fell back. With a single stroke, Connor plunged his sword into Balafre's midsection and pulled it free.

Balafre toppled to the floor, a look of absolute amazement frozen on his face as he breathed his last breath.

Clutching his sword, Connor snatched up Balafre's knife from the floor and dashed for the wall. His fingers found the latch that triggered the secret exit de Villiers had discovered. A loud click sounded and part of the wall swung inward, revealing a cramped passageway.

Connor stepped inside and started forward, wrapping one edge of his cloak about his mouth to try and keep out the smoke and ash that seared his throat with each breath. At the end of the hall was a single, small door. He threw his shoulder against it, but it held fast. He heard Laurien scream and he tried again. This time it gave way, tumbling him headlong into the chamber.

The small space was as hot as an oven. He scrambled to his feet and saw that the staircase in one corner had collapsed, along with part of the floor, destroying any hope of a way out. A writhing column of fire shot up through the opening to blast at the ceiling.

"You will not take what is mine!" de Villiers screeched, backing away, clutching Laurien against his chest as a shield. She struggled and kicked and bit. His every step carried them closer to the flames. "If I die I take her with me!"

Laurien jabbed an elbow into de Villiers's midsection and twisted to one side. Taking quick aim, Connor threw Balafre's knife. It struck de Villiers in the stomach, and the comte screamed, the sound shrill against the roar of the flames. He stumbled backward, hitting the wall, still holding Laurien by one arm.

Suddenly the wall gave way under de Villiers's weight. He grabbed for the skirt of Laurien's gown as he fell, dragging her with him. Connor leaped forward and caught her about the waist. De Villiers teetered at the edge, gripping the silk with both hands. The skirt ripped. His bellow of pain and rage was suddenly cut short.

Then he plunged into the column of flames.

The door, the hallway, and more than half the chamber were now a solid wall of fire. Connor desperately pulled Laurien toward the window, their only hope of escape. They embraced each other, both trembling, for an all-too-brief moment. Then Connor pushed open the shutters and they leaned out, gasping in what air they could as smoke poured over their heads and into the night sky.

The tops of the distant trees were far below. Even farther below, Laurien could see the fire reflected on the waters of the glassy-smooth loch.

Connor turned to her, and she lay a hand on his face, caressing his cheek, which was smudged with soot and streaked with blood and sweat.

The slightest shadow of his crooked grin crossed his features. "You have experience in this sort of thing, do you not?"

She shook her head wildly. "We are much too high, Connor—"

He silenced her with a kiss, a hard, deep kiss that tasted of saltiness and smoke. The next minute he caught her about the waist and lifted her onto the window ledge, jumping up beside her. He covered her hand with both of his.

She looked at him one last time.

Then they jumped.

Laurien's scream was the only sound in the sudden silence. Her stomach was in her throat. Yet her thoughts were startlingly clear, She felt the exquisitely sweet coolness of the air, the heat of Connor's hand grasping hers, and then just as suddenly the wrenching impact of her body striking the water. It hurt so much she thought for an instant they must have hit the ground instead of the lake.

But then she felt the dark, winter-cold waters of the loch pulling her down and closing over her head.

Chapter 27

The air felt delightfully fresh, clear, and, most of all, cool.

The sheets were soft against her naked skin, and sleep felt best of all. But, thirsty for a draught of that precious air, Laurien inhaled deeply. She came awake all at once, coughing. Smoke, she remembered. She had breathed in a great deal of it. Opening her eyes and sitting up, she found herself in Connor's chamber, in his bed. Alone.

Where was he? she wondered in sudden panic. Sweet Mary, what if he had been killed! And her father and Aidan—

Then she heard the knocking. "Come in," she said quickly, clasping the sheets to her, her voice rasping in her dry throat.

The door opened, and Aidan entered timidly. Thank God he was alive. He bowed to her and smiled hesitantly. "Good morn, milady." He was dressed in silk, white surcoat over green tunic and leggings. "I was told to let you sleep as long as you like, but the others are waiting."

"Waiting?" She turned her head, realizing from the sun pouring in the window that it must be late in the day. The fall must have knocked her unconscious. She turned back to Aidan. "Are they all right, Aidan? Your father and Sir Malcolm—where are they?"

379

The lad smiled. "Aye, they are well. But where they are is supposed to be a secret. If you will dress, milady, I will await you outside." He indicated with a nod a green silk gown draped over the foot of the bed. Bowing again, he closed the door behind him.

Laurien felt a wave of relief and quickly slipped from beneath the sheets. Her eyes still stung and her every muscle ached, but she found to her surprise that she had not suffered much damage in the fall. She picked up the gown. It was lovely, the bodice embroidered with tiny pearls and golden threads, the long sleeves wide at the wrist to reveal a white satin lining. There were slippers to match, And someone had been thoughtful enough to provide a hairbrush. Her curiosity thoroughly piqued, Laurien brushed her hair, then hurriedly donned the gown and slippers.

She paused only to splash her face with water from the bedside basin and take a soothing drink, then she stepped into the hall.

She was surprised to find Aidan gone. "Aidan?" she queried softly. Where had he gone?

Going below to the great hall, she again found herself alone. A fire burned brightly on the hearth, but there was no sign of anyone. Even Ranald and Mara and Aileen were absent. Mayhap when Aidan had said "outside" he had meant outdoors. She went out the portal, down the stairs, and into the bailey.

There she found the lad, waiting beside the handsomest horse she had ever seen. It was a creamy white mare bedecked with satin fittings on the bridle and saddle, a garland of flowers about its neck.

"She is yours, milady," Aidan explained, fairly beaming. "My father has told me to take you wherever you wish to go. Or you can follow where I will lead you."

Without hesitating, Laurien graciously accepted hi

1elp in mounting. She smiled down at him. "Lead on,
hen, sir."

He eagerly led the horse at a trot through the castle
3ates, over the causeway, and into the fields beyond.
There, he turned from the path and into the woods. A
.hort journey brought them to a clearing in the forest.

A number of tents had been set up, their bright colors
ike scarlet and yellow and green flags against the muted
»rowns of the autumn trees. She could see people mill-
ng about—Connor's guards, his servants, and towns-
»eople. And out of the crowd came Connor himself,
.triding forward to meet them.

He was dressed in an outfit that matched Aidan's, and
s he drew near Laurien, his smile rivaled the sun for
»rightness.

"Well done, my son." He gave Aidan an affectionate
lap on the back. "Now if you hurry, you might get
ome of the food before Sir Malcolm eats it all."

The boy set off at a run, and Connor turned his gaze
o Laurien. She returned his warm smile in full measure.
teaching up, he swept her down from the saddle and
.eld her to him.

"Thank God you are unhurt," she said. Then she
:ood back to look him up and down. "You are unhurt,
re you not?"

"Aye, quite fit—"

"What is that?" She touched a rather angry-looking
ruise on his chin. "Is that from our fall?"

"Nay, 'tis naught." He winced despite his words and
.ulled her hand away, holding it in his.

"And Malcolm and Henri—they are safe?"

"Aye, your brother and your *father* are well." He
rinned when Laurien looked at him in surprise. "Aye,
ialcolm told me. I am glad for you, Laurien. And for
.e."

"For you?"

"Aye, 'tis one more reason for you to stay in Scotland," he said firmly. "As for your brother, he turned out to be quite a hero. Malcolm and Aidan were halfway down the passage out of the prison cell when it became blocked. Henri freed them and got them to safety."

Satisfied that everyone was unharmed, Laurien threw herself into Connor's arms and hugged him tightly. " was so afraid. When the floor collapsed and the whole chamber was afire, I thought it was the end for all o us—"

"Shhh, 'tis over now." He stroked her hair. "Between de Villiers's guards and Ceanna, we were able te piece together the comte's real plan. He meant to take the French throne, and Scotland's as well. But we have put an end to that. His guards—the few left after m men finished with them—told us that the alliance ha been signed already. De Villiers had it with him when he left France. We found it in his travelling chest. needs only Balliol's signature to be complete."

'Then Scotland is safe?''

"Aye, for now. We havena heard the last of the En glish. But at least we will have a fighting chance."

"And Ceanna?"

"We have turned her over to Balliol's justice," h replied. "Mayhap he will take pity upon her and simpl banish her from Scotland forever."

Laurien looked up at him, feeling such a mixture c relief and joy and love that she did not know what t say next. She frowned at him with mock ire. "When awoke alone, I feared that you were . . ." She could nc bring herself to say it. "Were . . ."

"I amna so easy to get rid of." He chuckled. "Afte Mara and Aileen assured me you were not hurt, I cam here straightaway to start this." He indicated the tent with a sweep of his arm. They started to walk towar the waiting crowd.

"So sure were you that I would choose to come with Aidan rather than ride off?"

"Aye," he said smugly.

"I am becoming entirely too predictable. I must remember to be disagreeable more often, else you are going to be impossible to live with. And by what magic did you find the gown and the horse?"

"I sent Ranald scouring the countryside to buy just the right horse. And Mara and Aileen worked into the morning on the gown."

She smiled wryly. "They know how impatient you can be."

Connor stopped short, turning suddenly serious. "You're right, Laurien. I can be difficult to live with. I amna always patient, and I dinna say 'please' very often, and I can be too demanding. And I might forget, more often than not, to say that . . ." He looked away, then turned back to her and held her gaze. "To tell you how much I love you. But I want you to be my wife. And, by God's teeth, woman, if you find some reason to say nay, I shall . . . I shall lock you in my chamber until you agree! Will you marry me, Laurien?"

He said it so adamantly and so earnestly that Laurien was utterly bemused. She had not realized until this moment just how much Connor really loved her. The thought of this man doing something desperate over a woman, over her, was quite a striking image.

She smiled up at him, but rather than say any of the bright or witty or teasing things that came to mind, she settled for the most sensible answer to the most eloquent proposal she had ever received.

"Aye."

With an elated shout, he caught her in his arms and swung her about, laughing with a pure, complete joy that warmed Laurien's heart. By the time he finally returned her feet to the ground, she, too, was laughing

and breathless. She placed her hand firmly in his, and
they walked into the waiting crowd of well-wishers, who
cheered as they entered the circle of tents. Henri came
forward, and Laurien hugged him.

"Oh, Henri, I am so relieved that you are safe!"

"I have only just been able to breathe again, dear
sister, and if you keep squeezing me so tightly, you shall
choke from me what little air I have managed to in
hale."

"Men!" she huffed, releasing him. "You cannot stand
the least show of affection, any of you."

He grabbed her as she started to pull away. "Nay,
hug me then."

"Henri," she said seriously when he let her go. "I
have a gift for you."

"On your wedding day you are to receive gifts, not
give them."

She shook her head. "Nay, this one I wish to give
away, and I can think of no one else I would see have
it. My lands, Henri, I give you my lands. When you
inherit Louis's lands, unite them with our mother's es
tates and live there and raise a *happy* family."

"But, Laurien, it is too generous a gift. Might you
not wish to keep your lands, for your own children?"

Laurien glanced at Connor, then shook her head,
smiling. "Nay, Henri. My children and I will have all
that we need, all we could ever want, here in Scotland.
This is my home now."

Henri nodded, his shining eyes expressing his grati
tude. "I accept your gift, then. But I might not be re
turning to France just yet. I find much that is . . .
attractive about this Scotland of yours." He smiled at a
pair of young ladies on the edge of the crowd. One re
turned his smile while the other blushed and giggled.
"If I may impose upon your hospitality?"

Laurien looked at Connor, who frowned and rubbed his chin thoughtfully.

"What *is* that bruise on your chin?" she asked with concern. "Does it pain you?"

"No more than mine did, I imagine," Henri jumped in before Connor could reply. "That is my fault, Laurien. I repaid him for that little tap he gave me in the forest."

"I *allowed* you to repay me," Connor corrected.

"You *let* Henri hit you?" Laurien asked, at first surprised, then pleased and proud of Connor for his sense of fair play. " 'Twas most generous of you."

" 'Twas before I knew he had such a good right punch," Connor muttered. "But I suppose we have room for him at Glenshiel, if he would like to stay," he added grudgingly.

Laurien lightly kissed his bruised chin. "Thank you, my love."

Connor sighed. "Now if there are no more good deeds to be done today, may we proceed with the wedding?"

"Not just yet," Malcolm interrupted from behind them, slipping between Connor and Laurien to place a protective arm about his daughter's shoulders. He held a mutton chop in his other hand, which he waggled at Connor. "You seem to have forgotten something, lad."

Connor set his teeth in frustration. "And what might that be?"

"Why, to ask her father for her hand, of course," Malcolm stated, grinning at Laurien.

Looking to the sky in supplication, Connor gave in without a struggle. "May I have your daughter's hand in marriage, Malcolm?"

"Well, now, 'tis an interesting question," Malcolm said, thoughtfully chewing on the mutton. "I suppose I could be persuaded. Shall I be allowed to visit whenever I like?''

"Aye," Connor agreed readily.

"And you shall be generous with your foodstuffs?"

"Granted."

"And your ale?"

"Done," Connor ground out.

"And . . ." Malcolm paused to think. "I shall be freely allowed to bounce my grandchildren upon my knee?"

"Aye," Connor fairly growled. "Aught *else?*"

Malcolm turned to wink at Laurien. "Aught else?"

"Not that I can think of." She smiled back.

"Then 'twould seem I have no choice, lass, but to hand you over to this rogue. But first." He withdrew something from his tunic, a small package wrapped in velvet. "I would give you this. Consider it your dowry."

Laurien unwrapped the package and gasped in surprise. "It is my knife. But how—"

"Nay, 'tis not exactly. It is the other knife from the pair. You see, they are Viking blades. My father won them in the Norse wars and passed them on to me. One I gave to your mother the day I left her." His voice caught for a moment before he continued. "This one, I have kept locked away all this time. I couldna even look upon it. Until today." He kissed her forehead. "Until I found you."

Laurien hugged him, unable to express how much his gift meant to her, how much *he* already meant to her.

Malcolm pointed to the runic lettering on the hilt. "The inscription on the one you had read, 'May the gods protect you.' And this one reads 'Until we are united once more.' ''

With tears in her eyes, Laurien hugged him fiercely and kissed his cheek. "Thank you, Father. Thank you so much." She stood back so she could look at him. "I have so much I want to talk with you about. About Mother, about your—our—family—''

"Laurien," Connor interrupted, "your trouble is that you always want to talk when there is something much better to be done.''

With that, Laurien found herself scooped up in Connor's arms.

He grinned down at her, carrying her toward a garlanded arch where a priest awaited. "I have tried to be patient, but I seem to be a complete failure at it. I simply canna wait any longer to make you my wife.''

Laurien threw her arms around his neck, and he kissed her soundly. A cheer went up from the crowd.

It was long past midnight by the time they managed to steal away from the wedding feast. A cool breeze ruffled the leaves, and the moon ran silver ribbons along the forest floor. Connor rode his black stallion at a lazy pace as Laurien nestled in his lap, his cloak wrapped about them both. Her white mare trailed behind.

Snuggled against his chest, Laurien was surprised to hear a strange sound rumbling there.

He was humming, actually humming. She giggled.

"And what amuses you so, my lady wife?''

"I was thinking that this is the way we started—you on a black horse and me in your lap. It seems I am forever in your lap.''

"I find it a very rewarding position.''

"I, too," she agreed, her finger tracing the mat of hair at the opening of his tunic.

"If you are not careful, we willna make it back to the keep, wife.''

"You would ravish me here on the forest floor?''

"In a trice.''

"And do you know what comes of that?'' Her voice turned suddenly serious.

He looked down at her in puzzlement.

She gazed up at him uncertainly. "You did promise my father grandchildren to bounce upon his knee."

"Aye, that I did." He stopped the horse and kissed her softly, teasingly. "I think I could make do with ten or twelve. What think you of the name Adelle for a girl?"

Laurien's eyes misted with tears at his thoughtfulness. "Connor, how did I ever find you?" she asked in wonder.

"You are simply very lucky." His voice grew husky. "Besides, I found *you*, remember?" His lips traced a path along her jaw to her throat, then he lifted her in his arms and slid from the horse.

The moon shone down on them, new and silver-bright against the night sky, as he lowered her to the carpet of leaves. Laurien knew that she would treasure this night, this feeling of being utterly content, at peace, and complete for the rest of her life. She had found her way home at last.

She slipped her arms about Connor's neck and pulled him down for another kiss. "I love you, husband."

His indigo eyes shone with his response, but he said it aloud anyway.

"And I love you, my Lady Laurien of Glenshiel. Forever."

The Timeless Romances
of New York Times Bestselling Author
JOHANNA LINDSEY

SAVAGE THUNDER   75300-6/$4.95 US/$5.95 Can
Rebellious against Victorian England's fusty etiquette, voluptuous
Jocelyn Fleming wants to experience the unbridled spirit of the
American frontier—wild and virgin—like herself!

WARRIOR'S WOMAN   75301-4/$4.95 US/$5.95 Can
A coup on her planet forces Security Guard Tedra to flee to a strange
new world, where she encounters, and challenges, an unbearable
barbarian of a man. But her initial outrage turns to desire for this
gorgeous, infuriating man.

DEFY NOT THE HEART	75299-9/$4.50 US/$5.50 Can
SILVER ANGEL	75294-8/$4.50 US/$5.95 Can
TENDER REBEL	75086-4/$4.95 US/$5.95 Can
SECRET FIRE	75087-2/$4.95 US/$5.95 Can
HEARTS AFLAME	89982-5/$4.95 US/$5.95 Can
A HEART SO WILD	75084-8/$4.95 US/$5.95 Can
WHEN LOVE AWAITS	89739-3/$4.95 US/$5.50 Can
LOVE ONLY ONCE	89953-1/$4.95 US/$5.50 Can
TENDER IS THE STORM	89693-1/$4.50 US/$5.50 Can
BRAVE THE WILD WIND	89284-7/$4.95 US/$5.95 Can
A GENTLE FEUDING	87155-6/$4.95 US/$5.95 Can
HEART OF THUNDER	85118-0/$4.95 US/$5.95 Can
SO SPEAKS THE HEART	81471-4/$4.95 US/$5.95 Can
GLORIOUS ANGEL	84947-X/$4.95 US/$5.95 Can
PARADISE WILD	77651-0/$4.95 US/$5.95 Can
FIRES OF WINTER	75747-8/$4.50 US/$5.50 Can
A PIRATE'S LOVE	40048-0/$4.95 US/$5.95 Can
CAPTIVE BRIDE	01697-4/$4.95 US/$5.95 Can

KAREN ROBARDS

THE MISTRESS OF ROMANTIC MAGIC
WEAVES HER BESTSELLING SPELL

MORNING SONG
75888-1/$4.50 US/$5.50 Can
Though scorned by society,
theirs was a song of love
that had to be sung!

TIGER'S EYE
75555-6/$4.95 US/$5.95 Can
Theirs was a passion that could
only be called madness—but
destiny called it love!

DESIRE IN THE SUN
75554-8/$3.95 US/$4.95 Can
Love wild, love free—dangerous,
irresistible, inexpressibly sweet!

DARK OF THE MOON
75437-1/$3.95 US/$4.95 Can
The sweeping tale of a daring woman,
a rebellious lord, and the flames
of their undeniable love.

Avon Romances—
the best in exceptional authors and unforgettable novels!

SILVER CARESS   Charlotte Simms
76179-3/$3.95 US/$4.95 Can

GABRIELLE   Leta Tegler
75616-1/$3.95 US/$4.95 Can

HEART OF THE FALCON   Diane Wicker Davis
75711-7/$3.95 US/$4.95 Can

CHERISH THE DREAM   Kathleen Harrington
76123-8/$3.95 US/$4.95 Can

SEASWEPT   Laura Halford
75736-2/$3.95 US/$4.95 Can

SPELLBOUND   Allison Hayes
76214-5/$3.95 US/$4.95 Can

PLAYING WITH FIRE   Victoria Thompson
75961-6/$3.95 US/$4.95 Can

MOONLIGHT AND MAGIC   Rebecca Paisley
76020-7/$3.95 US/$4.95 Can

MOONFEATHER   Judith E. French
76103-3/$3.95 US/$4.95 Can

BRAZEN WHISPERS   Jane Feather
76167-X/$3.95 US/$4.95 Can

FALCON ON THE WIND   Shelly Thacker
76292-7/$3.95 US/$4.95 Can

SPITFIRE   Sonya Birmingham
76294-3/$3.95 US/$4.95 Can